"Buffoonery and Easy Sentiment":

Popular Irish Plays
in the Decade Prior to the
Opening of The Abbey Theatre

Frontispiece: Frank Breen [Dublin City Library and Archive] Caricature by Harry Ireland of Breen as Feeney in Boucicault's *Arrah-na-Pogue*. A highly accomplished comic actor, he played the villains and character leads in Kennedy Miller's and other companies.

"Buffoonery and Easy Sentiment":

Popular Irish Plays
in the Decade Prior to the
Opening of The Abbey Theatre

by Christopher Fitz-Simon

Carysfort Press

A Carysfort Press Book

'Buffoonery and Easy Sentiment': Popular Irish Plays in the Decade Prior to the Opening of The Abbey Theatre
by Christopher Fitz-Simon

First published as a paperback in Ireland in 2011 by
Carysfort Press Ltd
58 Woodfield
Scholarstown Road
Dublin 16
Ireland

ISBN 978-1-904505-49-5

Typeset by Carysfort Press Ltd

Printed and bound by eprint limited
Unit 35
Coolmine Industrial Estate
Dublin 15
Ireland

Cover design by Adrian Fitz-Simon

This book is published with the financial assistance of
The Arts Council (An Chomhairle Ealaíon) Dublin, Ireland

For

Sanford V. Sternlicht

CONTENTS

ACKNOWLEDGEMENTS

The author acknowledges with thanks the help and encouragement of the editors of Carysfort Press, Dublin: Lilian Chambers, Eamonn Jordan and Dan Farrelly. Thanks too to the University of Ulster at Coleraine and to Professor Gerry McCarthy, formerly of the Department of Media and Performing Arts, and to Ms Kathryn Johnson, Curator, The Lord Chamberlain's Plays in the Manuscripts Department of the British Library which provided by far the greatest amount of access to the plays considered. Other libraries whose staff contributed enormously were those of Trinity College, Dublin; the National Library of Ireland; the Dublin City Archive; the Belfast Central Library; the Linen Hall Library, Belfast; the Cork City Library; the Limerick County Council Library; the Mayo County Library; the Denbeighshire County Library Service; the Mitchell Library, Glasgow; the Liverpool City Library; the Manchester Central Library; the Westminster Library Newspaper Department; and the National Theatre Society Archive at the Abbey Theatre, Dublin. Special thanks are due to Dr Máire Kennedy, Divisional Librarian, Special Collections, Dublin City Library; Dr Mary Clark, Dublin City Archivist; and Ms Patricia Walker, Heritage Manager, Libraries NI. He also thanks Micheal Johnston for permission to reproduce the extract from *The Old Lady Says 'No!'* by Denis Johnston on p. 64. Every possible effort has been made to trace the owners of other copyrights.

ILLUSTRATIONS

INTRODUCTION

During the late nineteenth and early twentieth centuries there was immense activity in the theatre in Ireland. This was largely due to the enterprise of British managements. British touring productions of opera, operetta, West End comedy, music-hall variety and drama – both classical and contemporary – appeared in the leading playhouses of Dublin, Belfast and Cork. The latest plays of Maeterlinck, Pinero, Shaw, Suderman and Wilde were seen in these Irish cities – not in small *avant garde* theatres but in the largest commercial houses. Artistes such as Mrs Patrick Campbell, Coquelin, Henry Irving, Ellen Terry and Herbert Beerbohm Tree were frequent visitors. No year passed without the presentation of several of Shakespeare's plays by major 'Cross-Channel' companies.

Alongside this international (or colonial) largesse there had evolved a vibrant vernacular tradition of professional playwrighting and production. Gradually consolidating through the 1880s and absorbing the Irish repertoire of London-based dramatic companies, new works of historical and patriotic disposition were presented. Mainly written in the currently popular mode of melodrama these Irish plays differed from the majority of fashionable English plays in that their subjects were covertly or overtly political, envisaging a time when Ireland would be independent of English rule. Social criticism, both implicit and explicit, was a distinguishing feature. Production values were high, rendering these plays economically viable through extensive exposure on the British, and sometimes the North American and Australian, circuit. Dramas as different as Hubert O'Grady's *The Eviction*, J.W. Whitbread's *The Ulster Hero* and Dan Fitzgerald's *The Rose of Rathboy* achieved as many as 5,000 performances each due to continuous touring to metropolitan centres outside Ireland.

Thirty-four such plays that were performed in Ireland during the decade leading up to the opening of the Abbey Theatre in 1904 have been read and described here in their theatrical as well as their social and political context. (The longer-lasting Irish plays of Dion Boucicault are only discussed in passing because they have been adequately assessed elsewhere.) Several others, which have not survived in manuscript, have at least been identified through advertisements and reviews.

A number of misconceptions have been corrected – such as that the writing was invariably 'crude', that stage presentation was of the 'barnstorming' kind, and, more importantly, that Irish characters were favourably depicted and English unfavourably: in fact almost all the 'villains' were Irish, especially those who betrayed their country or oppressed its people as dishonest land-agents, unscrupulous rent-collectors or political opportunists and informers.

The chapters that follow stem in part from an invitation to give the Ernest Blythe Memorial Lecture at the Abbey Theatre in 1999. I chose as my title: *Before the Abbey Theatre: can there have been such a time?* and I subsequently gave a reconsideration of this talk as the keynote address at the conference *Nationalism and a National Theatre: 100 Years of Irish Drama* at the University of Indiana, Bloomington, in the same year. Later, I completed a thesis called *Popular Irish drama in the decade leading up to the opening of the Abbey Theatre* at the University of Ulster. This book is a distillation of that very lengthy study.

Very little has been written about the theatre in Ireland in the years prior to the establishment of the Abbey Theatre except in matters relating to the forces that led to the creation of that institution, where the literature is voluminous. While some theatre historians mention the better remembered plays of Hubert O'Grady and J.W. Whitbread and provide varying degrees of critical analysis, the tendency has been to ignore completely the work of other popular dramatists. Three scholars have contributed outstandingly in more recent times to the recognition and appraisal of such work: they are Professor Stephen Watt of the University of Indiana who published the text of O'Grady's *The Famine* and the first act of the same author's *Emigration* in the *Journal of Irish Literature* in 1985; Dr Cheryl Herr of the University of Iowa whose selection of four late nineteenth and early twentieth century melodramas relating to the Insurrection of 1798 contains two of the plays by

Whitbread which are a part of the present review – *Lord Edward, or, '98* and *Theobald Wolfe Tone* – under the title *For the Land they Loved* (1991); and Dr Desmond Slowey whose acute development of the theme encapsulated in his title *The Radicalisation of Irish Drama* (2008) treats of this particular sector of the Irish theatre, *inter alia*, in a most illuminating way.

Shortly before his death, when W.B. Yeats was pondering over his early play *Cathleen ní Houlihan* (1902) he asked himself

> Did that play of mine send out
> *Certain men the English shot?'* [1]

It is perfectly reasonable to suppose that it may have done so. However, at that electrically charged three-night-run in St Theresa's Convent Hall, when Madam Maud Gonne played the Old Woman, only 300 people saw the play each evening and audiences at subsequent performances in the Abbey Theatre were comparatively thin when there was less remarkable casting. Yet when one considers how many thousands saw the patriotic dramas that were staged in the commercial theatres one begins to comprehend what must have been the extent of the influence of the popular theatre as a political force: if any plays sent out men and women whom the English shot it is much more likely to have been those that were seen at the Theatre Royal and the Queen's Theatre in Dublin, the Theatre Royal and the Grand Opera House in Belfast and the Opera House in Cork. This is, of couse, a matter of unproveable statistics. In practical terms, Yeats's literary theatre did not wish to know about the popular theatre and the popular theatre had no interest at all in the literary. The cultural *maelstrom* that resulted in the formation of the Irish Literary Theatre and its natural successor the National Theatre Society – the Abbey – remained distinct from the existing popular professional theatre, to the detriment of both.

IRISH PLAYS PROFESSIONALLY PRESENTED IN LICENSED THEATRES IN DUBLIN, BELFAST AND CORK DURING THE DECADE LEADING UP TO THE OPENING OF THE ABBEY THEATRE

A = Abbey Theatre
ACR = Antient Concert Rooms
G = Gaiety
LH = Leinster Hall
Q = Queen's Theatre
TR = Theatre Royal
TRB = Theatre Royal Belfast
GOH = Grand Opera House Belfast
COH = Cork Opera House

Engagements are for one week unless otherwise stated.
(1) = Premier (2) = Irish Premier (O) = Opera/Operetta. Except for those marked (1) and (2) the plays were in constant production and revival prior to and during the period of this study.

1. DUBLIN

Week	Theatre	Title	Author	Management

1895

Week	Theatre	Title	Author	Management
1 Jan	Q	The Nationalist	JW Whitbread	Kennedy Miller Co
7 Jan	Q	Shoulder to Shoulder	JW Whitbread	Kennedy Miller Co
15 Jan	Q	Lord Edward, or, '98	JW Whitbread	Kennedy Miller Co
22 Jan	Q	Lord Edward, or, '98	JW Whitbread	Kennedy Miller Co
14 May	Q	Muldoon's Picnic	Walter Reynolds	J. Cassidy's Co
3 Jun	Q	The Famine	Hubert O'Grady	Marcus Hughes
10 Jun	Q	Emigration	Hubert O'Grady	Marcus Hughes
25 Jun	Q	Rogue Reilly (2)	EC Matthews	EC Matthews Co
12 Aug	Q	On Shannon's Shore (2)	Frederick Cooke	Frederick Cooke Co

2 Sept	Q	The Colleen Bawn & Born to Good Luck	Dion Boucicault Tyrone Power	Kennedy Miller Co
9 Sept	Q	Arrah-na-Pogue	Dion Boucicault	Kennedy Miller Co
28 Dec	Q	Lord Edward, or, '98	JW Whitbread	Kennedy Miller Co

1896

6 Jan	Q	The Shaughran	Dion Boucicault	Kennedy Miller Co
15 Jun	Q	Rogue Reilly	EC Matthews	EC Matthews Co
21 Jun	Q	The Wearin' o' the Green aka The Boys of Wexford	EC Matthews	EC Matthews Co
1 July	Q	The Gommoch aka The Wild Irish Boy	Hubert O'Grady	Webster & Enright
24 Aug	Q	The Colleen Bawn	Dion Boucicault	Kennedy Miller Co
31 Aug	Q	Arrah-na-Pogue	Dion Boucicault	Kennedy Miller Co
7 Sep	Q	The Victoria Cross (1)	JW Whitbread	Kennedy Miller Co
28 Sep	Q	On Shannon's Shore	Frederick Cooke	Frederick Cooke Co
26 Oct	Q	The Irishman	JW Whitbread	Ellam & Dempster
23 Nov	G	Shamus O'Brien (O)	CV Stanford JS LeFanu H Jessop	S O'B Opera Co

1897

4 Jan 1 night	L H	The Lily of Killarney (O)	J Benedict Dion Boucicault J Oxenford	Arthur Rousby Opera Co
17 Mar	Q	Bally Vogan	Arthur Lloyd	None advertised
19 Ap	Q	Lord Edward, or, '98	JW Whitbread	Kennedy Miller Co
7 Jun	Q	The Shamrock & the Rose	Walter Reynolds	J Rice Cassidy Co
23 Aug	Q	Arrah-na-Pogue	Dion Boucicault	Kennedy Miller Co
30 Aug	Q	The Colleen Bawn	Dion Boucicault	Kennedy Miller Co
6 Sep	G	Shamus O'Brien (O)	CV Stanford JS LeFanu GH Jessop	Ben Greet
27 Dec	Q	The Irishman	JW Whitbread	Kennedy Miller Co

1898

11 Apr	Q	Lord Edward, or, '98	JW Whitbread	Kennedy Miller Co
18 Apr	Q	Peep o' Day	Edmund Falconer	None advertised
25 Apr	Q	The Streets of London	Dion Boucicault	None advertised
30 May	Q	The Green Bushes	John Buckstone	Kennedy Miller Co
17 Jun	Q	Caitheamh an Ghlais (2)	Chalmers Mackey	Howard & Mackey
25 Jun	T R	An Irish Gentleman (2)	DC Murray & JL Shine	Globe Theatre Co, London
29 Apr	Q	The Colleen Bawn	Dion Boucicault	Kennedy Miller Co
5 July	Q	Arrah-na-Pogue	Dion Boucicault	Kennedy Miller Co
14 Nov 1 night	T R	The Lily of Killarney (O)	Benedict Boucicault Oxenford	English Opera Co
26 Dec	Q	Theobald Wolfe Tone (1)	JW Whitbread	Kennedy Miller Co

1899

2 Jan 3 wks	Q	Theobald Wolfe Tone (1)	JW Whitbread	Kennedy Miller Co
3 Apr	Q	Lord Edward, or, '98	JW Whitbread	Kennedy Miller Co
17 Apr	G	Our Irish Visitors	FJ Conyngham	Pitt Hardcastle
8 May 3+3 nights	A C R	The Countess Cathleen (1) The Heather Field (1)	WB Yeats Edward Martyn	Frank Benson Co/ Irish Literary Theatre
22 May	Q	A Fast Life	Hubert O'Grady	George Littleton Co
3 July	Q	The Shaughran	Dion Boucicault	Kennedy Miller Co
3 July	T R	Arrah-na-Pogue	Dion Boucicault	E Marie Loftus
24 July	T R	The Colleen Bawn	Dion Boucicault	EC Matthews Co
24 July	Q	The Lily of Killarney (O)	Benedict Boucicault Oxenford	FS Gilbert Opera Co
21 Aug 2 wks	Q	Theobald Wolfe Tone	JW Whitbread	Kennedy Miller Co

5 Sep	Q	The Irishman	JW Whitbread	Kennedy Miller Co
11 Sep	Q	The Green Bushes	J Buckstone	Kennedy Miller Co
2 Oct	Q	The Famine	Hubert O'Grady	Hubert O'Grady's Co
6 Oct 2 nts	G	The Rebels (2)	JB Fagan	Mrs Lewis Waller's Co
23 Oct 3 wks	Q	The Rose of Rathboy (2)	Dan Fitzgerald	HWSheldon Co
23 Oct 1 nght	T R	The Lily of Killarney (O)	Benedict Boucicault Oxenford	Moody Manners Opera Co
27 Nov	Q	Caitheamh an Ghlais	Chalmers Mackey	Howard & Mackey
25 Dec	Q	Arrah-na-Pogue & The Irish Tutor	Dion Boucicault Earl of Glengall	None advertised

1900

8 Jan	Q	A True Son of Erin	JW Whitbread	Kennedy Miller Co
11 Feb 3 + 3	G	The Bending of the Bough (1) Maeve (1) & The Last Feast of the Fianna (1)	G Moore E Martyn Alice Milligan	Irish Literary Theatre with Frank Benson's Co
27 Feb	Q	The Patriot's Wife/ The Rebel's Wife (2)	Fred Jarman	Alfred Wood's Co
16 Apr	Q	Rory O'More (1)	JW Whitbread (after Lover)	Kennedy Miller Co
7 May	Q	The Shaughran	Dion Boucicault	'A Special Company'
3 June	Q	A Fast Life	Hubert O'Grady	Mrs O'Grady's Co
9 July	Q	Shoulder to Shoulder	JW Whitbread	Mrs O'Grady's Co
16 July	Q	Emigration	Hubert O'Grady	Mrs O'Grady's Co
3 Sep	Q	Lord Edward, or, '98	JW Whitbread	Kennedy Miller Co
17 Sep	Q	The Green Bushes	J Buckstone	Kennedy Miller Co
24 Sep	Q	Arrah-na-Pogue	Dion Boucicault	Kennedy Miller Co
15 Oct	T R	The Devil's Disciple (2)	George Bernard Shaw	J Forbes Robertson Co
15 Oct	Q	The Famine	Hubert O'Grady	Mrs O'Grady's Co
22 Oct	Q	The Fenian	Hubert O'Grady	Mrs O'Grady's Co

26 Nov	Q	Caitheamh an Ghlais	Chalmers Mackey	Howard and Mackey
31 Dec	Q	The Irishman	JW Whitbread	Kennedy Miller Co

1901

18 Jan	Q	The Colleen Bawn	Dion Boucicault	Kennedy Miller Co
18 Feb	Q	The Colleen Bawn	Dion Boucicault	Kennedy Miller Co
22 Apr	Q	The Rebel's Wife/ The Patriot's Wife	Fred Jarman	Alfred Wood Co
17 Jun 3 + 3	Q	The Shaughran & The Colleen Bawn	Dion Boucicault	EC Matthews Co
23 Jun	Q	Peep o' Day	Edmund Falconer	Kennedy Miller Co
15 July	Q	The Boys of Wexford (2)	EC Matthews	EC Matthews Co
22 July	Q	Rogue Reilly	EC Matthews	EC Matthews Co
12 Aug	Q	Caitheamh an Ghlais	Chalmers Mackey	Howard & Mackey
19 Aug	T R	A Daughter of Erin (1)	Miss LeFanu Robertson	Louis Calvert
26 Aug	Q	Lord Edward, or, '98	JW Whitbread	Kennedy Miller Co
2 Sep	Q	Arrah-na-Pogue	Dion Boucicault	Kennedy Miller Co
9 Sep	Q	Theobald Wolfe Tone	JW Whitbread	Kennedy Miller Co
16 Sep	Q	Shoulder to Shoulder	JW Whitbread	Kennedy Miller Co
21 Oct	G	Diarmuid and Grania (1)	G Moore & WB Yeats	Irish Literary Theatre/ Frank Benson
		& Casadh an tSugáin (1)	Dubhghlas de hÍde	ILT/Connradh na Gaelige Co
25 Nov	Q	The Fenian	Hubert O'Grady	Mrs O'Grady's Co
16 Dec	Q	The Colleen Bawn	Dion Boucicault	James O'Brien's Co

1902

6 Jan	Q	The Irishman	JW Whitbread	Kennedy Miller Co
13 Jan 1 night	T R	The Lily of Killarney (O)	Benedict Boucicault Oxenford	Moody Manners Opera Co
28 Jan	Q	Emigration	Hubert O'Grady	W.Faulkner Cox Co
31 Mar 2 wks	Q	The Insurgent Chief (1)	JW Whitbread	Kennedy Miller Co
16 Jun	Q	The Octoroon	Dion Boucicault	John Tully Co
7 July 3 nts	Q	The Shaughran	Dion Boucicault	Kennedy Miller Co
10 July 3 nts	Q	A True Son of Erin	JW Whitbread	Kennedy Miller Co
21 July	Q	The Gommoch	Hubert O'Grady	Robert Barton Co
15 Aug	Q	The Insurgent Chief	JW Whitbread	Kennedy Miller Co
1 Sep	Q	Lord Edward, or, '98	JW Whitbread	Kennedy Miller Co
8 Sep	Q	Arrah-na-Pogue	Dion Boucicault	Kennedy Miller Co
15 Sep	Q	Theobald Wolfe Tone	JW Whitbread	Kennedy Miller Co
6 Oct	Q	The Famine	Hubert O'Grady	Mrs O'Grady's Co
14 Oct	Q	Shamus	DBAylmer	Calder O'Beirne Co
17 Nov	Q	The Fenian	Hubert O'Grady	Robert Barton Co
22 Dec 2 ngts	Q	The Insurgent Chief	JW Whitbread	Kennedy Miller Co
24 Dec 4 nts	Q	The Green Bushes	John Buckstone	Kennedy Miller Co

1903

5 Jan	Q	The Colleen Bawn	Dion Boucicault	Kennedy Miller Co
12 Jan	Q	The Ulster Hero (1)	JW Whitbread	Kennedy Miller Co
13 Ap	Q	The Old Land (1)	Robert Johnson	Kennedy Miller Co
13 Apr 1 nt	T R	The Lily of Killarney (O)	Benedict Boucicault Oxenford	Moody Manners Opera Co
20 Apr	Q	The Shaughran	Dion Boucicault	Kennedy Miller Co

20 Apr 1 nt	T R	The Lily of Killarney (O)	Benedict Boucicault Oxenford	Moody Manners Opera Co
4 May	Q	A Fast Life	Hubert O'Grady	Faulkner Cox's Co
13 Jun	Q	The Insurgent Chief	JW Whitbread	Kennedy Miller Co
24 Aug	Q	Lord Edward, or, '98	JW Whitbread	Kennedy Miller Co
31 Aug	Q	Arrah-na-Pogue	Dion Boucicault	Kennedy Miller Co
7 Sep	Q	The Ulster Hero	JW Whitbread	Kennedy Miller Co
14 Sep	Q	The Old Land	Robert Johnson	Kennedy Miller Co
5 Oct	Q	The Famine	Hubert O'Grady	Mrs O'Grady's Co
12 Oct	Q	The Wild Irish Boy	Hubert O'Grady	Mrs O'Grady's Co
7 Dec	T R	Muirgheis (1)	O'Brien Butler	Olive Adair's Company
21 Dec 1 nt	T R	The Lily of Killarney (O)	Benedict Boucicault Oxenford	Moody Manners Opera Co
14 Dec	Q	Shamus, or, Speidhóir na Glanna	DB Aylmer	Miss Olive Adams Co
26 Dec 2 wks	Q	The Sham Squire (1)	JW Whitbread	Kennedy Miller Co

1904

4 Jan	Q	Theobald Wolfe Tone	JW Whitbread	Kennedy Miller Co
25 Jan	Q	The Green Bushes	J Buckstone	Kennedy Miller Co
4 Apr	Q	The Irishman	JW Whitbread	Kennedy Miller Co
4 Jun	Q	The Shaughran	Dion Boucicault	Kennedy Miller Co
4 July	Q	The Colleen Bawn	Dion Boucicault	Kennedy Miller Co
11 July	Q	Rory O'More	JW Whitbread	Kennedy Miller Co
22 Aug	Q	Arrah-na-Pogue	Dion Boucicault	Kennedy Miller Co
29 Aug	Q	Lord Edward, or, '98	JW Whitbread	Kennedy Miller Co
5 Sep	Q	The Insurgent Chief	JW Whitbread	Kennedy Miller Co
31 Oct	Q	The Famine	Hubert O'Grady	Mrs O'Grady's Co
7 Nov	Q	The Fenian	Hubert O'Grady	Mrs O'Grady's Co
19 Nov	T R	The Lily of Killarney (O)	Benedict Boucicault Oxenford	Moody Manners Opera Co
19 Nov 3 + 3 nights	Q	The Shaughran The Colleen Bawn	Dion Boucicault Dion Boucicault	Kennedy Miller Co

26 Dec	Q	Sarsfield (1)	JW Whitbread	Kennedy Miller Co
27 Dec	A	Spreading the News (1) On Baile's Strand (1)	Augusta Gregory WB Yeats	National Theatre Society

2. BELFAST

1895

11 May	T R B	The Green Bushes	John Buckstone	Isabel Bateman Co
29 July	T R B	Our Irish Visitors (2)	Thomas E Murray	Pitt Hardcastle
18 Aug	T R B	McKenna's Flirtation	Edgar Selden	Pleon & Garth
30 Sep	T R B	Lord Edward, or, '98	JW Whitbread	Kennedy Miller Co
23 Dec	T R B	My Native Land	Wm Manning	Not known

1896

20 Jan	G O H	Rogue Reilly (1)	EC Matthews	EC Matthews
17 Feb	G O H	The Shaughran	Dion Boucicault	Leonard Yorke Co
16 Mar	G O H	The Shamrock & the Rose	Walter Reynolds	Compton Comedy Co
5 Oct	T R B	On Shannon's Shore	Frederick Cooke	Frederick Cooke
2 Nov	T R B	Shamus O'Brien (O) (2)	CV Stanford FS LeFanu GH Jessop	Shamus O'Brien Opera Co
16 Nov	G O H	The Victoria Cross	JW Whitbread	Kennedy Miller Co
23 Nov split week	G O H	Arrah-na-Pogue The Colleen Bawn	Dion Boucicault	Kennedy Miller Co
7 Dec	T R B	Lord Edward, or, '98	JW Whitbread	Kennedy Miller Co

1897

8 Mar	T R B	Muldoon's Pic Nic	Harry Pleon	Wood & West's Co
20 Sep	G O H	Shamus O'Brien	CV Stanford FS LeFanu GH Jessop	Ben Greet Grand Opera Co
30 Oct- 1 Nov 2perfs	G O H	Kerry	Dion Boucicault	Edward Terry

1898

11 Apr	T R B	Muldoon's Pic Nic	Harry Pleon	Wood & West's Co
18 Apr	G O H	Lord Edward, or, '98	JW Whitbread	Kennedy Miller Co
11 Jul	G O H	McKenna's Flirtation	Edgar Selden	Pleon & Garth
5 Dec	G O H	Muldoon's Pic Nic	Harry Pleon	Wood & West's Co

1899

6 Mar 2 perfs each	T R B	Arrah-na-Pogue The Colleen Bawn The Irishman	Dion Boucicault JW Whitbread	Kennedy Miller Co
21 Aug	T R B	Muldoon's Pic Nic	Harry Pleon	John Cassidy's Co
16 Oct	T R B	A Fast Life (2)	Hubert O'Grady	Hubert O'Grady's Co
21 Nov	G O H	The Shaughran	Dion Boucicault	Kennedy Miller Co
11 Dec	T R B	Caitheamh an Ghlais	Chalmers Mackey	Chalmers Mackey's Co

1900

29 Jan	T R B	Theobald Wolfe Tone	JW Whitbread	Kennedy Miller Co
19 Mar	T R B	The Patriot's Wife	Frederick Jarman	Wood & Princeps Co
27 Aug 2 perfs. each	T R B	The Shaughran The Colleen Bawn Rory O'More	Dion Boucicault JW Whitbead (after Lover)	Kennedy Miller Co
26 Nov	T	Arrah-na-Pogue	Dion Boucicault	Kennedy Miller Co
3 Dec split week	T R B	Shoulder to Shoulder A True Son of Erin	JW Whitbread JW Whitbread	Kennedy Miller Co

1901

25 Mar	T R B	Dear Hearts of Ireland	Myles McCarthy	Myles McCarthy Co
29 Apr	A B	Muldoon's Pic Nic	Harry Pleon	Nono Bland & Nono
27 May	T R B	The Fenian	Hubert O'Grady	W Faulkner Cox Co
18 Jun	T R B	The Shaughran	Dion Boucicault	John S Chamberlain

1902

22 July	T R B	The Shaughran	Dion Boucicault	Kennedy Miller Co
28 July	T R B	The Irishman	JW Whitbread	Kennedy Miller Co
13 Oct	T R B	The Famine	Hubert O'Grady	Mrs O'Grady's Co
21 Oct	T R B	Theobald Wolfe Tone	JW Whitbread	Kennedy Miller Co
15 Dec	T R B	On Shannon's Shore	Frederick Cooke	Frederick Cooke Co

1903

2 Jan	TRB	The Ulster Hero	JW Whitbread	Kennedy Miller Co
18 May	TRB	The Old Land	Robert Johnson	Kennedy Miller Co
20 July	TRB	The Shaughran	Dion Boucicault	Kennedy Miller Co
27 July	TRB	The Colleen Bawn	Dion Boucicault	Kennedy Miller Co
3 Aug	TRB	Arrah-na-Pogue	Dion Boucicault	Kennedy Miller Co
24 Aug	TRB	Shamus	DB Aylmer	Olive Adair's Co
21 Sep	TRB	Lord Edward, or, '98	JW Whitbread	Kennedy Miller Co
7 Dec 5 perfs.	TRB	The Ulster Hero	JW Whitbread	Kennedy Miller Co
12 Dec TRB 1 perf. Griffin Centenary		The Colleen Bawn	Dion Boucicault	Kennedy Miller Co
14 Dec	TRB	The Insurgent Chief	JW Whitbread	Kennedy Miller Co

1904

There were no plays in this genre professionally presented in Belfast in 1904. This is an entirely accidental quirk of programming, as the sequence resumed the following year.

3. CORK

Although the Palace Theatre opened in 1897, presenting drama, variety, opera and pantomime, all the plays under review were given at the Opera House

1895

28 Jan 4+2 perfs	C O H	Lord Edward	JW Whitbread	Kennedy Miller Co
		The Irishman	JW Whitbread	
13 May	C O H	Our Irish Visitors	FJ Conyngham	Pitt Hardcastle
12 Aug 2+2	C O H	The Shaughran	Boucicault	O'Brien/
		The Colleen Bawn	Boucicault	Gibson Combination
		The Eviction	Hubert O'Grady	
2 Nov COH 1 perf as afterpiece in West End season		Kerry	Dion Boucicault	Edward Terry Co

1896

13 Jan 2 nights each	C O H	Lord Edward	JW Whitbread	Kennedy Miller Co
		The Irishman	JW Whitbread	
		Arrah-na-Pogue	Dion Boucicault	
16 Nov	C O H	Shamus O'Brien	CV Stanford	Ben Greet
			J Sheridan	
			FS LeFanu	
			GH Jessop	

1897 There were no Irish plays in this genre presented in Cork in 1897.

1898 There were no Irish plays in this genre presented in Cork in 1898

1899

Date		Play	Author	Company
23 Jan	C O H	Wolfe Tone	JW Whitbread	Kennedy Miller Co
24 Apr	C O H	Our Irish Visitors	Thomas E Murray	Pitt Hardcastle
7 Aug Mon	C O H	Lord Edward	JW Whitbread	Kennedy Miller Co
Tue				
Wed		The Shaughran	Dion Boucicault	
Thu		The Irishman	JW Whitbread	
Fri		The Colleen Bawn	Dion Boucicault	
Sat mat		Lord Edward	JW Whitbread	
Sat eve		Wolfe Tone	JW Whitbread	

1900

Date		Play	Author	Company
19 Feb one night each	C O H	Wolfe Tone	JW Whitbread	Kennedy Miller Co
		The Irishman	JW Whitbread	
		Lord Edward	JW Whitbread	
		A True Son of Erin	JW Whitbread	
		The Colleen Bawn	Dion Boucicault	
		Arrah-na-Pogue	Dion Boucicault	

1901

Date		Play	Author	Company
15 Apr one night each	C O H	Lord Edward	JW Whitbread	Kennedy Miller Co
		A True Son of Erin	JW Whitbread	
		Rory O'More	JW Whitbread	
		The Shaughran	Dion Boucicault	
		The Colleen Bawn	Dion Boucicault	
		The Green Bushes	John Buckstone	
19 July	C O H	The Fenian	Hubert O'Grady	Faulkener Cox Co

1902

Date		Play	Author	Company
21 Apr 4 nts 1 nt 1 nt	C O H	The Insurgent Chief	JW Whitbread	Kennedy Miller Co
		Arrah-na-Pogue	Dion Boucicault	
		The Colleen Bawn		
8 Sep	C O H	The Wild Irish Boy	Hubert O'Grady	Robert Barton Co

27 Oct 2 nts 2 nts 1 nt 1 nt	C O H	The Insurgent Chief Lord Edward The Shaughran Wolfe Tone	JW Whitbread JW Whitbread Dion Boucicault JW Whitbread	Kennedy Miller Co
7 Nov COH 1 perf as after- piece in West End season		Kerry	Dion Boucicault	Edward Terry Co

1903

11 May 2 nts 2 nts 1 nt 1 nt	C O H	The Old Land The Ulster Hero The Colleen Bawn Lord Edward	Robert Johnston JW Whitbread Dion Boucicault JW Whitbread	Kennedy Miller Co

1904

11-13 Jan Mon Tue & Wed Thu Fri Sat mat Sat eve	C O H	The Colleen Bawn The Sham Squire The Insurgent Chief The Shaughran The Green Bushes Wolfe Tone	Dion Boucicault JW Whitbread JW Whitbread Dion Boucicault John Buckstone JW Whitbread	Kennedy Miller Co
15 Aug one night each Sat & Sun	C O H	The Colleen Bawn The Shaughran Arrah na Pogue The Green Bushes Rory O'More	Dion Boucicault Dion Boucicault Dion Boucicault John Buckstone JW Whitbread	Mrs Glenville's Representative Irish Co

14 Nov I perf only	C O H	Kerry	Dion Boucicault	Edward Terry
12 Dec one night each	C O H	Lord Edward, or, '98 The Insurgent Chief The Shaughran The Irishman The Colleen Bawn Wolfe Tone	JW Whitbread JW Whitbread JW Whitbread Dion Boucicault Dion Boucicault JW Whitbread	Kennedy Miller Co

1 | THE BACKGROUND TO PERFORMANCE

Theatregoing: what was on offer?

Authors of innumerable studies of the theatre as it existed in Ireland at the turn of the twentieth century generally ignore the popular theatre, dwelling at length on aspects of the 'literary' theatre and the playwrights and performers who nurtured and sustained it. It goes without saying that Yeats, Synge, the Fay brothers – to name but four – were deliberate innovators, and from their achievement grew the great tree of Irish drama which, with its numerous branches, developed, changed and flourished for the next hundred years, and continues to flourish in a way that would undoubtedly have surprised its initiators – not only on account of its durability but more especially because of its acceptance by a very extensive public in Ireland and abroad. Today's 'popular' theatre in Ireland is an evolution from Yeats', Synge's and the Fays' fairly arcane 'art theatre', which in itself could not have existed without nineteenth century precedents mainly in France and northern Europe.

At the time of the Irish Literary Theatre and other less remembered *théâtre à côté* groups, the components were completely self-contained. The easy manner that exists today where an actor (for example) moves regularly from one genre to another, playing this month in a revival of an esteemed international classic and next month in an entirely experimental local piece, was not then the norm. (Even more so because of technical developments: an actor playing on the stage this month appears next in the film or television studio.) Except in rare cases a hundred years ago the components were mutually exclusive. Actors who made their living on Shakespearean tours rarely, if ever, appeared in the West End comedy troupes and never on the variety stage.

When the Abbey Theatre opened in 1904 its plays were not noticed in the Entertainments columns but on the pages devoted to the much more protean Home News and Fashionable Intelligence, for the work was considered to be somewhat above discussion on the 'popular' pages. Furthermore, the movement which would, in time, become the backbone of the Irish theatre was treated with scant regard by the only periodical dedicated solely to the theatre, the *Irish Playgoer,* which concentrated on showy productions graced by such visiting luminaries as Madame Sarah Bernhardt, Dame Ellen Terry and Dame Clara Butt, juxtaposed in its pages with the distinctly home-grown work of Hubert O'Grady, Dan Fitzgerald, Howard & Mackey, J.W. Whitbread and others. It appears that whereas the Sarah Bernhardts and Hubert O'Gradys shared the soubriquet 'professional' in the *Playgoer's* pages, Yeats and his circle were seen as well-meaning dilettantes whose idealistic dedication to sowing the seeds of a different kind of 'national' drama would result in little more than a romantic harvesting of neo-Celtic corn.[2]

Scholarly studies of the Irish theatre tend to ignore the background of what was happening on the popular stage, whether local or imported. An outstanding example of this kind of myopia is Sam Hanna Bell's *The Theatre in Ulster* (1972) in which the otherwise diligent author gives the impression that there was no theatrical activity in Belfast beyond what was provided by the Ulster Literary Theatre, the Northern Drama League, the Ulster Group Theatre, and the Lyric Players. It therefore appears that the Belfast public lacked access to national companies that were touring plays, opera and dance, imports from the West End of London and Christmas pantomime, when in fact the nightly patronage of such shows, in theatres as opulent as any in London or New York, hugely outnumbered attendance at the sporadic productions of the groups treated in Bell's book. We know that his interest was in indigenous play production, but it did not occur to him that this should be seen against the wider theatregoing scene, or even that the existence of such a scene should be acknowledged.

The principal dramatic substance during the decade prior to the opening of the Abbey Theatre in 1904 arrived at the theatres of Belfast, Cork and Dublin (and to a limited extent Derry, Limerick and Waterford) *via* managements operating out of London, with a very small minority of productions from Paris and New York. It would therefore be reasonably correct to generalize that what

Newcastle, Glasgow and Leeds saw this week, the Irish cities would see in the following weeks. Colonialism ruled, though the use of such a term would have been neither popular nor profitable.

The theatres and licensed halls in Belfast at the time were the Theatre Royal, the Alhambra, the Ulster Hall, the Empire (from 1894) and the Grand Opera House (from 1895). In Cork, there were the Opera House, the Assembly Hall and the Palace (from 1897). Other buildings in both cities were used for professional performances from time to time. It was an era of extensive theatre construction, with houses of immense charm and distinction appearing with remarkable rapidity. Cork's Viennese-Baroque Opera House, formerly the Athenaeum, was, according to *The Era*, 'one of the handsomest theatres in the provinces', until the opening of its Hindu-Gothic counterpart in Belfast, arguably Frank Matcham's architectural masterpiece.

When Belfast's Grand Opera House was opened on 23 December, 1895, the proceedings began (according to the *Irish News*) with the singing of 'the National Anthem by the Entire Company' after which Lord Arthur Hill, MP, speaking from a box, declared the house open. These solemn proceedings completed, the invited audience was treated to a performance of 'Dottridge and Lydon's Original, Farcical, Comical, Funny, Christmas Pantomime *Blue Beard, or, Is Marriage a Failure?*' At the Theatre Royal, four city blocks distant, the fare was *My Native Land,* an Irish-American drama by William Manning: but readers seeking a political nuance amounting to rivalry between the two houses – the colonial and the local – will be disappointed, for the two theatres were owned by the Warden family, the Grand Opera House being their latest venture.

In Dublin there were over 6,500 seats on sale each night – to which should be added a further 6,500 on Saturdays for matineés. The licensed theatres at the turn of the century were the Theatre Royal a rebuilding of the inadequate Leinster Hall which had replaced an earlier Royal – the Gaiety, the Queen's Royal Theatre, the Empire Palace (later renamed the Olympia) and the Lyric, the latter two catering almost exclusively to variety. (The Rotunda Concert Hall and the Antient Concert Rooms were also licensed and were mainly devoted to music.) Other smaller venues, such as the Mechanics' Hall (rebuilt as the Abbey Theatre in 1904) were occasionally licensed for professional productions, though usually with limited concessions.

The Theatre Royal, with 2,001 seats, attracted the most successful West End operettas, the larger opera companies, one-night celebrity concerts, plays with star performers and plays of enduring popularity such as those of Shakespeare and Boucicault. The fare at the 1,100 seat Gaiety was very similar except that the scale of presentation was slightly smaller; one has the impression that the Gaiety was considered to be the more fashionable house by patrons residing in the wealthy suburbs of Ballsbridge and Rathgar. No theatre was given over exclusively to any one type of attraction – much depended upon what was available from touring companies and whether a house's calendar was full or otherwise at the time of offer, so that in spite of its reputation as 'the Home of Irish Drama', the Queen's Royal Theatre's programme for at least three quarters of the year was English *boulevard* drama with fashionable titles such as *Her One Great Sin* and *A Woman's Revenge,* interspersed with light opera and pantomime. The Queen's had 680 seats, the Empire Palace 1,600 and the Lyric (which changed its name to the Tivoli) 1,252.[3]

There was a local perception that Dublin audiences were more 'discerning' than others on the British commercial circuit. This may have been one of many myths perpetrated by Dubliners who liked to believe that their's was still 'the second city of the Empire'. However, a scrutiny of the newspaper advertisements and a comparison with those of the largest British cities outside London shows that (for example) Mrs Patrick Campbell's celebrated performances in Sudermann's *Magda,* Maeterlinck's *Pelléas and Mélisande* and Pinero's 'interesting play' *The Second Mrs Tanqueray* were seen on alternate nights at Dublin's Theatre Royal over a period of two weeks in February 1899, while only one week each was accorded to Newcastle and Glasgow and these productions did not visit Leeds at all. In June of the same year Coquelin appeared at the Gaiety in Rostand's *Cyrano de Bergerac* and Molière's *Le Tartuffe* and *Les Précieuses Ridicules*: what is extraordinary is that the management of such a large house could even contemplate risking seven performances in French.

It is easy to pick out impressive examples that demonstrate the abundance available to the Dublin public, but the fact is that the choice was much more varied then than what is available in the twenty-first century. In the year in which the Abbey Theatre opened, Sir Herbert Beerbohm Tree visited the Theatre Royal in *Hamlet, Twelfth Night, Julius Caesar, The Merry Wives of Windsor* and *The*

Merchant of Venice; Sir Henry Irving was seen in *The Merchant of Venice* (in a week at the same theatre that included plays by Tennyson, Bulwer Lytton, Leopold Lewis and Boucicault's adaptation of Casimir Delavigne's *Louis XI*); Frank Benson was at the Gaiety in *Hamlet, Richard II, Othello* and *Macbeth*; and Martin Harvey gave *Hamlet* for a full week at the Theatre Royal. True, these were not 'runs', but in effect one-night-stands of each play, but they were sumptuously mounted, great attention was given to the speech, and Dublin had the heady experience of being able to compare the Hamlets of three leading English actors in one year. Where nowadays one is lucky to hear six fully staged operas and perhaps two more with reduced forces in a year, in 1904 Dublin heard the Elster-Grimes Grand Opera Company in *Maritana* for a week, followed by a week of *Faust,* at the Queen's; two nights each of the Moody Manners Opera Company in *The Bohemian Girl, Carmen, Faust, Rigoletto, Tannhauser* and *Tristan and Isolde* over a fortnight at the Gaiety; and one performance each of *The Bohemian Girl, Carmen, The Daughter of the Regiment, La Traviata* and *Il Trovatore* by the Carl Rosa Opera at the Theatre Royal.

It is the broad choice of theatrical fare that has been ignored by most historians. When, for example, Hubert O'Grady's *The Famine* was enjoying an apparently well merited revival at the Queen's in the autumn of 1900, patrons with little taste for Irish historical melodrama might select the London production of George Bernard Shaw's historical quasi-melodrama, *The Devil's Disciple,* at the Gaiety; 4 when *The Famine* was followed by O'Grady's *The Fenian,* the alternatives were the D'Oyly Carte Opera Company at the Gaiety and Fred and Julia Neilson Terry in Paul Kester's *Sweet Nell of Old Drury* at the Royal.

Managements, Companies and Tours

A distinction should be made between Theatre Managements and Theatre Companies. All the licensed theatres in Dublin, Belfast and Cork were 'receiving theatres': they rarely staged their own productions, even importing companies to provide their Christmas pantomimes. The Queen's was also in this category: although noted for its Irish plays, these were produced by external companies on a rental or percentage basis. A confusion may have been created for historians by the fact that many of the Irish plays by J.W. Whitbread were presented at the Queen's during the period when he was also the theatre's manager (1883-1907) but the actual productions were given by other companies, most notably by the J. Kennedy Miller Combination.

Occasionally leading amateur and semi-professional groups were accommodated in the licensed houses. There was the annual production by the Dublin University Dramatic Society at the Gaiety, and, at the same theatre, the culturally significant week in October 1901 when Douglas Hyde's *Casadh an t-Sugáin* was given by the Irish Literary Theatre with players from the Keating Branch of Connradh na Gaelige as an afterpiece to Frank Benson's production of *Diarmuid and Grania* by George Moore and W.B. Yeats. These groups simply rented the Gaiety for the required number of nights.

It is a very curious and interesting fact that at this time almost all the plays of Irish content – with the notable exception of most of those of Whitbread – were initially performed in Britain. This is because the British circuit was infinitely more extensive than the Irish.[5] Players could rehearse their newest piece – which might happen to be Irish – while on tour and open it in the next provincial English city. The majority of professionally produced Irish plays were born in this way. There were certain theatres in London where Irish plays were frequently seen, among them the Princess's in Oxford Street, the Imperial in Westminster, the Elephant & Castle Theatre, the Standard in Shoreditch, the Pavillion in Stepney and the Prince of Wales' in Kennington.[6] An interesting statistic was printed in *The Era* for October 28, 1893, showing that of the six productions which had taken the most money in the British Isles to date that year, three were on Irish subjects (and two by an Irish writer) – Dion Boucicault's *The Shaughran* and *The Colleen Bawn* and John Buckstone's bizarrely uncategorizable *The Green Bushes*.[7]

Demographically speaking it does not seem that the *immigré* Irish were particularly numerous in any of the London boroughs mentioned above; one must assume that the Irish plays were interesting enough to please the audiences regardless of subject. However, the theatres outside London in which Irish plays seem to have been most regularly presented were situated in the industrial centres where there certainly was a significant Irish population, rather than in Cathedral cities like Norwich or Lincoln. (It could be argued that the overall population was much greater in cities such as Manchester or Liverpool and that theatres were more numerous in those places anyway.) In 1900-04 there were 19,000 births registered to 'Irish' families in Glasgow so it is not surprising that Irish titles appear with unusual frequency in the entertainment columns of the Glasgow newspapers for the Grand, the Metropole and the Royal Princess's in the city, the New Century in Motherwell, the Lyceum in Govan and the New Gaiety in Clydebank.[8] When Kennedy Miller brought Whitbread's *Lord Edward, The Ulster Hero* and *Sarsfield* to Glasgow in 1905, the performance on 8 August was given under the 'Grand Patronage of the United Kingdom Delegates of the Irish Forester's Society', and the Lord Mayor of Dublin, Councillor Joseph Hutchenson, was present as General Secretary of the Society and guest of honour.[9]

Judging by the headings in newspaper advertisements for Irish plays presented in Dublin, Belfast and Cork, the most active London companies were Amy Ellam & Hugh Dempster's Combination, Robert Barton's Company, the Compton Comedy Company, Webster & Enright, E.C. Matthews, J. Rice Cassidy, Faulkner Cox and Morrell & Mouillot. There is no reason to believe that any of them had a particular interest in Irish drama, for their dates in Ireland were in small proportion to those on the (undifferentiated) English, Scottish and Welsh circuit. An enthusiastic reception was not always guaranteed in Ireland, especially when the Irish characters were portrayed by patently non-Irish actors assuming 'Irish' accents which the audience had difficulty in comprehending.

The actor-manager Frank Fay, while contributing as a critic to the *United Irishman* prior to his highly influential role as producer in helping to create the 'Abbey style of acting', castigated the Scottish management Morrell & Mouillot for their production of Boucicault's *Arrah-na-Pogue* at the Theatre Royal, Dublin, in July 1899: 'The present company may pass muster in Glasgow, but it is not good enough for Dublin'!

The professional companies producing exclusively Irish work spent most of their year on tour in Britain. The sheer extent of the popularity of well presented Irish plays may be seen in the advertisements in *The Era*. In September, 1899, for example, an announcement shows that Hubert O'Grady's Irish National Company would be making *return* visits of a week each with *The Fenian, The Famine* and *The Priest Hunter* to London (Elephant & Castle), Sheffield (Theatre Royal), Derby (Grand), Leicester (Opera House), Greenwich (Morton's), Hull (Theatre Royal), Nottingham (Grand), Stockton (Theatre Royal), Ashton-under-Lyme (Theatre Royal), Belfast (Theatre Royal), Dublin (Queen's), Reading (County), London (Dalston), Stockport (Theatre Royal), Glasgow (Grand), Stratford-on-Avon (Theatre Royal), Birkenhead (Theatre

Royal), Liverpool (Star), Portsmouth (Prince's) Stoke-on-Trent (New Garden), Newcastle (The Theatre), Oldham (The Theatre) and Warrington (Court). With the exception of the Dalston Theatre in a north London suburb, these were all major houses, in many cases the leading theatre in each city.[10]

The only Irish-based company producing Irish plays exclusively from 1889 until well after the opening of the Abbey Theatre was the Kennedy Miller Combination, a well-organized ensemble which spent at least three quarters of the year outside Ireland. According to the *Irish Playgoer* of 15 March, 1900, Miller was born in Scotland and spent many years in various capacities 'on the circuit'. It is not clear when he first met J.W. Whitbread, the manager of the Queen's in Dublin and soon to become a prolific playwright, but small pieces of evidence suggest the earliest arrangement for Miller to produce a play by Whitbread was in 1889 with *The Irishman*. Thereafter, Miller directed and toured Whitbread's *The Nationalist, Lord Edward, The Victoria Cross, Theobald Wolfe Tone, Rory O'More, The Insurgent Chief, The Ulster Hero, The Sham Squire* and *Sarsfield* all over the British Isles. He also directed revivals of Boucicault and Buckstone at the Queen's and elsewhere. No record has been found of his involvement during the period in any but plays by Irish authors, or plays with an Irish setting by non-Irish authors. In 1899 Miller became General Manager of the Queen's under Whitbread, while continuing to produce plays that almost invariably opened there.

Frank Fay was far from euphoric when he reviewed Miller's production of Boucicault's *The Shaughran* in the *United Irishman* for 12 May, 1900, remarking that 'except for the obvious want of rehearsal, the interpretation which *The Shaughran* receives is not at all bad. I do not care for Mr Frank Breen's Harvey Duff, which, to my mind, is arrant clowning; but the audience took to him immensely, and, to his point of view, that is of more importance than his attaining any standard of excellence. Mr Tyrone Power is fairly good as Conn, and, when he has had longer experience, he will learn to deliver Conn's description of how he stole Squire Foley's mare without the effort that was only too visible on Monday evening ... Mrs Glenville, as Mrs O'Kelly, was nearly all that could be desired. It is the best thing that I have seen her do. Needless to say, she is an immense favourite with the audience ...' Allowing for Fay's deep desire that Irish actors should attain a standard comparable with the best from London, and that Irish dramatic writing should not of necessity be relegated to the second class, this is a remarkably favourable critique.

Fay's review is in the same spirit as the comments made by J.M Synge four years later when he saw Kennedy Miller's company (with some changes of cast) in the same play at the same theatre:

> The characters of Conn the Shaughran, and in a lesser degree those of Mrs O'Kelly and Moya, as they were played the other day by Mr Kennedy Miller's company, had a breath of naïve humour that is now rare on the stage ...

He liked the performance of James O'Brien, who was now playing Conn: '... in listening to him one felt how much the modern stage has lost in substituting impersonal wit for personal humour.'[11] O'Brien and Frank Breen, another leading comedian, were the only actors to be accorded single-line billing in the advertisements for Kennedy Miller's productions.

It would be impossible for there to be a theatrical production or incident in Dublin during the period without Joseph Holloway confiding an opinion to his journal. In the entry for 11 January, 1900, having attended a revival of Whitbread's *The Nationalist* at the Queen's, he wrote, 'The play was interestingly interpreted by Kennedy Miller's very capable company of Irish players who each and all seem to know the pulse of the popular audiences to be found in this theatre ...'[12] What is most significant is his phrase 'very capable company of Irish players', for, judging by reports in all sections of the press throughout the decade, Kennedy Miller's players were precisely that: 'capable', not 'wonderful'; and they were 'Irish players', not strollers from over the water. Taken with Synge's favourable comment written in the year of the first productions of *In the Shadow of the Glen* and *Riders to the Sea,* it does seem more and more extraordinary that Yeats, Martyn and their colleagues should have gone to the London actor-manager Frank Benson for players to interpret their early work when there were experienced professional Irish actors based in Dublin. Benson's company had to travel from London for *The Countess Cathleen, The Heather Field, The Bending of the Bough, Maeve* and *The Last Feast of the Fianna.*

It can not be stressed strongly enough that companies such as Kennedy Miller's, Hubert O'Grady's and Howard & Mackey's were highly professional ensembles, carrying three to six productions with at least two dozen actors and technicians and many tons of scenery. The staging of these productions required metropolitan theatres with flying facilities and a resident orchestra. In her book

Ireland's National Theatres (2001) Dr Mary Trotter describes Kennedy Miller's Combination as 'a fit-up company'.[13] This was far from being the case. Fit-up companies carried very rudimentary sets and, when they did not have their own portable booth, they played in parish halls, seaside pavilions and (later) in small town cinemas. The Kennedy Miller Combination played in city centre theatres and opera houses.

Companies visiting Ireland usually gave an 'early house' at 6 pm on the final Saturday night, following a matinée at 2 pm or, quite often, in the morning – hence the use of the term. This gave time for the 'take-down' and 'get out' in order to catch the last steam-packet. Occasionally there are newspaper references to a boat being 'held' in order to accommodate such-and-such a major company; and often two or three theatrical and operatic companies, along with acts from the music halls, might be seen travelling on the same boat from North Wall to Liverpool or Glasgow. The railway junction at Crewe was the recognized Sunday meeting place when news of engagements and the prospect of future tours was exchanged. As most of the steamship companies, including the London Midland & Scottish 'Mail Boat' which plied between Kingstown and Holyhead, ran overnight services, the incoming troupes arrived on Sunday evenings or Monday mornings, depending upon the length of the rail journey from the city of their previous engagement, their members spending the day seeking 'digs', usually in the Brunswick Street and Ringsend area of Dublin.

In Belfast, all the packet-boats lined up on the north bank of the Lagan, the berths designated with huge signs visible from the Queen's Bridge indicating the places of destination – Ayr, Ardrossan, Douglas, Glasgow, Greenock, Heysham and Liverpool. Theatrical digs were to be found in the neighbourhood of Albert Square and Ulster Street, no more than five minutes' walk from the Alhambra, Empire and Theatre Royal. When the Grand Opera House opened in 1895 householders in the adjoining Murray Street started taking in actors and stage staff: this arrangement continued until at least 1959. In Cork, theatre folk stayed in houses in the narrow streets between Lavitt's Quay and Patrick Street, only a quarter of a mile from the berths for Bristol, Milford Haven and Liverpool at Penrose Quay and Horgan's Quay.

Crossings were at best uncomfortable and at worst perilous. In the last week of 1895, having completed a lengthy tour in Bolton, the entire cast of Whitbread's play *Lord Edward* was feared lost on the voyage from Liverpool to Waterford, the ship being two days overdue. 'Much anxiety as to the safety of the members of Mr Kennedy Miller's company' was expressed in the *Waterford Star* of 30 December, but the paper was able to reassure its readers that the ship had at last arrived, and the company would be in a position to present Mr Whitbread's famous play that very evening.

The Players

The names of a dozen or more leading actors dominate the playbills of companies producing popular Irish plays in the years leading up to the opening of the Abbey Theatre – and for some time thereafter, for the popular style did not expire until after the arrival of the cinema. Programmes and newspaper reports disclose several names of younger players later to become synonymous with the Abbey but who spent prentice seasons at the Queen's and elsewhere: W.G. Fay appeared in Whitbread's patriotic melodrama *Shoulder to Shoulder* long before he joined his brother Frank in creating the semi-professional troupe which was to evolve as the earliest National Theatre Society ensemble; and later leading lights of the Abbey such as PJ Carolan, May Craig, Barry Fitzgerald (*né* W.J. Shields) and F.J. McCormick (*né* Peter Judge) all worked at the Queen's. F.J. McCormick appeared there under his own name as Gallopin' Hogan in a revival of Whitbread's *Sarsfield* in 1922 and Frank Fay appeared in a touring version of Whitbread's *The Nationalist*.[14] Players such as these may be seen as forming a 'bridge' between the two traditions – 'popular theatre' and 'art theatre' for want of more appropriate terms.

Most of the professional Irish actors of the time were associated with the continuously operational companies run by Hubert O'Grady, J. Kennedy Miller and Howard & Mackey. Many more were attached for periods of two or three years to long-running tours of the Boucicault plays whether or not under the author's managership. Names of actors may also be traced as moving from one company or production to another, as their talents grew or diminished in demand, or as casting arrangements altered due to age or other circumstances. Almost all the plays of the time needed very large casts: Whitbread's *The Ulster Hero* is quite typical, requiring twenty actors for speaking parts – crowd extras were taken on locally when touring. In 1900 there would have been at least a hundred leading and supporting professional actors employed simultaneously in Irish plays, the major proportion always being on tour 'across the water'. Some of these actors were patently not Irish but those who took the leading parts almost always were.

When, in 1903, Frank Fay and his brother William undertook to form the acting company of the National Theatre Society from the existing membership of seriously-minded amateur and semi-professional performing groups, they would find, for a time, an artistic *milieu* in which to create a more literate 'national' drama than anything which might have been imagined on the stage of the lamentably commercial Queen's Theatre. The pity is that the talents of the professional Irish actors, musicians, stage managers and scenic artists who were employed in the companies supplying productions to the vast commercial circuit were not automatically absorbed into the exciting and innovative venture that was taking shape across the river from the Queen's Theatre at the Abbey. A few players did later find their way there, but not as the result of any articulated recruitment policy or co-operative plan, and so the professional theatre and the art theatre remained mutually exclusive for at least another half-century.

2 | THE PLAYWRITING TRADITION

Ireland on the English language stage

There is little discernible difference between the way in which Irish and English playwrights from the Restoration until the beginning of the nineteenth century depicted their Irish characters, though Thomas Sheridan was at pains to show that Captain O'Blunder's apparently uncooth manners were a mere external, and that the man was in fact ' a true gentleman'. Among those created by Irish-born writers were George Farquhar's Roebuck and Foigard, Richard Brinsley Sheridan's Sir Lucius O'Trigger, O'Connor and O'Dawb, Charles Macklin's O'Bralligan and Mrs O'Dogherty and John O'Keefe's Dermot, Darby and O'Hanlon. Among those created by English writers were Captain O'Cutter in George Colman the Elder's *The Jealous Wife*, Sir Patrick O'Neale in David Garrick's *The Irish Widow* and Major O'Flaherty in Richard Cumberland's *The West Indian*. All were intended primarily to amuse the London audience.

Many of these stage Irishmen merely performed the function of the rustic Englishman dazzled by the sophistication of London. A first rate example may be seen in John O'Keefe's comedy *Tony Lumpkin in Town* (1773) where the Dublin playwright makes use of a favourite character created by his contemporary, the Longford playwright Oliver Goldsmith. This Tony Lumpkin endearingly makes a fool of himself on his first visit to the metropolis; he is English but he is really no different to the succession of unrefined yet good-natured Irish visitors to London encountered in so many plays.

Almost all the plays in which Irish characters appeared were set in England. The Stage Irishman is seen generally to fall into one or other of two categories – the lazy, crafty, and (in all probability) inebriated buffoon who has the gift of good humour and a nimble way with words, and the braggart who is likely to be a soldier or ex-soldier, boasting of having seen a great deal of the world when he has probably been no further from his own country than some provincial barracks. The former is an Irish naturalization of the parasite-slave character and the latter an adaptation of the *miles gloriosus* of classical comedy. There are overlapping variations of the two types.

The press in Ireland was often absurdly touchy about the portrayal of Irish characters, and of scenes set in Ireland. Throughout the nineteenth century there were innumerable instances of critical fury. On 26 July, 1881, after the first Dublin showing of Boucicault's *The O'Dowd* by a London company at the Gaiety, the *Freeman's Journal* observed that the actor who played Colonel Muldoon, was 'most objectionable ... It may be fairly stated without too much national vanity that no Irishman, and especially no Irish gentleman, ever presented such an appearance or conducted himself in such a fashion ... Of the crowd of ragamuffins who appeared as the bold peasantry, the less said the better. One would have fancied that outside a London music hall such caricatures of the Irish race had no existence.' The *Evening Herald* of 18 April 1899 found that Thomas E Murray's *Our Irish Visitors* at the Gaiety 'at times descends to the utterly ridiculous, especially in the Irish characters. These individuals, indeed, are such as one never meets off the stage'. The *Freeman's Journal* of 14 April, 1903, felt that Robert Johnson in his Whitbread Award play *The Old Land* at the Queen's displayed a 'tendency to follow on the line of the Stage Irishman and Irishwoman, a creation never popular with Irish audiences, and now even less so than ever'. This was in regard to the writing, but critics often confused writing with acting, or with the casting, when the supposedly Irish accents assumed by English actors proved unacceptable.

Towards the end of the eighteenth century Irishmen and women started appearing in Irish landscapes rather than English townscapes. The prolific and now undeservedly neglected John O'Keefe (1747-1843), as well as comparatively minor playwrights (but major theatre personalities) like Tyrone Power I (1797-1841), Samuel Lover (1797- 1868), Anna Maria Fielding (1800-1881) and Edmund Falconer (*né* O'Rourke; fl.1856-87) set the scene for the far more accomplished Irish plays of Dion Boucicault (1820-1890). None of O'Keefe's romantic Irish comedies such as *The Shamrock*

(1777) survived on the professional stage into the period of this review.[15] Tyrone Power I was said to be the son of the Marquess of Waterford; he was brought up by his mother in England and 'ran away' to join a theatre company at an early age. After a Nickelbyesque apprenticeship he accidentally landed the part of O'Shaughnessy in William Macready's *The Bank Note* and then quite quickly rose to leading roles in Shakespeare and modern dramatists and to running his own company. He enjoyed immense success in his own utterly fanciful Irish plays, most of them no more than burlesques. One was *O'Flannigan and the Fairies* (1836) which Boucicault later adapted as an afterpiece.

One of Tyrone Power I's most popular roles in Ireland, Britain and America was Conor O'Gorman in Anna Maria Fielding's *The Groves of Blarney* which that lady dramatized from a short story of her own. If there is an archetypical romantic Irish melodrama this is it.[16] Power's more sober melodrama *St Patrick's Eve* (1832) is set in Prussia during the reign of Frederick II; in it a Major O'Doherty, a wise Irish gentleman in the *miles gloriosus* mould who is instrumental in saving the lives of the juvenile leads, provides a diverting selection of anecdotal Irish country lore.

Tyrone Power I had another huge success in 1837 as Rory O'More in Lover's stage adaptation of his own three-volume novel of that name.[17] The O'More/O'Moore of history was a leading spirit in the Rising of 1641, but Lover used the historical incidents as mere background, though at the same time attempting to show that the recorded atrocities of the era were due to a few desperadoes and were not typical of the Irish people as a whole. The stage character of O'More is a strange mixture of *braggadocio* and whimsicality. According to the introduction to the published text Power was Lover's best interpreter, receiving 'hurricanes of laughter', especially for his narration of the speech about 'the fox of Ballybotherem'. J.W. Whitbread made a new stage version of *Rory O'More* in 1900. The script has not survived, but the critical response was that this was an inferior work and the wonder was he had not decided to revive Lover's script. It is interesting that Power's great-nephew, Tyrone Power II, played the part in Whitbread's adaptation; his performance was described in the *Irish Playgoer* of April 26 as 'ungenial'. The *Evening Telegraph* of 29 April referred significantly to 'buffoonery' – that term of contempt that Augusta Gregory and W.B. Yeats had used in their Irish Literary Theatre manifesto only two years earlier, in regard to Irish plays the titles of which they did not choose to specify.

The Importance of Being Boucicault

Dion Boucicault's position in the Irish stage picture of his time is central and unassailable. His work has been ably assessed by eminent scholars, yet it would be unthinkable not to remind the reader of his importance in the context of work by Irish contemporaries and also by English and American playwrights writing on Irish themes in the same era. Curiously, some commentators seem to be under the impression that all nineteenth century Irish melodrama was written in imitation of Boucicault but the fact is that many Irish melodramas pre-date his famous Irish plays.[18] As has been seen, all of Tyrone Power I's Irish plays, as well as the immensely successful *Rory O'More* by Lover and *The Groves of Blarney* by Anna Maria Fielding, which Power popularized, came out long before Boucicault's earliest Irish play of significance, *The Colleen Bawn* (1860). John Buckstone's *The Green Bushes*, which may be regarded as the progenitor of much that is quaintly and uncompromisingly bizarre in Irish melodrama, came out in 1845.

Briefly, Dionysius Lardner Boucicault was born in Dublin, probably in 1820. His mother was Mrs Anne Boursiquot (*neé* Darley). His father is more likely to have been Dr Dionysius Lardner than Mr Samuel Smith Boursiquot.[19] His dubious parentage and the presence of a 'second father' puts one in mind of Bernard Shaw, whose background was also of the Protestant professional class, a generation later. Boucicault was acquainted with the Wildes of Merrion Square who shared the social background and in later years he was helpful to their son Oscar when he was seeking theatrical introductions in the United States. He died in New York in 1890 following a career during which he was undoubtedly the most widely performed dramatist in the English speaking world after Shakespeare.[20]

Boucicault's apprenticeship in the theatre in London and provincial England was remarkably similar to that of Tyrone Power. After his first playwrighting success with *The London Assurance* in 1841 he proceeded to write more than 120 stage works – many of them adaptations of other writers such as Dickens and Dumas *père* – comedies, tragedies, tales of horror, historical dramas – as well as burlesques, farces and afterpieces. He was evidently an engaging character actor, especially in the Irish roles which he created for himself. He was by frequent turns a highly successful and spectacularly unsuccessful manager, making and losing several fortunes. The embodiment of the entrepreneurial actor-dramaturg-manager of the day, much of his work was hastily written to serve a particular obligation. Of the non-Irish plays on which he spent considerable time and thought, *The London Assurance* (which resembles an 18th century comedy of manners), *Jessie Brown, or, The Siege of Lucknow*, and *The Octoroon, or, Life in Louisiana*, are remarkably assured. *The Octoroon* was still appearing on the stages of America, Britain and Ireland at the turn of the twentieth century.

The intense popularity of Boucicault's misleadingly termed 'Irish trilogy' during his lifetime and for at least twenty years after his death left an impression that they were not only his most typical but also his best plays: such a view is perfectly justifiable. Time has shown that Boucicault was most 'comfortable' as a dramatic author with *The Colleen Bawn* (New York, 1860, inspired by Gerald Griffin's novel of 1829 *The Collegians*), *Arrah-na-Pogue* (Dublin, 1864) and *The Shaughran* (New York, 1874). The revival of interest in these plays, rather than in any other of his stage works, since the 1960s, endorses this view.

The Colleen Bawn is a prime example of first class adaptation from prose fiction to stage fiction. *Selection* is an important component of the process: selection of the essentials of plot and of the more vivid characters, and, conversely, the removal of extraneous narrative detail, didacticism and moralizing. *Substitution* is another essential component – such as substitution of dull passages of dialogue for pithy repartee. All this points towards the most important element, technically speaking, that of *dramatic compression*. Boucicault's greatest contribution to the success of this play was something less technical and more creative, something which only a unique talent could supply, and this was the sudden yet smooth transitions from lively action to moments of quiet emotion, from derring-do to genial wit. (O'Casey absorbed this trick for his 'Dublin trilogy', 1923-6.) Sentimentality is effectively cut short by humorous sallies, as if the dramatist were saying 'This is preposterous: I must introduce an immediate antidote'. The vehicle is usually the central comic character – here Myles na Coppaleen, originally played by the author – who is free to address the audience and, if necessary, raise an eyebrow at the ridiculous shenanigans. The sheer theatricality of this device comes from a confidence in the machinery of involving the public and stems very much from the tradition of pantomime. In the Irish context, as David Krause succinctly remarked, *The Colleen Bawn* depends 'more upon comic dialogue than wild situations for its triumph, in which the language itself, the Irish wit and rogueish blather, become merry weapons with which the characters defend and amuse themselves'.[21]

Boucicault had clearly 'found himself' as author-producer-actor with *The Colleen Bawn*. It broke London records for a first run with 260 performances. Queen Victoria attended three times, which ensured further popularity as well as respectability. Four years later, with tours of *The Colleen Bawn* proliferating, *Arrah-na-Pogue, or, The Wicklow Wedding* came out at the Theatre Royal, Dublin, to almost equal acclaim. (This was Boucicault's only play to be premiered in his native city.) Set at the time of the Insurrection of 1798, there is a strong political/historical motif, but this is diffused by the much stronger elements of comedy and characterization. Beamish McCoul is a 'rebel' hero somewhat in the mode of Lover's *Rory O'More*, but the plot seems to be Boucicault's own invention. The comic interest centres on Shaun-the-Post (the author's role) who gradually exerts more and more influence on the outcome, particularly in contriving his escape from prison and in his impertinent – not to say daring – answers in the courtroom.[22] The introduction of the traditional ballad *The Wearing of the Green*, rewritten by Boucicault with inflammatory phrases, did not cause objection until a Fenian-inspired explosion in Clerkenwell Prison in 1867 caused the authorities to request its removal, to which Boucicault evidently agreed.[23]

Ten years and some thirty plays later, *The Shaughran* appeared in New York with the author as the eponymous and prototypical garrulous Irish comic vagabond. Now entirely in charge of his material and the means of displaying it, Boucicault must surely have taken an enormous risk in setting the piece during the years of the comparatively recent Fenian uprisings – that is, if he wished to perform the play in Britain. Not only did he do so with impunity, but he also organized special performances in provincial venues in aid of the Fenian prisoners in British jails. (It is an extraordinary tribute to the broadmindedness of the British public that they should have supported a fund for the relief of convicted felons.) Yet we must constantly bear in mind with Boucicault's Irish plays, as well as with the numerous patriotic Irish melodramas by other writers, that if a play was seen to be worth attending on its merits as dramatic entertainment, its Irish provenance was of no consequence to the

British audience. Furthermore, since the potentially subversive element in *The Shaughran* is so encompassed by pungent dialogue and drollery at all social levels, by whimsical story-telling (as in the tale of Foley's horse), by comic situations (as in the wake scene when the corpse sits up, very much alive), any 'harm' was remarkably well concealed. There is something rather 'Irish' about entertaining one's enemy while excoriating him at the same time.

Boucicault bequeathed to the Irish stage three outstanding figures who may be ranked with the following century's Christy Mahon, Joxer Daly, Fluther Good, Monsewer, Pats Bo Bwee, Jimmy Jack and many others. Far from being stereotypes, Myles, Shaun and the Shaughran are each highly individual. Tyrone Power II was taken to task by the vigilant Frank Fay for his apparently unsuccessful attempt to play them as if they were the same character.[24] The nominal heroes of the three plays are absolutely inferior in worldly comprehension, executive action and vivid expression to what, in Irish playwrighting prior to Boucicault, would have been supporting comic roles. Boucicault also left an influential legacy in his combination and juxtaposition of comic and tragic elements; this specifically prefigures O'Casey's tragic satire, and more generally the inability of so many twentieth century Irish playwrights to produce 'pure' comedy or 'pure' tragedy.

Boucicault's three famous Irish plays did not vanish from the stage as so often happens shortly after the death of a playwright. As a matter of statistics, in Dublin in the decade leading up to the opening of the Abbey Theatre *The Colleen Bawn* and *Arrah-na-Pogue* were each seen twelve times and *The Shaughran* eleven times – 'number of times' may be taken as signifying a week's run at a commercial theatre, so thirty-five weeks were given over to these plays. In Belfast during the same period *The Colleen Bawn* and *The Shaughran* were presented for five weeks each and *Arrah-na-Pogue* for four. In Cork, where these plays were usually given for one or two nights only as part of a varied six-night programme, nine separate performances of *The Colleen Bawn* were given, six of *The Shaughran* and four of *Arrah-na-Pogue*. Productions in major theatres became less and less frequent as the twentieth century progressed, with the Abbey Theatre, to most people's surprise, setting the scene for rediscovery in 1967.

It is reasonable to suggest that without the example of the Boucicault trilogy the playwrights who are the principal subject of this study (O'Grady, Whitbread, Howard & Mackey, Fagan, etc) would not have been stimulated to seek 'serious' Irish subjects, nor might they have found the confidence to do so in the context of the commercial theatre of the English-speaking world.

Fig 1. Theatre Royal, Dublin [Dublin City Library and Archive] The third theatre on the Hawkins Street site, and the largest in Ireland at the close of the 19th century. Interspersed among West End tours of opera, drama and variety were London productions of Irish plays.

Melodrama – and Melodrama, Irish style

Irish melodrama was a unique and distinctive genre within the conventional melodramatic form.

The term 'melodrama', which came to denote plays of excessively dramatic content containing exaggerated episodes of duplicity, violence and horror but with virtue ultimately triumphant, originally meant exactly what it suggests: music drama. Music, as background to the spoken passages of an opera , or separating incidents in a play and emphasizing the emotional pitch, came to be employed more and more towards the end of the eighteenth century, most famously in Germany by August Kotzebue (1761-1819) and in France by Guilbert de Pixérécourt (1773-1844). Pixérécourt's *Coelina, ou l'Enfant de mystère* (1800) was adapted by Thomas Holcroft (1744-1809) as *A Tale of Mystery* at Covent Garden in 1802 and is said to have been the first English stage production thus described.

The material was often adapted from prose fiction and tended to ramble. Constant juxtaposition of pathos and comedy make for a hybrid type of theatre; real tragedy is absent, for in melodrama ostensibly tragic acts are set very much in the public arena and there is none of the inner conflict which conspires towards the fall from grace that constitutes the tragic hero in the Aristotelian sense. In present day parlance a 'melodramatic' play suggests one that relies on cheap sensational effects, but originally the term was not intended as one of disparagement.

Essentially, melodrama attracts the attention of the audience by the immediacy of its swift-moving story and by its instantaneous appeal to the most basic human concerns. The author does not waste time on niceties of verisimilitude or on the believability of the situations: he uses a kind of dramaturgical shorthand, rarely filling in the thematic or psychological interstices. It is left to the actors to create an enveloping style which will lessen the sense of improbability and create a momentary *frisson* of rapt involvement. In other words, the players – and indeed the orchestra – must paper over the authorial cracks. The style is rhetorical – it had to be, for nineteenth-century building technology was creating larger and larger theatres where naturalistic speech and gesture could hardly reach the furthest recesses of back stalls or gallery. The actor had to convey feelings by magnified vocal and physical means – by way of declamation, and by exaggerated gestures and glances. The performance style, therefore, was larger than life.

What distinguished Irish melodrama from its counterparts in the English speaking theatre was its vividly patriotic sentiment, both as expressed in the dialogue and as embodied in the action. The lovely – and generally witty – Irish heroine was much more than a wronged Maria Marten (of *Murder in the Red Barn*) or Isabel (of *East Lynne*): whether peasant or gentlewoman, to some degree she was almost invariably an embodiment of Ireland, albeit less subtly drawn than in the work of the *aisling* poets of a hundred years earlier. The hero of Irish melodrama was, if not determinedly taking the road to the gallows in order to assuage his country's wrongs, at least striving to create some measure of political or social reform; there was a strong tendency for the central male character to be presented as a figure with whom the audience could readily identify – such as the fictitious Hervy Blake in J.B. Fagan's *The Rebels* or the history-inspired Henry Joy McCracken in J.W. Whitbread's *The Ulster Hero*.

The Irish villain was quite different from the mustachio-twirling toff intent on securing the hapless village maiden or society beauty for his own sexual or social gratification. It is remarkable that he was almost always an Irishman: the conniving agent of an absentee landlord or, worse, an informer against those of his countrymen who were seeking to beat a path towards liberty. The villain in these plays was hardly ever an English officer or a Justice of the Peace under the colonial regime.

In Irish melodrama, the servants and rustics who aid and support their masters are, as a matter of course, aiding the cause of national liberty. Their use of language is far more allusive and colourful than the speech of the servants or peasants in any English or American play of the same type which the present author has come across.

As early as 1886 we find a clear appreciation of the above traits in an article in a 'popular' newspaper, where the reviewer of JW Whitbread's first play *Shoulder to Shoulder* bestows 'the highest praise' on the dramatist for overcoming the difficulties set by imitators of Boucicault. 'It is true we are asked to renew acquaintance with the broken-down swell, the villainous agent, his no less villainous factotum, the virtuous Irish maiden in dire distress, the comical and resourceful Irish manservant together with the comical and resourceful maidservant, and so forth ...'[25] A decade later a Belfast reviewer enumerated some of the more obvious traits of the genre as exemplified in Walter Reynolds' *The Shamrock and the Rose:* 'Of course it leans to comedy, but there is also much emotional drama in it ... It acquaints us with excellent types of the prominent Irish characters of the present day Irish society ... We have the over-generous peasant, the land agent, the devil-may-care labourer, the quack doctor, the R.I.C. constable, etc, all done to the life ...'[26]

The following year the inveterate Dublin theatregoer Joseph Holloway was writing in his journal that 'patriotic sentiment was cheered and the villains hissed all over the place' – this was in a revival of Whitbread's play about Lord Edward Fitzgerald.[27] Holloway was stirred by some of the major scenes, which he found 'quite poetical'; but he put his finger on the inconsistent nature of melodrama by adding that some other scenes were 'farcical to the point of absurdity'.

Most of the thirty-four plays discussed in this book – like the Irish plays of Dion Boucicault which are only touched upon here because they have been richly analysed by other authors – are true melodramas or are in some sense melodramatic. The element that binds these very disparate and individual works is the way in which they provide dramatic entertainment suitable for the satisfaction of a vast and largely uneducated audience. Authors such as Hubert O'Grady, J.W. Whitbread, J.B. Fagan and the Chalmers Mackey & Walter Howard partnership were responsive to the latent feelings of that audience and gave expression, often in an extraordinarily overt manner, to problems which were vexing the minds of Irish men and women in the street, to matters of national concern, and thence to aspirations of nationhood.

3 | A PATRIOTIC (OR SUBVERSIVE) THEATRE

Public and press reaction: to applaud, question or ignore

From a review in *The Era* of Whitbread's *The Irishman* at the Elephant & Castle Theatre, London, 2 November, 1889:

> The great British public of recent years have had a pretty good reason to give expression to a sense of weariness with the everlasting Irish grievances which have asserted themselves or been asserted in a way to give few other grievances a hearing; but we think it may be truthfully said that the British playgoer is not yet weary of Irish drama.
>
> Dion Boucicault, who gave sentiment and fun to the Irish character, and who, in his time, proved himself unrivalled in the matter of stagecraft in this direction, may be somewhat played out, but his old work has lost little of its popularity, and we fancy the day is far distant when such pieces as The Colleen Bawn and Arrah-na-Pogue will fail to create laughter and to exact tears. In new Irish drama we may perhaps not look for the Boucicaultian skill of construction or wit or pathos; but humour and interest are by no means wanting in the piece above, which on Monday evening met with the hearty approval of the large audience assembled ...

The critic went on to describe the plot of this early play of Whitbread's, and to praise most of the actors, the only objectionable element being 'the silly will business in the second act'. The (Irish) patriotic sentiments did not in the least displease. This review is in line with hundreds of others that appeared in newspapers throughout the British Isles over a period of a quarter century. Only a few keen-eyed British journalists noticed something more insidious and quite alarming.

One of these was *The Era's* own editor who, in the issue of 29 July, 1880, had accused Dion Boucicault of 'making political capital out of his dramatic child' – *The Shaughran,* now six years before the public. To this the playwright spiritedly replied a week later, denying the suggestion, and adding:

> you also say that my Irish plays 'are all flavoured with the sentiment of oppression, the love of the shillelagh and battered crowns, the hatred of the red coat and the steadfast devotion of "The Boys"'; I beg that again you are in error. No such incidents or language are to be found in any of my works. I challenge a single quotation.

Boucicault was clearly chancing his arm, for *The Shaughran* is certainly 'flavoured with the sentiment of oppression'; he probably sensed that the editor was unlikely to bother to rise to his challenge. Continuing to take a high moralistic tone, Boucicault went on to claim for the drama 'as broad a right to deal with social and political subjects as the Press enjoys, and will acknowledge only one censor – the public.' *Touché.*

The fact was that 'the sentiment of oppression' which the editor detected in *The Shaughran* was so well disguised by good-humoured blather and striking incidents that his readership was clearly no more uneasy than the people enjoying the play in stalls and dress circle. The play was the thing. It was also the thing in Scotland. In early February of the same year, the paper's Glasgow correspondent was more than a little taken aback by the content of Hubert O'Grady's *The Eviction,* which had enjoyed a three-week run at the magnificent Princess's Theatre and which the general public enjoyed without question. Noting that the play 'is cunningly put together and abounds in effective situations, which on Monday evening called forth loud cheering from the audience,' this reviewer was dubious about the suitability of theme. 'Dealing largely as it does with recent unhappiness in the sister isle, the play cannot fail to become popular with a certain section of playgoers, but it may fairly be questioned whether the production on the stage of such scenes as exaggerated heartless evictions and agrarian outrages is likely to prove instructive or amusing, or whether the play containing them can be considered a welcome addition to the literature of the stage.'

Had this Scottish reviewer been reading reports in the *Dublin Evening Telegraph* or the *Freeman's Journal,* he or she would hardly have described the scenes in *The Eviction* as 'exaggerated'. It is strange, too, that in a country where mass clearances had taken place within living memory, that the connection with *The Eviction* does not seem to have been made in the press. Others in Glasgow were more observant, for during the first run of *The Eviction* the *Evening Times* of 29 January printed a short piece headed 'The Distress in Ireland', when the Lord Provost presided at a meeting that resulted in a fund being set up to help alleviate such distress, to which the Provost himself subscribed £50 and others quickly followed suit, £100 being the highest figure donated on that date.

It may be instructive here to look more closely at *The Eviction* and its reception both in Ireland and other parts of the British Isles. This play, in spite of its superficially entertaining melodramatic story, is at its centre strongly critical of the regime that countenanced and indeed perpetrated the social disorders and upheavals reflected by the title, and also by the titles of most of O'Grady's plays. When produced at the Grand Theatre, London, in August, 1880, *The Era's* critic found that 'the entire drama may be pronounced completely successful', in spite of his reservation that

> the owners of land in Ireland can hardly be expected to take such a sentimental interest in Irish grievances ... In the pathetic scene of the eviction, which was managed with no little artistic skill, making an admirable and effective tableau, the fierce invective of the sensitive Dermot and the passionate address of the dying mother moved the audience deeply ... and the curtain fell amidst deafening applause.

This London critic's remark about the likelihood of Irish landlords having a different view to the one expressed by Dermot McMahon in the play brings into focus a phenomenon that permeates productions of most of the 'political' Irish drama of the time: these plays were interesting enough *in themselves* to attract an audience which might very well disagree with sentiments articulated by the characters and as shown by their actions; yet applause was clearly merited for the manner in which the possibly objectionable material was presented. Certainly the present writer has not found any reference to serious objection to this play in Britain, whether popular or official. In any case, the Lord Chamberlain had physically placed his stamp of approval on the script. Reaction to *The Eviction* in Ireland was of course quite different; but in England the report of an eviction (most likely in an industrial city in times of economic uncertainty) simply had to do with the matter of non-payment of rent and did not carry the same political or ethnic loading. English audiences could feel for the plight of the McMahons and O'Haras in their remote island: being turned from your home was surely a matter for universal sympathy, whatever the background.

The history of *The Eviction* in Ireland was, naturally, more explosive. The paucity of records regarding the early productions is frustrating in the light of the possibility that officials at Dublin Castle may have attempted to have the piece repressed.[28] The first performance in Dublin was on 6 June, 1881, eighteen months after the Glasgow premiere, the production having been on tour for most of the intervening period and described in the publicity as 'the greatest Irish drama of the present day'. By this time it was so widely promoted that the name of the National Theatre Company had been altered on the billboards to read 'Mr. and Mrs. HUBERT O'GRADY and their EVICTION COMPANY'.

No subject could have been more topical. The *Freeman's Journal* of the same date reported evictions in Ballina, Ballinasloe, Ballyshannon and Listowel, and the editor praised the Bishop of Meath, Rev Dr Thomas Nulty, for his outspoken objections to the Land Bill, which 'the patriot bishop' believed contained 'splendid principles' but many 'limitations and exceptions'. Three nights after the opening at the Queen's the same paper's critic wrote that 'nightly the house is packed from pit to gallery by an audience which certainly seems to thoroughly appreciate the play and sympathize with the evicted ones in it ... The 'Eviction' scene is most realistic, and gives a perfect picture of what is now almost a daily occurrence in the country ...' The reviewer proceeded to mention the players and the settings, but, as was the custom, did not provide any real analysis of the play's content.

The *Irish Times* and the *Evening Mail,* Unionist newspapers, did not trouble to review *The Eviction*. One wonders therefore if the Castle authorities were even aware of its explosive content, or if it was decided that the prudent course was to ignore it. However, eighteen years later *The Era* printed a comprehensive obituary of Hubert O'Grady in which it was stated that O'Grady 'was requested to withdraw the piece from the Irish stage. This was the means of giving the drama an extra boom, and made the business everywhere extraordinary.' As this obituary is imprecise on a number of points the statement may have been founded on hearsay; certainly reports in the Dublin press at the time of the production have not been found – unless reportage was also suppressed. A return visit of the same production in September 1881 was also very successful, but no report can be found even of an attempt to ban the play. Stephen Watt, in *Joyce, O'Casey and the Irish Popular Theatre* tantalizingly states that the Castle, 'as Dublin newspapers reported, threatened *The Eviction* in 1881 with a censurious (*sic*) notice'. Unfortunately Professor Watt has been unable to find the source of his notes on this issue – and there must have been an issue, on the 'no smoke without fire' principle.

A search in the Dublin Metropolitan Police Reports for 1881 has disclosed nothing further – but the police may not have been involved. Nor does the matter appear in the files of the Chief Secretary's Office where there is most likelihood of mention and where an anonymous letter is preserved dated 21 October 1881 in which 'A Loyal Irishman' draws the Chief Secretary's attention to a play which 'appeals strongly to the disloyal and excitable minds of an angry populace': this turns out to be a production of *The Shaughran* by a visiting London company! and there is no note to indicate if the Chief Secretary took any action; certainly the daily advertisements show that the play was presented without interruption.

As will be seen, the degree of political or social criticism varies considerably in O'Grady's other plays. In a play like *The Gommoch*, for instance, anything of the kind would hardly have been noticed outside Ireland; but in this country the presence on the stage of 'landlord' and 'police' would immediately have created an implication. References to the 'hard times' would have been picked up. When the local fortune-teller, Molly McGuire, speaks of her diminishing number of clients she is wondering if the young people are becoming wise to her hokum; but on another level her remarks may be seen as referring to the ever-increasing rural depopulation. This would not have been missed, for example, at the Theatre Royal in Belfast, when on any night much of the audience in gallery and pit would have been made up of economic migrants from Fermanagh and Donegal. When Larry O'Brien mentions 'the raising of the rents and the pulling down of houses' his words as a 'gommoch' may seem incidental rather than inflammatory, but they would have struck home to those with an ear to hear.

The gossip columnist in the *Irish Playgoer* of 8 January, 1900, declared in a passing reference to O'Grady that 'the palm for steering clear of political gunpowder cannot be awarded to him ... *The Famine* and *Emigration* have had long runs and always may be relied on to furnish situations hot and strong and vigorous...' The titles of these plays immediately signal their content. The leading character in the former believes that all the 'trials and troubles' of his time – which include agrarian disturbances and emigration - 'can be traced to the great distress during the Famine' and certainly this play does everything possible to support his thesis. Though it might seem from the deposit of 'ballad and story, rann and song' that the Irish had an exclusive right to bemoan the trauma inflicted by emigration, at this period Welsh, Scots and English folk were all contributing to the rise in population of North America and the Antipodes, and those who attended the English-language theatre in those places had been through – or their parents or grandparents had been through – the experience of what was far more than a simple matter of residential relocation.

America is seen in *Emigration* as the 'land of liberty', where 'the poor of Ireland will have the freedom that is denied them here at home' – this is the only line in the play that refers directly to the current conditions in Ireland that make emigration inevitable or even desirable – though what we have of the piece (only one of two acts survives) conveys the same idea in its general tone.To audiences in Philadelphia or Melbourne this theatrical testament must have come with an unwritten codicil: they would have to equate the aspirations expressed by the emigrants in the play with the reality of their new life. Had immigration proved, for instance, that America *was* the 'land of liberty'? Did Jerry Naylor's remark that 'when the emigrant leaves home, nothing but trouble and hardship meet him at every step' create a special resonance?

O'Grady's remaining two Irish plays, *The Fenian* and *The Priest Hunter,* both come with a handwritten 'disclaimer' on the mss. Of *The Fenian,* the author wrote, 'This Drama is simply a Romantic Irish Love Story, and has nothing to do with Patriotic, Political or Local evils' – except its *title*, one might respond; or, as one discovers, with a fair proportion of the action. It is likely that O'Grady was playing games with the Lord Chamberlain's reader, trusting that because of this sincerely phrased disclaimer the official would not trouble to scrutinize the text very carefully. There are curious omissions from the descriptions of the characters in the cast list. It is not stated that Jack Lynch is leader of the local Fenian brotherhood; his name is given but not this affiliation: to omit the name of one of the two principal male characters would have looked like deliberate carelessness – but O'Grady did omit the names of two other characters, O'Brien and Larkin, who are leading Fenian activists.

The persistent problem of 'loyalty' in pre-1922 Ireland (*Loyalty?: to whom?*) is interestingly raised in the second act of *The Fenian* where those attending the secret meeting object to the reported intention of their leader's sister, Ellen Lynch, to marry an officer in the British army. 'Let me tell you,' her brother Jack replies, 'there's many a true Irish heart beats beneath the uniform of a British soldier.' This statement is fairly well taken by those present, with only two seriously dissenting voices; those of Larkin and O'Brien. One thinks of the general tone of *The Silver Tassie* forty years later. The arrest of Fr Kelly on a trumped up charge, quite shocking in itself, would have been very shocking indeed to an Irish audience.

It may be considered strange that the duplicitous O'Grady used so provocative a title, for, as he so carefully states in his submission, the play is merely 'supposed to take place' at the time of the Fenian movement, which was, he strongly implies, twenty years ago and now thankfully forgotten. This is promotional fudge: if the author really felt that the title *The Fenian* would be detrimental in any way, he would not have used it. Clearly, he knew that this title on the billboards in Ireland would arouse tremendous interest, and in England would ring some kind of tocsin in the minds of prospective patrons who would then expect an exciting story for their money's worth.

The Priest Hunter was not, so far as has been ascertained, performed in Ireland; probably O'Grady imposed self-censorship, believing that the subject would be too inflammatory. A disclaimer is written on the first page of this mss. as well, to the effect that the play contains no 'political or religious element' (which is untrue) and that it is 'simply a romantic Irish love story' (which is only partly true). In appearing to accept the official line on what could or could not be presented on the stage by demonstrating, in the play's final moments, English benevolence to 'our poor country' – the period, though unstated, must be that of the late eighteenth century Catholic Relief Acts – O'Grady was surely fully aware that the overall effect of this piece is in complete contradiction to its fatuous conclusion. He would certainly have known that members of any audience would carry away with them a memory of the cruelty and dishonesty of the Penal Laws and, by extension, of the British presence in Ireland, rather than of the magnanimity of the government in partially rescinding the laws which it had itself imposed.

O'Grady was the most considerable dramatist to write on Irish subjects in the thirty years separating Boucicault's *The Shaughran* (1874) from Shaw's *John Bull's Other Island* (1904). It is quite extraordinary that given his deeply felt and often overtly expressed nationalistic concerns, and his stagecraft, his work has received such sparse attention from academic commentators in this or the last century.

Irish topics: material for a diversity of Irish, English and American playwrights

While O'Grady's *The Eviction* was having its stupendously successful initial three-week Dublin run, a glance at the newspapers reminds one of the variety of socio-political strands which made up the fabric of the country's daily existence. The Gaiety Theatre was pleased to announce that 'His Excellency the Lord Lieutenant and Countess Cowper will honour the Theatre by their attendance tonight' - the play was T.W. Robertson's *School,* a West End success. The following day the *Freeman's Journal* reported that 'Their Excellencies were greeted with mingled cheers and hisses.' (It is needless to surmise what reception they would have received had they attended *The Eviction* at the Queen's: but did they deliberately steer clear of it, or had the Viceregal household even heard of it?) On 18 June, Carlisle Bridge was renamed O'Connell Bridge, as the result of an overwhelming vote of the City Corporation, but without any special ceremony. The Ladies' Land League was founded; at this time the leader of the league, Michael Davitt, was in prison. The sculptor John Lawlor completed his statue of Patrick Sarsfield, Earl of Lucan, for erection in the Peoples' Park, Limerick; and the memorial to Cardinal Cullen by Thomas Farrell was unveiled in St Mary's Pro-Cathedral, Dublin. The second volume of Standish J. O'Grady's *History of Ireland: Cuculain and his Contemporaries,* was available at all good bookshops. Mrs S.C. Hall, who with her husband had written the influential travel book *Ireland, its Scenery and Character* and who as Anna Maria Fielding had written the popular melodrama *The Groves of Blarney,* died in England; and the poet and playwright Padraic Colum was born in Granard, Co Longford. The latter event was not noted in any newspaper and naturally there was no way of knowing how it presaged a changing Ireland.

Several 'Irish' plays which contain an appreciable nationalistic slant that were not written by Irish born authors or authors resident in Ireland were performed during the precise period of this study. Among the more interesting are Frederick Cooke's *On Shannon's Shore* and Arthur Lloyd's *Bally Vogan*. Both authors must have been struck by the vogue for genuine Irish melodrama and the commercial potential for new work in this vein. Cook and Lloyd were English playwrights; Cooke's *Under the Czar* was a West End hit. *On Shannon's Shore* takes place in Limerick and its surroundings at a time when agrarian reform was sought by violent means. Cooke is quite vague about what subversive organization 'the boys' may have belonged to, and because of this it is not possible to identify the exact period in which the action is laid. The play was almost continuously on tour from 1895 until 1904, but only played in Ireland for three (separate) weeks. The *Irish News* twice took the author to task for lack of essential knowledge of recent Irish history.

Paucity of historical research, however, did not prevent Cooke from writing a play in which nationalist sentiments were strongly expressed. If Gerald O'Neale is 'a supporter of the law of the land', his romantic nationalist nephew Hyacinth is quick to point out that the same law 'has never oppressed him'. Hyacinth O'Neale states that his feelings are 'with those who, heedless of their own advantages, risk death itself in an honest endeavour to place Ireland where it should be, in the front rank among the nations.' In an English-composed melodrama one might expect to see Hyacinth admit the error of his views in a final scene, but this does not happen; in the end Hyacinth achieves his greatest wish which has nothing to do with politics – the hand of Norah O'Riordan, the innkeeper's lovely daughter. Hyacinth's uncle Gerald, a man of property, is the intended victim of the principal subversive, Shaun, who is probably a Moonlighter; but at length Shaun is unsuccessful in his dire endeavour. Barney, the O'Riordan's comical handyman, is a 'Boccal na Sleeve' (*Buachaill na Sliabh,* or Mountain Boy); at one time he was imprisoned for his activities, apparently on scant evidence. Though there are plots and skirmishes, no one gets killed; those who seem to have been murdered exhibit a quite magical propensity for turning up later, quite unscathed. The convoluted action must certainly have gripped an undemanding audience, but as a drama of genuine Irish character and situation *On Shannon's Shore* ultimately fails to satisfy.

Bally Vogan, though also spurious in its Irish trappings, is not so heavy-handed. It appeared on the Irish stage on several occasions to a good reception. Irish jigs are danced on the village green, but the rustic flavour is patently Cotswoldian. In Ireland, the home of the local landlord is never referred to as 'The Hall'; a policeman would have been sent from Dublin, hardly from London – but instances like these are minor. The attitude to the 'Irish question' is quite positive, though a cynic in the audience would have found it all too naïve. Sir Gerald McMahon is an improving landlord; he spends most of his time and money in Ireland and has never evicted a tenant. It is McCrindle, his agent, who conspires to remove the O'Sullivans from their cottage, unbeknownst to Sir Gerald and due to McCrindle's own pique at having been rejected as a suitor by Norah O'Sullivan. Norah and her mother agree that 'if all landlords were like Sir Gerald our poor country would never have seen such trouble and distress!'.

Fortunately Lloyd did not attempt to put 'Oirish' speech in the mouths of Norah and the other rural characters. There are several references to the contemporary political situation. Bobby, the archetypal Englishman abroad, expresses the hope that by the time the landlord's son, Gerald McMahon, reaches his father's years, 'we shall have what all true-hearted Irishmen have prayed for for generations' – an undisguised reference to Home Rule even if not fully articulated.[29]

Arthur Lloyd seems to be attempting to portray a prosperous countryside which could be the prototype for all rural Irish communities once the 'trouble and distress' had been alleviated by a measure of self-government. It could be that the author, who does not appear to have written other plays on Irish subjects, had been looking for a topic of public interest in order to lend some kind of substance to a light drama; the Home Rule bill was accorded extensive coverage in the British as well as the Irish press, and was the subject of widespread debate.

A far better play is *Caitheamh an Ghlais*. In it the Irish elements are genuinely understood and portrayed – undoubtedly because the co-author and leading player, Chalmers Mackey, was Irish. If it is extraordinary that as early as 1898 a full-length play at a commercial Dublin theatre should be advertised with an Irish language title and play to full houses, then it is doubly extraordinary that the same should be the case at the Theatre Royal, Belfast. Clearly, a statement about 'Irishness' was being made. There is a less overt linguistic manoeuvre in O'Grady's *The Priest Hunter* which only those with a knowledge of Irish could have picked up: in the text, the eponymous villain is named as Paddy Mulloney, but by the time the play reached London this had been changed to Mickey Macanaspie – Mac An Easpaigh meaning 'Son of the Bishop'. Was this a coded ironic message to the audience to the effect that this persecutor of the Roman Catholic clergy during Penal times was in fact a Bishop's son? If so, the message could hardly have reached many people, for the play was not, as far as can be ascertained, performed in Ireland. Or was it a private joke among the members of the company? Whichever it may have been, it opens the interesting and unanswerable question as to whether O'Grady was an Irish speaker.

If the chief characters in *Caitheamh an Ghlais* are stereotypes, they are stereotypes who experience innate as distinct from imposed emotions. There is the landlord who is more concerned about preventing his son from marrying a peasant girl than he is about her family's connection with a subversive organization; there is his conniving land agent who is intent on improving his own way of life at all costs, including that of murder; there is the son of the dispossessed family who is fighting for his rights – and what he believes to be his country's rights – in the only way he knows; there is the witty and resourceful rustic, Shawn, who is capable of outwitting the most obdurate representatives of officialdom. They have all been seen before, but rarely exposed as persons of real flesh and blood.

In spite of its description as 'an Irish operatic comedy-drama' the performance style of *Caitheamh an Ghlais* is surprisingly unforced. The language is remarkably natural; it becomes terse when basic issues are at stake, as when the dodgy lawyer, Martin, informs Shawn (in prison) that he has been sentenced to death for the unlawful killing of Sir George Courtenay. Shawn refers to his own impending execution as 'murder':

MARTIN: Murder?
SHAWN: Aye, murder.
MARTIN: The law calls it justice.
SHAWN: Ireland has almost forgotten the meaning of that word. But there is one word she will never forget.
MARTIN: And what is that?
SHAWN: Oppression.

It is indeed curious that plays in which sentiments of this kind were openly expressed were passed by the Lord Chamberlain for performances in Britain. Whether used, abused or ignored, the absence of a similar mechanism in Ireland is even more extraordinary. If it is unclear whether the Castle did attempt to prevent a production of O'Grady's *The Eviction,* it is certainly clear that the attempt was unsuccessful. Can it be that the officials were simply unaware of what was going on in the popular theatre, and of the power of the theatre to contribute to the moulding of public opinion?

Irish heroes and scoundrels

Of the patriotic melodramas of the late nineteenth and early twentieth centuries those by J.W. Whitbread are the most often referred to by theatre historians. As has been suggested, the titles of some of these plays are such that one is quite surprised that the Castle authorities do not seem to have been interested. Whitbread's early plays are somewhat in the mode of Boucicault's *Arrah-na-Pogue* – domestic drama with a strong political background. When one of his earliest, *The Irishman,* arrived in Dublin after a week's showing in London the *Dublin Evening Telegraph* was pleased that the British public had been shown 'a representation of an Irish eviction', and that 'the casting out on the roadside of an aged and dying man is not an impossible incident in Ireland.'[30] In Whitbread's *The Nationalist* Paddy Finnigan boasts of delivering 'twenty-seven ejectments' in one day. We are not shown actual evictions or subversive gatherings in this play, yet the incidence of both offstage is constantly referred to. The young landlord, Phil Hennessy, is a member of the 'National League'; when visiting Australia he had been in contact with a proscribed group known as 'The Dynamitards'. This is balanced with unusual care by the introduction of Lieutenant Walpole, R.N., who is on a posting from the government in order to report on the situation in rural Ireland - which he is obviously going to carry out sympathetically; he is accompanied by an official photographer. Their presence is fairly understated, and they are quite subtly integrated with the domestic elements of the plot.

A play of Whitbread's in quite a different mould is *The Victoria Cross.* The title leads one to suppose that this must have been one of his plays that were initially presented in England, but such was not the case: once again one is reminded of the diversity of topics that were acceptable to Dublin audiences. It is set in England and colonial India, and contains one memorable Irish character in the courageous and beguiling person of Private Andy Cregan. The *Freeman's Journal* found it 'a capital production ... splendidly staged'; a *resumé* of the plot was printed, and there is not a trace of a suggestion that the home-and-colonial ethos of the piece was at all inappropriate on the stage of the Queen's Theatre.[31] When J. Kennedy Miller's company took *The Victoria Cross* to the Grand Opera House, Belfast (16 November, 1896) the week-long engagement was advertised as being under the 'Distinguished Patronage of Field-Marshall the Right Hon. LORD ROBERTS, V.C., G.C.B., G.C.I.E., Commander of the Forces in Ireland, and LADY ROBERTS.'[32] The nationalist *Irish News,* in an unusually brief review the following day, said that it had 'just the right dash of comicality to relieve the gloom of the main plot, the indispensable Irish soldier being in evidence', but the company was a 'harmonious ensemble' and there were 'scenes of varied beauty, principally in the neighbourhood of Cawnpore.' Surprisingly, the unionist *Northern Whig* was not greatly taken by the mildly Empire-building theme; on 17 November he or she found 'the elements of interrupted love, baffled hate and triumphant heroism very obvious.'

Arguably the now totally forgotten *The Victoria Cross* was Whitbread's best play: but his reputation during his lifetime was assured by the later group of plays which he built around the lives of Patrick Sarsfield, Lord Edward Fitzgerald, Theobald Wolfe Tone, Michael Dwyer and Henry Joy McCracken. These are not 'history plays' in the accepted sense of the term, but fictionalized accounts of crucial moments of decision and action leading up to the death, banishment or emigration (as the case may be) of the heroes whom Yeats would later collectively recall in the mesmeric phrase 'all that delirium of the brave'.[33] Whitbread's prototype was Boucicault's relatively unsuccessful melodrama, *Emmet.* Under critical analysis these plays now appear superficial, repetitive, often ill constructed, occasionally sentimental; in spite of the constant stage activity they contain passages that are woefully flaccid. Yet when considered a century after their composition they still retain a theatrical consistency and buoyancy and an irrepressible sense of certitude. In the special context of their theatre and audience they are far from risible. They create an emotional impact which only the determined cynic could disparage.

Because the shared motif in these later plays of Whitbread is nothing more nor less than that of the single-minded individual who believes in the concept of 'liberty, equality and fraternity' in an Ireland freed from the blight of foreign domination and who is prepared to lay down his life for the land he loves, they cannot be considered as anything but political statements. Their audience was not concerned with literary or intellectual issues, and for this reason political content was largely ignored by writers of serious dramatic criticism throughout the British Isles. The exception was Frank Fay in *The United Irishman;* this weekly must have been pored over by harassed and uncomprehending officials in Dublin Castle, but as Fay's chief interest was theatrical the political asides in his reviews would not have caught the eye of the government inspector intent upon identifying subversion.

Occasionally critics in the Irish dailies departed momentarily from writing the kind of reviews that were really little more than extended puffs in which every participant was given a mention. This occurred more often in Belfast than in Dublin or Cork. When Whitbread's *The Ulster Hero* reached the Theatre Royal, Belfast, on January 26, 1903, after two weeks at the Queen's in Dublin where it enjoyed business sufficient to warrant a return only nine months later, there was a predictable divergence of opinion between the *Irish News* and the *Northern Whig*. The latter pointed out with perfect fairness that what was 'euphemistically styled "a new Irish historical drama" is in reality the old familiar play with the traditional plot and the same characters disguised by other names'. In other words, McCracken might just as well have been Tone or Dwyer for all the difference it made. Unfortunately the *Whig* review was dismissively brief but the writer did mention that 'there was no mistaking the fervour and enthusiasm with which it was received by the greater portion of the audience' – as if to say the yobs from the Falls Road. The actors were praised, and so were the pictorial settings – Cave Hill, McArt's Fort, High Street, the Exchange – so this was not the kind of review which set out to denigrate any Dublin import, whatever its nature.[34]

The *Irish News* took it upon itself to beat the national drum in a prose style that was distinctly *passé*. Instead of imaginatively employing the cool prose style of the United Irishmen who appear in the play, the sentimental rhetoric of Lady Wilde and other contributors to *The Nation* newspaper was preferred, almost to the point of parody: the play's reception was seen as being 'proof positive of the faithfulness with which the memory of the dead is preserved amongst all that is pure and valiant in the Irish national character. In Belfast, more than in any other part of Ireland, does this lofty admiration for the heroes of a hundred years ago prevail with an intensity of feeling that can nowhere else be excelled, for was it not here that Henry Joy McCracken and the gallant band of Irish patriots conceived the glorious but alas! unsuccessful idea of freeing their country from the yoke of the foreign invader? It was only natural that the production on the stage dealing with the episodes and life of the Irish martyr should meet with a worthy reception in his native city ...'[35]

Clearly 'the greater portion of the audience' was of like mind that evening, for 'time after time the house applauded and cheered to the echo his [the actor Alfred Adam's] utterance of the sterling sentiments of the character. His reception was particularly warm when he delivered his speech to the United Irishmen before the rising near Antrim.' This might lead one to suppose that the actors rose to the heady atmosphere by overplaying the patriotic lines; but if we turn back to the *Whig* reviewer, who praised where praise was due, it appears that the performance was highly disciplined.[36]

When reading through *The Ulster Hero* it is impossible not to feel that little has changed in Belfast, not merely in the hundred years that divide the subject matter from the production but in the further hundred years that divide the production from more recent events. The constant watchfulness, the searches of houses, the necessity for moving home, the 'lifting' of suspects, the attempted shootings and stabbings, the undercurrent of betrayal, the constant fear of reprisal, the lack of comprehension shown by members of the British forces, the small and revealing acts of humanity: all these give the second act of the play in particular a disturbing feeling that we have been witnessing the same thing over again.

A 'relevancy' of this kind was spotted by Joseph Holloway in 1902 when he attended a performance of *The Insurgent Chief* in Dublin. Holloway noted a resemblance between Michael Dwyer and the South African politician, soldier and big game hunter Christian de Wet. The second Anglo-Boer war was then at its height, with reports appearing daily in the Dublin press. The most interesting of these appeared regularly in the *Evening Telegraph,* whose South African correspondent was Michael Davitt. Davitt naturally presented quite a different view to those of the reporters from the *Irish Times* and the Irish edition of the *Daily Express*. Holloway remarked in his journal:

> The manner in which he [Whitbread] manages to get his hero, Michael Dwyer, out of every tight corner in which he places him, suggested to all who followed his chequered career on the stage the present day De Wit (*sic*) in South Africa. No matter what trap the Yeos (*sic*) lay for him he gets clear off, and furthermore the Yeos, like their present-day prototypes, run like frightened deer when they learn of his approach, so much so that many people were heard to exclaim that 'it was a rale (*sic*) Boer War they were seeing'. This similarity of incidents in the Irish patriot's career to those taking place each day in the Boer commando Bg. [Brigade] in South Africa, added a great interest to the new drama.[37]

It would be easy to view these hero-based plays as a deliberate incitement to rebellion, were it not for the fact that in no way do we get the impression that the admittedly shadowy figure of J.W. Whitbread had anything more subversive in mind than maintaining a profitable playhouse. It appears to have been the view of all sections of the press that Mr Whitbread was respectability personified. In the view of the Castle – if the Castle took a view in this matter – it would have been noted that he was of English birth and professional experience, that a Lord Lieutenant had attended one of his productions and that HM Commander of the Forces had attended another. Against this, can the Castle have been aware that under Whitbread's management a benefit performance of *The Insurgent Chief* was advertised at the Queen's Theatre for the evening of 22 December 1902 from which the entire proceeds were donated to aid 'the erection of a national memorial to Michael Dwyer and Samuel McAllister' – the latter known in the play as 'Antrim Jack' – and that two years later the memorial was unveiled in the main square of Baltinglass? Unless the intelligence service was very much at fault it must have been aware of this, and the policy must have been to do nothing about it.

If 'factual' or 'documentary' history showed that Patrick Sarsfield's defence of Limerick culminated in the momentous migration known as the Flight of the Wild Geese, that the French expeditions to Bantry Bay and Kilalla ended in sheer disaster and ultimately led to the suicide of Wolfe Tone, that Michael Dwyer's guerilla campaign in the Wicklow mountains earned the insurgent chief a free ticket on a ship to New South Wales, folk history saw these events and their leaders in a different way, substituting epithets such as 'bold', 'noble' and 'heroic' for less complimentary official descriptions. Whitbread in his later plays went a step further, presenting the ingrained deposit of the localized folk memory in a tuppence-coloured panorama of *tableaux,* interspersed with music and racy dialogue, and given human interest by the introduction of enthralling marital and domestic trivia, all of which could be seen and relished by thousands on payment of sixpence at the box office. Unpalatable facts were simply ignored in these plays, unless they were capable of giving additional emotional impetus to the drama. *Theobald Wolfe Tone* ends in Brittany to the huzzas of the crowd as the hero embarks on the voyage that will free his native land. History tells us that this voyage resulted in nothing of the kind and that Ireland was plunged into worse turmoil, but Whitbread stops short of the historical *dénouement* and all is flag-waving and optimism. In *The Ulster Hero* he follows McCracken right onto the scaffold, presenting a horrifying physical conclusion because there could be none other. The whole thrust of this play demonstrated McCracken's sincerity, honesty, modesty and bravery, and it is clear that a moral victory has been won: the cause of the United Irishmen has triumphed over death and Ireland will, it is implied, be free.

Dr Cheryl Herr suggests that Whitbread gave an alternative 'take' to the dominant perception that the Insurrection of 1798 was a failure: 'By emphasizing the positive achievements of 1798, the Queen's Theatre writers asserted against historical fracture and stronger typological coherence that the Society demanded of itself'.[38] In some respects the Queen's Theatre enjoyed the position that a popular tabloid newspaper or television channel would occupy a hundred years later. An appreciable section of the audience, if not statistically illiterate, certainly would not have been reading the political commentators of the *Freeman's Journal,* but would have discovered in their attendance at the theatre the essence of such comment alive upon the stage. The theatre, therefore, served as a means of keeping in touch with the spirit of nationalist opinion: it was a kind of arena where the like-minded met informally to consolidate a view.

While the British crown may be seen as the ultimate baleful influence, this is usually by implication and, because depersonalized, quite a long step removed from the real and ominously present perpetrators of evil, those Irishmen who sought to use the political *status quo* to further their own interests and thus betray their neighbours, dependents and, in the final account, their country. Betrayal is therefore a significant theme. The most perfidious villains in almost all the plays of the genre are upwardly mobile Roman Catholic Irishmen of the lower middle class. Dr Mary Trotter seems to have entirely missed this point when she asserts that 'the Irish characters are kind and generous' – some are, but the real scoundrels are all too Irish.[39] It may be that Dr Trotter believes that names like Turner, Blake and Higgins denote Englishmen, but they and their like are perfidious Hibernians.

All Whitbread's principal scoundrels are Irish – Richard O'Cassidy, the land agent in *Shoulder to Shoulder* and Felix Blake the land agent in *The Irishman;* Patrick O'Flynn, attorney, Matthew Sheehan, land agent and Paddy Finnigan, server of eviction notices, in *The Nationalist*; Francis Magan and Sam Turner, Castle informers, and Francis Higgins 'the sham lawyer' in *Lord Edward*; the same Turner with Joey Rafferty, another Castle informer, in *Theobald Wolfe Tone*; Brander Byrne, the informer in *The Insurgent Chief*; and Danny Niblock, a Falls Road factory clerk and informer in *The Ulster Hero*. The Anglo-Irish landlords, where they appear, are mainly secondary figures; the most prominent are Squire O'Neil in *Shoulder to Shoulder,* an entirely sympathetic country gentleman wronged by his land agent, and Captain Airely in *The Insurgent Chief* who actually hands in his army commission and declares his support for the principles of the insurgents. Several of the British soldiers such as Major Sirr in *Lord Edward* (he also appears as the chief villain in Boucicault's *Emmet*) were of Irish birth. The English Captain Carr in *The Insurgent Chief* is, however, a real bounder - perhaps he is the proverbial exception who proves the rule.

The majority of O'Grady's villains are also Irish – McCauley, a squireen, and Hicky, 'a cadger' in *The Gommoch;* Rooney, a bailiff in *The Eviction;* Naylor, a land agent in *Emigration;* Sadler, a public works timekeeper in *The Famine;* Brannigan, a porter in *The Fenian;* Mulloney in *The Priest Hunter*; Harry Maxwell in *The Fenian* is a traditional cad who may or may not be Irish. Of the Anglo-Irish landlords, Lord Hardman in *The Eviction* finally rejects the cruel practice of the play's title; the only irrevocably hard line Anglo-Irish tyrant is Lumley Sackville in *The Famine,* and the author puts a stop to his direful gallop with a bullet. Of the British military and colonial administrators, Colonel Tracey is experiencing a change of heart when shot by Maxwell in *The Fenian*; and Sir John

Oliver Cromwell in *The Priest Hunter* alters his attitude when the partial repeal of the Penal Laws becomes government policy.

The ancestors of O'Casey's indigenous 'pimps and informers' are also to be found in plays by lesser dramatists than Whitbread and O'Grady: Stephen Purcell the tithe-proctor and his dire accomplice Black Mullins in Falconer's *Peep o' Day,* the spy Jack Daly in Jarman's *The Patriot's Wife,* the land agent Norry Boyle in Manning's *My Native Land* – they are all Irish born and bred. It cannot be stressed too strongly that the perception among most British and American commentators that the villains in these plays are *de facto* high ranking members of the British forces and judiciary is altogether erroneous.

Fig 2. National Standard Theatre, London [*The Era*] One of several very large metropolitan theatres that received touring productions of Irish plays.

Dramatic entertainment and dramatic literature

> SPEAKER: How long, ah, Sarah, can I say how long my life will last?
> SARAH: Cease boding doubt, my gentlest love; be hushed that struggling sigh ... Ah, Robert, Robert, come to me!
> SPEAKER: I have written my name in letters of fire across the page of history. I have unfurled the green flag in the streets and cried aloud to all the people of the five kingdoms: 'Men of Eire, awake to be blest! Rise, Arch of the ocean and Queen of the West!' I have dared for all Ireland and I will dare again for Sarah Curran.

This is not a typical piece of dialogue extracted from a late nineteenth century melodrama about Robert Emmet and Sarah Curran but a pastiche written by Denis Johnston in 1926 for the play which was produced three years later as *The Old Lady Says 'No!'*[40] Yet these speeches and those that follow are actually rather more than pastiche: they constitute a *collage* of quotations taken from lyrical verses by the poets Callanan, Drennan, Mangan, Moore, Todhunter and several others and put into the mouths of two actors in what is supposed to be a second-rate theatrical fit-up company, and performed by them in an overblown romantic style. It was Johnston's intention to give a brief and atmospheric glimpse of an old-fashioned Irish play as a prelude to the main body of his satiric modernist comedy; those in the audience who recognized the quotations might have the satisfaction of experiencing an extra *frisson*.

In all the thirty-four Irish melodramas considered, few contain passages as interesting, inventive, amusing and indeed moving as the opening scene from which the above lines have been extracted. The language is vibrant, allusive, atmospheric, melodious (where it needs to be) and eloquent. Johnston was creating – whether the thought crossed his mind or not – dramatic literature that also happened to be entertaining. A generation earlier Fagan, O'Grady, Mackey, Whitbread and others were creating dramatic entertainment – often interesting, amusing and indeed moving, yet none of their plays may be confidently claimed for literature. Their language, quite high flown at times, their style, their intellectual grasp of topic and material, were distinctly of their era and do not survive beyond the confines of that era. Johnston's play is also very much of its era, for it is written in the prevailing mode of German expressionism but it transcends the surface particularities of its time and survives vividly in print as well as on the stage. The popular late nineteenth century Irish playwrights possessed many gifts and, in varying degrees, they understood how to put a play together, how to tell a story winningly on the stage and how to amuse and involve a very large audience, but they fundamentally lacked the gift of eloquence that might sustain their work over the next hundred years.

Language: the defining gleam

What surprises, on first approaching these plays, is the absence of stereotypical 'melodramatic language'. For example, in only one play of those studied (Whitbread's *Sarsfield,* and only once in that) does one come across a phrase such as 'She little suspects that I know ... (etc)!', spoken in a subdued hiss to the audience from behind a white-gloved hand. What Allardyce Nicoll described as 'would-be dignified but bathetic conversations' amongst people of rank and education are another stereotype of melodrama, and these are certainly to be found in any of the plays mentioned here in which the nobility and gentry are depicted.[41] This is more a matter of the obtrusion of these authors' social background – they tended to come from relatively modest homes. This is patently not so in J.B. Fagan's *The Rebels,* where the Bagenals of Dunleckney House speak and behave with ease and decorum, and the reason must surely be that Fagan (an Old Clongownian) came from a landed family in the Queen's County and therefore transcribed the appropriate mode of speech without feeling the necessity for highfalutin' language. However, while the speech of the landed and officer class is usually fairly stilted, when a sardonic effect is intended – which is frequent – this works well, as in much of the dialogue between Lady Honor and Lady Rose in Whitbread's *Sarsfield:*

> ROSE: Your General, Honor, evidently is attaining to the highest pinnacle of fame, the love of the lower orders.
> HONOR: Which at heart is honest – not like our own, leavened with hatred, malice and all uncharitableness. But I wish, Rose, you would not so continuously harp on the same string. Sarsfield is no more 'my' General than he is yours.

When the difficulties of transcribing speech informed by birth and class are ignored by the playwrights, conversations between high-ranking persons become less linguistically strained, especially when pressing professional matters are under discussion.

Of a quite different quality are many strongly worded – and strongly felt – speeches to be found in the midst of much fustian prattle in most of Whitbread's and O'Grady's plays. Such speeches tend to contain well balanced argument or opinion harmoniously expressed in admirably poised phrasing. The following example is from *The Nationalist,* when the journalist Joe McManus addresses the land agent and his dubious accomplice outside the prison in Act II Scene 2:

> JOE: You and men lie you resemble the snail: wherever you go you leave behind you a trail of slime; whatever you touch you defile. You clog up the lungs of the country, undermine its constitution, wither up its fair surface – and the sooner it is free of your polluting presence the sooner it will breathe again.

An excellent example of this antithetical speech may be found in Act I Scene 2 of *Theobald Wolfe Tone,* where the Castle spy Rafferty dilates on the difference between the Patriot and the Informer:

> RAFFERTY: The patriot schemes, works, delves, builds for the regeneration of his country, the informer steps in and reaps the reward; the patriot is starved, exiled, bayoneted or hanged, the informer retires to his country seat a rich gentleman, respected by the community at large and there ends his days peacefully and quietly like the honest man he is.

This speech, and others like it, possess both a lively rhythm and an ironic sparkle that would be worthy of Shaw.

Some of the most agreeable elements in most of these plays are the exchanges between members of the lower orders, or speeches addressed by a member of the lower orders to his or her superior – such dialogue is often peppered with what the Edgeworths called 'Irish bulls' and what a know-all provincial type in Somerville and Ross described as stemming from 'rustic ignorance'[42]. In Whitbread's earlier plays the language of the Irish peasant tends to be more exuberant than in his historical dramas. Says Denny to Matthew Sheehan (in *The Nationalist*) of his meanness: 'You'd steal the gum off a postage stamp to make soup with!' Says Denny of Peggy's garrulousness:

> DENNY: Her speech is like the Shannon: it occasionally overflows, and, as the quality's good, I'd like to dam it.

An alarmed Peggy exclaims to Denny:

> PEGGY: I'll be a widow before I'm married to you!

Many of the working-class or peasant characters, through formally uneducated, seem to have inherited a love of the lengthy words and archaic expressions that their parents or grandparents would have brought back from the hedge school, where Greek, Latin and Gaelic terms were tumbled about with current English. Magisterial Johnsonese Latinisms are especially evident (as they are evident to this day in speeches made by local politicians). Says Flynn of Joe McManus the journalist in *The Nationalist:*

> FLYNN: He's a perambulatin' encyclopaedia of gineral intilligence.[43]

These people relish an arresting turn of phrase as much as Christy Mahon's audience in *The Playboy of the Western World.*

Some of the longer speeches in *The Nationalist* and other early plays by Whitbread are as florid as anything in O'Casey. It would not be fanciful to suggest that the latter's theatregoing in Whitbread's Dublin may have influenced the kind of highly tinted word clusters, alliterations, mispronunciations and Malapropisms which he put into the mouths of the likes of Mrs Madigan and Mrs Grigson – or at least that his visits to the Queen's Theatre would have confirmed in the back of his mind that such a liberality of loquacity was legitimate on the professional stage. Says Peggy to Mathew Sheehan, the land agent in *The Nationalist:*

> PEGGY: Yeer very prisince is contagiously contaminatin' to a dacent girl, and I lose my indignity when I spake to ye at all. Gintlemen – kape him at a disrespectable distance or he'll defile ye with the dirthy pitch of his own conglomerfication!'

When viewed on the page, written out phonetically (as in the published text of O'Casey's plays) such utterance looks like nothing other than bucolic blather at its most irritating, but when spoken by skilled actors the effect is invariably amusing and often devastating. It is, however, the *flow* of such dialogue, rather than individual words and phrases, that gives it its vitality on the stage. Here are Eilly Blake and Terry 'Gallopin' Hogan discussing General Patrick Sarsfield in Whitbread's play of that name:

> EILLY: Oh, Terry, agra, my heart's glad to see ye. An' how's his honour – have you seen him?
> TERRY: Seen him? Faith, I have. Bedad, her ladyship must have given him a fine ould wiggin to put him in such a tunderin' passion.
> EILLY: Is he that?
> TERRY: Throth, he is. He came jumpin' into the boat like an avalanche ov snow on Mount Vesuvious; sure I tought the bottom was goin' clane out ov it altogether. "Is that you, ye blayguard" says

he; "it is" says I. "What are yez doin' here?" thunders he. "Waitin'
for you", says I... an' in I jumps wonderin' what was comin' next.
An' thin I heard a great big sob, and thin his voice as tender as
ever, say. "Terry, me boy, me heart's broke," and his head fell on
me shoulder, an he cried, acushla, as only a strong man can cry
when his heart is breaking wid the sorrow.
EILLY: Ochone! Ochone! And did he send ye here?
TERRY: He did that. "See Eilly", says he, when he grew calmer, an'
got his articulo mortis undher proper control, "axe her how her
mistress is, get all the information ye can, and join me in
Limerick." Arrah, what's the manin' ov it all?

Spicy vernacular terms taken directly from the Irish language
pepper the dialogue of many of these plays, especially those of
O'Grady and Whitbread. In *Sarsfield,* words such as 'girsha'
(*girseach,* 'a young woman'), 'mulvathered' (*méarbheallach,*
'confused'), 'doch ah dorrish' (*deoch an dorais,* literally 'a door
drink', meaning a parting toast) could quite easily have been
inserted by other hands and in the case of the English-born
Whitbread probably were, though it is entirely possible that his keen
ear picked them up from his theatre and domestic staff. His use of
'collops' (*colpa,* 'shin') predates that of John B. Keane by three
quarters of a century. In Falconer's *Peep o' Day* many Irish words
issue naturally from the mouths of the speakers, such as 'prashkeen'
(*práiscín*) for apron, 'caubeen' (*cáibín*) for hat, 'nabocklish' (*ná bac
leis*) meaning 'it's of no consequence'. In the same play there is a
location called 'Foil Dubh' (*Fál dubh*) 'a dark enclosure'.

As will be seen, the English-born playwrights writing on Irish
topics generally do not have the facility with vernacular dialogue
that is a mark of their Irish (or *immigré* Irish) counterparts. The
rural Irish people of the English playwrights are more in the
'country bumpkin' mould than the rooted-in-the-soil characters that
appear in truly Irish plays like Chalmers Mackey's *Caitheamh an
Ghlais.* The genuinely Irish characters, too, seem to be able to
express real emotion without descending to sentimental drivel.
When the agonized Shamus McDermott in Caitheamh an Ghlais
pines for his lost Norah McGrath – who may be seen as a symbol for
Ireland and who, it appears, has flown to the arms of another – he
attempts to console himself with a charming metaphor drawn from
nature:

SHAMUS: When the wings of the bird are tired, when its strength
is spent and its heart is bruised, it wanders back to its first nest,
and 'tis here my Nora will wander back.

to which the more realistic Biddy Maginn observes,

> BIDDY: Aye, when her lover has left her and the people point the finger of scorn at her she will come back – and what will you do then, Shamus?'

Shamus declares that he will welcome her. Shamus – a member of an unnamed illegal organization – sums up his position in a perceptively written speech that concludes

> SHAMUS: I am the last of a long line whose misfortune it has been to fight on the losing side, and as a result our own roof is to be torn from us and we are to be expelled from the homes of our kindred ... It would be a blessing if the vast estates of our land would be ruled by men who would spend their rents not in London or Paris but from among the people from whom they are ground, and on the land from whence they are raised ...[44]

Vernacular speech? Well, not exactly; for, in the hands of the professional playwright, when real emotion is introduced rude rusticisms give way to deliberately heightened language. There is a thin line to be drawn between this spare type of speech and the declamatory style which is usually associated in the reader's mind with the notion of melodrama, and which certainly tends towards the bathetic.

Declamatory speech of another kind – in the sense of the intentionally rabble-rousing patriotic diatribe – is absent from most of these plays, for the very good reason that had it been there the Lord Chamberlain would not have granted a licence for performance in England, Scotland or Wales, and in Ireland the authorities might have found a way of revoking a theatre's performing licence for some technical reason.[45] The anti-colonial content is not of the diatribe variety, but is generally expressed in the day-to-day vernacular speech of the ordinary characters. It is more often than not cloaked in rustic sallies that a censor would have had difficulty in interpreting in the handwritten text – but in the mouth and gesture of a skilled performer would scatter the mist of misapprehension like a bolt of lightning, wherever there was an audience willing enough to be struck by it.

This leaves us with plays the very titles of which should have alerted the authorities – *The Fenian,* for example, or a play bearing the soubriquet of a revolutionary leader such as Henry Joy McCracken, 'the Ulster hero'. That the authorities did not react would have been due to an astonishing failure to grasp what was going on in these plays, and also from fear of stirring the noxious

Irish pot of broth; the disclamatory notice may be seen at source in the way O'Grady wrote outrageously misleading introductory notes on his manuscripts, stating that, for example, 'This drama does not deal with the Political or Religious element of the time', the mendacity of which was not appreciated by the censor who, satisfied that there would be no harm in it, did not then trouble to read the play; or in the apparently conciliatory speeches at the final curtain of many of the plays – such as in *The Insurgent Chief* where the British army captain apologizes for his rough treatment of Dwyer (which was made in the course of duty); Dwyer is pardoned for not actually taking part in the Insurrection of 1798 and accepts the verdict of transportation – while, naturally, never forgetting 'the dear land I loved so well'. Such compromise goes entirely against the grain of the preceding two hours traffic of the stage, and it is that which members of the audience would have carried out with them into the street and into their homes, to meditate upon during the long nights after Samhain.

Fig 3. Royal Princess's Theatre [Bruce Peter: *Scotland's Splendid Theatres* Glasgow] Hubert O'Grady's *The Eviction, Emigration* and *The Fenian* opened here and many other Irish plays appeared here on tour. It is now the Citizens' Theatre..

4 | HUBERT O'GRADY: REFORMER DISGUISED AS A GOMMOCH

Hubert O'Grady (1841-1899) was the author of the most original and also the most politically and socially provocative body of Irish plays that were first seen during the final quarter of the nineteenth century. They continued to be performed regularly until well into the twentieth. Though he made use of the prevailing popular theatrical mode it would be a mistake to categorize him purely as a writer of melodrama for much of his work is imbued with deeply felt humanitarian concerns – all the more poignant for being cloaked in improbable incident and capricious comedy.

O'Grady's plays are *The Gommoch/The Wild Irish Boy*, *(The) Eviction*, *Emigration*, *The Famine*, *The Fenian*, *The Priest Hunter* and *A/The Fast Life*. Plays attributed to O'Grady which were not performed in Ireland and may not have been performed at all were *The Maid of Erin*, *The Chief Secretary* and *The Land Grabber;* in any case no mss. of these titles has been found. *The Land Grabber* may have been an alternative title for *The Eviction*. There are contemporary press references to what seem to have been short music-hall sketches, but it has not been possible to find any trace of these either in manuscript or in print.

Had a journal or diary been preserved, the details of O'Grady's work in the theatre would make fascinating reading. That his professional life was crowded with incident can only be gauged from chance newspaper comments, from reviews of plays, and from obituary notices. He may have considered that his career was so typical of the playwright-actor-manager of the time that a written record would be of no interest to future generations. His beginnings were quite ordinary – so ordinary, indeed, it is some wonder he did not invent something more colourful for himself in the manner of so many other theatrical figures. He was born in Limerick in 1841 - this much is agreed by the writers of his obituaries.[46] *The Era* gives the fullest account of his life, stating that he attended the Christian Brothers' school in Limerick, where he showed aptitude in singing and in playing the 'cello. Evidently his parents discouraged his entering the musical profession, and so he was apprenticed to an upholsterer, but 'on completing six years and a half he ran away to Liverpool'.[47] 'Ran away' may be a euphemism for 'emigrated'. He worked for two years in Compton House,[48] a large draper's shop which seems to have been more like a department store – one surmises as an upholsterer – while accepting musical and theatrical engagements in the evenings.

It may have been in deference to his employers that he performed as 'Hubert Watson', a remarkably uninspired stage name. At this period he formed a double-act known as 'Watson & Coyne, Negro Minstrels and Acrobatic dancers'.[49] If his stage partner was Irish, as the name (O Cadhain) suggests, there is some ironic satisfaction to be gained from the notion that two young Irishmen chose to appear as belonging to the most marginalized of all the immigrant groups – but in practical terms Negro Minstrelsy was then at the height of its popularity. He became a member of the 'Forest Eclipse Minstrels' and the 'Butterworth Minstrels'. He played Cariboo, the Desert Island King in a pantomime in Dundee, and

> at the conclusion of this engagement he decided to give up the Nigger business altogether and wrote an Irish sketch for himself and his wife, and toured the Music Halls under their real names, Mr and Mrs O'Grady, the only native Irish comedians, Mrs O'Grady making her first appearance on any stage.[50]

Whether Mrs O'Grady was Irish-born, or came from the *immigré* Irish community, or had no connection with Ireland, it has not been possible to discover; but she played Irish parts successfully throughout her career. Critics in Ireland were unceasing in their scorn for non-Irish actors attempting Irish accents, and as no such comment was made about Mrs O'Grady, it is reasonably safe to assume that she had an Irish background of some kind. On her husband's death in 1899 she took over the management of his Irish National Company.

Mr and Mrs O'Grady appear to have been continuously employed on the halls – of which there were over 500 in England alone – until 1874 when their sketch *Molly Bawn* was seen by Boucicault who was looking for an actor to play Conn, the part he had created for himself, in the earliest touring production of *The Shaughran*. Mrs O'Grady (she was always billed thus, in the period manner favoured by Mrs Patrick Campbell and many others) was cast as Mrs O'Kelly.[51] This production opened at the Theatre Royal, Edinburgh, on January 21, 1876, touring for eleven months and finishing at the Gaiety Theatre, Dublin, in Christmas week of the same year.[52] Boucicault told the manager of the Glasgow Theatre Royal, a Mr Knapp, that O'Grady was more suitable for the part than he was himself.[53] With curious serendipity this *Shaughran* was seen by a Dublin schoolboy, Joseph Holloway, at fifteen a pupil at Castleknock College. The young Holloway recorded details of all the plays and operas which he saw in very neat handwriting and without comment; his small notebook shows that the actors Frank Breen and Tom Nerney, who would figure in many future Irish plays, were the Donovan and Duff in *The Shaughran* respectively.[54]

The Shaughran was the turning point in O'Grady's career: at thirty-five he was playing the lead in one of the most popular plays of the day. It was while performing in Dublin that he formed his own company to continue the *Shaughran* tour, making the arrangement with Boucicault's agent. It is said that O'Grady wrote his first play, *The Gommoch*, during this tour. [55] It is very definitely 'School of Boucicault': the Boucicault cadences – and indeed the story and situation – would have been in his head while he was immersed in the part of Conn each night.

The Gommoch opened at the Theatre Royal, Stockton-on-Tees, on 16 March 1877 and toured in tandem with *The Shaughran* for two years, appearing in such fashionable houses as the Theatre Royal in Manchester, the Theatre Royal in Newcastle-upon-Tyne and the Royal Princess's Theatre in Glasgow – all venues which the company would visit many times over the next quarter-century, and a huge upward step from the countless Hippodromes and Empires to which the O'Gradys had been accustomed. Press billings announced 'Hubert O'Grady's Irish National Company', the earliest example of the kind of title which would proliferate in Dublin a decade or so later as an adjunct to the Irish Literary Renaissance.[56] During the period 1877 to 1880 Boucicault's *The Colleen Bawn* and *Arrah-na-Pogue* and Edmond Falconer's well-tried *Eileen Oge* were added to the touring repertoire.[57]

Viewed with hindsight, O'Grady's next plays may be seen to comprise a trilogy on socio-political issues. None of them was billed as such – allowing audiences to discover the content for themselves. If nothing else, this demonstrates O'Grady's comprehension of the need to keep on the right side of the Lord Chamberlain, who, it may be fairly assumed, never troubled to attend a play once the licence had been issued. *The Eviction* was brought out at the Royal Princess's Theatre, Glasgow, on 24 January, 1880; after a three week run it joined the company's touring programme, playing twice in London, at the Olympic and Standard Theatres. In Dublin it was sensationally successful following its first performance at the Queen's on 6 June, 1881; it then proceeded to the United States and Canada. The second play of this 'series', *Emigration,* was cunningly billed as 'a nautical drama' – which at some stretch of the imagination it is; it also made its first appearance at the Royal Princess's in Glasgow (14 May, 1883). The third, *The Famine,* was the only play of O'Grady's to have its premiere in Dublin – this was at the Queen's on 26 March, 1886. It gave the author what turned out to be his best-remembered role, Sadler, the 'Emergency Man'. For five consecutive years *The Famine* was the 'Bank Holiday Attraction' at the spacious Court Theatre in Liverpool.[58]

In spite of its provocative title, his next play, *The Fenian,* was presented all over the British Isles at a time when the Fenian uprising was a comparatively recent memory, opening at the Royal Princess's Theatre in Glasgow on 1 April, 1889. Its description as 'a romantic Irish love story' is not entirely misleading, for it is something of a return to the Boucicault mode of comedy-drama, though, as in Boucicault, it contains a definite 'patriotic' motif. It played continuously up to the time of the author's death, and then sporadically into the early years of the twentieth century. *The Priest Hunter* was first produced at the Queen's Theatre, Manchester, on 3 April, 1893, prior to two years of almost continuous touring, though apparently not in Ireland. If the absence of Irish exposure can be attributed to the title, the title could surely have been changed, but a search of the theatre columns has not revealed a play on this theme under another name. O'Grady is said to have claimed that it was 'the first religious play produced in England'![59]

O'Grady's last play, *A Fast Life* (Operetta House, Rhyl, 26 October, 1896), was billed as 'an original drama of English life' and has no Irish content other than the name of a minor character, Burke. It was given at the Queen's Theatre, Dublin, in June 1900 and at the Theatre Royal, Belfast, in October of the same year, by Mrs Hubert O'Grady's Company. It is very much in the 'ripping good yarn' category, a comedy thriller about a London financier who robs his own bank and flees to Australia – O'Grady had played there in his Irish repertoire, when he must have collected some local allusions. *A Fast Life* is in some ways a 'better' play than the more characteristic O'Grady works – it moves more swiftly, there are no heartfelt effusions upon the state of the peasantry or the infamy of the landlords and the dialogue is free of colourful Boucicaultesque digressions: quite a well made play, in fact, somewhat in the style of Tom Taylor's *The Ticket of Leave Man*. It is easy to see why it was popular, though it leaves no sense in the reader's mind – and probably not in the theatregoer's either – of any original thought or real emotion. However, an English provincial critic enthused that 'The working out of the details show Mr O'Grady to be a master, not only of the literary but of the stage knowledge necessary to the successful mastership of the theatrical craft. The humorous element comes adroitly and naturally into each scene. From the rise of the curtain to the end of the last act there are a succession of exciting situations ... The play is capitally mounted and its interpretation is rendered by a most capable company.'[60]

When he saw *A Fast Life* in Dublin in 1900 Joseph Holloway was not so impressed. Although he had enjoyed O'Grady's Irish plays, he found this one to be 'a crudely constructed improbable melodrama' – improbable, yes, but one can not agree that it is all that crudely constructed. It may have been that Mrs O'Grady's company was less proficient than the now defunct Hubert O'Grady's National Irish Company, exaggerating the dramatic moments and therefore giving an appearance of crudity. Holloway's private memoir records that 'they shout their thoughts in soliloquy straight out at the audience whenever they get the chance'![61]

A Fast Life did not want for engagements. An advertisement in *The Era* for September 1899 shows a full programme of bookings up to Easter 1900, by which time Mrs O'Grady had taken over the management. Thirteen of these bookings were *repeat* engagements, from the handsome Elephant & Castle Theatre in suburban London to the Star in Liverpool.

According to regular advertisements in *The Era,* O'Grady settled in his later years at Hubertstown House, Rhyl, at which address theatre managers were urged to contact him by the latest electric means of communication, the telegram. In his obituary, the same paper stated that he built himself 'a magnificent dwelling place there at a cost of £2,000', but neither his name nor that of his house are listed in the local directories for that time.[62] It is clear that he was exceptionally active right up to the time of his death, with *The Famine*, *The Fenian* and *A Fast Life* simultaneously on tour. *The Era's* Liverpool correspondent reports the re-opening of the Rotunda Theatre in the first week of September 1899, describing the 'electrical illuminations' and the expensive decorations which included the carpeting of the grand staircase and foyers in peacock-blue Axminster – 'an effect of richness, elegance and comfort ... The reopening performance on Monday was patronized by a crowded audience, the selected piece being *The Fenian*, in which the author (Mr. Hubert O'Grady) gave his racy representation of Barney ...' Three months later O'Grady was dead, at the age of fifty-eight.

O'Grady's productions were not based in any specific theatre building. He and his company spent their working lives as lodgers in other men's houses. He was very much in the tradition of the flamboyant actor-manager, his advance publicity promoting his personality as much as his productions. His posters, upon which his figure almost invariably appeared – as Hughey in *Emigration* or Sadler in *The Famine* – show a distinct appreciation of the bold image of the costumed thespian as eye-catching publicity. The theatre historian Peter Kavanagh refers to O'Grady's work as having appealed 'to that section of the public for whom the wolfhound and the round tower were the highest and purest symbols of Ireland', but his assessment falls so far short of the mark one wonders if he can have seen any of O'Grady's plays – they were still current when he was a young man in Monaghan – or indeed have read them. It is clear that Kavanagh was not aware that O'Grady was known to a very wide public in other Anglophone countries including the United States, and that all but one of his plays (*The Famine*) received their premier productions in metropolitan theatres in England and Scotland.[63] Both *The Famine* and *The Fenian* were revived in Dublin in the month preceding the opening of the Abbey Theatre.

The Gommoch

The occasionally used title *The Wild Irish Boy* has confused one modern critic who believes that they are two distinct plays.[64] A third title, *Larry and the Leprehaun*, was used at the Queen's Theatre in Dublin in 1889, possibly because the management felt that audiences would not wish one of their countrymen to be described either as a 'gommoch' – the Irish language term *gamach* is generally taken to mean a simpleton or clown – or as being 'wild' in the sense of 'uncivilized', though one might have thought a leprehaun would have been just as slighting. None of these titles, however, gives any idea of the charm and vitality of the piece, which puts it alongside the plays of Tyrone Power I for sheer ridiculous enjoyment. The action takes place in the King's County hard by the picturesque ruins of the Seven Churches of Clonmacnoise. Other blatant opportunities for scenic indulgence include 'a Mountain Pass', 'a Lakeside Bridge' and 'the Exterior of the Barracks by Night'. The period is unspecified but would seem to be contemporaneous with the first production. There is in fact a feeling of timelessness, of an Ireland poised in a never-never-land set between fairy tale and severe reality. While Boucicault anchored his Irish plays to a definite time or to a political event, and though the influence of Boucicault is palpable throughout *The Gommoch,* O'Grady had not yet learned how to moor his own vessel so as to give the audience a solid deck (so to speak) upon which to observe the action. The play has one serious flaw, that of combining the role of the romantic lead with the principal comic character – something Boucicault would never have done – but this does not seem to have caused difficulties for either audience or critics who clearly took the whole shenanigans on its entertainment value.

Larry the Gommoch is 'a quare boy, fond of fairies'. He is engaged to Norah, daughter of Brian McCarthy, a small farmer of intense probity and goodwill. The local squireeen, McCauley, whose advances to the charming Norah have been repulsed, intends to dispossess McCarthy of his farm and to that end employs the services of Nicky Hicky, 'a cadger'. Among the cast of 'dacent boys', 'spalpeens', police, pipers, fiddlers and singers, are two notable eccentrics, Dr Dyonisius O'Donovan and Molly McGuire. Dr O'Donovan is a bonesetter who dresses in the ethnic garments of distant Spain, from which country he has recently returned; the garrulous Molly describes him as 'looking like either the Lord Lieutenant or a leprehaun'. She is a fortune-teller and interpreter of dreams who, in the current 'hard times', forsees her own future as bleak, for her young clients have a general wish for emigration. She gives Larry a positive account of what is in store for him: there will be money as well as happiness after severe difficulties. Larry surmises that he will find a cache of gold in the ancient castle.

Hicky plants false deeds in the McCarthy house showing that the tenant has no right to the property. McCauley invites Dr O'Donovan to inspect the ruins of the castle where, because of his strange attire, he knows that the gold-prospecting Larry will take him for a leprehaun and hold him prisoner. The oddball doctor gives Larry a large sum of money for his release but at the height of the merrymaking to celebrate Larry and Norah's engagement and the former's new found wealth McCauley has Larry arrested for attempted murder and robbery. In court, trumped up evidence is produced to prove his guilt; the McCarthys are evicted and Larry is condemned to solitary confinement from which he escapes by a clever ruse. McCauley proposes marrriage to Norah – she refuses, there is a skirmish and McCauley and his accomplices are sent packing. The crowd pursues Hicky – the go-between – and in the ensuing chase he is wounded by police, but he informs on McCauley who is revealed as the cause of all local ills. McCauley flees, but is shot in a spectacular *coup*.

A prosaic synopsis of the plot unfairly stresses the absurdity rather than the integrity of the piece which, like a Christmas pantomime, should be assessed in the context of its audience's expectations. *The Gommoch* is skilfully structured. Within barely fifteen-minutes of the opening we are made aware of the background of land-grabbing and evictions – and also of the principal movements of the domestic action: McCauley's intention to take McCarthy's property as well as his daughter, is established. The sides are clearly drawn. The elements of drama and fantasy are quite deftly dovetailed – McAuley's wicked schemes and Larry's innocent aspirations. McAuley is the traditional villain of melodrama, with the important extension of being the representative of a usurping external power; the latter is the charming young suitor, mildly amplified here as the representative of a downtrodden race – and clearly not as simple as his sobriquet 'gommoch' implies.

Scenes of high tension and comic business alternate. The scenes of conviviality at the engagement party come at just the right moment to increase the suspense: will Larry be arrested? The merrymaking may seem drawn-out in the text, but audiences would have expected an appropriate musical *divertissement*: a parallel may be drawn with the introduction of dance in opera. The dramatic moment comes, of course, at the height of a full dance number, when the police burst in and Larry is forcibly removed.

The Court House and Barracks scenes have distinct similarities with the scenes in *Arrah-na-Pogue* in which Shaun is tried and convicted as a rebel and then escapes dramatically by climbing down the ivy of his prison wall. In O'Grady's court scene the hapless Dr O'Donovan is treated to the continuous guffaws of the crowd when he relates the story of how he was mistaken for a leprehaun: here O'Grady may be commenting on the absurdity of his own plot. Following Larry's incarceration O'Grady moves the play into a rather darker mode, no doubt giving value for his patrons' money, but losing the initial feeling of a charming rural comedy interspersed with derring-do.

The characters, with one important exception, are well drawn, considering that this was the playwright's first full-length work. McCauley is the prototype villain, but with the difference that here he is the instigator but not the enacter, it being left to Hicky to carry out his infamous designs. Hicky's part is much larger and much more interesting; he is seen as obsequious and devious, but also fearful, hesitant and anxious about his standing in the community. He is an early example of the class of native-born informer who plays a centrally mischief-making role.

Brian McCarthy is more conventional – the distressed parent with the grasp of the political situation which he is powerless to change – a figure epitomizing the frustration of the articulate rural dweller. His daughter Norah has less of the bucolic coyness and more moral determination than is usual in the female juvenile lead. Molly McGuire and Dr O'Donovan are the eccentrics, and success in those roles would have been entirely dependent upon the comic capabilities of the actors.

The leading figure is less well drawn. Droll, good-natured, loyal, Larry O'Brien does not really possess the characteristics of the well-meaning simpleton. The story does not unfold as a consequence of Larry's *gommoch* condition. O'Grady did something fairly extraordinary in combining the qualities of chief comic with that of romantic lead. Larry is at once the hero and the artful peasant. The amalgamation of two conventional types could be praised as innovative, but we do not know if it resulted from any critical consideration or if the author was simply attempting to give himself an extraordinarily juicy part. He never did this again. It does, however, tell us something of what a talented actor O'Grady must have been in order to make such a curious hybrid viable on the stage, as the play's popularity for over twenty years with the author in the lead surely demonstrates.

The topic of eviction, and the possibility of being rendered homeless in one's own land, is touched upon in *The Gommoch,* but in his next two plays O'Grady would make it his central theme.

The Eviction, or, The Mountain House

This play is an advance on *The Gommoch* in every respect. The outstanding question is how it managed to receive the stamp of approval in the Lord Chamberlain's office where it was passed as fit for public performance on 10 November, 1879. It was not the business of the Lord Chamberlain's readers to comment upon the literary and dramatic qualities of a play, though they often did, but to determine whether the content might be deemed seditious or irreligious and whether a performance might lead to a breach of the peace. *The Eviction* contains numerous remarks, as well as physical incidents, which, one should have thought, would quite definitely lead to such a breach. It remained in the repertoire of Hubert O'Grady's Irish National Company until the mid-1890s.

The thought strikes one that because the original manuscript is so ill penned the Lord Chamberlain's reader may have given up after a few pages; certainly it has an amateurish appearance and might well have been considered as unlikely to find a producer. Can it be that the unfortunate official leafed through the work until he came to the final page, taking on face value the *faux-naïf* message that if all landlords were to behave with generosity of spirit Ireland would be at peace? Who would gainsay such a sentiment? Cursory examination of script submissions leading unforgivably to rejection are not unknown in modern times[65] – but this examination led to acceptance.

The title, of course, should have rung warning bells. O'Grady could have chosen something innocuous (such as *Hardman Castle*, or, *The Landlord's Atonement*) but, as his title boldly announces, *The Eviction* was a highly topical work.[66] Coverage of the Evicted Tenants debates at Westminster, in which the Irish party took the initiative, was widespread in the British press. The play would have been regarded by its audiences as very much of the moment, though in fact no 'period' is ascribed to the action either on the manuscript or, subsequently, in newspaper advertisements.

The first performance of *The Eviction* at the Royal Princess's Theatre, Glasgow, on 24 January, 1880, was described by the correspondent of *The Era* as an improvement on *The Gommoch* 'both as regards construction and literary merit ... Dealing largely as it does with recent unhappy occurrences in the sister isle, the play cannot fail to become popular with a certain section of playgoers, but it may fairly be questioned whether the production on the stage of such scenes as exaggerated heartless evictions and agrarian outrages is likely to prove either instructive or amusing ... It must be conceded that *The Eviction* is cunningly put together and abounds in effective situations which on Monday evening called forth loud cheering from an audience completely filling gallery and pit ...'[67] None of the actors were named though 'the parts were capitally sustained'; the scenic designer, Mr Small, received special commendation.[68]

The dramatic critic of the *Glasgow Evening Citizen* described 'the turning out of a poor family from their holding in the depth of winter. Accompanying this there are, as usual, the stock ingredients of love and jealousy; while a bailiff and process server of the Michael Feeny type gives characteristic piquancy to the piece'. Not only was this critic familiar with Boucicault's villain in *Arrah-na-Pogue,* but he expected his readers to appreciate the allusion. He added that:

> the dialogue is freely interspersed with powerful denunciations of the hard-hearted landlords, the want of leases, and the great advantage to be derived from emigration to America, "the land of the brave and the free", all of which sentiments were loudly applauded by the audience ...[69]

The play opens in the sylvan setting of the Castle Hardman estate where the newly rich merchant Downey and the bailiff Rooney dilate on Lord Hardman's financial difficulties. Downey is prepared to offer a large sum for a five-year lease. In disclosing his plan to marry Hardman's daughter Eveleen, Downey is surprised to learn that he has a rival in a Dr Chessman – but he may do a deal with Eveleen's father. Rooney promises to obtain further financial and matrimonial intelligence for Downey provided the latter will use his influence with Hardman to evict a dozen tenants in order to 'better the land'. It may be, however, that his lordships problems will be resolved if his mare wins an important race. 'We'll stop her gallop!', declares Rooney.

Dr Chessman is at present without a practice and therefore an unsuitable candidate for the irascible Hardman's daughter. Chessman further undermines his position by asserting, in regard to the rumoured evictions, that 'there should be a law to punish those who trifle with the poverty of their fellow creatures'. Hardman informs his daughter that he is accepting Downey's offer and has also agreed to the evictions. This horrifies Eveleen who declares that it was the tenants' industry that made the estate what it was, and they may take a justifiably violent revenge.

Dermot McMahon and Molly O'Hara, son and daughter of tenant families, delay their marriage until the eviction issue is clearer. The McMahons are not in arrears but Dermot surmises, correctly, that the rent will be increased to an unreachable figure. They face emigration. Dermot is perplexed when Rooney, 'secretly' confirming the evictions, gives him a pistol as if to show he is on their side and implying that Dermot should use it when the moment comes. The priest advises the tenants not to resort to violence but when Rooney arrives with a warrant, stating that he is merely 'an instrument of authority' Dermot elects to resist 'tyranny and aggression'. He is seized by the hired men as the houshold belongings are thrown out of the window. When Hardman arrives Dermot's ailing mother emits a long and vile curse before collapsing. The priest takes a firmer line with Hardman than might have been expected from his earlier stance – to which the landlord replies that he has a right to do as he pleases with his own property. The police arrive. Hardman instructs them not to leave a stone standing. Police enter the bedroom and remove the bed with the aged woman on it, presumably dead. Dermot is led away as the house is demolished. Snow begins to fall.

The image of the old woman being carried on her bed from the tumbling remains of her home is one which remains vividly in the reader's mind – how much greater must have been the image left in the minds of theatre audiences. If the material is visually strong, the play is even stronger in regard to its remarkable political commentary. When *The Eviction* was first produced in Dublin eighteen months after the Glasgow opening there were daily reports of evictions in the press, so that the play must have had the effect that a cinema newsreel would have conveyed half a century later. Not an issue of a daily paper of the time lacks a description of a similar atrocity in some part of the country.

Downey pays Hardman the promised sum but Hardman still hopes to regain his estate following the result of the horse race. Rooney reports that the horse is ailing. For want of a veterinary surgeon Dr Chessman is approached; Hardman apologizes for his earlier intemperate words and Chessman does what he can. Rooney, of course, is systematically doping the horse. Downey convinces Rooney that she should give the mare 'another dose', which Rooney agrees to do for £100. If the mare loses the race Hardman will remain in debt and will be more likely to make a bargain about Eveleen.

Meanwhile Dermot is reported to be crazed because his evicted parents have died. He is 'keeping company with wild boys' – this type of association will surely bring him to harm. He arrives at his fiancée's house with some of the 'wild boys', among whom is the two-faced Rooney. The 'fire of patriotism' is kept alive by the singing of patriotic songs. A meeting develops and drink is taken. Rooney discloses that Lord Hardman is going by train to Dublin to find a real vet and lots are drawn as to who will pick Hardman off. Dermot draws the black bean. Molly observes a commotion outside – the police are coming and will undoubtedly arrest all present for unlawful assembly. *Exeunt omnes* by the back door as the police enter by the front to find an empty room.

At the Railway Station, Dermot, Rooney and others watch the approach of Hardman accompanied by two policemen. Rooney lets off a pistol 'by mistake', alerting the police. Dermot accuses Rooney of playing them false, and shoots him. Wounded, Rooney aims at Dermot, misses, and hits Hardman. Police seize Rooney. Eveleen and Dr Chessman appear, enquiring who fired the shot. A constable replies correctly that it was the bailiff. Eveleen rushes to her father, who is hardly hurt. Chessman reports that he has cured the mare and the rascal who sought to destroy her is discovered. Dermot states that his intention was to shoot the landlord, but 'I winged that blackbird instead. Order my arrest if you please!' but Hardman has had a change of heart and admits that the evictions were wrong. Downey has been arrested for having persistently cheated the Revenue. Hardman has a cottage built for Dermot and Molly, regretting that he can not bring Dermot's parents back to life. 'But *I* can!' interposes Eveleen brightly – and she reveals that she had the ailing couple conveyed to a room in the castle where their health and composure have been restored. At this Lord Hardman declares that he is proud to be her father, bestowing her upon the attendant Dr Chessman. Dermot McMahon has the final word:

> If all other landlords follow your example, that ugly word that's
> a stain on our nation may be wiped off the page of Irish history.
> I mean the hateful word 'Eviction'!

Strong words – but a diappointing dénouement. The final actions are of the kind that might seem credible in a motion picture – on the principle that seeing is believing. The concluding scenes do not deliver the promise of what has gone before. Where O'Grady sticks to the point made by title and sub-title, he produces atmospheric drama of a quality that is far superior to what was usual in the popular touring theatre of his time; but he loses concentration and resorts to padding with extraneous actions, and, worse, he reneges on the pledge, implicit at the outset, of providing a critical and topical *exposé* of the situation in his own country. The final speech in the play may be seen as an avoidance of the issues: everyone behaves nicely after all. That having been said, it may fairly be argued that O'Grady went as far as he could.

The conventional trappings of melodrama (or, presciently, of the motion picture) include the story of the horse, the shootings that ensue, the connection between this and the betrothal of the heiress to the doctor who stands in as a vet, and thence to the main story of the dastardly landlord who will not allow his daughter to marry an apparently impecunious but honest young man, and who, by a brutish extension of his nature, ill-treats his tenants to the extent of forcibly removing them from their homes.

Yet *The Eviction* has several admirable qualities. It is a remarkably 'modern' piece in so far as it treats of contemporary traits and types. Downey has been made rich by dealing in corn; he is one of a new breed, the middle-class Catholic entrepreneur. Rooney, the bailiff, is a middle-class Catholic with ambiguous allegiances. Much is made of the Railway as a means of swift communication.[70] The unities are observed in so far as the time scale is brief, the place is confined to one townland and the action is continuous. The transitions to and from castle to woodland to cottage to railway station are smooth. The ensemble scenes are well composed: the secret meeting in the O'Hara home, where lots are drawn for who will do away with the landlord, where 'rebel' songs are sung and where there is a police raid, must have been spellbinding. The scene of the eviction, when the apparently dying woman-of-the-house is carried out on her own bedstead as her home is demolished around her, must have been affecting wherever the piece was played, but in Ireland it was sensational.

The critic of the *Freeman's Journal* wrote:

> 'The "Eviction" scene is most realistic,' wrote and gives a perfect picture of what is now almost a daily occurrence in this country... Last night, at the end of each act, the players were called before the curtain, and the sufferers from the mimic eviction loudly cheered while the landlord, mealman and bailiff

were liberally hissed ...'[71] What more explicit proof of *The Eviction* touching the national nerve could there have been?

Fig 4. Belfast Poster For *Emigration* [Riddell Collection/Belfast Central Library] The shipboard image from the second act fails to give an indication of the strength of the play; it is in the typically 'Hibernian' graphic style of the time.

Emigration

The copy of *Emigration* submitted to the Lord Chamberlain for approval on 5 July 1880 was as ill penned as its predecessor. Certainly one forms the opinion that this was a deliberate ploy on the part of the author, designed to exasperate the censor who may have been glad to stamp the wretched document and be done with it – who would ever have the patience to produce, let alone read, such an untidy, not to say illiterate, work?

As a text *Emigration* is in some respects O'Grady's least impressive play, but it bears certain marks of distinction which, in a later era of stage presentation, might have elevated it to critical acclaim as a *symboliste* piece. The reader absorbs a certain feeling that there is something other than what is apparent lurking here and that O'Grady lacked the prescience to understand that he was on the verge of tumbling into a new mode of expression. One is further assailed by the outlandish thought that if Paul Fort or Lugné-Poë had come across it and put it into rehearsal they would have revealed an intense interior drama, paring it of its all too glib dialogue and developing its substantial core of connecting images – for example, the slow progress of the cart carrying its mournful occupants across the barren moonlit landscape, leading to O'Grady's carefully described choreographic sequence of the fight in the turf bog. In these scenes there is a deep current of feeling for those on the verges of existence – people who have no meaningful present and possibly no future at all.

Be that as it may, the sober fact is that we have only one act of the three-act play which was first produced at the Royal Princess's (now the Citizens') Theatre, Glasgow, on 14 May 1883 and toured sporadically in Britain and Ireland for almost twenty years thereafter. One assumes that the Lord Chamberlain was provided with only the first act as if it were a one-act play and that, once approved, O'Grady appended the rest. The extant opening takes place in the Irish midlands and in Dublin; according to press reports and posters the second act is on ship-board and the third is in the United States. The surviving act was reprinted in the Journal of Irish Literature but the editor did not disclose that this was anything other than a one-act play.

The *dramatis personae* are Paddy Burk, a small farmer, his wife Biddy and his daughter Kitty; Hughey, Kitty's suitor (the author's part); Biddy, a milkmaid; Jerry Naylor, an agent, and Skinner, his clerk; Flanagan, a carter; and two scoundrels, Moriarty and O'Brien. There are sundry police, dockers and emigrants. (The characters we do not meet because the script has been lost are Captain Breeze of the emigrant ship, Justin Mooney, described as 'an agitator', and Grace Hamilton, an heiress.) Hughie's 'exciting adventures on board the coffin ship' are adverted to in the *Freeman's Journal* – a provocative phrase regarding the play's content which includes 'scenes on the emigrant ships provided by the British government on which so many people died of sickness and overcrowding'.

The billing in some newspapers as a 'musical drama' is somewhat misleading but may have been part of a public relations exercise designed to remove any potentially depressing taint from the title – and there certainly must have been songs other than the ballad sung by Hughey as the emigrant ship casts off.

The play opens in the Burk cabin where Paddy Burk reads out newspaper accounts of the 'general distress' of the country. A large number of emigrants are reported to have left for America. Paddy and his daughter Kitty are considering emigration, but Mary is totally against it. Kitty is unsure as to whether Hughey (not yet her fiancé) wishes to go – 'I never know when he is joking or in earnest'. She notices Hughey chatting with Biddy the milkmaid outside: this heightens her sense of indecision. When Hughey enters the house he discloses himself as a light-hearted young fellow who takes life as it comes, but a serious discussion follows, and the cost of passage is estimated. Hughey offers to contribute £10, and will travel with them. He hopes Kitty will consent to marry him – which she does, with parental blessing.

Naylor, Hughie's rival for Kitty, makes plans to prevent her departure, but if he does not succeed he will have the cynical satisfaction of knowing that as 'emigration brings hardship at every step' the couple will hardly prosper. With the connivance of Skinner he plans to pick a quarrel with Hughey and 'provoke him to strike me. And then I can have him locked up.' Hughey overhears the plot and strikes Naylor – exactly what the latter hoped for. Kitty appears and informs Naylor that she knows exactly what he is capable of. He retorts by declaring that Hughie is 'buying' Kitty by paying her passage.

On a desolate stretch of the Bog of Allen Naylor's hired thugs, O'Brien and Moriarty, conceal themselves to rob migrant family by night. The ass-cart carrying the three Burks and their scant worldly goods draws up to wait for Hughie. Naylor's signal pistol shot is heard. The two thugs overpower the Burks but the driver makes off with their goods, returning later to help Hughie overpower O'Brien and Moriarty. An extended melée ensues, culminating in Kitty pelting their adversaries in a bog-hole with sods of turf as Hughey aims his fowling-piece at Naylor.

If the fight in the Bog of Allen resembles a dance, then the scene on the North Wall quay where prospective emigrants mingle with crowds of dockers and police is like the opening of an opera. A band plays as passengers mount the gangway. The carter drives on bearing the Burks, Hughey and their baggage. Hughey informs a constable of the previous night's incident. Naylor, unscathed, arrives with his two accomplices. They agree that it will be possible to effect the robbery during the confusion of embarkation. The constable notes the movements of the would-be robbers who snatch the Burks' box as they approach the ship, arresting Naylor and O'Brien. Moriarty escapes but is later caught. There is much congratulation as the dastardly trio are led away to the cheers of the crowd. The gangway is raised and the ship moves off, bound for the New World. Hughey sings a 'Farewell to Ireland' ballad, the passengers and the crowd on the quay joining in.[72]

The plot of *Emigration* is linear and the action highly consequential. The style is almost that of the strip-cartoon, so rapidly do events follow one another, each incident reduced to its essentials. There is no sub-plot. The point is made quite openly that the necessity for emigration is a disagreeable fact of life. Most of the characters are little more than cyphers, though the two leading parts are interesting. Like other O'Grady heroines, Kitty has a mind of her own that is admirably out of keeping with the usual run of young women in popular plays of the time. Hughey, as Professor Watt has deftly pointed out, is 'neither a servant, nor a confederate of a country gentleman, nor a Fenian on the run'. He is a member of the dispossessed class of tenant farmer who has retained more than a modicum of self-reliance in a world of destitution and despair, and he has a surprisingly resilient sense of humour to go with it.

What we have of *Emigration* – in its subject matter, in its attitude towards its subject matter and in its physical projection on the stage – bears an extraordinary resemblance to James McKenna's *The Scatterin'* as directed by Alan Simpson for Pike Theatre Productions at the Metropolitan Hall during the Dublin International Theatre Festival of 1960 – a time when emigration was as much a fact of life as when O'Grady was writing eighty years earlier. There is the sense in both plays of emigration being not just the inevitable but also the accepted way for young people to create a future for themselves, the sense that those who remain behind are committing themselves to a life of dull decrepitude, and the extraordinary sense of exhilaration – in spite of the sadness of parting – at a huge adventure that is about to happen. These features are shared by the two plays, as is the musical component: in *Emigration* the music appears to be incidental, in *The Scatterin'* it is a formal score, but both plays are, ultimately, melodramas.

THE LATE MR. HUBERT O'GRADY AS SADLER.

Fig 5. Hubert O'Grady as Sadler in *The Famine* [*Irish Playgoer*/National Library of Ireland] O'Grady wrote small but telling comic parts for himself as villains in his socially critical plays, presented by his Irish National Company.

The Famine

The Famine was the only play of O'Grady's to open in Dublin. This was at the Queen's Theatre on 28 April, 1886 – a Wednesday rather than the usual Monday because of the technical rehearsal required to try out the new scenery – which was evidently considered worthy of mention in the publicity.

> The following well-known scenes will be presented: The Village of Swords, St Doolough's, The Butcher's Wood, the Phoenix Park and the Exterior of King's Bridge Railway Station'. The press advertising announced '...for the first time on any stage/by Mr. and Mrs. O'Grady's/IRISH NATIONAL COMPANY/Including the talented actor Mr. W.H.HALLATT/of an entirely new and original Drama in a/Prologue and Four Acts, entitled/FAMINE/written by Mr. Hubert O'Grady'.

Hallat, a guest artiste with the company, was the only actor apart from O'Grady to receive billing. O'Grady played Sadler, 'a timekeeper'. This was to become one of his two most celebrated roles, the other being Conn in Boucicault's *The Shaughran*.

The run continued for a second week from Monday 3 May. It paid its first return visit to Dublin for the week commencing Monday 6 December of the same year, when it was described in the press advertisements as 'The Hit of 1886' and 'The greatest of all modern Irish dramas'. It was then retained for a second week from Monday 13 December, when Frank Breen took over the part of Sadler, 'due to the severe illness of Mr O'Grady'.[73] During the decade leading up to the opening of the Abbey Theatre, *The Famine* was given in Dublin in 1895, 1900, 1902, 1903 and 1904; in Belfast it was given for a week in 1902. It appeared regularly in British centres throughout that period as part of Hubert O'Grady's, and subsequently Mrs O'Grady's, touring programme.

Three Prologue scenes take place during what one assumes is the period of the Great Famine of 1845-1849. The main body of the play is set 'fifteen years later' when the spectre of famine was still stalking the land. The younger characters have matured and there is an opportunity for them to seek retribution for cruelties at the hands of the local landlord. Professor Watt has shown that the Prologue should take place in 1881 because of the reference to the 'No Rent Manifesto' of the Irish Parliamentary Party, and this accords with the reference to the Land League, which was founded in 1879. On this assumption, therefore, the main body of the play must be set in 1896 – in other words in the *future*, the play's first production being

1886.[74] However, the *feeling* of the Prologue is very much of the 1845-49 famine at its height. During the rest of the play there is little sense of the action taking place in a speculative future, as Professor Watt's undoubtedly correct view of the chronology makes necessary; rather, we are being shown a picture of incidents which could have taken place fifteen years after the famine – in other words c.1860-64, long before the Land League and the No Rents Manifesto.

There is no real answer to this – beyond the likelihood that O'Grady was not too greatly concerned with the political chronology and was providing a fictive truth rather than a documentary one. (One thinks of the Anglicization of the names of townlands by officers of the 1832 Ordnance Survey in Brian Friel's *Translations,* where a strict adherence to historical fact has been sublimated by a more generalized poetic verity, described by historians as 'inaccuracies'!) In any case, since the title of the play is *The Famine,* one may suppose that audiences assumed they were observing a Prologue set during that very famine which still had the power to cause a shudder of terror and disgust at its very mention.

The prologue is presented in three vivid scenes and reads more like a first act than a conventional prologue. In the village of Swords in north County Dublin, Sir Richard Raymond, a Poor Law Inspector, enquires of Father Barry why he is being followed by a crowd, to which the priest replies that the people believe he will distribute alms. Sir Raymond explains that it is only within his power to help those who intend to emigrate. Father Barry feels that the money allocated towards assisted passages would be better spent on the alleviation of immediate hardship; both believe that the relief schemes are useless for those who are too weak to work.

Sir Raymond urges Lumley Sackvill, a young landlord appointed to oversee police works, to distribute relief justly; Sackvill retorts that his family has suffered from unruly and ungrateful tenants, describing how Vincent O'Connor, an agitator in the 'No Rent Manifesto' movement, has caused his family immense financial loss and personal grief. Sadler, the timekeeper, reports that he has dismissed O'Connor and some other men for lateness. When O'Connor pleads to be reinstated, refusing to place his wife and children in the workhouse, Sadler sends him packing and reveals in cynical monologue that he wished to marry O'Connor's sister but was turned down 'because I was a loyal subject and not a patriot!'

In their hovel Mary O'Connor, surrounded by her starving children, is seen to be unwell. She falls asleep. Vincent arrives with a loaf followed shortly by Sackvill and Sadler who have evidence that he stole it. Vincent does not deny the theft and is arrested. When he attempts to bid farewell to his wife he finds that she is dead.

This extended prologue provides a most unusually dramatic opening for any play and is imaginatively larded with Sadler's ironic remarks – yet it is so dramatic one wonders if the author will be able to keep up the tone, not to mention the pace. What must surely have been the author's own view is put forward with Father Barry as mouthpiece: '... And I hope that we may live to see this country with her own Parliament controlling her domestic affairs, and Eviction, Famine and Emigration banished from our native land.' (One wonders if the priest was aware that he was employing the titles of three of Hubert O'Grady's plays is a single sentence!) The final scene of the prologue, which culminates in the death of Mary O'Connor, has an intensity of atmosphere unlike anything in Irish drama prior to the appearance of Synge.

Fifteen years later: Sackvill will marry Sir Richard's daughter Alice. Sackvill discloses to Sadler that he became 'entangled' with a servant, the late Vincent O'Connor's daughter Nelly, whom he foolishly promised to marry. He commissions Sadler to pass £100 to Nelly on condition that she emigrates and Sadler must be sure to see her off at the railway station – but Sadler tells the audience he prefers to observe the wedding: 'I wasn't invited – but then I wasn't told to stay away!' The festivities are interrupted when Nelly O'Connor appears and denounces 'the scoundrel who is passing for a gentleman!' She accuses Sackvill of having ruined her – but he coolly declares that she is mad. Nelly gives him back his money – £50: it is clear to the audience who kept the other £50.

During the intermission between acts one and two Sackvill has evidently explained to general satisfacion that Nelly is insane. Alice, the new Mrs Sackvill, kindly sends her carriage to convey Nelly to the railway station but the carriage is diverted to the house of Dr Kildare who, for a payment of £1,000, pronounces Nelly to be a lunatic and has her removed to the Asylum. Sadler is ordered from the Sackvill demesne when it becomes obvious that he retained £50 of Nelly's fee; he, in monologue, berates himself for not taking the whole £100 and departing for America himself!

Sadler meets Dr Kilmore and lets him know he is aware of the deal. The doctor – who, it emerges, was a rival for the hand of Alice – bribes Sadler to keep quiet and also to arrange Sackvill's death. Nelly's brother John, discharged from the army, seeks his sister and is horrified to learn from Sadler that she is in the Asylum, and why. The authorities refuse to discharge Nelly and O'Connor vows to kill Sackvill; this pleases Sadler as it will relieve him of the same task! The assassination will take place at a ball – Sadler gleefully informs the audience that he will spend some of his fee on 'superfine black so that I may appear respectable at Sackvill's funeral!'

A compelling revenge motive has now taken over but it does not compensate for the loss of the emotive social criticism of the early scenes. John O'Connor shoots Lumley Sackvill but is arrested and condemned to death. Local opinion is that O'Connor would not have been capable of such an act but even if he were an effort must be made to rescue him *en route* to the scaffold. The *coup* is effected by night on the road to Kilmainham Jail. The meaningful location and the realistic staging – the prison with its clanging doors, the dark street where the horse-drawn van is hijacked – supply a much-needed element of atmospheric action to what has degenerated to a thin text. The earnestness is relieved by some humorous sallies such as when one of the helpers, disguised as a priest, is instructed that in the event of his being recognized by the police he is to say that he's on his way to perform as Father Tom in an amateur production of *The Colleen Bawn*!

In the fourth and final act it emerges that O'Connor did not murder Sackvill – but who did? Nelly is released from the Asylum due to the kindly intercession of Sackvill's widow who engages her as a maid. At a meeting in a pub Dr Kilmore declares that by shooting Sackvill prematurely Sadler has effectively prevented him from receiving the £1,000 promised for committing Nelly to the madhouse. A row ensues between the two men and they are removed by the barman, but not before he has absorbed enough of their conversation to enable him to report them to the police, adding the information that they are even now boarding the American Mail Train at King's Bridge station. Detectives, in the nick of time, arrive at the station accompanied by Sir Richard Raymond and John O'Connor. Sadler and Kilmore are arrested. Appropriate recriminations are made by O'Connor and his sister ending with Sir Richard complimenting the latter for having risked his life on his sister's behalf. O'Connor makes a graceful speech in return, concluding, 'And if you will only look back to the years gone by, you cannot but be convinced that all our trials and troubles can be traced to the great distress during The Famine!'

John O'Connor's final lines remind us of the play's sombre and thoughtful prologue, and of its title – a reminder that is fully justified, for the many fraught occurrences that have taken place during the fifteen-year interval have obscured the peg upon which the drama has been hung. This is a major disappointment in a play which has much to recommend it as a genuine theatrical experience.

O'Grady's *The Famine* is cited by Dr Chris Morash in a survey of plays concerning the Irish famine. Morash is much concerned with O'Grady's manipulation of past and present, tending to agree that the title would have cast the collective mind of the audience back to the 1840s, but adding the suggestion that the food shortages of 1879 and 1880 and the land war of the same time would have provided a special immediacy. He states that 'there is no doubting the political effectiveness of constructing a carefully defined memory of the past as justification for action in the present', and concludes that 'as an intervention in the struggle for land in the 1880s, it is superb.'[75]

Audiences in Ireland, from the first production of *The Famine* in 1886 up to the time of the opening of the Abbey Theatre in 1904 when the play still held its place on the commercial stage, were acutely aware of the land question and would immediately have empathized with John O'Connor's final speech. Audiences outside Ireland would have been largely unfamiliar with the background so the play must have been effective as drama irrespective of its historico-political context. O'Grady's picture of privation, of the problems experienced by those who should have been in a position to alleviate suffering but were powerless to do so in the face of an uncomprehending bureaucracy, and his notion that the agrarian difficulties of the 1880s sprang directly from the famine, are all intensely projected in the prologue to the play but are diluted in the consequential action of standard melodrama that comprises most of the following four acts.

The Fenian

The Fenian opened at the Royal Princess's Theatre, Glasgow, on 1 April 1899. It had been licenced by the Lord Chamberlain following a handwritten submission of 112 pages at the head of which is another of O'Grady's *faux-naïf* forewords stating that

> This drama is simply a Romantic Irish Love Story, and has nothing to do with Patriotic, Political or Local evils. It takes the title from the fact that the scene is laid in Ireland and is supposed to take place during the Fenian movement which

gives the opportunity for the Villain to accuse the Hero (Lieut. Tracey) of complicity with the [indecipherable word which may be rebels] in order to have him removed so that he may more easily possess the hand of the heroine (Ellen Lynch), the Coastguard's daughter.

This description is not entirely hokum insofar as it deals with the 'romantic' element in the plot; but what O'Grady describes as 'Patriotic, Political or Local evils' have everything to do with the 'Irish Love Story'. 'Do not trouble to dwell on these evils, they are merely there as colourful background!' O'Grady is clearly advising the censor, and the censor equally clearly took his advice for the licence was granted on 3 November, 1888.

A cast of fifteen characters is listed as well as 'soldiers, sailors, college boys, city police, constabulary, etc.' Eight further named parts are given for a run at the Grand Theatre, Glasgow, in 1899; whether the piece had been greatly amplified or whether the management was simply granting printed status to some of the supernumeraries is impossible to discover for none of these people is mentioned in the notices. What we do discover on reading the play – and what was disclosed to the audience by two additional players – is the presence of important Fenian activists, O'Brien and Larkin. This blatant sleight of hand on O'Grady's part makes a complete mockery of the censorship process and demonstrates that members of the Lord Chamberlain's staff can never have followed up their decisions by going to see the plays they had approved.

Naturally, therefore, Jack Lynch is not described on the cast list as 'leader of the local Fenian Brotherhood', which he turns out to be. It is extraordinary, however, that O'Grady used so provocative a title as *The Fenian* – but here again he may have been ultra-subtle in seeming to show that there was nothing to hide, for, as he states, the play is merely 'supposed to take place' at the time of the Fenian movement in Ireland, which was, he seems to imply, twenty years ago and now thankfully forgotten.

In spite of its daring title, *The Fenian* is, stylistically, something of a return to the comedy-drama mode of *The Gommoch*. It lacks the sense of involvement, and the explosions of real anger, of *The Eviction*, *Emigration* and *The Famine*. 'It can scarcely be said to be by any means the most representative of this prolific author's dramatic works,' remarked the *Irish News*, yet pointing out that any deficiencies in the writing were amply compensated for by 'the well-balanced company'.[76] O'Grady was universally complimented for his performance as Barney Brannigan, a college porter; a Glasgow newspaper praised his playing as 'so very distinctive from that of the average Irish comedian.'[76]

The action takes place in a coastguard station at Malahide in north Co Dublin, in the city and in the Dublin mountains. Lieutenant Frank Tracey hopes to marry the coastguard's daughter, Ellen Lynch, but the match is strongly opposed by his father, Colonel Tracey, a magistrate. The union of Frank and Ellen is further complicated by the persistent importuning of Ellen by one Harry Maxwell, probably an Englishman, who may best be described as the typical period cad or bounder. For reasons that are entirely to do with class Colonel Tracey favours Maxwell. When Ellen's brother Jack makes representations to the Colonel on behalf of his sister's marriage to Frank the Colonel refers to 'the absurdity and impropriety' of his son contemplating marriage to 'a person of lower degree'. Jack points out that a coastguard's daughter is (financially) 'comfortable' but the Colonel becomes abusive and Jack is removed from the house. Naturally the young lovers become more determined; they obtain the support of the parish priest, Father Kelly, who agrees to marry them. He does, however, call on the Colonel, hoping for a change of heart, but the latter is obdurate.

Maxwell, learning that the marriage will take place, calls on the priest not to proceed. Father Kelly will not listen and there are harsh words. Maxwell reports that the priest threatened him and urges the Colonel (magistrate) to have him arrested for using 'treasonable language'. It is one of several improbabilities of plot that the order is given to have the priest arrested. There is undoubtedly an unscripted implication that to the colonial administration the priests were implicated in 'rebel' activities and that the Colonel-magistrate is using his office to give the people a warning. The result is a dramatic scene when the crowd reacts vociferously and the constable refuses to carry out the order. Father Kelly is, however, removed to jail by a military sergeant. Declares Jack Lynch: 'Father Kelly, they may brand your garment with the broad arrow, but they can never brand your heart!'

To audiences in Ireland, where the figure of the priest would stand for the Roman Catholic people and that of the magistrate for the British administration, the political implication would have been obvious, but an audience in any part of the British Isles would have found the arrest of a clergyman quite shocking. (One is reminded of the decision of the board of the Abbey Theatre in 1907 not to produce Synge's *The Tinker's Wedding* because of the rough treatment meted out on the priest.) The immediate outcome is that Jack Lynch and his father attempt to bail out Father Kelly without success. Jack stows two pistols in his belt and departs – his father and sister assume he intends to shoot Colonel Tracey. Ellen informs her fiancé that his father's life is in danger and he should make a plea for clemency to the Fenian Brotherhood. Maxwell observes Frank setting forth and commissions Barney Brannigan to follow him.

In the cave used by the Fenians for their meetings we find Jack, who now appears as the leader of the local Fenian Brotherhood, describing how the priest has been arrested on a false charge. Larkin considers that Colonel Tracey has exceeded his duties: 'Is he to be removed?' They all cry 'Yes!' O'Brien then says they are given to understand that Jack's sister is to marry the Colonel's daughter – a redcoat. Jack argues that she intends to marry the man and not the coat. All draw their pistols as a whistle is heard outside. Frank Tracey appears. To the accusation that he is a spy, he replies that his mission is purely personal, to plead for his father's life. The men state that he is too late, for the sentence of death has already been passed. Frank humbly begs them to reconsider, and Jack supports his plea. A vote is taken, all but two (Larkin and O'Brien) agreeing to drop the death sentence. It is decided that there must be a condition that Frank will never divulge the secret of the meeting place, or ever 'recognize' any of those present. Frank agrees, and is formally sworn.

Maxwell informs the Colonel that Frank is in thrall to the Fenians. This is confirmed by Brannigan who reported what he observed at the cave. If the Colonel fails to institute proceedings against his son the information will surely emerge by other means and the Colonel will be accused of withholding intelligence that is likely to be a serious danger to the realm. At a soirée where there is singing and dancing a captain suddenly enters and delivers a warrant 'for Lieutenant Frank Tracey on a charge of complicity with the Fenians!' Before being handcuffed, Frank informs the assembly that this is a false charge brought by 'some secret foe'. Ellen, not surprisingly, faints.

The military 'At Home' is similar to the wedding scene in *The Famine* where there is a mood of gaiety that is suddenly shattered by the arrival of one bearing unwelcome news; and also to the engagement-party in *The Gommoch* where the police burst in at the height of the merriment: these are well-worked formulae. What is different in this play is that the comic Irish character is unsympathetic. O'Grady wrote the comparatively small part of Barney Brannigan for himself; he does not appear until the second act and has few lines, but those he does have are entertaining in the expected way, such as when describing the close of the scene where Frank visits the cave: '... When all of a sudden a blast of wind set up the sand in a whirell-my-gig and nearly blinded me, and when I saw him again he was out of sight.'[78]

Learning on a visit to his son in prison that the latter was in the Fenian hideout in order to plead for his father's life, the Colonel is distraught. He begs forgiveness, which is granted provided he will consent to Frank's marriage to Ellen. He readily consents and declares that he is confident that he will secure a reprieve for Frank. When Maxwell hears from Brannigan of the likelihood of Framk's release he pays Brannigan to engage a criminal called Flannigan to rob the mail car that will carry the reprieve document. An argument arises when Flannigan states that unless he is allowed an assistant to overpower the driver he will disclose the plan to the police. A deal is reluctantly agreed, Maxwell announcing to the audience, 'That's one of the biggest ruffians I ever met!'

Jack Lynch calls to see the Colonel to tell him that he was tipped off about the mail robbery, intervened, and managed to snatch the reprieve document, which he now hands over. The Colonel is surprised and mollified that a well known Fenian activist should act thus. A shot is fired through the window and the Colonel falls dead. Jack immediately realizes that he will be accused of the assassination – but he remembers to keep the papers in his possession. All fear that Jack committed the murder. Jack tells Father Kelly that he is unsure whether the bullet was meant for the Colonel or for himself. He gives the papers to the priest for safe keeping and leaves to hide in the mountains. Father Kelly hastens to the prison – just in time, as Frank Tracey is about to be executed. He presents the reprieve to the officer in charge who pronounces the word 'Pardoned!' to the cheers of the crowd.

The saving of the hero from execution at the last minute was a familiar device of melodrama, used again with a real sense of relish by George Bernard Shaw in *The Devil's Disciple* nine years later. There is one anomaly, which must have been addressed in a production copy that we do not have, and that is the reappearance of Fr Kelly. There is no explanation as to what occurred at his trial for treason, so it must be assumed that he was acquitted or the case dismissed.

The final scenes move swiftly if incredibly. Brannigan delivers the morning paper to Maxwell; the reprieve of Frank Tracey is reported as well as the murder of his father, for which Jack Lynch is said to be chief suspect. Flannigan and his accomplice Delaney come for payment but Maxwell declines to pay the balance as they failed to secure the letter of reprieve. However, he re-engages the two men in a plan to abduct Ellen; and he writes to Ellen as if from Frank asking her to meet him at 'the Quarry Road'. The two criminals proceed to the Quarry Road but decide to turn Queen's evidence because they believe that the present assignment is merely Maxwell's trick to get rid of them without paying. They decide to turn Queen's evidence, and depart. Maxwell and Barney appear, Maxwell berating Barney for failing to ensure that Flannigan and Delaney turn up. Ellen arrives. Maxwell accosts her, disclosing that he wrote the letter as he intends to have her by foul means since he could not do so by fair! She cries for help as Maxwell and Barney bind her and lead her off to where a carriage awaits.

At a disused stable in the Dublin mountains Jack soliloquizes that it is hard to have to hide for a crime that he did not commit. He observes the arrival of a carriage and Maxwell and Brannigan carrying Ellen into the building. Jack shoots and wounds Maxwell. Police appear, followed by Frank Tracey and Father Kelly. Maxwell is arrested. Coolly demanding why this should be so, a policeman replies, 'For the murder of Colonel Tracey!' Maxwell immediately states that the murderer is Jack Lynch. Brannigan gives evidence against Maxwell, to the latter's immense chagrin, but Brannigan is also arrested. Jack then addresses Frank, commenting that the course of love never did run smoothly and his has been a rough course 'with plenty of breakers ahead'. Various vivid storm metaphors are drawn upon until Father Kelly finally declares, 'Yes, and when the squall's over, Frank will tell the story of his life and how he was mistaken for a Fenian!'

The concluding scenes of *The Fenian* are less well structured than in O'Grady's three previous plays. There is an unusual number of extraordinary coincidences, the most incredible being Jack hiding in a remote mountain stable where, a few seconds later, Maxwell and Brannigan turn up with the abducted Ellen. Barney Brannigan's turning against Maxwell is hard to accept, but at least O'Grady did not attempt to whitewash him at the last minute. It is a feature of

O'Grady's writing of parts for himself (in all his plays after *Emigration*) that he obviously relished roles of ambiguous morality, for which the gallery responded with hisses.

One cannot believe that the final line of the play is a naïve remark: surely immense irony is intended. It is true that Frank Tracey did *not* take the Fenian oath – he only swore not to disclose the existence of a Fenian cell in the locality – so he *was,* quite literally 'mistaken for a Fenian', but his friendship with the leading Fenian activist, and his imminent marriage to the daughter of the principal Fenian family in the neighbourhood, hardly suggests revulsion for the ethos of that organization. The effect would have depended for its force upon the manner of delivery of certain lines; and audiences in Ireland would have heard what they were listening for.

The symbolism of the British army uniform introduces an attractive sense of ambivalence. It becomes increasingly likely, the more one delves into O'Grady's work, that in relation to issues of nationalism and censorship he may be justly regarded as the prototype *Tadhg an dá thaoibh*.[79] Thus the declaration in the Preface to *The Fenian* that the play is no more than 'a romantic Irish love story' and has 'nothing to do' with politics may be seen as an amusingly impudent – not to say intrepid – snub to the office of the Lord Chamberlain, demonstrating that the playwright had by now divined that the censors were not only easily taken in but were less than thorough in their duties.

The Priest Hunter

Like its predecessor *The Fenian*, the script submitted to the Lord Chamberlain begins with a disclaimer:

> Notwithstanding the strong title (which is necessary nowadays) the drama does not deal with either the Political or Religious element of the time, but is simply a ROMANTIC IRISH LOVE STORY. The play takes its title from the fact that the villain of the piece tries to have the priest, who is about to marry the hero and heroine, arrested, so as to prevent their marriage – he having the law on his side, for the priest is a proscribed one, and forbidden to land on Irish soil.

This requires no further comment as we are by now conversant with O'Grady's sly method of pulling the wool over the apathetic censor's eyes.

Fig 6. Poster for 1919 Revival of *The Fenian* [Dublin City Library and Archive]
Hubert O'Grady's plays continued to be played at the Queen's Theatre, Dublin,
up to the 1920s. Peter MacCormac, aka F.J. McCormick, and May Craig, later
Abbey Theatre players, were in this Ira Allen production.

The action takes place in an unidentified 'wild coastal region', at Sir John Redmond's country house, Shamrock Hall, and at the headquarters of the Governor of Ireland, Sir Oliver John Cromwell. The Cromwell name suggests that we are in the seventeenth century but it quickly becomes apparent that this Cromwell is not the Lord Protector nor is he intended to be a portrait of that historical figure. Though not the villain of the piece, Sir Oliver is the villainous influence; O'Grady probably wished to create an antipathetic feeling towards the character by use of the surname. However, as *The Priest Hunter* does not appear to have been performed in Ireland the Cromwell reference is odd: audiences in Britain, where the play was constantly on tour following its opening at the Queen's Theatre, Manchester, on 3 April 1893 until O'Grady's death in 1899, would not have the received Irish view of Oliver Cromwell as the epitome of evil.

The play is about constitutional religious discrimination. At the final curtain the good news is brought that 'the dark cloud of persecution has passed for ever', and priests are no longer to be prevented from performing their religious duties. This suggests that the action must take place at the close of the period of the Penal Laws, probably at the time of the Catholic Relief Acts of 1778, 1782 and 1792 – but there is a vagueness about the political background throughout, and it may be that O'Grady was trusting that his audiences would accept a gallous story and not waste thought on anything so dull as historical exactitude.

In the character of the priest hunter Paddy Mulloney (aka Mackinaspie on some playbills) O'Grady wrote yet another small yet definitive and catalystic part for himself. The reviewer in *The Era* described Mulloney as 'a brutal, corpulent and intemperate peasant' and O'Grady's performance as giving a 'marvellously vivid and amusing effect'.[80] Here again O'Grady was presenting a comical villain, in this case his authorial and acting creation cleverly drawing attention to the absurdity of the prevailing law. The interlacing of the comic with the dramatic – which removes the kind of solemnity that the title of the work might lead one to expect – is quite skilfully achieved; Mulloney's asides to the audience reveal a personality powered by a hatred so manic that it demonstrates how ridiculous – in the sense of being unachievable – was the notion of stamping out Roman Catholicism in Ireland, or indeed anywhere.

In a characteristic scene the fugitive Father O'Flaherty has secretly let it be known that he will make a brief appearance to commit a deceased man's body to the earth. Mulloney learns of this and insinuates himself into the crowd of mourners. The burial takes place at night by lantern-light and there is every possibility that having perfomed his Christian duty the priest will disappear into the gloom before Mulloney has time to denounce him and have him arrested. Mulloney mistimes his *coup*. He signals the soldiers, the priest jumps onto a wall, Mulloney grabs his cassock which slips off and Mulloney tumbles into the open grave. The symbolic nature of his fall is not lost on the crowd and the soldiers have the temerity to laugh. Priest and mourners melt into the landscape as Mulloney clambers out of the grave, a buffoon revealed.

Sir John Oliver Cromwell despises Mulloney. He expresses the opinion to his associates that Mulloney has made the administration the laughing stock of the kingdom for allowing the same priest to escape on several occasions. Major Robert Redmond, a Catholic turned Protestant and one of the more hotheaded upholders of the anti-Catholic laws, cannot deny that Father O'Flaherty enjoys the support of the peasantry. Father O'Flaherty is – as well he might be – a shadowy figure, something of a cypher. He is described by Sir Oliver as 'notorious' but O'Grady resists the temptation of making him a Scarlet Pimpernel figure; all the priest does is administer the sacraments wherever and whenever possible, almost always in disguise.

A much more interesting figure is the Reverend Mr Gordon, the peace-loving non-conformist minister who is physically attacked by Robert Redmond when the clergyman defends the right of Robert's sister, Rose, to allow 'one of the forbidden sort' into their home. Subsequently the Reverend Gorden is accused of defending 'disloyal rebels'. When questioned he states that he will 'continue to act as a gentleman and a Christian'; he does not believe that the proscriptive law will lead his 'poor countrymen from the error of their ways' and maintains that 'the present persecution will recall fearfully against us in the future'. The sentiments expressed by Gordon introduce a note of the kind of ecumenism that formed one of the essential precepts of the United Irishmen of the same historical period in which *The Priest Hunter* appears to be set. In a dramatic moment when violence is about to erupt Gordon holds up his hand to the soldiers (representig the official regime) and to the crowd (the plain people of Ireland), a gesture symbolising the play's central motif, that of the need for moderation and respect for one another's beliefs.

The story of the play concerns the love of Captain Arthur Cromwell, the Governor's son, for Rose Redmond, a well born Irishwoman of the Roman Catholic faith. Sir Oliver does not object to the match provided Rose will embrace the Reformed church. The young couple believe that after marriage they can continue to observe the religious practices to which they were individually reared. Father O'Flaherty has been conveyed by ship from the continent by Rose's brother Frank to perform the marriage ceremony, and also the marriage of a young peasant couple, Rody and Nancy, whose courtship is amusingly chronicled in a parallel sub-plot; and it is upon the difficulties that emerge from their situations and the ensuing intrigues of the official religious spy or informer that the plot develops. There are opportunities for mistaken identity, personation and disguise.

When Frank Redmond arrives at his sister Rose's house with Father O'Flaherty both men are disguised as 'farmers'. Rody and Nancy join them as they await Arthur Cromwell who will confirm a date when he can absent himself from the barracks for a double wedding. This is soon decided for the following day at a mountain location, but Arthur fears that his father has become aware of their plans. Rody proposes that the priest stay the night with Mulloney's sister – this woman is as staunch as her brother is traitorous. Rody has bought a new gun which he declares he will use if need be, 'for I'm ready for anything, either murder or mischief!'

Frank Redmond and Father O'Flaherty install themselves with Biddy Mulloney who rails against her renegade brother to whom she declares she has permanently given 'the wrong side of the door'. Mulloney appears at the window as she shows her visitors to the inner room. Responding to a knock, Biddy is surprised and alarmed to see her brother. They have an argument during which Mulloney moves stealthily towards the bedroom door; there is a tussle during which Biddy throws her brother off, enters the room and bangs the door. Mulloney bangs on the door which suddenly opens revealing Major Redmond, but, completely unfazed, Mulloney throws him aside and enters the chamber. The priest runs out but falls over a chair and Mulloney catches him by the throat. Biddy strikes her brother with a spade and he falls stunned; the priest rushes from the house; Mulloney recovers and makes to follow but Frank forestalls him with a knife. Then Rody arrives and shoots Mulloney with his brand new gun.

This sequence is very carefully worked out. We are given the detailed choreography in a way that is absent from most of O'Grady's manuscripts except *Emigration* and which gives substance to the view that the existing texts are not the finished work. Visual effects are of exteme importance: the reaction of the audience to Mulloney's face at the window, and the subsequent slaying of this dastardly informer after a series of leaps, runs and feints, can well be imagined.

News of the murder is brought to Sir Oliver Cromwell. Though no admirer of Mulloney's methods, he will give no quarter to the perpetrator. He sends for his son who incenses him by suggesting that Mulloney's murder may be a blessing for the country! Arthur accuses his father of mercilessly hunting Father O'Flaherty purely on account of his own decision to have his marriage performed by a Roman Catholic priest. As Arthur leaves Sir Oliver mutters that if he can't catch the priest he'll catch the girl. Major Robert Redmond reports that he has sent a detachment to find the murderer. Sir Oliver approaches him on the subject of Rose, whom Robert now declares not to be his sister as long as she maintains her 'superstitious' adherence to her religion. Perhaps Rose could be removed to 'a place of safety'? Sir Oliver directs Robert to inform O'Rourke the gauger (customs officer) that he may let two Dutch smugglers go free if they will transport Rose Redmond to the continent by ship.

Sir Oliver has reckoned without the gauger's native sense of justice, for O'Rourke immediately informs Frank Redmond of the plan. Frank and Rody disguise themselves as the smugglers, and, in lighthearted mood, practise Dutch accents. Robert Redmond arrives with six soldiers to help the 'Dutchmen' on their mission. Rose is informed that she will be taken to the mountain retreat to meet Father O'Flaherty prior to her much delayed wedding but she is terrified when in fact she is seized by the soldiers and handed over to the smugglers. Later, an embarrassed sergeant reports to Sir Oliver that he accompanied the woman and the smugglers to the wharf where the Dutchmen, in very good English, told him his company was no longer required – whereupon 'a crowd fell on us and nearly murdered us!' A peasant boy delivers a note to Sir Oliver: it is from his son Arthur stating that all his evil plans have been foiled. Instantly Sir Oliver mobilizes his forces: a rigorous search will be made for Arthur, Rose, Frank, O'Rourke and Father O'Flaherty.

In the Hag's Valley – 'Romantic mountain scenery, moon shining between mountains. Ripple on lake below ruins of old Church' – a crowd congratulates the two newly-wedded couples. O'Rourke the gauger rushes in to announce that troops under Major Robert Redmond are on their way. The priest and women conceal themselves behind rocks, while the men line up to confront the soldiers. Father O'Flaherty begs that there be no bloodshed. There is 'march music' as the soldiers enter. Major Robert Redmond declares that he has it on good authority that the priest is here; receiving no reply, he orders the soldiers to raise their guns. Father O'Flaherty rushes forward. The major charges him with being 'a proclaimed priest on Irish soil, against the laws of the land, and also for proposing an illegal marriage here tonight'. Arthur and Rose step forward and announce that they are already married.

Suddenly Sir Oliver Cromwell appears and cries 'Hold!' There is news from Dublin Castle: the priest must be released! 'The law against proscribed priests has today been revoked!' he announces. There is wild cheering. Arthur forgives his father. Father O'Flaherty addresses the crowd:

> We must all forgive our enemies ... Friends and fellow countrymen, this is the happiest day of my life. The dark cloud of Persecution has passed forever, and that [sic] bright days are in store for our poor country. The wedding that we have celebrated here tonight will shine as a brilliant example of the fidelity of our people in this country and [sic] their creed!

In spite of the conventional high-flown action interwoven with comical turns the subject of religious discrimination is treated with an outspokenness that one should consider surprising in a melodrama designed for the 'popular' touring circuit – were one not already aware of O'Grady's social concerns from reading all his plays consecutively. Early on in *The Priest Hunter* Sir Oliver Cromwell refers unambiguously to 'the disloyal set', meaning all those who do not conform to English ways through failure to embrace the reformed religion. Major Robert Redmond fearlessly describes Roman Catholicism as 'superstitious'. (Members of the Free Presbyterian Church in Northern Ireland still employ the term.) Sir Oliver declares that Arthur's marriage to Rose would deprive him of his 'property and position' unless she were to change her faith. (Arthur's riposte is quite pungent: 'If she is a pauper, who made her so but the cruel bloody laws of which you are an upholder!') These are but passing examples, for it is the general thrust of the work that is astonishingly courageous.

The evil of religious discrimination is, by generalized implication, extended to include British rule in Ireland. By having the drunken, deluded Irish priest hunter Mulloney shot, O'Grady effectively removes the element of ironically humorous political/religious ambiguity which surrounds his personality, transferring the focus to the English Governor (there never was such an office) as the chief perpetrator of evil in Ireland. Then, by a curious alteration of the dramatic convention, Sir John Cromwell himself becomes the *deus-ex-machina* through whom the news of the relaxation of the Penal Laws against priests is conveyed. Father O'Flaherty then makes a flowery speech welcoming a new dawn for Ireland.

There are two ways of interpreting this ending: either the actor who plays the priest uses a cynical tone of voice to convey the opposite of the speech's apparent message – which would go very much against the grain of the happy ending expected of melodrama – or, which is much more likely, the happy ending is allowed and we see O'Grady as bowing to political correctness; but he has made his point.

The Priest Hunter may not be O'Grady's best play – that is surely *The Eviction* – but it is certainly his most theatrically effective and his most daring in terms of its subject matter.

Hubert O'Grady's later career

A popular playwright, an accomplished actor, an out-and-out professional who never reached the topmost rung of the ladder in either discipline, O'Grady was nonetheless more creative than any of the other Irish playwrights of the years which separate the era of Boucicault from that of Synge. The very small body of serious criticism seems to tell us that he was content to satisfy the undemanding taste of the lower middle and working class theatre-goer: but the fact is we do not *know* if he was satisfied with his commercial success, or if he had aspirations towards something better. What we can glean from a reading of his plays is that he was much more than a mere spinner of exciting and amusing theatrical yarns: his genuine feeling for the deprived and the dispossessed, his anger at unjust laws and, in spite of an almost lifelong residence in England, his innate sense of nationality, continually break through the shell of his playwrighting in the prevailing popular style.

O'Grady's plays were filling the Queen's Theatre in Dublin at the precise time that Augusta Gregory, Edward Martyn and William Butler Yeats were discussing the possibility of a new type of Irish drama that would 'express the deeper thoughts and emotions of Ireland'. We do not know if O'Grady was aware of their plans – for one thing, he did not reside in Ireland – nor is it possible to imagine whether he would have taken their *recherché* stage productions at all seriously.

Hubert O'Grady died in December 1899. In May of that year Yeats' *The Countess Cathleen* and Martyn's *The Heather Field* had been produced in Dublin. In October O'Grady appeared yet again in Dublin in *The Famine*. One reviewer noted the familiarity of the piece, but took the line that the production was as fresh as ever, admiring 'Mr O'Grady's amusing impersonation of the character of the very scrupulous steward of Lawley Sackville' [sic].[81] His death occurred while on a visit to Liverpool. His brother Frank, who had played supporting roles in some of his plays, now took on Hubert O'Grady's parts, with Mrs Hubert O'Grady as producer.

The obituary writer of *The Era* stated that 'Mr. O'Grady claimed that his success had been attained by hard work both mentally and physically, sobriety, attention to business, and a determination to succeed, combined with a good constitution, a level head, and a good wife who entered into all his enterprises with enthusiasm ... For twenty years he toured his Irish dramas only, a fact unparalleled in the history of the stage... [He] was the first to take an entire company, scenery and properties to America.'[82] The Irish newspapers devoted very little space to news of his death, undoubtedly because he was known more as a visiting artiste than as a local figure. One obituary writer made a key point in stating that *The Eviction* was 'a sermon preached from behind the footlights'.[83] In his native Limerick, O'Grady's death passed almost unnoticed, with a nine-line paragraph which does not even mention the title of any of his plays.[84]

The *Irish Playgoer* redressed the balance somewhat, the columnist Hokey Pokey (who may have been Joseph Holloway) recalling memories of several of O'Grady's performances. 'Shall we ever see *The Shaughran* so brilliantly performed again?', he wrote. 'I fear not! I have now waited three and twenty years and failed to find even an approach to it in all-round excellence.' He mentions having seen several of O'Grady's plays, but does not attempt a critical evaluation of any of them – an obituary would hardly have been the place. He does provide information on the circumstances of O'Grady's death on Tuesday, 19th December; it occurred in Liverpool, 'where, on a visit to a friend, he contracted a chill that developed into death-dealing pneumonia ... The last time poor O'Grady was playing in Dublin I chanced to drop into the Queen's, on Tuesday, October 10th, 1899 [when] the play was *The Famine*, never dreaming that it was the last time I was to see him act. The tightly packed scrummage reminded me of the old times ere the *queue* system was ever thought of ... Seldom have I seen the Queen's so full. And now the poor fellow is no more and he only 58 years of age. Pneumonia when it claims a victim gives very little grace, and in O'Grady's case 10 days was all!'[85]

5 | J.W. WHITBREAD: ENTREPRENEUR IN JOHN BULL'S OTHER ISLAND

James W. Whitbread (1848-1916) made his home in Ireland at the age of thirty-six. While it may not be true to say that like the descendants of the Anglo-Norman invaders he became 'more Irish than the Irish', his plays from the mid-1880s were almost entirely Irish both in subject matter and – curiously for an Englishman – political stance. Whether the latter was the result of a cynical eye for the main chance or whether it sprang from a genuine wish to right Ireland's wrongs through the medium of the public stage, the following may help to elucidate. He was fortunate in forming a collaboration with the producer J Kennedy Miller without whom his sequence of patriotic plays might never have materialized in the spectacular way they did.

Attempts have been made by Stephen Brown, Allardyce Nicoll, Peter Kavanagh and Séamus de Burca[86] to list the first productions of all of Whitbread's plays, but the task is really impossible because unless an author had reached a high degree of eminence his or her name was rarely given in newspaper advertisements and hardly ever printed on playbills for pantomimes, burlesques or adaptations of novels. As far as can be ascertained, Whitbread's plays and dramatic adaptations were, in order of production: *Shoulder to Shoulder, (The) Race for Life, True to the Last, Miss Maritana, Hero of Heroes, The Irishman, All Hallow's Eve, The Nationalist* (aka *A True Son of Erin), The Spectre of the Past, Lord Edward, The Victoria Cross, Theobald Wolfe Tone, Rory O'More, The Insurgent Chief, The Ulster Hero, The Sham Squire, Sarsfield, The French Huzzar* and *The Soldier Priest.* Of these, only Whitbread's Irish plays will be treated here.

Briefly, his non-Irish plays were (*The*) *Race for Life*, which does have an Irish connection in that it was first produced at the Queen's Theatre, Dublin, in 1887.[87] A conventional story of a secret marriage, bigamy and a separation, its only distinguishing elements are the presence of a treadmill at work, described as 'one of the most realistic scenes ever witnessed on the stage', and a French detective who, by a very lengthy stretch of the imagination, might be described as a precursor of Hercule Poirot. *True to the Last*[88] was first performed at the Elephant & Castle Theatre, London, in 1888. It has no Irish content. No copy of *Hero of Heroes* seems to have survived; it was first produced at the Queen's in Dublin in 1889 where the advertising promised that it would prove to be 'Replete with Interest/Brimful of Fun/Full of Intense Pathos/Thrilling Interest/Powerful Situations/And Sensational Effects' – qualities shared with (for example) *Hamlet*. *Miss Maritana* was an 'operatic burlesque' written in collaboration with a Lieutenant George Nugent of the Grenadier Guards and has a tenuous Irish element in that it parodies the work of one of Ireland's best known operatic composers, William Vincent Wallace.[89] It was performed as an afterpiece in 1890 at the Theatre Royal, Dublin, 'under the patronage and presence of their Excellencies The Lord Lieutenant and the Countess of Zetland and their serene highnesses Prince and Princess Edward of Saxe-Weimar'. The occasion demonstrates how easy it was in the Dublin of that time to move about the labyrinthine sectors of Irish society: we have the *immigré* English author Whitbread, who had already produced a highly patriotic Irish play, *Shoulder to Shoulder,* lending his professional services for the amusement of the colonial regime at its most elevated level.

All Hallows Eve[90] has no Irish content. It was written in collaboration with an Hon Mrs Forbes who was undoubtedly a member of the society that revolved around Vice-Regal Lodge. It was performed at the Queen's in 1891, and does not seem ever to have been seen again. Unfortunately there does not appear to be a surviving script of *Spectres of the Past,* which was first presented at the Queen's in 1893. This should have been a significant event in production terms because it was the second occasion on which a play by Whitbread was announced as having been produced by 'Mr Kennedy Miller's Company' and therefore demonstrates that Kennedy Miller's handling of *The Nationalist* in the same year must have been fruitful to both parties. The reviews show that it is the story of a man who betrays the widow of a dead friend and robs their child of her inheritance. There was a burlesque sequence which was evidently a shortened version of the *Cinderella* tale as imagined in a delirium by the poor orphan girl. The *Irish Times* stated that 'the Cinderella interlude would be ludicrous were it not for the excellent production'.[91] This comment is fascinating in the light of the involvement of Kennedy Miller and his company.

The French Huzzar appears to have been lost or else was not submitted to the Lord Chamberlain – possibly Whitbread did not intend to tour it outside Ireland. It was first performed at the Queen's in 1906 and was announced in newspapers of the previous week as having been dramatized from Charles Lever's *Tom Burke of Ours* (1844). Finally, *The Soldier Priest* was licenced for the Theatre Royal, Wolverhampton, in 1916, by which time Whitbread was dead and his now outrageously *passé* melodramas were superseded by the Abbey Theatre which by this time had produced at least one masterpiece of international dimension in JM Synge's *The Playboy of the Western World* (1907) as well as several other important plays such as George Fitzmaurice's *The Country Dressmaker* (1907), St John Ervine's *Mixed Marriage* (1911), Lennox Robinson's *The Whiteheaded Boy* and George Bernard Shaw's *John Bull's Other Island* (both 1916).[92] The manuscript of *The Soldier Priest* is of interest because it is the only one seen upon which an actual comment was made by a member of the Lord Chamberlain's staff:

> It is fairly well written for the sort of rubbish. In spite of the hero being a priest, I did not think there is anything offensive to Catholics. The character is of course entirely sympathetic and though naturally there is a certain amount of priestly local colour, so to speak – the play ends with the angelus and a prayer – it is quite reverent.'

The writer of this succinct critique signed himself *G.S. Street*.

We are therefore left with eleven melodramas of varying quality for which Whitbread should be fittingly commemorated in the pantheon of Irish dramatists.

Whitbread's Life

Various press reports over the years mention that Whitbread was born in Portsmouth in 1848. Kavanagh confirms this in *The Irish Theatre* (1946). However, a search made in 2002 at the General Register Office in London denies any birth of that name in Portsmouth in that or contiguous years. Either he was not born there, or he was born there at quite a different date, or his parents failed to register his birth: the possibilities for speculation are endless. *The Era* states that he took up residence in Scarborough 'when quite a boy'; and it was there that he died on 10 June 1916. He became involved in the theatre in Scarborough, probably first as an amateur actor. He subsequently acted with numerous touring companies, none of whose names are relevant to his Irish writing

Fig 7. The Queen's Royal Theatre, Dublin [Dublin City Library and Archive] Schematic drawing of the theatre in Brunswick Street at the time of J.W. Whitbread's management. It was rebuilt in 1908 and housed the Abbey Theatre from 1951 to 1966. It was demolished in 1969.

career.[93] He is said to have played every part in *Hamlet* and *Macbeth* except the name parts – this suggests that he must have realized he was not destined to become a leading actor, and so moved into management.[94] He became manager of the Theatre Royal in Scarborough c.1876 and, alike with managers of all the receiving theatres, had his finger on the pulse of whatever was circulating in the profession. He may have had financial involvements in other houses – certainly he produced the pantomime *Dick Whittington and his Immortal Thomas* for the Queen's Royal Theatre, Dublin, in 1882.[95] The following year he bought the Queen's from its current owner, Arthur Lloyd. An article in an English newspaper six years later recalled that prior to his taking over the venerable Dublin house, 'the plays were low, the actors vile, the audiences rough exceedingly ... Mr Whitbread purchased the going concern, and by main energy, patience, wisdom and expenditure of money, dragged all out of the mire'.[96] Whitbread moved to Dublin with his family. We know from an illuminated address presented to him and his wife by the theatre staff on the occasion of their silver wedding on 8 October, 1897, that he had two daughters, by now grown up as their portraits in small medallions show. Their names are not given, and Mrs Whitbread is not even accorded an initial.[97]

Whitbread's earliest play (and earliest Irish play) was *Shoulder to Shoulder*, which opened at the Theatre Royal, Limerick, on 8 November 1886, before arriving at the Queen's the following week. Undoubtedly there is a hint of the 'out of town' preview before facing the metropolitan crowd. From *All Hallows Eve* onwards all *premiere* performances of Whitbread's plays, whether Irish or English in background, were given at the Queen's. *The Nationalist*, later entitled *A True Son of Erin*, appeared there on 21 December, 1891. It survived on the stage for at least twenty years and was also taken on by amateurs, presumably because a paper edition was published in Dublin in 1892.[98] The actor-director William Fay, who with his brother Frank was largely responsible for creating the acting style which became synonymous with the new Abbey Theatre, toured for several months in a fit-up production of *The Nationalist*.[99] Although *Shoulder to Shoulder* and *The Nationalist* were perennially successful, to the extent of entering that category which allows of the numbing description 'tried and trusted', they are, by comparison with the plays which Whitbread produced from 1894 onwards, fairly turgid examples of stock-in-trade melodrama.

On 20 March, 1894, the Queen's saw the first production of *Lord Edward*, a much livelier piece altogether. *The Victoria Cross* upsets the neat sequence of Irish plays – it opened at the Queen's on 7 September, 1896. It was followed two years later by *Theobald Wolfe Tone*, specifically mounted to coincide with the nationwide commemoration of the Insurrection of 1798. *The Insurgent Chief*, which follows incidents in the life of the historically more shadowy figure of Michael Dwyer, came out at the Queen's on 31 March, 1902, and immediately joined its predecessors on the road. This was followed on 12 January, 1903, by yet another play of 1798, *The Ulster Hero*, which must have been the earliest by many authors on the revolutionary leader Henry Joy McCracken.[100] (Tone appears in it as a minor character.) *The Sham Squire*, described as 'concerning the iniquitous Francis Higgins', is also set in 1798; it did not enjoy the popularity of the other 1798 plays, and no copy seems to have been preserved.

The year 1904 was an *annus mirabilis* in the Irish theatre. The first production of Whitbread's *Sarsfield* coincided with the dress rehearsal for the Abbey Theatre's inaugural night on 27 December. Set during the Siege of Limerick of 1690-91, *Sarsfield* is a sturdy work, displaying some of the faults but more of the virtues of historical melodrama. 'Hasn't Mr Whitbread turned the attention of many a previously indifferent young Irishman to the history and literature of his country?' enquired an anonymous correspondent to the *Irish Playgoer* in a piece headed 'Irish Drama by an English Writer' – 'and hasn't he shown aspiring Irish dramatists that they've plenty of groundwork here in their own land for their writings? Probably the Irish Literary Theatre Committee think these Queen's Theatre dramas have "no class"... But I'd rather see young Irish writers follow the footsteps of our genial English friend in this direction, than those of our great literary lion George Moore ...'[101] Alas for the correspondent, time has shown George Moore – though an indifferent dramatist – to be a far greater writer than Whitbread, but the comparison is an unfair one, for the two had quite dissimilar aims. The point about seeking inspiration 'in their own land' is, however, very much in accord with the thinking of Moore's circle – which this correspondent would not have known at the time. This is yet another example of the failure of the literary and the popular streams in the Irish theatre to coalesce at the period in question – something which did not happen until Yeats and Gregory had perforce to embrace playwrights like George Shiels and Brinsley Macnamara in the 1920s.

At the conclusion of the performance on the first Saturday night of the two-week run of *The Insurgent Chief* in April 1902 Whitbread appeared on the stage and offered a prize of £100 for 'the best Irish drama written by an Irish man or woman, born of Irish parents and residing in Ireland'. This generous sum, provided by the acknowledged leading living author of Irish dramas, who was neither born in Ireland nor of Irish parentage, shows how conscious he must have been of his position as a successful *immigré* with a real devotion to the Irish stage; he would also have realized that he could not go on writing these plays for ever, and that a successor or successors must be found to retain the name of the Queen's as 'the home of Irish drama'. The winner, Robert Johnston, was awarded the prize a year later for *The Old Land,* a play which has not survived. [102]

As manager and lessee of the Queen's, Whitbread did not produce – in the modern sense of 'direct' – his own plays: this responsibility was almost always given to Kennedy Miller, who ran the company that quickly became almost synonymous with the house. In 1900 Miller became Whitbread's deputy, assuming artistic control of the theatre as well as of his own company. It was a most fortunate collaboration, and the success of Whitbread's plays clearly owed an enormous amount to Miller's sense of stagecraft.

Shoulder to Shoulder

Whitbread's first significant Irish play did not open at the Queen's Theatre, Dublin, as some sources specify, but in Limerick. The touring management involved was Claude Shaw's Dramatic Company, which transferred the play to the Queen's the following week. The advertisement in the *Limerick Chronicle* which announced the opening for 8 November, 1886, provided the information that the piece was 'by Mr J.W.Whitbread, Manager, Queen's Royal Theatre, Dublin' and listed the 'Magnificent Stage Effects!' and the 'New and Beautiful Scenery!' as follows: *'Act 1. Shamrock Dale, Co Wicklow. Outcasts on the Wayside. – Act 2. Kate O'Brien's House, Dublin. Love defeats Villainy. Act 3. Scene 1. A Garret on the Coombe. Escape of Gerald. Scene 2, College Green, the Bank of Ireland. Scene 3. The River Liffey. Terrible Collision with a North Wall Steamer. One of the most realistic scenes ever witnessed. Act 4. Scene 1. House on Rogerson's Quay. The Murder. Scene 2. The Custom House by Night. Shoulder to Shoulder!'*

Only Act I has been preserved in manuscript but a forty-four page novelette of the same name, printed in Dublin two years later, gives us the missing part of the story.[103] The only surviving Limerick press notice is a wonderful example of period provincialism, bemused as it is by the wonders of the visiting production yet emphasizing any local involvements wherever possible: of James O'Brien in the comic role of Mike Rooney the critic noted that 'Mr O'Brien, we believe, graduated in Limerick, and Limerick ought to give him a bumper'. The actors are praised, but this critic takes his calling seriously, eschewing the Dublin trend of giving polite mentions only: J.R. Walton as Richard O'Cassidy (the villain) 'has talent combined with a striking figure. We would venture to give him this advice, however, that his mannerisms are a little too pronounced, and detract from his general performance'.[104] The reviews of the Dublin opening do not give any indication as to whether Mr Walton took this advice. The same Limerick critic commented admiringly on the staging:

> The scenery is really good – the best that we have seen in Limerick for a long time. College Green by moonlight is a really pretty and effective picture, but the terrible collision on the North Wall is one of the most realistic we have witnessed in the provinces; indeed it is a triumph of the stage-carpenter's art.[105]

Thus, in a few words, we have a lively picture of the provincial touring scene, with a typical play in a typical presentation. We learn from the *Irish Times* the following year that *Shoulder to Shoulder* enjoyed 'an exceptionally successful tour in England and Scotland' before appearing for a further three weeks at the Queen's. Fourteen years later Frank Fay attended a visiting English production at the Queen's. As he was to be the chief advocate for the National Theatre Society in employing Irish actors in Irish plays, it is no surprise that he dismissed this performance: 'The lines of the parts corresponding to those in the Boucicault Irish plays would sound absurd if spoken by anything but an Irish actor. That was Boucicault's secret; an Irishman may master it; an Englishman cannot, and Irish drama is impossible without it ...'[106]

The critic of the *Irish News* shared Fay's view that 'one never does feel satisfied at hearing the rebellious patriotic young scion of an ancient Irish home talking about 'dear old Ireland' in an English accent' – this in reference to the unnamed English actor playing the part of Gerald O'Neil in Belfast.[107]

The scene is Shamrock Dale, the O'Neil country seat south of Dublin, where Nelly O'Neil keeps house for her widowed father. It appears that both she and her brother Gerald believe that their father has grown too much under the influence of his land agent, O'Cassidy, with whom young Gerald has had a number of bitter arguments in relation to the management of the estate. Nelly discloses that O'Cassidy has been making unwelcome advances to her. O'Cassidy informs his employer that he will no longer accept Gerald's insolence, proposing that he send him packing, which O'Neil reluctantly attempts to do. He refuses to give his daughter's hand in marriage to O'Cassidy but agrees to tell her of O'Cassidy's feelings (which she already knows and fears) but he will not force her to accept him. Gerald's college friend D'Arcy, who has a genuine understanding with Nelly, determines to intervene and offers to help Gerald remove O'Cassidy from the house.

It emerges that O'Cassidy has a 'hold' on O'Neil because some years back he was witness to O'Neil murdering a Mr O'Brien, father of Kate O'Brien to whom Gerald has now formed an attachment. It is, to say the least, a difficult family situation, bound up with the shaky financial affairs of the country estate. There is a definite sense that O'Neil did not commit the murder, but apparently O'Cassidy has proof and this is a stone which must, for the sake of everyone, remain unturned. At a fraught family gathering O'Neil states that he has 'every confidence in O'Cassidy' but his looks belie his words. The young people are astonished at his obduracy.

The situation and relationships are well set up in the first act, which is all we have of the play.

Audiences would have sensed early on that O'Neil did not murder Phil O'Brien in the years gone by, that he would eventually be vindicated and that O'Cassidy would be revealed as the villain that his initial appearances suggest. This indeed proves to be the case, as the novelette of 1888 discloses, but not before there have been a number of exciting escapades including a scene on the North Wall in Dublin where Gerald is knocked senseless by two dastardly boatmen and his body consigned to the waters of the River Liffey – from which he is rescued by his faithful servant Mike. Moments later a steamboat slices the rowing boat in two.

Such physical occurrences, one might suppose, must have been additions to the story as published rather than a part of the action of the play – yet the reviews refer to the 'excellence of the mechanical effects employed', including 'the terrible collison on the North Wall'. How this was achieved one can only surmise; but the effects must have been quite ingenious in order to satisfy a critical audience, demonstrating how proficient the staging must have been.

The Irishman

Whereas Whitbread's earliest known play, *Shoulder to Shoulder,* was tried out in the relative obscurity of Limerick, *The Irishman* was accorded a much riskier London opening. Although the Elephant & Castle Theatre was situated on the New Kent Road there is no sense of its being hidden away in a place from which news of a disaster would be unlikely to reach Dublin, where it was due to appear the following week. The Elephant & Castle was in fact one of several splendid new theatres designed by Frank Matchham.[108] It seated

2,203 patrons and drew its audience from the recently developed suburbs of Camberwell and Dulwich, as well as the West End, which was now easily accessible by underground *via* Blackfriars Station. Yet why, one might wonder, did Kennedy Miller's company choose to open this Irish play on the other side of the Irish sea? The answer is quite simple: the company was currently on the road in England. The London opening took place on 4 November 1889, and the play remained in the repertoire of Kennedy Miller's company until well into the first decade of the twentieth century.

The Kavanaghs of Coolgamartin are an indigenous aristocratic Roman Catholic family. (They would have been disparagingly referred to as 'Castle Catholics' by co-religionists.) 'I brought you up a Tory,' exclaims the irascible Sir Owen to his charming nephew and heir, Owen, 'and you have become a ranting nationalist!' The period is not stated, but the feeling is definitely Victorian. Reference to 'the popular party' of which young Owen is a member is not elaborated upon – it is unlikely to mean Parnell's Irish Parliamentary Party for, if so, there would be no basis for Owen's arrest; a subversive group is vaguely inferred. This play is unusual in that there are two comic male servants – Larry O'Rourke, the indefatigable family retainer, and Mickey Whelan, the clever poor boy who is the villain's highly outspoken 'creature'; the two comics are well differentiated. The villain is the Kavanagh's land agent, Felix Blake. Nora Desmond, beloved of Owen, is an orphan who dwells in the Kavanagh home – 'orphan' was often a euphemism for the child of some unmarried member of the family. A somewhat worldly couple, Sir Owen's mature niece Kate Kearney and her gentleman caller, Captain Delehunt, provide a distinctly ironic comment on the proceedings which open, for all their conventionality of the components, intriguingly.

Blake has given his servant Mickey a message to deliver to Coolmagartin: the hapless Mickey returns to say that Sir Owen 'kicked me out', Larry O'Rourke 'kicked me across the lawn', Master Owen 'whipped me' and Miss Desmond 'laughed at me'. Mickey is nothing if not candid in reporting what these persons have remarked about Blake: thus the lines of conflict are effectively and amusingly drawn. Larry O'Rourke has overheard Blake instructing Mickey to take a letter to the magistrate which should ensure that a warrant is issued for the apprehension of Owen for his membership of 'the national league'. If Owen is jailed it will clear the way for Blake to approach Norah. Larry discovers the contents of the letter which he reports to Sir Owen who immediately quizzes Blake. Blake grovellingly replies that it was due to his wish not to 'drag Sir Owen's name through the mire'. The latter crisply replies that if the allegations are true, then the letter must take its course, but he dismisses Blake. Blake reveals that young Owen has not been passing on the rents; Sir Owen declares this to be a lie – 'He [Owen] may sport sedition, but he could not descend to robbing his own uncle!' Sir Owen agrees to pay off Blake; £1,000 is agreed, but Blake (in an aside) intends £1,000 *per annum*.

Owen's engagement to Norah is announced amid much rejoicing. Kate informs Owen that his uncle is in a terrible rage and feels it his duty to let the authorities know of his membership of 'the popular party'. She urges Owen to leave the country; Norah declares that as she is 'an Irish girl' she understands his motives and will endure his absence for a while. Kate jokingly suggests that Owen should first 'thrash' Blake – suddenly they notice Blake eavesdropping and Owen pursues him, encouraged by Captain Delehunt to whom Blake shouts that he will report him to his commanding officer. There are shouts of affray (off). Sir Owen emerges to address the victorious Owen: he will put up with his nephew's politics but not with his thieving – for Blake has provided evidence of a shortfall in the accounts. Owen explains that he paid some of the rents himself because the tenants were 'too poor', giving the money to Blake, from whom he did not request receipts. Sir Owen immediately retracts his accusation. Redcoats appear, escorted by Blake. Owen stands firm. Larry levels a pistol at Blake and challenges him to repeat his political accusation against Owen. Tableau.

A short time passes during which the Kavanaghs' finances have disimproved. Owen has been jailed for membership of an illegal organization. Blake has effectively taken over the estate and Sir Owen has gone into a decline. He has disowned Owen. Says Larry: 'That owld uncle should be boiled down for charity soup!' Norah again refuses Blake's proposal of marriage. He produces a letter in which she appears to accept: it would be catastrophic if Owen set eyes on it – but Owen, escaped from jail, believes her true explanation that it was a schoolgirl exercise written several years previously to an imaginary gentleman.

The Kavanaghs are evicted from Coolmagartin for non-payment of rent. Blake, as agent, takes possession, vowing that he will remain in residence until Norah becomes his wife. A rapid sequence of events discloses Sir Owen writing his will, into which, when the old man is momentarily absent, Blake inserts his own name as beneficiary. Sir Owen returns, confronts him, and Blake stabs the old man. Owen, acceding to his uncle's summons (when he should have been informed that he is reinstated) finds the corpse and is accused of murder by Blake. Unknown to both, Larry has witnessed the full proceedings from behind a convenient arras. Blake subsequently reports Owen to the police, but Owen escapes – disguised as Father Kelly, the priest who has just married himself and Norah!

The complicated business of forging the will, the murder, and the ensuing concealments of almost everybody at different times and sometimes simultaneously, as well as the various confrontations and skirmishes that follow, are so physical they make for tedious reading, but they clearly provided riveting spectacle on the stage. The comic *dénouement* of the second act, which comes as much needed light relief, has Blake's unfortunate servant, the tipsy Mickey Whelan, hoisted into the air by an unknown force – Larry having slipped a rope around him – providing a welcome pay-off to all this improbable activity as if the author were puckishly declaring that his tongue has been partly in his cheek throughout.

Kate Kearney and Captain Delehunt discuss her legal position – if she marries before she is twenty-five the house on the Coolmagartin estate in which she lives will revert to the nominal owner, who is now Blake; she decides to delay her wedding till the last moment in order to vex him – which Delehunt finds not a little frustrating. Blake announces that he is going to evict three families for arrears of rent. Delehunt offers to pay on their behalf but Blake points out that this would place him among the lawbreakers. Blake further declares that he will be calling on Delehunt as an officer to assist in asserting 'the majesty of the law'. Delehunt advises forbearance. 'What will prevent me?' enquires Blake. 'This!' cries Larry, brandishing a voluminous document. 'The will you stole the night you murdered Sir Owen Kavanagh!'

This sensational pronouncement is typical of curtain lines in so many of these plays. Often there is no follow-up in the succeeding scene and it takes some time to discern what followed – in this case it turns out that Larry had the wrong document and Blake is free to continue his ill disposed plans. He supervises the evictions and uses a battering-ram to knock down the side of a cottage. An elderly peasant is carried out on a shutter to die. Father Kelly cries out that Blake will suffer eternal torture for his actions.

There is a multiple setting for the final scenes in and surrounding Kate Kearney's house. Two interiors, one above the other, are on view, as well as the garden with a lake in the background.[109] Norah is staying in the upper room and Blake has made it plain that he will spend the night with her: 'Tomorrow will see her with her reputation sullied for ever!' Blake is so incensed that his servant is closely trailing him that he fires a shot which frightens poor Mickey who tumbles into the lake. Owen and Larry arrive by boat. Upstairs, Norah meets Blake – 'what brings you to my chamber at this hour of the night?' she enquires. Says Blake: 'Revenge! Revenge for your coldness, your insults, your contempt!' When Blake lays hands on her she shouts for help and Owen rushes in. Larry rises out of the water below with what is evidently the drowned corpse of Mickey. The author appends a stage direction to the effect that 'this must be regulated so that the double picture occurs simultaneously'.

Next day Father Kelly congratulates Owen for saving Norah from a fate worse than death.

They expect that Mickey, who has survived his dowsing in the lake, will accuse Blake of attempted murder. In the final scene in the library at Coolmagartin, Blake, expecting to be accused of attempted murder by the very much alive Mickey, pays the latter off handsomely. 'What's this intrusion?' he cries when almost the entire cast, plus constables, enter. Owen accuses Blake of murdering Sir Owen Kavanagh. Will Larry testify as witness? Yes. Will Mickey? No. Blake points to Owen as the murderer – but Larry has found the will which Blake forged and shows that the watermark on the paper is of recent date and can not be Sir Owen's original. Blake is arrested. It is likely that he will be convicted and hanged, with the hapless Mickey as an accomplice. The play ends with Owen taking Norah's hand and inviting the audience's approval.

The use of multiple staging for the final scenes is imaginative. The writing is brisk and to the point. The exchange leading up to the anticipated rape is packed with tension. Owen's providential arrival in the bedroom just as Larry saves Mickey from drowning is presented with a real sense of theatricality. Thereafter the piece dwindles into a typically fragmented series of incidents and pronouncements. The disclosure of the watermark in the will is a nadir of authorial barrel-scraping. The sub-plot concerning the sophisticated couple Kate Kearney and Captain Delehunt has been forgotten – one assumes that the director would contrive for them to appear for the final tableau, or at least arrange them together for the final tableau. The eviction and its consequences are not alluded to, which makes one all the more certain that the scene was a later insertion to give emotional substance to a sagging plot. It is not beyond the bounds of possibility that Whitbread attempted to model it on the heartrending central scene in O'Grady's eviction play.

This scene impressed the *Evening Telegraph* reviewer when *The Irishman* reached Dublin a week after its London opening:

> The resistance to the invaders is vividly illustrated ... and until the huge battering ram is brought on and part of the wall brought down, the evictors had but small success against the vigorous resistance ... Add to this story plenty of smartly written dialogue, some light love incidents, a good deal of fun, and a constant change of scenes [and] it will easily be seen why *The Irishman* pleased the large audience.[110]

The last sentence is a fair enough assessment of the play in the terms of its time – we are still in the 1880s. Ten years later in his *United Irishman* column Frank Fay acknowledged its continuing popularity but pointed out how very old-fashioned it had become:

> Before the first act was through, all my old friends, whom I never met outside melodramas, had made their appearance. Being one of those who prefer that *rara avis*, the dramatist who endeavours to put into his characters something of the heaven and hell that is in each of us, the melodramatist's libels on human nature are quite outside my sympathy. I never can understand how the common-sense of an audience tolerates them ...'

What interested Fay about *The Irishman* was the effectiveness of the eviction scene, but here again he felt that Whitbread relied on the predictable emotional response of his audience and failed to take the incident further than its physical enactment: for him the scene did not convey the human tragedy. In the hands of an author of 'artistic aim' the piece 'might have mirrored the truth about the land agitation, and been intensely dramatic at the same time'.[111] Neither Fay, nor any other critics seen, made a comparison with Hubert O'Grady's vastly superior play, *Eviction*.

The chief fault with *The Irishman* is surely that Owen Kavanagh – generous, selfless and honest to the point of nobility – lacks the charisma which one would expect from a character bearing the burden of such a title role. He is not by any means colourless – he simply lacks stature. Within a comparatively short time Whitbread would solve the inherent difficulty of the portrayal of dramatic heroes by employing those who came ready-made from the multicoloured pages of history.

MISS ANNIE HYLTON

Fig 8. Annie Hylton as Kate Kearney in *The Irishman* [*Irish Playgoer*/National Library of Ireland] A leading member of the Kennedy Miller company, Annie Hylton was Eileen O'Moore in *A True Son Of Erin*, Lady Honor in *Sarsfield*, Anne Chute in *The Colleen Bawn*, etc.

The Nationalist, also known as *A true Son of Erin*

Whitbread was well established both as author and manager when *The Nationalist* came out on St Stephen's Day, 1891. This play has the distinction of being the only one of Whitbread's for which an original published version has survived.[112]

The Nationalist was well received. The *Irish Times* predicted that it would have a successful run, 'and it will certainly be received with as much favour in England' – an interesting comment.[113] The *Evening Telegraph* found it to be 'absolutely free of bewilderment', presumably meaning that there are no unbelievable situations – and this is a moot point, for in fact it seems to be as replete with the latter as any in the *genre*.[114] The *Telegraph* gives more attention than is usual to the performances, demonstrating that comparatively colourless dialogue can be made quite vibrantly entertaining in the mouths – and gestures – of accomplished actors. A verbal tussle between Phil's manservant Denny and the dishonest lawyer Flynn in Act I passes as faintly amusing in the script but was evidently very funny indeed when played by James O'Brien and Frank Breen, the two most experienced comic actors in the Kennedy Miller company.

Joseph Holloway saw the play nine years later when it appeared under its new title *A True Son of Erin*. He found that

> the piece abounds in sensational tableaux which invariably bring down the curtain amid great excitement and applause from the front. A plentiful supply of popular humour made the mixture truly palatable, while the villanies of the villains at times were such as to arouse the house to storms of hissing. The play was interestingly interpreted by Kennedy Miller's very capable company of Irish players who each and all seem to know the pulse of the popular audiences ...[115]

Once again we are reminded of Whitbread's debt to what we would now call his Artistic Director. Theatrically, then, the piece survived – due, one feels, to the sensitive attention of Miller and his men and women. As a piece for the study, however, it has its *longueurs*: so much so that it may not be too unfair to describe it as a very protracted play indeed.

The action takes place mainly on the country property of the charming Phil Hennessy who has recently returned from a visit to Australia where he has been seeking the support of the Irish immigrant community for a Society that very closely resembles the factual Land League. He is accompanied on his return by Joe McManus, photographic reporter of the *Daily Exposer,* and meets Lieutenant Walpole who has been sent by the government at Westminster to report on the 'state of the country'. The other main characters are Matt Sheehan, Phil's land agent, and two associates of Sheehan's, Paddy Finnigan and Patrick Flynn – the latter an attorney-at-law. The chief ladies are Eileen O'Moore, to whom Phil is engaged, and Lady Rose O'Malley, a wealthy neighbour. The chief comic parts are Denny O'Hea, Phil's manservant, and his sweetheart, Peggy Donohue. There are numerous supporting characters with names such as Swivel-eyed Donegan and Nobby-nose Doherty, and the essential priest, Father O'Rourke.

Peggy Donohue is insulted by Matt Sheehan and Paddy Finnigan who have been frustrated in the serving of a writ for eviction upon her because she paid her rent at the last minute; they suspect she was helped by someone else. Finnigan then serves an ejectment order on Denny O'Hea; Denny is incensed because Finnigan suggests that Peggy is being 'looked after' by a secret lover; there are fisticuffs and Finnigan ends up in a tub. When Lady Rose arrives on a walk with Eileen Moore and Father O'Rourke she discloses quite openly that it was she who paid the rents of 'the poor peasants'.

From the land agent's point of view this is not at all as it should be. It emerges that under his late father's will Phil can not dismiss his agent (Matt Sheehan) until he attains the age of twenty-five. Sheehan and Finnigan overhear the latter described by Phil as 'a cringing sycophant to his superiors and a bully to his inferiors'. Walpole delivers a government letter to Sheehan requesting him to help in his information-gathering. A fierce argument develops between Phil and his agent when Sheehan speaks disparagingly of the tenants; when Phil raises his whip Sheehan provocatively shouts 'murder!'.

Denny invites Phil into his cabin so as he won't be seen passing 'League' documents to Joe McManus but Finnigan listens to their discussion. Denny catches him eavesdropping and sees him off. Denny then takes charge of the documents because he is sure Finnigan will elaborate on the conversation and the reporter may be arrested. Denny has found some bank notes, which he believes Phil or Joe must have left behind, or someone may have planted them: on the spur of the moment he gives them to Lady Rose for safe keeping. The police arrive, Finnigan having informed them and the attorney Patrick Flynn of subversive conversation and a theft; he declares that the money will be found on Denny O'Hea but no money is found. Matt Sheehan accuses Phil of having documents relating to an 'extreme section, the Dynamitards'. Denny announces that the bank notes will be found on Sheehan: and they are! Evidently Sheehan planted the notes in Denny's cabin, Denny gave them to Lady Rose who gave them to the attorney and Flynn gave them back to Matt Sheehan. 'And there they are!' cries Denny, snatching them out of Matt's pocket!

Phil is incarcerated in Ballyhoolit Jail on account of papers connected with a Dynamitist plot having been planted on him and discovered by the police. He has succumbed to prison fever. (The visiting Lady Rose is constrained to remark on the 'insanitary state of our wretched prisons!') Denny is also in jail, having given Patrick Flynn a severe thrashing so that he'd be arrested and placed next to his young master. Matt Sheehan is overjoyed to hear that Phil is dying, for he will inherit the estate under the terms of Phil's father's will, Phil being unmarried and having no progeny. Sheehan believes that once he is owner, Eileen O'Moore, whom Phil is shortly expected to marry, will turn to him.

Phil, however, recovers. Sheehan requests to see him alone, but Danny lingers behind a panel and observes Sheehan pour something into Phil's medicinal wine. When the doctor returns, Danny steps forth and denounces Sheehan as a poisoner!

In her home, Ballyrassel Castle, Lady Rose is giving a party. Lieutenant Walpole tells her they've brought along Matt Sheehan, who was not invited, in the hope that he will inadvertently expose himself. In the course of the evening the attorney Patrick Flynn has too much to drink and attempts to embrace Lady Rose; she seizes a whip and lashes him. He drunkenly declares that he'll have the law on her, but she has further recourse to the whip when Joe McManus appears and photographs the scene. News is brought from Dublin to the delight of Peggy that Danny's sentence has been remitted. When the room clears of guests Matt Sheehan searches Lady Rose's desk; he finds a bank draft from Australia made out to Phil in favour of the National League: he decides to cash it so that Phil will be accused of embezzlement – but he has reckoned without Eileen, who has entered silently and observed his actions. She takes up a pistol, points it at him, and orders him out of the house.

Outside the prison, Matthew Sheehan and Patrick Flynn expect to see Phil released and rearrested on false information which they have supplied. Phil has been instrumental in having Flynn struck off the attorneys' roll. He emerges disguised as a warder and is hustled away by Danny and friends. The warder appears, disguised as Phil: Sheehan and Flynn identify him to the police who move to arrest him, but the warder reveals himself to the immense discomfort of the two schemers.

Peggy Donohoe attends to her aged father in her kitchen, while at the same time engaging in an amusing love dialogue with Danny as she attempts to bake a cake and he tries to help, with disastrous culinary results. We learn that Lady Rose has invited Phil to conceal himself in her castle but he, concerned for her safety, has chosen to hide in the Old Mill until Joe secures a vessel to convey him to France. Father O'Rourke will marry Phil and Eileen and the couple will travel together. While the couple are left alone for a tender exchange, Patrick Flynn enters with Matthew Sheehan: the latter impertinently asks for Eileen's hand: there is a scuffle, the priest and Joe appear and in the *melée* Sheehan shoots at Phil but misses and hits Father O'Rourke. Joe photographs the incident.

On the road to the Old Mill, Flynn tells Sheehan he has stowed Eileen there – having seized her following the previous *débacle*. They do not know that Phil has concealed himself in the same building. When they have moved on, Denny and Peggy enter: she is fearful for their lives. Lady Rose and Joe McManus appear, with the news that Father O'Rourke is merely injured. It emerges that Lady Rose and Joe have been seeing a great deal of each other and are to be married. Lieutenant Walpole arrives to help in the search for Eileen and to organize the apprehending of Matt Sheehan.

Two men are digging a grave in the Old Mill as Matthew Sheehan attempts to get Eileen to accept him: failing, he locks her into a room. Patrick Flynn arrives with four accomplices; they leave with Sheehan to continue plotting as Denny arrives in search of Phil, who breaks down the door where Eileen is held captive. The noise disturbs the plotters who return just as Phil hides in a box and Denny in a barrel. Police alerted by Lieutenant Walpole arrive; Phil and Denny jump out of their hiding places and all point pistols at the plotters. Finally Phil grabs Sheehan by the throat. There is a note in the text designed for future producers advising that this tableau should be arranged according to poster.

Phil and Denny search for papers in Flynn's office. They hide when Flynn – apparently having escaped from the earlier incident – enters, takes money from a safe and stows it in a portmanteau. Flynn then inadvertently locks Denny in the safe. Matthew Sheehan appears: Phil then emerges and confronts him at gunpoint, requesting a written confession that he and Flynn forged the documents implicating him in 'hideous crimes for which the authorities have issued a warrant for my capture'. Sheehan goes to the safe, and when he opens it Denny steps out! Enter Lieutenant Walpole, Joe McManus, Lady Rose and Eileen. Joe states that many of Flynn and Sheehan's vile deeds are recorded on film. Sheehan declares that Paddy Finnigan forged the documents, but Finnigan, who has been concealed thoughout, steps forth and accuses Sheehan of lying. Finnigan states that all the money robbed from Phil is in the safe. The portmanteau of documents is seized by police who arrive advertently, appropriate arrests are made and Father

O'Rourke, recovered from his ordeal, congratulates Phil – 'the true Nationalist'.

The first act of *The Nationalist* suffers from what should have been an easily remedied structural deficiency – one which occurs in so many of these plays – that of ill-contrived exits and entrances as the various sets of characters are introduced, necessitating the padding of dialogue and slowing down the action all too measurably. The concealments and exchanges of documents and bank notes, which seem so complicated in the script, would have been quite easily comprehended when observed as part of the stage business. The action is less sluggish in the subsequent three acts. An incident referred to by Holloway which does not occur in the script is the attempted drowning of Phil by Flynn in the mill race: this is proof, if any be needed, that these plays were in what television producers refer to as 'continuing script development'. Such a scene must have appeared to regular theatregoers as amazingly similar to the attempted drowning of Gerald O'Neil in *Shoulder to Shoulder*. The internal furnishings of *The Nationalist* are more interesting than its rather awkward architecture, epecially in the way Whitbread gives us an exciting story with a 'nationalist' background yet does not portray the physical appurtenances of 'nationalism'. The fact that nationalist elements are active is made manifest in Phil's interest in the work of the 'Leaguers' and in the references to a nationalist element known as 'the Dynamitards' which apparently finds its support in Australia: Whitbread never introduces a Leaguers' meeting, nor do the Dynamitards make an appearance, but the presence of all this *offstage* activity is keenly felt.

The presence of Lieutenant Walpole as a sympathetic government inspector is an innovation, and his integration into the plot as Lady Rose's chosen suitor gives a little additional colour. Joe McManus, the English photographic journalist, is also a novel character. (The use of photography as a means of providing police evidence may have been inspired by the same device in Boucicault's *The Octoroon* (1859) which was still regularly played in Dublin and elsewhere.) Otherwise the characters in *The Nationalist* are mainly of the hackneyed variety to which audiences had become accustomed – except for Lady Rose who combines the brisk assurance of the experienced *châtelaine* with something of the exaggerated philanthropy of a Lady Bountiful. Her prolonged use of the horse-whip upon her would-be abductor has alarming implications which would have been of distinct interest to Sigmund

Freud. Phil Hennessy, 'the true son of Erin', is a more than usually self-righteous hero, his heart so generously and compassionately in the right Hibernian place.

Fig 9. H. Somerfield Arnold as Phil Hennessy in *The Nationalist* [Dublin City Library and Archive] In Kennedy Miller's company he played Lord Edward Fitzgerald in Whitbread's play, Captain Molyneux in *The Shaughran*, Owen Keegan in *The Irishman*, etc. He died a few weeks after this picture was taken.

The Victoria Cross

The Victoria Cross, 'an entirely new military drama', was first produced at the Queen's Theatre, Dublin, on 7 November 1896. If Whitbread's name were not on the manuscript – or were he not praised as author in the reviews – one might easily suppose that it had been penned by a superior hand, for the first act – with the exception of some rustic drolleries from the servants – reads like an English society drama by Henry Arthur Jones or Arthur Wing Pinero. However, the succeeding acts do disclose many of Whitbread's stock contrivances such as escapes, hectic chases, sudden changes of fortune, denunciations and (so to speak) black and white characterization. It is set in England and India and has no Irish reference save for the important presence of Andy Cregan, servant to Captain Richard Maynard, who possesses, to an almost Kiplingesque degree, that intrepid quality which, in spite of dislocation, was evidently a characteristic of Irish recruits 'a-serving of Her Majesty the Queen' in 'India's sunny clime'.

None of the reviews seen draws attention to obvious similarities with Boucicault's *Jessie Brown* (1858) which is set during the Siege of Lucknow of 1857 – Boucicault's opportunism in bringing out a play on so topical a subject so quickly is typical of the man. While Boucicault relied on contemporaneous press reports of the Indian Mutiny for his background, almost 30 years later Whitbread could have used any number of books on the same subject. Whitbread is certain to have seen *Jesse Brown* for it was on the circuit for many years. Both playwrights treat Nana Sahib as the arch villain, both make much of the exotic oriental location, and both employ daring displays of military might for climax – in Boucicault's play this is the Relief of Lucknow by a Highland regiment, pipes a-skirl and kilts a-whirl, and in Whitbread's the Massacre of Cawnpore, fortunately most of it offstage.

Joseph Holloway attended the premiere and recorded his observations in a diary entry.

> The house was packed, and became quite excited as the night wore on and the play proved a capital one of the sensational kind, exceedingly well written and most interesting. Incidents of the Indian Mutiny formed a picturesque background into which the plot of the drama was ingeniously woven. Mr Whitbread was called twice before the curtain amid great applause ...

Holloway then described the principal actors of the Kennedy Miller Combination, particularly complimenting H. Somerfield Arnold, who played Jack Raynton 'with restraint and marked effect', Frank Breen's Andy Cregan and Clara Russell's Kate Maynard. '... The scenery and staging were all that could be desired, especially effective being the Indian scenes'.[116] He noted that the play was 'over' at 11.15 pm – a running time of three and a quarter hours.

A review in the *Freeman's Journal* stated that it was a 'capital production', 'splendidly staged', 'well acted', and that there were 'hearty plaudits' throughout the evening.[117] There is not a trace of any suggestion that the 'home and colonial' ethos of the work was inappropriate on an Irish stage, the *Freeman's* reviewer treating it on its merits and not from his newspaper's political viewpoint.

The Victoria Cross is set on the Aubrey family demesne in the Home Counties and in the neighbourhood of Cawnpore in 1857-8. The 'young squire', Richard Aubrey, returns to England after a decade serving abroad, to accept the title and property of his late father. Richard has a childhood friend, Jack Raynton, now the gamekeeper, whom he does not know is his half brother. Richard's widowed mother does not 'recognize' the Rayntons. Richard has hopes of marrying Kate Maynard, daughter of a neighbour, Colonel Maynard – but it emerges that he has a rival in Jack Raynton. The opening act, in which some highly complex family history and relationships are set forth, is remarkably taut and benefits enormously from the stage design in which the interior and exterior of the house are seen at the same time, allowing an easy flow of action. The dialogue is particularly sharp, from the light repartee of the servants to the snobbish declarations of the aristocracy. Some of the socially pointed exchanges have a hint of Shaw, reminding us that Whitbread, a much travelled manager, would have seen *Widowers' Houses, The Philanderer* and *Arms and the Man,* the latter in Dublin.

Jack Raynton receives a legacy through the Aubrey family solicitor enabling him to improve himself by studying for the bar in London. He is uneasy about his social position, unburdening himself to Kate, who reassures him. When Lady Aubrey, Richard's aunt, observes them kissing she is appalled. In a confrontation Kate declares – mainly to vex the dowager – that she is a Socialist. Kate's father takes her subsequent engagement to Jack in his stride. In a parallel situation below stairs in the neighbouring houses Andy Cregan and the milkman vie for the attentions of Phyllis, the

Aubrey's housemaid. Colonel Maynard is displeased to note that Richard (now Sir Richard and out of the running in regard to Kate) may be making surreptitious advances to Phyllis. Richard is gradually revealed as quite a slimy operator rather than the stock patrician dastard of melodrama.

A number of skeletons come clattering out of the Aubrey family closet at the reading of the will, the chief bone to pick over being the disclosure that Richard and Jack are half brothers. There is a strange clause by which the solicitor and Colonel Maynard are to manage a trust until such time as the 'legitimate heir' shall reach his thirtieth birthday. Jack makes an impressive 'God stand up for bastards!' speech. He decides that he must end his engagement to Kate as their marriage would result in her being socially ostracized. He enlists in the army.

About a third of the way through the play the scene changes to India where Mrs Railton, Kate and the maid Phyllis are to be found established in Cawnpore. This is by no means a device of the author's to increase the involvement of the female members of the cast for reasons of plot, for it was common for 'the womenfolk' to travel with the male members of their families throughout the Empire. Kate is taunted by Richard for her continued attachment to Jack on account of his rank – he is a lowly sergeant-major. The British garrison is in a hopeless situation surrounded by the army of Nana Sahib, leader of the Sepoys and 'the arch fiend'. He offers free passage to the British troops and their train if they vacate the city. Richard makes a deal with an Indian of dubious background, Pandeen Khan, to have Jack murdered and to plant a letter on his corpse, the contents of which should alter Kate's attitude. Andy Cregan overhears the plot and informs Jack who reports the nature of Pandeen's involvement as a kind of broker for Nana Sahib to General Wheeler's more trustworthy officers who find incriminating documents belonging to Pandeen: the General orders Richard to have Pandeen shot – a well-considered irony on his part – but Richard later reports that he has escaped. The General promotes Jack to Lieutenant: he is now on an equal social footing to Richard.

A letter arrives from England to announce the death of Lady Aubrey. Mrs Raynton exclaims 'No! Lady Aubrey lives!', informing her astonished hearers that she is the first and true Lady Aubrey, giving the complex reasons why this had been kept dark for so long. Turning to Richard, she says, 'Yes, and you are the bastard!'

Nana Sahib's 'safe passage' is a ruse. Nana will in fact allow the evacuation to happen 'with all colours flying' but his Sepoys will shoot at the boats once they set forth on the Ganges. They will take whatever women are not drowned – but he will ensure that they capture Kate, for whom he has a great desire, before she boards. As the principal characters prepare to leave, Pandeen announces that there is a special boat for ladies only, but the ladies wisely disregard the offer. Shots are heard. They realize that they have been betrayed. Jack fires at Pandeen who screams 'Death to the Ferringheens!' and disappears into the crowd.

The tone of the play has by now altered. Incidents are numerous and fast moving. In the midst of the alarms and excursions of the Indian Mutiny a quasi-Arabian Nights mode of speech is introduced for the 'natives': '... By the beard of my adopted father, I tell thee that none of these cursed bulldogs of Ferringheens shall live!'. The positive aspect is the heightened visual interest – the exotic scenery and the costumes characteristic of the mixture of races in the Ganges valley contrasted with the elaborate mid-Victorian fashions of the English ladies and the vivid uniforms of the officers – which would match the heightened dialogue and action.

A river, temple and wood by night. Mrs Raynton, Phyllis, Andy and an Indian servant, Ruslan, have avoided the boating disaster but tremble for Kate and Jack who have not been seen. Andy and the servant arm the ladies and leave them in the temple while they go on a search. Richard arrives with Pandeen; he requests Mrs Raynton to take back the lie that he is not the Aubrey heir; when she refuses he stabs her. Richard leaves, and as Pandeen goes to finish off Mrs Raynton, Phyllis threatens him at gun point and forces him to carry her into the temple.

Nana learns that a force under General Havelock is on its way. He naïvely supposes that, if Jack is disposed of, Kate will begin to smile upon him. Jack and Kate are brought in. They embrace – this enflames Nana who orders Jack to be tortured, but the British regiment approaches and Nana takes flight. Andy and Ruslan rush in to free Jack and Kate. 'Hurroo! Ireland for ever!' shouts Andy, somewhat illogically. Mrs Raynton seems little the worse for having been stabbed.

So much is happening that the audience is inevitably distracted into accepting the range of activity.[118] The dialogue is sparse, but what there is remains true to the established personalities. 'I'm as dumb as a dead cockle!' says Andy when he hears that Kate is being held for Nana Sahib. 'Art thou fond of the sight of blood?', enquires the latter of Kate. 'I dread it less than the sight of you!' retorts the brave British lass. 'Then thou wilt see thy lover's!' promises Nana, irked.

It is something of a relief to return to the sylvan setting of Aubrey Manor, but all is not as it should be. Richard is present with Pandeen, the Indian now attired in an English suit. They believe Jack died in Cawnpore and that Mrs Raynton was disposed of in the Ganges with hundreds of other corpses. Richard discusses his position with the family solicitor who confirms that although Jack may be dead Richard is still the illegitimate son. Richard threatens the lawyer, but Colonel Maynard enters with police, followed by Kate, Andy and Phyllis. Kate enumerates Richard's misdeeds with the obliging servants as witnesses. Then Jack and his mother appear. 'Alive!' croaks Richard.

Jack and Kate, as well as Andy and Phyllis, have in the meantime married. Kate is now Lady Aubrey. Pandeen has been used by the police to draw Richard into this trap. Discovering this, Richard attacks Pandeen and Jack but Pandeen stabs Richard fatally. In the midst of the attempted *grande tuerie* an important messenger is announced bearing a letter from Windsor. The letter states that due to his bravery under fire in succouring his men, 'the bestowal of the Queen's own hand of that coveted soldiers' prize for British valour and noble deeds – ' He does not need to conclude, for Kate finishes the sentence for him: ' – the Victoria Cross!'.

The Victoria Cross is an unusually entertaining play. It may be churlish to complain that its promise as a society drama is not fulfilled and that it evolves as standard melodrama. Actors came relatively cheaply, hence the unnecessarily lengthy cast list. As far as dramatic function is concerned, the roles of Colonel Maynard, General Wheeler and General Havelock could be one person – there is no reason for Kate's father, Colonel Maynard, to go to India, but once he is there he could easily fulfil the duties of General Wheeler; nor is there any need for the appearance of General Havelock, even though he was an historical figure associated in the popular mind with the Relief of Lucknow. It seems that Whitbread may have been thinking along this line, for Colonel Maynard is twice addressed as 'General' – but perhaps he had received promotion.

The fact that in the midst of his 'patriotic Irish' playwrighting phase Whitbread could, apparently effortlessly, embrace a 'colonial' subject and enjoy success with it on the Irish stage, demonstrates firstly that he had the creative adaptability which the true dramatist must possess in order to enter the minds of a particular set of characters, no matter how bizarre; and secondly that the audience at the Queen's Theatre was as adaptable as any other in recognizing a well fashioned play, whatever the milieu portrayed.

The Victoria Cross stands outside Whitbread's customary canon not merely on account of its foreign setting but because it is better written than most of his Irish plays, save perhaps *Sarsfield*.

6 | TRUE GREEN: WHITBREAD'S IRISH HEROES

The phenomenal success of Whitbread's *Lord Edward* throughout the British Isles two years before he took a moment's respite from Irish subjects to write *The Victoria Cross* must have convinced him that there was an immense and almost unexcavated vein of drama to be mined in tales which had an acknowledged national hero as the eponymous leading figure – a kind of Hibernian biopic before the invention of the commercial cinema. Boucicault's relatively unsuccessful *Robert Emmet* (1884) had paved the way.

Two of Whitbread's hero-plays have recently been meticulously reprinted from the Lord Chamberlain's copies and included in a volume of four Irish melodramas set during the Insurrection of 1798 – *Lord Edward* (1894) and *Theobald Wolfe Tone* (1898).[119] Whitbread's other plays in the *genre* are *Rory O'More* (an adaptation from Samuel Lover's 1837 play of the same name, 1900), *The Insurgent Chief* (concerning Michael Dwyer, 1902), *The Ulster Hero* (Henry Joy McCracken, 1903), *The Sham Squire* (Francis Higgins, 1903) and *Sarsfield* (1904).

Some of the historical figures portrayed in the first of this series, *Lord Edward,* are found in other plays by Whitbread that are set in the same revolutionary period, taking a larger or smaller part in the action as the subject requires. The faithful Neilson and the iniquitous Turner in *Lord Edward* also appear in *Theobald Wolfe Tone*. The Higgins of *Lord Edward* takes part in *The Sham Squire* and Neilson appears again in *The Ulster Hero*. Tone has a minor role in *The Ulster Hero,* and the eponymous McCracken has one in *Theobald Wolfe Tone*. Individual actors in the Kennedy Miller company did not necessarily play the same historical figure as projected in the various plays. On a tour of Scottish cities in 1905 we find *Lord Edward* and *The Ulster Hero* playing night about but with different actors as McCracken in the two plays in which the Ulster hero is portrayed!

Lord Edward, or, '98

The leading characters in most of these plays remain familiar to those with even a small recollection of history from primary school level today but at the time when *Lord Edward* was in Kennedy Miller's repertoire the audiences which enjoyed the drama – especially in Britain where it received its widest exposure – would have known little of this particular past and would have taken the characters and their story at face value. Such pedantic matters as historical accuracy, or the efficacy or otherwise of the transition from historical sources to script, did not greatly trouble the reviewers; not only did the bookish Joseph Holloway forebear to quibble with the author's manipulation of the facts and personalities of the era of the United Irishmen, he did not even mention them.

Lord Edward opened at the Queen's on 26 March 1894. The *Evening Herald* noted that '... if one were to judge by the reception accorded to it last night, it bids fair to rival *The Irishman* in popular appreciation'. The critic goes on to praise the 'excellent staging', and the 'picturesque scenery, which is specially painted'.[120] When *Lord Edward* returned to the Queen's in April of the following year the *Evening Telegraph* remarked that 'the play is a very popular one and needs no recommendation to the Dublin public'.[121] Still on the road a year later, the *Irish News* – whose reviewer had seen the play twice in Belfast – observed that 'the secret of its unparalleled success' was twofold, '... the subject appeals to the people, and Mr Kennedy Miller's company give it just such a liberal interpretation as the public deserve' – whatever that may mean.[122]

Joseph Holloway went to see it again in April 1897 to find 'a mixed to middling performance'. As he was not writing for publication he did not have to choose his words with discretion. It is more than likely that the company was tired of repeating this – and other – plays over a period of three years; the problem of keeping a production 'fresh' is one that besets touring managements to this day, and nineteenth-century companies that played a different show each night of the week simply did not have time for 'workouts' and 'reassessments'. Holloway went on to remark that the audience received the work as enthusiastically as ever. He was interested in the unevenness of the writing – 'sometimes quite poetical, and at other times melodramatic or farcical to the point of absurdity' – a feature which must strike the reader of almost all the plays in the *genre*.[123]

Lord Edward Fitzgerald (1763-1798) is described in the cast list as 'one of the noblest figures of Irish history'. Samuel Neilson is 'his faithful adherent'. Fitzgerald's wife Pamela has a surprisingly large part for such a male dominated drama and we are also given unusually vivid glimpses of their domestic life – indeed, the hero is frequently to be found dilating upon his campaign in their private apartments. Napper Tandy, 'a General in the Irish Army of Rebellion', plays a comparatively small part. Thady McGrath, 'a boy of the right sort', and his sweetheart, Katey Malone, form the faithful and amusing below-stairs interest. The extensive rogues' gallery of informers, scoundrels and desperados are all Irish; the most villainous is Samuel Turner; Francis Higgins, attorney-at-law, and Francis Magan, barrister-at-law, are clearly delineated as persons of position and education whose malevolence ill becomes them. (Like the three senior officers in *The Victoria Cross*, Turner, Higgins and Magan virtually fulfill the same dramatic purpose; while it may be convenient to have two registered villains who can argue the course of their villainy, three seems excessive.) Major Henry Charles Sirr is described as 'the Fouché of Dublin'. Important French characters include the Comtesse de Genlis and General Hoche.

The first act, set in Paris in 1791, resembles an extended prologue. Throughout the rest of the play the noble, almost too-good-to-be-true, Fitzgerald makes a number of entrances in which to urge on his men in the cause of Ireland; upon each, his immediate henchmen deftly contrive to save him from the dozen awkward scrapes into which he tumbles for (far too many) theatrical effects.

The second act takes place seven years later, mainly in Leinster House, Fitzgerald's residence in Dublin. There is news from Paris that the Directory has promised 5,000 men in three frigates for an invasion of Ireland. Fitzgerald informs Magan of this not knowng that he will immediately pass the intelligence to the Castle. Magan, it now appears, is secretly in love with Pamela and has expectations that once Fitzgerald is arrested she will turn to him. (The convention of the villain showing an unseemly interest in the wife or fiancée of the hero is greatly overdone in this play for it is impossible to believe, from the presentation of Pamela's character, that she would give such a person a moment's notice.) Soldiers commanded by Major Swan – as it happens, a former suitor of the beautiful Pamela – invade the house. Fitzgerald escapes through a secret panel and Swan is taken aback to find a calm domestic scene with Pamela surrounded by her children and servants. Swan is apologetic, Pamela haughty and Thady satiric. A further foray by Swan is accompanied by a moment of frightening suspense as the panel refuses to open; Fitzgerald seizes Swan, his pistol falls to the ground, Pamela snatches it and covers the intruders as Fitzgerald makes his escape.

In the street, Higgins and Magan recognize the disguised Fitzgerald but pretend not to, altering the iniquitous gist of their conversation so that he overhears their good intentions. Fitzgerald reveals himself to these 'friends', but they become uneasy when he shows that he is armed. He resumes his disguise when Major Sirr appears and engages Higgins in conversation; when Sirr asks Higgins the name of his companion, the latter is discomfited and excuses him as 'a country cousin'. Sirr leaves, and Higgins and Magan are left with the supposition that Fitzgerald may now suspect them of being informers.

In a different disguise, Fitzgerald commands a detachment of pikemen as they await orders to march on Dublin from the north. He is now certain that Higgins is a spy; Higgins seems nervous but becomes less so when they are joined by Magan. Fitzgerald openly accuses Higgins of spying and, when challenged, removes his disguise. Higgins is astonished not to have recognized him and terrified when Magan turns against him – as he must, so as not to to give himself away: Fitzgerald addresses Magan with apparent irony as 'my trusted friend'. The pikemen call for Higgins' execution but Fitzgerald will not hear of it. Pamela brings news that the Castle is aware of Fitzgerald's part in the insurrection. The act ends with his delivering a rousing speech that ends, 'Tonight, boys, we write a glorious page in Ireland's history!' The band plays and there is an appropriate tableau.

The third act is set in a 'safe' house in Denzille Street where Fitzgerald is lodging, though temporarily absent. Magan and Higgins are hoping to have Fitzgerald captured so that they can share the reward – over which they quarrel. Magan has not yet issued the proclamation announcing this reward for he feels that if Pamela discovers that he is in charge she may look upon in with less favour – one can imagine the raucous laughter of the audience at his self belief. After Higgins departs Pamela arrives, distraught to find Magan; she sees the reward money which she describes to Magan as 'the price of your treachery'. Magan, ostensibly deeply hurt, claims the money has been collected to help the cause: Pamela can only apologize. Magan believes he is 'progressing' with her.

Fitzgerald arrives with the children and servants; all are unsure about Magan's allegiance. Pamela urges Fitzgerald to withdraw from the insurrection, which has failed in some counties. Soldiers arrive, and there is another attempted arrest of Fitzgerald which Magan appears to resist, indicating a secret door concealed by a picture, of which Fitzgerald makes immediate use. Just before Major Sirr enters, Magan gives Fitzgerald's hat and cloak to Thady, who puts them on, and when Sirr orders the soldiers to take him, Thady discloses himself, to the officer's immense mortification.

The Fitzgeralds and their supporters move to the house of a Mr and Mrs Moore. In the street Higgins and Magan await the arrival of soldiers who will surely take Fitzgerald this time, while Pamela and Kitty watch from an upper window for Fitzgerald's return. When Major Sirr and two soldiers are observed, Kitty leaves with a note warning Fitzgerald to stay away, but she is questioned and drops the note, which Sirr reads. Fitzgerald approaches, accompanied by the Moores and other supporters. Sirr apprehends him and there is a fierce tussle. A military detachment is observed approaching; Fitzgerald's supporters cry 'Fly!' He flourishes his sword, shouts 'Follow if you dare!' and leaves. Pamela is seen at the upper window, crying.

Act Four opens in Thomas Street outside the house of Mr Murphy, a feather merchant. Thady answers Neilson's knock and assures him that Fitzgerald is safe. Swan arrives with soldiers. They question Neilson and Thady, who give false names but are left under guard as Swan and other men enter. Kitty arrives and, in her alarm, almost reveals Neilson and Thady's identities but she manages to extricate them from possible arrest by confusing the soldiers with comic trivialities. Thady works the same way on Swan when the latter re-emerges, not having found Fitzgerald.

We learn from Thady and Kitty that Fitzgerald was all the time hidden in a feather mattress. Magan arrives, 'glad' to hear that Fitzgerald is safe, and purporting to have a message for him from Pamela which he must deliver in person. Neilson pretends he also has a message, so as he can follow Magan to the Moore's house.

While Fitzgerald is reading a letter which Kitty has brought from Pamela, Swan enters the Moore's house quietly. When Fitzgerald looks up, Swan orders him to surrender in the King's name. Fitzgerald snatches a pistol, but it misfires. Swan again orders him to surrender, but Fitzgerald says he will die first. Officers enter. There follows an elaborate fight, during which Fitzgerald stabs Swan. Major Sirr runs in and shoots Fitzgerald, who falls.[124]

Thady McGrath, from an upstairs window of the Dog and Duck tavern, overhears Magan say that now Fitzgerald is in prison he has only to fear his servants, whom they should have shot. Thady, outraged, reveals himself, and Magan shoots him through the window; he collapses inside. A patrol arrives, and Higgins informs them that they'll find 'a rebel' inside – 'Lord Edward's servant man; he fired ... on this gentleman, who was reluctantly compelled to return his fire'. The soldiers enter the tavern but Thady reappears – having counterfeited being hit – and points the soldiers in the direction of the departing Magan, whom he describes as 'the real blackguard!'

Magan arrives at Moira House, where Pamela is now residing, to inform her that Fitzgerald is mortally wounded. He is delighted when she faints into his arms. When she revives, he entreats her to be his friend, informing her that Thady betrayed Fitzgerald because he had knowledge of the household. He pretends to be on his way to the prison to engineer Fitzgerald's escape, and exits. Thady and Kitty come in and Pamela unjustly excoriates them. Thady manages to convince her that Magan is a complete liar. All conceal themselves when Magan and Higgins are seen returning; they observe the final 'blood money' transaction, and hear Magan say he is leaving for France, offering all the United Irishmen's papers to Higgins for £1,000. Pamela, in a fury, comes forth. Higgins, leaving, taunts her for having got rid of her husband for the sake of her lover! She shouts vituperations at Magan, while the sound of an angry crowd is heard outside, but he is calm, believing he now has her alone in the house. He tells her he is taking her to France. She cries out. Tony, Fitzgerald's black serving boy, rushes in and Magan shoots him. Thady appears and stabs Magan several times, as Neilson, followed by supporters, enters the house. Neilson enquires if Magan has escaped. 'No, he lies there!' replies Thady. All cheer.

While the dramatic faults made evident by the relatively flimsy structure and threadbare conventions of the second and third acts persist into the fourth, they are less obvious due to the genuine suspense generated in the scenes preceding Fitzgerald's arrest, the excitement of the arrest itself and the well contrived minor turns of plot in the scenes at the Dog and Duck and Moira House.

An opportunity was missed by having Fitzgerald's concealment in the feather bed related rather than enacted, but with so much physical business, one incident less may perhaps be seen as an advantage. There is a kind of tongue-in-cheek fun in some of the wilder dramatic moments. Whitbread was too much of a professional not to realize that – for example – Pamela's rage at the machinations of Magan has its humorous side, building on this by having her faint into his very arms. Thady, having overheard Higgins describe him as 'a gom' can not restrain himself from putting his head out of the window and shouting insults at Higgins and Magan, resulting in his being shot at by the latter; this is a comic exchange, even though it has an apparently heartrending outcome. (We discover later that Thady escaped the bullet – a comic revelation in itself.) The comedy in this, as in other of Whitbread's plays, is not by any means confined to the rustic drolleries of the peasant class. It is curious that the only critic who has systematically analysed *Lord Edward* and *Theobald Wolfe Tone* has remained impervious to its comedic ironies – or perhaps has not found them to be worth mentioning.[125]

The fifth and final act is of but five minutes duration and is more like an epilogue. Fitzgerald is dying of his wounds in Newgate Gaol, seated in a chair and attended by his wife, brother and aunt. Major Sirr and the 'shamado' Higgins are also present. Higgins would rather Fitzgerald left the world by means of the scaffold. He has the effrontery to mention that Pamela had a tryst with Magan – whom, he reports, was not killed and is recovering. Pamela hisses at him – 'Would you dare – dare to lie in the presence of death?' but Higgins' response is to throw a paper on the table, declaring to the dying man that his estate will go to the King because he'll be convicted of High Treason. Fitzgerald dies before this course can be accomplished. Major Sirr shows his abhorrence for Higgins by stating that when he dies his grave will be 'an object of hatred and contempt'. Fitzgerald bids a dignified and affectionate farewell to his family and expires.

This is a remarkably concise conclusion. Rather than introducing a crowd of patriotic mourners, not to speak of a heavenly choir – elements which would be perfectly in order for the *genre,* as in Hollywood biopics of a later era – Whitbread allows the tensions and betrayals of the earlier part of the play to coalesce in the chamber of death. While it may seem fortuitous to bring on Lady Louisa Connelly (*sic*)[126], without introduction, to exclaim 'Oh, go, go!' to Higgins – who is she? members of the audience might well ask – and also to give a line to Fitzgerald's brother who has never been seen before in the play, it is a bold and effective measure to bring Higgins into the scene to continue his anti-United Irishmen campaign. There is also the effectively dramatic irony of phrases such as Higgins' 'The Rebellion will die with you!', for the rebellion's spirit clearly lived on in the minds of the theatre audience a hundred years later. Each character continues in his or her preordained manner, there are no incredible changes of heart, and no passionate oratory around the deathbed. This is a real advance in Whitbread's dramaturgy; indeed, the whole play, in spite of its inconsistencies and improbabilities, can be accounted a *tour de force*.

Historically speaking, Fitzgerald's death scene was quite different, for neither family nor friends were allowed to visit him. Lord Clare, the Lord Chancellor, recognizing a fretful situation, took Lady Louisa Connolly and Lord Henry Fitzgerald to Newgate Gaol and had them admitted a few hours before Fitzgerald died, but there were no relatives present when death came, as Tom Moore made clear in his biography upon which Whitbread based the play. Fitzgerald's death scene, as restaged by Whitbread, is dramatically effective and satisfying.

Theobald Wolfe Tone

The announcement of a St Stephen's Night opening signalled an important production, for 26 December was the most prestigious theatrical date in the year. Since Whitbread's most recent plays had been major successes it must have been reasonable to suppose that *Theobald Wolfe Tone* would follow suit, and in the event this proved to be the case for it achieved a four week initial run into January 1899, something out of the ordinary in Dublin. While the production of *Lord Edward, or, '98* had anticipated the centenary of the Insurrection by four years, *Theobald Wolfe Tone* may be said to have been written to celebrate it. Patriotic sentiment was at its height, encouraging the diverse strands of political and cultural renaissance.[127] *Wolfe Tone* (as the play will henceforth be named) was back in Dublin for two weeks in August, having been on the road in Britain with other Kennedy Miller productions in the interim.

MONDAY, 1st OCTOBER,

AND DURING THE WEEK,

Grand Production by

KENNEDY MILLER'S

CELEBRATED IRISH COMPANY,

The Most Famous Representative Company of Irish Players now before the Public

Including the Popular Character Actor,

Mr FRANK BREEN

And the Successful Young Irish Comedian,

Mr TYRONE POWER

The Romantic Irish Drama, In Five Acts, entitled—

LORD EDWARD or '98

SEVENTH YEAR OF TOUR.

(Depicting the Vivid Scenes and Vicissitudes in the Life of Lord Edward Fitzgerald). Founded on the Revelation in W. J. Fitzpatrick's Work, "Secret Service under Pitt."

By J. W. WHITBREAD.

Lord Edward Fitzgerald, One of the noblest figures of Irish History	Mr Fred Lloyd
Major Sirr, the Fouche of Dublin	Mr Edward Shelton
Major Swan, Assistant Town Major	Mr Chas. H. Herberte
Captain Ryan	Mr Alfred Danes
Francis Higgins, an Attorney-at-Law, nicknamed the "Shamado"	Mr Frank Breen
Francis Magan, a Barrister-at-Law—an Informer	Mr Frank Lyndon
Neilson, a faithful adherent of Lord Edward	Mr St. John Beecher
Tony, a Negro—Servant to Lord Edward	Mr Henry Richardson
Thady M'Grath, a Boy of the right sort—True to the Core	Mr Tyrone Power
Mr James Moore, Merchant, 119 Thomas Street	Mr Kenneth Mure
Mr Murphy, a Feather Merchant, 151 Thomas Street	Mr A. O'Neill
Palmer } Clerks in Moore's {	Mr Joseph Bebb
Gallagher } Employ {	Mr G. Kinsella
M'Cabe	Mr W. J. O'Connor
Napper Tandy, a General in the Irish Army of Rebellion	Mr R. Payne
General Hoche, of the French Army	Mr Charles Boyle
Sam Turner, an Informer	Mr J. Duffy
Lord Henry Fitzgerald	Mr D. Haslam
Pamela	Miss Annie Hylton
Madame de Sillery, the Comtesse de Genlis	Miss Mabel Veriton
Lady Louisa Connolly	Miss P. Maynard
Edward, Son of Lord and Lady Fitzgerald	Little Mollie Miller
Mrs Moore	Miss Ada Turner
Miss Moore	Miss Ella Nourse
Katie Malone	Miss Monica Kelly

Soldiers, Peasants, &c.

Fig 10. 1901 Glasgow Playbill for *Lord Edward* [Mitchell Library] J. Kennedy Miller's production of Whitbread's play had been on the road for seven years with Frank Breen in his original role, Tyrone Power II having taken over James O'Brien's part.

The only penetrating review seen was published in *The United Irishman* that August, signed by Frank Fay. He described it as 'an exceedingly effective play' in spite of the use of 'primitive and well-worn devices'. He was also pleased by the absence of 'sensation scenes'. Most interesting is the following:

> I scarce think he was wise in writing a play of this type around Wolfe Tone. I doubt whether a playwright of greater ability than Mr Whitbread possesses would have been successful with the theme, and I do not think an Englishman, no matter how able or sympathetic, could evolve from it a drama that would be satisfactory to a critical Irish audience; but he might succeed in giving us something of the atmosphere of the time and enable us to realize the terrible trial which the close of the last century brought to Ireland. I cannot say that Mr Whitbread has done this, and probably he did well not to attempt it, even if he thought of such a thing ...[128]

Fay was wishing for the impossible, a serious Irish history play from the pen of a writer of melodramas. When Fay refers to a 'critical' Irish audience, he means an audience made up of the various components of the intelligensia – the kind of audience which, within the span of the next decade, he would help to bring in to the Abbey Theatre. In spite of some misgivings, Fay thought that *Wolfe Tone* was Whitbread's best play to date. Holloway, who caught up with it in June, 1902, also had misgivings, especially about the earlier scenes which he thought 'very clap-trap melodrama', but he found the interview between Tone and Buonaparte to be 'a dramatic gem' and 'the best scene J.W. Whitbread has ever written'.[129] For Holloway the star of the night was James O'Brien as Shane McMahon, 'a comedian of genuine comicality', demonstrating that as a member of that intelligensia he was not disgusted by the comic element in plays on serious subjects.[130]

The action takes place in Ireland and France in 1789-98. Nine leading members of the Society of United Irishmen appear, though most of them merely as tokens – those who were not featured in *Lord Edward* are Bond, Emmet, Jackson, Keogh, McCracken, Rowan, and Russell.[131] There are two unmitigated scoundrels – Samuel Turner, a United Irishman whom we have met before as an informer, and his accomplice, Joe Rafferty, 'an attorney-at-law and a Castle spy'. An important character in every respect is General Napoleon Buonaparte; his charming wife, Josephine, plays more than a supporting role for she befriends Tone's wife, the former

Susan Witherington; however, both these ladies are somewhat colourless compared with Mrs Tone's maid, Peggy Ryan; she is the beloved of Shane McMahon, a Trinity College porter, and their relationship, as well as their entertaining repartee, mirrors that of Kitty and Thady in *Lord Edward*. Nothing is made of Tone's Quaker background or of the fact that he had previously published *An Appeal on Behalf of the Catholics of Ireland* and was Secretary of the Catholic Committee; and the audience is not given even an inkling of his final humiliation and death.

In the first act the political motif is subdued, with the author's description 'an Irish romantic drama' very much the prevailing mode. The demarcation between the honest citizens – Tone, Russell, Susan, Shane and Peggy – and the scheming blackguards – Turner and Rafferty – is strongly established. Thomas Russell of the Society of United Irishmen seeks directions to Wolfe Tone's rooms from the Trinity College porter, Shane McMahon, from whom we learn that Tone is always 'to the fore' at 'larnin', dhrinkin' or larkin' with the petticoats'. As if to confirm the latter, Peggy Ryan is simultaneously delivering a letter for Tone from Miss Susan Witherington. A pert relationship develops between Shane and Peggy. Turner and Rafferty appear and Russell speaks up for his friend Tone in a passing altercation. We learn that Tone is not favoured by Witherington *père* as a suitor for his daughter because of his lack of funds. Turner and Rafferty inform Witherington that Susan is in constant communication with Tone so the anxious parent removes her from his town house to his country estate at Rathfarnham, five miles away, but Tone and Susan secretly marry. Turner is intent on having Tone arrested 'for debt' but the good-natured Shane helps him out with money collected from students' tips.

As in *Lord Edward*, seven years pass between what in this play is an unimpressive first act and the much livelier second. Tone is now a family man with three children living in Irishtown, Dublin, in respectable penury. A number of UI activists attend a frugal dinner at the Tone home at which important political developments are examined; John Philpot Curran's anti-Penal Laws speech in the Irish House of Commons is discussed. Turner is present and in the course of the evening infers to Tone that Susan is engaged in a torrid affair with Russell. Tone is aware that Turner is not to be trusted in anything and that spies are adept at causing personal distress in order to crack the morale of those being spied upon. Turner later admits to Rafferty that his scheme to implicate Susan with Russell has not worked.

The dinner at the modest house gives an absorbing picture of the cameraderie of the members of the UI. It is not until a formal meeting of the Society where letters from the continent are read that the urgency of their objectives becomes plain. Tone is dispatched to Paris as special emissary. Turner's objection that the Society should have to pay Tone's expenses is overruled. Later there is a showdown between Tone and Turner; soldiers arrive with an arrest warrant – but it is for Turner, not Tone! Tableau.

At Le Havre Turner and Rafferty observe preparations for what may be an invasion of England. It emerges that it was Rafferty who had Turner arrested following the meeting in Dublin so that the UI members would cease to be suspicious of him. Turner states that it is his greatest wish to see Tone's head on a spike in Dublin. They learn that the Minister for War has agreed to provide troops for Ireland.

Tone, registered as 'Mr Smith' but dressed as a French general, is overjoyed. He notes that Turner and Rafferty 'raise their hats with offensive politeness' to him. Shane – now married to Peggy – receives news from Ireland of the birth of a son, and also that Peggy and the child will accompany Mrs Tone to France. Turner and Rafferty balefully watch the warm welcome which Tone receives from the Emperor Napoleon and his gracious wife. Turner immediately arranges to have the Emperor informed that Tone is in reality an English spy. Still harbouring ill will towards Susan he makes plans to have her abducted by a Dutch slave trader named Hans to South America. Seeking the Tone's Le Havre address they enquire directions of a soldier in French uniform, not knowing it is Shane McMahon: he keeps responding annoyingly 'Oui, oui!' to all their questions.

In a house overlooking the harbour, Susan Tone expresses anxiety for their future. Tone reassures her with gallant and patriotic fervour until papers arrive from Ireland telling of the arrest of the entire Leinster committee of United Irishmen. Now Tone is near to despair, and this time it is Susan who restores their spirits. The Empress Josephine calls on Mrs Tone to inform her that she has arranged for a formal interview between Tone and the Emperor. Their chat is interrupted by Hans, who barges in to inform Susan that her husband wishes her to join him and the Emperor immediately on a ship bound for Brest: but Josephine knows her husband has no such plan and calls Hans's bluff. Hans is flabbergasted when he learns who she is, and Peggy has no difficulty in hooshing him off the premises.

Later, the stage lights go down to half as Hans, Turner and Rafferty enter the now empty room *via* the balcony. Peggy comes in and observes Rafferty pocketing a document. Hans immediately seizes and binds her – when Turner expostulates that he has captured the wrong woman Hans declares that he wants Peggy for himself! Hearing her maid's cries Susan enters, to be confronted by Turner who triumphantly informs her of her fate, adding that she'd have done better to have married him. Unobserved by the main participants a cloaked figure sneaks in through the window, creeps under the table and releases Peggy's bonds: it is Shane. She snatches the poker while Shane covers the assembly with his pistol just as Tone rushes in with soldiers.

Fortunately for Turner and Rafferty they were in possession of a safe pass from the Emperor. Rafferty blames Turner for the numerous contrary turns of events. They quarrel. The Emperor passes with his entourage, stops, and enquires about the reported break-in at 'Monsieur Smeeth's' lodging – Turner hands over papers which he says prove Tone is in the pay of the English prime-minister, to which the Emperor dryly enquires if Turner stooped to robbery in order to obtain the evidence. While Turner is trying to slide out of this Peggy rushes in and gives him a battering. She and Shane are mortified when they discover that the Emperor is present but Peggy recovers herself and declares that she saw Rafferty stealing the papers. Napoleon orders his men to escort Turner and Rafferty to their hotel while he questions Peggy and Shane further; they do not hestitate to give the worst possible account of Turner and Rafferty. Napoleon tells the audience he'll soon discover who is true and who is false.

Napoleon summons Tone to the military headquarters where Tone is able to show that the papers are irrelevant. Asked if he is 'an adventurer', Tone agrees that in a manner of speaking he is. He proceeds to speak eloquently of this moment being ripe for an expedition, citing the desirability of invading England from France while British troops are occupied in Ireland with the Insurrection organized by Lord Edward Fitzgerald. Tone is dismissed and Turner and Rafferty, who have been deliberately posted in the next room so that they'll overhear the foregoing, are admitted. Napoleon enquires if they still believe Tone is spying for Pitt? – they do, and the papers will prove it. Turner then realizes that Napoleon has innocuous papers; they distract his attention while substituting the 'right' ones. Napoleon seeks their advice as to what should be done with Tone: 'arrest and execution!' says Turner. When Tone is interviewed again he denounces Turner as a spy in the pay of the English administration in Ireland. It is clear that Napoleon is convinced, but is playing a game: he says to Tone that 'here are papers that condemn you', at the same time making a signal which results in guards appearing at every door. Napoleon then sends for Hans, who is brought in and confesses that he was engaged by Turner and Rafferty to abduct Mrs Tone as a means of destroying her husband. Turner is searched and letters signed by Pitt are found. Napoleon orders Turner and Rafferty to be shot at sunrise.

The action is now moving quickly, with the political/military strand in the ascendant, yet with domestic matters still allowed a substantial share: Whitbread would have understood the desire of the audience to identify with the family unit comprised of the Tones and their faithful servants in their precarious situation on foreign soil. There is, in fact, a very nice balance between momentous events and highly personal concerns. A real sense of suspense is introduced with the attempt to abduct Susan and this sub-plot is carried through to the theatrically effective scene where the plans go awry for the perpetrators, which is staged in a way that is more convincing than most scenes of violent action in Whitbread's earlier plays.

The stealing and confusion of documents seem to be an unnecessary complication to the story, which is complicated enough without it – but we must constantly bear in mind that what we have is a draft of the play and changes may have been made in production. What is especially well done is the constantly menacing presence of Turner and Rafferty – hiding in doors, skulking in laneways, poking and probing and denigrating Tone for reasons that are as maliciously personal as they are professional. Napoleon's apparent slowness to accept Tone's explanations, and Tone's almost childlike enthusiasm for the cause of Ireland's liberty, is the basis for a quite subtle exposition of two characters of very different demeanour and social standing in an extraordinary collaboration.

As an example of Whitbread's increasing mastery of his medium one must single out his treatment of Turner and Rafferty: instead of simply allowing these renegades to come to their inevitably sticky end, he pursues their uneasy relationship right up to the last moment, when each reveals himself in his individually muddy colours. Far from being projected as mere ciphers they appear as persons with their own particular foibles and anxieties.

The same is true of the two principal women, the Empress Josephine and Susan Tone. As far as the plot is concerned the Empress provides womanly friendship and thence a means of Tone gaining ready access to the Emperor, and Susan may be seen as underlying what Whitbread must have felt was the need to show the domestic side of Tone's life – but as well as this both ladies are revealed as persons of intellectual acumen. Dr Mary Trotter points out that 'the plot conflates the possession of Susan with the fight for Ireland' and that Susan's 'spirited reply to Turner's threat to make her literally a colonial slave embodies Hibernia's refusal to acquiesce to John Bull's control'. This is certainly important symbolism as far as it goes, but surely Susan's 'spirited reply' is more to do with 'the ignominy of being for one single instance your wife', which is a somewhat different matter. In any case, Turner is Irish, not English.[132]

The final act in the manuscript takes place at the camp outside Brest where Generals Kilmaine, Lemoine and Tone prepare for departure for Ireland. Tone is ecstatic about the outcome for his 'beloved country'. Susan Tone, who will remain in France under the protection of the Empress, has a presentiment that the expedition will fail. A haggard Turner and Rafferty are brought on in chains. Tone had earlier pleaded for clemency without success – 'Though they are such vile wretches, they are still my countrymen!' – and asks if they have last messages for Ireland. Turner only has curses, while Rafferty is too terrified to respond. A message then arrives from the Emperor with a reprieve for Turner, who then speaks contemptuously of Rafferty. Rafferty pulls a gun and shoots Turner. Rafferty then pleads for his life, but Tone, unfazed, refers to all those whom Rafferty has sent to the gallows in Ireland, and Rafferty is ceremoniously blindfolded, stood against the wall, and shot. 'So perish all traitors!', is Tone's last line, and that appears to be the end of the play.

Well, not quite the end, for the playbills show a further two scenes in the production as performed. Whitbread undoubtedly felt that the manuscript submitted to the Lord Chamberlain was sufficient to give an adequate idea of the piece, and certainly the short scene which is all that is given of Act IV does have a conclusion – a chilling conclusion in its utterence, if not as dramatic in its

staging as one might have been led to expect. It is certain that the
Lord Chamberlain would not have approved the work if his reader
had seen the final scenes as ultimately produced, but members of
his staff never appear to have bothered to attend performances of
plays which they had passed as fit for public exposure.

The two final scenes that are not included in the manuscript are
'On the Road to Embarkation' and 'The Embarkation of the French
Army for Ireland'. Séamus de Burca recalls 'the thrill of the Band in
the pit and the Band on the stage playing together'.[133] The latter was
advertised in the first production as the 'Brass Band of the City of
Dublin Workingmen's Club, Wellington Quay' – its headquarters
were only a quarter mile from the Queen's Theatre, and
advertisements disclose that it was not unusual for its members to
appear on the stage when a play required a band as part of the
action.

We have to imagine the stage picture – the ship sailing off just
before the fall of curtain, with those on board waving to the
Emperor and Empress and the assembled crowd, and the band
playing for all its worth. *Vive la France! Vive l'Irlande! Vive la
Liberté!* (Similarly, Whitbread's *Sarsfield* ends with the eponymous
hero sailing from Limerick for France.) The ship, of course, is not
the ship of history, but the ship of theatrical illusion. Whitbread was
giving his audience what it wanted to see.

Whitbread's evident *penchant* for scenes in which his hero, by
one means or another, extricates himself from what seem to be
hopeless situations, reaches its apogee in this play, for there are no
less than four occasions on which Michael Dwyer (1721-1826)
spectacularly eludes his pursuers. While most of these escapes are
the inventions of the dramatist, it is certainly true that during the
five years following the Insurrection of 1798 Dwyer managed to
evade several attempts by the British army to capture him. He had
many hideouts in the Wicklow hills, one of which, a cottage at
Derrynamuck not far from Baltinglass, was restored as a tourist
attraction in the 1960s. Whitbread's picture of Dwyer is as a kind of
Irish Scarlet Pimpernel, pre-dating that elusive hero of prose fiction
by three years. On the evening of 22 December, 1902, a performance
of *The Insurgent Chief* was given at the Queen's Theatre in aid of
'the erection of the national memorial to Michael Dwyer and Samuel
McAllister in Baltinglass'. The handsome piece of sculpture still
dominates the town centre.

The Insurgent Chief

Fig 11. 1798 Memorial in Baltinglass, Co Wicklow. [Author's Collection] The pikeman statue and marble plaque to Michael Dwyer and Samuel McAllister was erected partly from the proceeds of a performance of *The Insurgent Chief* at the Queen's Theatre, Dublin, in 1902

Whitbread probably obtained most of his source material from a popular work by John Thomas Campion called *Michael Dwyer, or, the Insurgent Captain of the Wicklow Mountains, a tale of the Rising in '98,* a book which was said to be found in every house in the county and was in the home of the present writer's grandparents. Many of the incidents are very similar to those in the play.[134]

The Insurgent Chief opened at the Queen's Theatre on 31 March 1902. There are certain difficulties for the reader which would not have applied to a member of the audience because in the theatre the physical appearance of the characters is sufficient identification, but in the script the fact that both Dwyer's faithful henchman and the villainous informer are named Hugh Byrne makes for some initial confusion. (Henceforth the former will be referred to as Hughie and the latter by his nickname 'Brander' Byrne.) Even if one did not see the playbill one would guess correctly that Hughie was played by Tyrone Power II and Brander by Frank Breen.) Mary Doyle (later Dwyer's wife) and Anne Devlin (Dwyer's niece and a devoted servant to Robert Emmet) are seen as very strong women with minds of their own, though the author allows Anne Devlin's role to become less and less important as the play proceeds. Dr Armstrong treats, and is on friendly terms with, people of all persuasions – 'the physician knows no politics!', he says. Captain and Mrs Airlie are Anglo-Irish of the landed class and are particularly well studied – they admire Dwyer and hope he will evade capture; Airlie, at the start of the play still an officer in the British army, remarks only semi-jokingly to his wife, 'Why, I do believe you're a rebel yourself!' to which she replies quite seriously, 'I do believe I am'. Captain Carr and Sergeant Agar of the Yeomanry are conventional officers, Carr with a more interesting dimension in that he is enamoured of Mary Doyle/Dwyer.

As for Dwyer, his entrance is built up to until the final moments of the first act when he makes an unexpected appearance. Throughout the play his moments on the stage are brief and he has few words. His exploits are almost all in the past or take place offstage. It quickly becomes clear that the play is less about him than about those who are touched by his actions and by the cause which he represents. At the centre of the piece are the nature of loyalty to a cause and the ambiguities of Irish life in relation to that (or any) cause. It is significant that Whitbread did not call the play *Michael Dwyer* – in the manner of *Lord Edward* and *Theobald Wolfe Tone*

– but the less personal *The Insurgent Chief*. Reviewers at the time of the first production did not make this point.

In the first act Brander Byrne informs Captain Carr that he knows enough about Dwyer 'to hang him ten times over'. Carr agrees to pay for further information. The Doyle farmhouse is indicated, which Carr subsequently surrounds with Yeomen who have orders to shoot the first man to emerge. He is insolent to Mary Doyle. Dwyer is not in the house but Mary knows he is on his way and asks a neighbour to warn him. Carr is suspicious and shoots at the neighbour, but misses; Mrs Airlie tells him he is a disgrace to his uniform. There is consternation as Dwyer briefly appears: he coolly approaches Carr who requests Captain Airlie to arrest him. Airlie refuses, declaring he is not on duty. Carr leaves, daunted by the moral superiority of those present. Dwyer has a brief moment with Mary: they are to be married that night. Dwyer departs with Mary as Carr and the Yeomen are seen returning – 'You're just in time to be too late!' remarks Anne Devlin.

In Act Two, several months later, Dr Armstrong attends to the wounded Dwyer who is concealed in Armstrong's pigstye. Captain Airley, disgusted with the behaviour of the British army, has handed in his commission. Mary Dwyer is offered a refuge at the Airley home, Crosby Hall. Dwyer leaves, dressed in Airley's clothes. When Captain Carr arrives he is surprised to see Airlie, enquiring 'Who is that fellow I saw with your wife?' Airley, knowing that by now Dwyer will have vanished into the hills, replies, 'Oh, that was that fellow Dwyer!'

Carr bemoans his ill-luck to Brander Byrne who passes on the information that Dwyer is now said to be hiding in St Kevin's Cave overlooking the lake at Glendalough. If this is so, Byrne will flash a signal by night. In fact, the cave has become the headquarters of the Wicklow insurrection. Dwyer addresses the insurgents in rousing tones. Byrne's arrival causes only mild suspicion for there is no evidence that he may be in the pay of Carr. Byrne drops an anonymous letter addressed to Dwyer in which Mary is described as engaging in an affair with Captain Airley. Byrne loses no time in flashing a lantern; when soldiers mount to the cave Dwyer picks off each as his head appears over the clifftop.

Back in the comfort of Crosby Hall there is a dinner party where allegiances are an awkward topic. Conversations are skilfully organized in separate parts of the room. Carr observes that Mary is 'too damned good for that brute of an outlaw' to which Airley responds that Dwyer is 'a gentleman in the truest sense'. Carr informs the audience that Mary is 'a splendid creature' and he intends to 'hang her husband and get possession of her'. Brander Byrne appears at a window to tell Carr that Dwyer is on his way. Later, Dwyer is glimpsed by the audience outside the window. Carr makes an insulting remark about Mary and Airley orders him out of the house. He goes, smirking. Airlie kisses Mary's hand by way of condolence just as Dwyer makes his entrance: he accuses Airley of being 'a miscreant in the garb of a gentleman and with the heart of a traitor!' Carr is seen outside the window, gloating. The guests withdraw as Airley invites Dwyer to partake of a sensible conversation but Dwyer remains vitriolic, throwing the offending letter on the table. Airley protests that it is a forgery, but Dwyer pulls a gun and at the same moment Carr aims through the window and shoots Airley.[135] All rush in to find Dwyer with a pistol in his hand and Airley on the floor. Dwyer realizes that Carr has set up the scene, goes to the window and whistles. At the same instant Carr calls for the Yeomen to put Dwyer in irons but before they have time Dwyer's men enter and cover the participants with their muskets.

This lengthy scene in the Crosby Hall drawingroom is central to the plot. All the previous scenes contribute to its cumulative effect. Up to and including this scene Whitbread shows greater structural expertise than in any of his previous plays – there is less extraneous action or irrelevant (especially comedic) material and less bombast. As for Michael Dwyer, it has already been noted that his appearances are brief – so much so, his relationship with Mary Doyle is bound to be sketchy.Yet in this act we are allowed to see that Dwyer harbours doubt in respect of his wife's fidelity, as a result of Carr's clever campaign to destroy the marriage. Dwyer may therefore be observed as something of a boor and this makes him more interesting than, for example, Fitzgerald or Tone, whose singleminded devotion to their respective spouses shows them as altogether whiter than white.

Unfortunately the plot from Act Three onwards becomes overloaded with physical incident as if the author did not feel confident in the strength of the central situation and in the personalities of his chief characters. About a year later – Dwyer and Mary now have a child – Brander Byrne is introduced as hiding in a barn where Dwyer, Mary, Dr Armstrong and a newcomer, Antrim Jack McAllister, appear to be taking refuge. Dwyer is suitably contrite about his past actions, praising Armstrong for Airley's recovery. A noise is heard and there is some talk of rats – a suspense-inducing device that is continued throughout the scene in which Byrne is constantly referred to as a likely informer. The approach of the 'Yeos' is signalled; all leave except for Anne Devlin who decides to confront them and demonstrate that the barn is not a hiding place. Carr arrives and his men make a search: they believe they have found Dwyer hiding in the straw, but it is Brander Byrne!

A busy scene takes place on the banks of the River Slaney where Dwyer addresses the insurgents following the execution of one of their number for the attempted murder of Mr Hume of Humewood House.[136] An officer of the Yeomanry, Lieutenant Fenton, stumbles on the meeting – those present are all for making an example of him but Dwyer stays them – 'we are not murderers, boys, but honest men fighting in defence of our liberty and our country'. When the crowd has dispersed, Carr and Byrne appear from behind a ruin; Byrne, believing nothing will hurt Dwyer more than the abduction of his wife, has arranged for twenty Yeomen to do this very thing. They retire, as Mary comes with her guide, Dan O'Brien, en route for Dwyer's latest hiding place. Having observed Byrne, Mary and Dan hide; just then, Dr Armstrong comes fishing and Byrne rushes out and stabs him. Mary and Dan run to help the doctor but Byrne shoots Dan. Mary bravely confronts Byrne. Valentine Case, one of the Insurgents, appears; when Carr arrives with the Yeos, Byrne changes his plan, saying that Case killed the doctor and that Mary helped him. 'Then, my beauty,' says Carr, 'you are mine at last!' – but Dwyer enters at the head of his Insurgent band. All cry, 'Dwyer!' and Dwyer stands before Carr, announcing, 'Aye, Dwyer! Now touch her if you dare!'

There are a number of similar incidents. The structure creaks ominously in this act, with too many instances of persons appearing from nowhere just in time to make a telling pronouncement or save an apparently irredeemable situation. (One can not help imagining that the entire cast is waiting in the wings, each one intent upon making a sudden entrance on any plausible or implausible cue.) Dwyer is made to appear more attractive, perhaps in recompense for his unwarranted suspicion of his wife in the second act.

The fourth act begins in Sergeant Agar's cottage where Carr and Byrne discuss the hanging of Valentine Case for the murder of Dr Armstrong: his head has been exposed on the Market House at Baltinglass, following a court martial. The recent coup has ultimately proved disastrous for the insurgent chief, for he later took refuge in the Agar cabin, fell asleep, was found by Agar and bound; he now rests in another room. Carr goes to get his men to escort Dwyer to the barracks, followed by Byrne. Hughey and Anne arrive, looking for Dwyer. Mrs Agar, who has felt sorry for Dwyer and believes the laws of hospitality should prevail: 'better poverty and a clear conscience', she says. Hughey and Anne release Dwyer, and Dwyer tells Mrs Agar that he forgives her husband 'because of the true Irishwoman he has for a wife'.

Carr, Byrne, Agar and soldiers plan to capture Dwyer at a meeting which they learn is to be held in the very pub where they are now drinking. They retire as Dwyer and Antrim Jack arrive, exhausted. 'Death, Jack, is near us all', says an unusually pessimistic Dwyer. 'Nearer than you think', mutters Byrne, concealed from them by the doorway. Dwyer and Jack sleep; Yeomen enter stealthily and Carr calls on Dwyer to surrender, but in the *melée* that follows he escapes. This scene and those preceding are as disappointing as those in the preceding act. A strong sense of approaching doom is created – this must surely be the lull before the storm of the final act. The storm, however, turns out to be little more than a squall.

The final act takes place at a house in Rathfarnham where Captain Airley has the news that Robert Emmet's insurrection has failed. He advises Mary Dwyer that it would be madness for her husband to continue the struggle. Mary believes that such a notion would strike Michael to the heart. Airley then discloses that he and Mr Hume have approached the Castle authorities for a pardon for Dwyer; he leaves to pursue this delicate matter. Carr appears and tells Mary that all is over for Dwyer: he has in fact been captured by his men and so she might as well accept Carr now – but Dan enters, proves this is a lie and says that Dwyer is in fact free. Mary is furious – 'You poltroon, to trade on a woman's fears!' – but Carr is called away to help search for Emmet. Dwyer arrives and discloses that he tried to prevent Emmet from proceeding on what was sure to be a disastrous course. Hughey then arrives to announce that Anne Devlin has been taken, and Dwyer calls for men to help him with her escape.

At an outdoor location in Rathfarnham, Carr, Agar and soldiers, with Byrne as hanger-on, have just abducted Anne Devlin. She refuses to disclose Emmet's whereabouts. She is threatened with torture, but declares, 'You may do what you like with my body, but you shall never put the black guilt of the informer on my soul!'

Dwyer and his followers arrive. Hughey seizes Byrne. Carr, covered by the Yeomenry, arrests Dwyer. Dwyer snatches Carr's pistol and says that if the soldiers attempt to fire, Carr is a dead man. Captain Airley and Mr Hume arrive and announce that there is a pardon for Dwyer and his followers – on a technicality, for they did not actually take part in the recent insurrection organized by Emmet – but they must leave the country. Carr is made to apologize. Dwyer announces that his work is done. 'Though henceforth broad seas will separate me from the dear land I have loved so well, I know she will ever cherish in her heart of hearts sweet thoughts and memories of her exiled son, Michael Dwyer!'

The *dénouement* is perfunctory. The story has been wound down in a rather dispiriting way, and though there is a physical tussle in the final scene it is rather less exciting than the many tussles which take place earlier on. More seriously, the announcement that Dwyer is to be granted a pardon comes almost out of the blue. Although we have been informed earlier that Airley and Hume have sought such a pardon, very little is made of it, and when the pardon does come it is dramatically deflationary considering the idealism, ambition and energy which Dwyer and his supporters have expended, and the deprivation which they have endured in their campaign for their country's freedom. Hume – mentioned earlier but not seen – appears here as the *Deus ex Machina*, and one can not help feeling that the device has been used because the author had run out of more imaginative or startling ideas with which to close his play.

Dwyer's declaration that his work is done, and his apparent acceptance of the suddenly introduced element of exile, is quite a feeble reaction. While the dramatist embarking upon a historical subject who sticks rigidly to the incidents and chronology as set down in the factual source is undoubtedly on course for producing a long-drawn-out and ultimately boring play, it does seem a pity that in this case Whitbread did not make better use of the extensive historical and folkloric material which was readily available to him.

There are curious anomalies. 'Brander' Byrne is not given his comeuppance: he simply fades from the scene – there is no retribution for the audience to gloat upon, and, more surprisingly, no grovelling exit speech for the actor. As this was Frank Breen, who relished boos and catcalls and used them as an element against which to react wickedly and amusingly, one's wonderment at Whitbread's short-changing of the finale is even greater.

All this leads one to surmise that Whitbread may have made improvements to the script between its submission to the Lord Chamberlain and its first production – but inspection of the chronology shows that the play had already been on the boards in Ireland for three months before a copy was sent to Whitehall, so we are probably in possession of the script as produced. *The Insurgent Chief* begins adventurously but loses its way in the later acts and reverts to the standard patriotic melodrama of Whitbread's early career.

Fig 12. Theatre Royal, Belfast [*Irish Builder* Magazine/Belfast Central Library] *The Ulster Hero* was given here in 1903 shortly after its Dublin premiere. The classical pediment and medallions were saved from the fire of an an earlier theatre.

The Ulster Hero

This is probably the earliest professionally produced play with Henry Joy McCracken (1767-1798) as principal character. There is some irony to be gained from the fact that the first showing in Belfast of a drama set entirely in Ulster and dealing with one of the major figures of Ulster history should have sprung from the pen of an English writer resident in Dublin, and be presented by a Dublin company – establishing a pattern which was to continue throughout the twentieth century when much dramatic writing on Ulster themes arrived in the Northern capital at second hand.[137]

The reaction of the Belfast press to this play has already been noted. In Dublin, Joseph Holloway found the presentation superior to the writing. 'The drama is full of exciting incidents mostly spoiled with improbable situations', he confided to his diary. He liked the treatment of the more personal scenes, citing McCracken's 'love for the factory hand Noral Bodel, and his cousin Mary Tomb's jealousy over the matter, and her own endeavour to get Norah out of her path at all costs', finding these to be 'accountable for many of the more dramatic passages of the play'; but he was not taken in at all by the 'now you got him now you haven't' aspect of the action, 'as each scene ends up with spies and soldiers foiled in their attempt to capture McCracken.'[138]

Thus we have Whitbread once again shortchanging the more knowledgeable members of the audience when one feels he could have pleased them as well as the groundlings without too great a loss to the latter. The early scenes of *The Ulster Hero* certainly show how capable he was of creating vibrant characters and a striking argument: but later he seems to lose energy, or interest, reverting to the more tattered tricks of the trade. In this play, however, he redresses the balance with a resounding final act.

The opening act, like that of *The Victoria Cross*, is immensely promising. Its expository scene is set in a cotton mill which immediately creates a feeling of the newly industrialized Ulster of the time.[139] If it is scholastically pretentious to suggest that this factory, where management and staff are constantly alert to political and military intrigue, is a metaphor for the Ulster of its time, then so be it. In practical terms the setting provides a forum for transactions of a commercial, social and political nature, and Whitbread deftly intertwines these elements in a way that exposes civil, domestic and military loyalties. Furthermore, class distinctions within this confined society are touched upon in an illuminating way.

The audience is immediately made aware that the main character, Henry Joy McCracken, is neglecting his business interests in favour of his involvement with the United Irishmen and that Society's objective of creating an egalitarian Irish state independent of British rule and based on precepts inspired from France and the United States. One of the mill employees, Danny Niblock, is spying for the military garrison and easily finds incriminating material in the office which is ill supervised by McCracken's light-hearted rural clerk, James Hope, who is more interested in flirting with one of the mill girls, Rosa Mullen. Another female employee, Norah Bodel, is in love with McCracken, but is unsure of his real feelings towards her; she finds the factory atmosphere insupportable because 'walking out' with a man from a 'superior' class engages the ridicule of her peers: the relationship is in fact made to appear scandalous by the conspiring Niblock. The third of the four women in the piece, Mary Tomb, is McCracken's cousin and is engaged to an English officer, Lieutenant (later Captain) Ellis – but she harbours intense feelings for McCracken and wonders if she should be marrying the captain at all; she is 'a staunch Unionist' but 'a staunch friend as well', and when Ellis is deputed to seek out McCracken she sends a warning to the UI *via* Rosa. Undoubtedly the most interesting of the women is Mary Ann McCracken; a free-thinker and a feminist long before the term came into use. She supports her brother's proposed marriage to a member of the working class and advises Norah to 'make yourself not only his wife but his independent companion as well'.

In no other play in the genre of Irish patriotic melodrama are the female characters given such prominence. Outside the work of Ibsen and Shaw the impact made by these four very dissimilar women, each with her own particular outlook and expectations, is beyond the ordinary, and there is a very pronounced initial feeling that we are about to follow the development of a play in which social issues both private and public will be addressed through lively argumentative dialogue, sustained by a strong story with a patriotic theme.

The other leading characters are much less interesting. Thomas Russell of the United Irishmen is depicted as the stock supportive associate for McCracken; Niblock and his *confrère* in malice, Hughes, are the stock duo of inefficient blackguards; the British officers Ellis and Fox display varying degrees of sympathy for the objectives of those involved in the Insurrection of 1798 but have their duty to perform.

The opening scene takes place in the general office of the McCracken mill on the Falls Road, Belfast. Men and girls who work at the machines are seen through the windows. Danny Niblock is surreptitiously examining papers on James Hope's desk. When Hope disturbs him a potential quarrel is cut short by the entrance of Mary Ann and Henry Joy McCracken who are clearly suspicious of Niblock; they retire to a private room to discuss a letter from Thomas Russell. In Niblock's view the factory is 'going to the devil' because of the McCrackens' interest in 'Defenders, United Irishmen, patriots and informers'. Mary Tomb, the McCrackens' cousin, comes in with Lieutenant Ellis – a friend of McCracken who is not ill-disposed to the aims of the United Irishmen – to whom she is engaged. Mary considers the UI ideals to be will-o'-the-wisps. Norah Bodel gives notice that she intends to leave the factory because she is jeered at for being 'walked home up the Antrim Road' by McCracken.

James Hope is visited in the office by a Captain Fox who is intent upon discovering whether Hope may provide information on the United Irishmen, but Hope will not do so. Having shown Fox out, Hope finds Niblock actually removing papers; he asks him to replace them 'like an honest man', to which Niblock enquires if it is 'honest' to incite rebellion?. McCracken returns, prevents a scuffle, but dismisses Niblock from the factory. Niblock leaves, causing a minor affray by shouting to the workers that Norah Bodel isn't a morally fit person to work with them. McCracken, aroused, strikes Niblock with a whip and announces to the astonished workers and the equally astonished Norah that he intends to marry her! The men turn against Niblock as a scandalmonger, threatening to throw him in 'the blue vat'! He begs mercy, is allowed to leave, but turns to shout to McCracken 'It won't be to a ducking in the dye-vat they'll be takin' ye, but to the gallows!'

On the slopes of the Cave Hill where a picnic of UI supporters is to take place, Norah wonders if McCracken was merely being kind to her in a difficult situation – does he genuinely want to marry her? Mary Ann encourages her to 'improve her mind, study life's enigmas and its duties'. Mary Tomb is tight-lipped, jealous of Norah. She does not divulge to her intended, Lieutenant Ellis, that members of the UI are in the vicinity. Niblock appears, besmirched with blue dye and followed by jeerers including Rosa who calls him 'a miserable little wretch of an informer'. Niblock informs Fox, who has a warrant for McCracken, that he and his associates are nearby. Norah whispers to Rosa to slip away to warn them while a troop under a reluctant Lieutenant Ellis is summoned.

On the summit of the hill at McArt's fort McCracken observes, 'What a scene is this! What a country! And what slaves its people!' The international political situation is adverted to. Tone is about to leave on his mission to France. All swear on their swords to pledge themselves to the cause of Irish liberty. They kiss their swords and disperse, having seen the redcoats gathering in the woods below.

The second act begins three years later in a cottage on the shores of Belfast Lough where Mary Ann and Mary Tomb refer to Norah Bodel, 'that poor girl who disappeared so mysteriously three years ago'. It is now 1798. A pedlar – Niblock in disguise – realizes that he has found McCracken's hide-away. He tells the ladies that Norah was in America but has recently returned. McCracken has been appointed to command the Insurgents in Co Antrim. John Hughes arrives to advise – needlessly – of military activity; in fact he is a spy. McCracken welcomes 'the grip of the sword' – 'And the grip of the rope', says Hughes, *sotto voce*. Hughes and Niblock quarrel over their shares of the reward offered for McCracken and Hope; Niblock is amusingly ironic, seeing himself as a 'legitimate loyalist' while Hughes is a double-agent. Alarums as the military approach; Niblock covers McCracken with his pistol but Hope enters behind and instantly seizes the gun which he hands to McCracken as both men escape.

It soon becomes plain that physical incidents of this kind, which lead to McCracken once again evading capture, are taking over the scheme of the play to the detriment of the emotional and political matter, very much in the manner of *The Insurgent Chief*. Few of these incidents advance the drama in any substantial way.

Fox dispatches Niblock to the barracks to get men to make a raid on McCracken's father's house where McCracken is said to be hiding. The kindly Ellis passes by with Norah, now back from America, escorting her to Mary Ann McCracken's house: Fox thinks there's 'some mystery here' and questions Norah; she says she was 'once McCracken's affianced' but Fox finds this is so preposterous, because of class, that he believes she must be astray in the head. Ellis admits he is a childhood friend of McCracken, to which Fox states that he'll have to report him 'for sympathy towards an insurgent'. Norah is sorry she led Ellis into this situation, to which he replies that Fox is only a bully, 'and bullies, you know, are like mongrel dogs, they bark but are always afraid to bite'. In McCracken's father's house Mary Ann McCracken and Mary Tomb discuss Norah – the former favourably, the latter not so. McCracken comes in – it is obvious to Mary Tomb that he still loves Norah. Niblock is seen (by the audience) outside the window. As Fox arrives with soldiers McCracken runs upstairs. The men search the house. 'Father!' exclaims Mary Ann as an elderly gentleman descends the stairs: it is McCracken in his father's clothes, but this time the ruse fails and the soldiers make to arrest him. He shouts 'Remember Orr!' – the name of a member of the UI whose execution had caused much public outrage, and a signal for the insurgents to rush in and hold the soldiers at bay.

In spite of numerous confrontations of this kind it is surprising how the central relationships continue to be presented in an absorbing way. Class distinctions have an effect though religious distinctions are not introduced; probably Whitbread felt that this would be going too far, even though his subject matter was a century old. Lieutenant (now Captain) Ellis, an Ulsterman and an officer in the British army, understands McCracken not just because of their early friendship but also because he has a respect for political views that are not his own. The other officer, Captain (now Major) Fox, being English, has no such understanding – and this is interestingly developed.

Their commanding officer, Colonel Montmorency, confers with Ellis and Fox on a Belfast footpath. A cordon has been placed around the city, but McCracken has not been found. Norah Bodel is reported to have been jailed as an accomplice – Montmorency orders her release and Ellis goes to attend to this. Fox implies to Montmorency that Ellis is not to be trusted: Montmorency affects not to believe him. When they have moved on McCracken appears, considering that his safest place is on the street in daylight where no one will expect him. He has a gun in his pocket and lets Niblock and Hughes know this when he happens to meet them, boldly forcing them to conduct him to the Antrim Road where he has a rendezvous.

McCracken magnanimously dismisses his escorts once he is safely beyond the city barricades. He is joined by Hope who is about to leave for Dublin with letters for Lord Edward Fitzgerald concerning the Ulster rising: McCracken bids him stay, as Fitzgerald is reported to be dying in prison. McCracken creates Hope his aide-de-camp. Antrim will rise! Down is assembling! *Exeunt*, to attend a secret assembly.

Rosa, on her way to join Hope – who is now her husband – at the same assembly observes the distressed Niblock and Hughes who are afraid to return to the city because of the 'rebellious spalpeens' at large in the hills. Rosa berates them and is soon joined in this by Norah, but Niblock and Hughes suddenly jump on them. Their shouts are answered by McCracken, Hope and others who hold the scoundels. McCracken spares their lives and sends them packing. The normally goodnatured Hope believes McCracken has been far too lenient. The scene ends with McCracken and Norah embracing at last: 'You are the pure, true, warmhearted girl I loved in the Falls Road!', declares he, as the curtain descends on the improbabilities of the third act.

At the Exchange, Montmorency, Fox and Ellis confer following the collapse of the insurrection. Only the leaders (if found) will be hanged. Fox is dismissive of the UI members 'constant carping about their rights'. Mary Ann McCracken and Mary Tomb approach and ask for news of McCracken. Montmorency courteously replies that there is none – and he would be sorry 'to have to see such a fine fellow mount the scaffold'. The ladies having gone, Niblock and Hughes arrive to announce that McCracken has taken refuge with Norah Bodel in a cottage on Cave Hill. Hughes is dispatched to escort fifty men thence. Niblock is annoyed when ordered to remain in Belfast because he expects Hughes to do him out of the reward. When Mary Ann and Mary Tomb return, Niblock warns them that McCracken's hiding place is known, suggesting they get a message to him to flee towards Carrickfergus. The ladies suspect Niblock's motives: in fact he does intend to go to Carrickfergus to intercept McCracken and claim the reward.

In the cottage on Cave Hill McCracken and Nora, now married, dilate upon their present state: he is now a hunted felon. Mary Ann and Mary Tomb arrive as expected: Mary Ann gives her brother money and urges him to fly to Carrickfergus. McCracken withdraws as Niblock appears and asks what money the ladies will give him to keep silent; he also makes a contumacious remark about McCracken's relationship with Mary Bodel. This is too much for McCracken who emerges from concealment and thrashes Niblock; he and Hope bind him and bundle him into a bed. When Hughes arrives with soldiers they believe the figure in the bed is McCracken but their cries of joy turn to exasperation when they pull out the quaking Niblock. Niblock and Hughes shout insults at each other, and in a further falling-out of thieves Niblock mortally wounds Hughes.

McCracken and Norah rest in a wood near Carrickfergus where they are discovered by Hughes' men, but Hope appears from behind a rock with a pistol and covers McCracken and Norah's flight. In an intimate scene, McCracken tells Norah she should always keep her marriage lines safe, because the minister

> who made us one died with his face to the foe in the market town of Antrim. Because the book in which our marriage was entered perished in the flames in the edifice set fire to by Lumley's infuriated soldiery. Because one witness [Orr] lies buried in his lonely grave on the side of Slemish mountain, and only those lines and Hope are left to prove that you are my wife.

The fugitives continue their journey. They are finally captured by the Yeomen under Corporal McGilpin – clearly a soldier with local sympathies – who enquires of his men if McCracken should be let free 'for the sake of his young wife'. The Yeomen unanimously agree. Captain Ellis arrives: this is a real quandary for him but he concedes to the general humanitarian wish and McCracken is released. Norah urges him to run. At this moment Major Fox arrives, counteracts the order and bids McCracken surrender. Declares McCracken: 'Never! Better a dozen bullets in my heart than death on the gallows!'

The repetitious nature of the action – now McCracken is held captive, now he has escaped, now prisoners are being taken, now they are being released – might be ascribed to the author's intention of creating a metaphor for the chaotic nature of the province in 1798. However, it is much more likely that Whitbread had lost track of the play's main thrust and was temporizing with a series of ruses, betrayals and comical interludes to hold the audience's attention. After the scene in which Niblock is hidden in the bed suspense evaporates, and this reader at least is left with the irreverent wish that the Ulster Hero would either succeed in making his way to some more hospitable clime or else mount the gallows without further delay. The moment when McCracken speaks sincerely to Norah Bodel about their marriage is genuinely touching, but is simply one example of a glowing scene within an insecure frame.

The last act takes place outside and inside the Exchange, which is being used as a temporary court and prison. Hope and Rosa wait among the crowd for news of McCracken's trial. There is severe shock when the announcement is made that he has been found guilty of treason and sentenced to death. Mary Ann appears and says that her pleas and those of her mother, backed by Colonel Montmorency, have been refused. Rosa is astonished by Mary Ann's composure; Mary Ann states that it is not the time for shedding useless tears and they must take whatever action is necessary – even going as far as bribing the hangman.

Inside the building the stage is divided between a corridor and the cell in which Mary Tomb and Captain Ellis are having an interview with McCracken. McCracken commends his cousin to Ellis and they leave – presumably to get married. Major Fox and Danny Niblock then enter. Fox has been sent to obtain the names of UI members who were involved in the insurrection: these McCracken refuses to give though the information might result in his reprieve. Fox leaves. In the corridor, Corporal McGilpin tries to have Norah admitted to her husband's cell, but Niblock – who now appears to have considerable authority – declares she is not his wife and tears up the marriage lines which she shows him, declaring the document a forgery. She tries to pick up the pieces and is forcibly removed. McCracken hears her voice, overcomes his sentry and comes into the corridor. They have a brave farewell, and the corporal leads Norah gently away. Fox gives orders for the hangman to be changed because he is suspicious that Hope has bribed the man assigned. Mary Ann McCracken arrives with Captain Ellis who has provided her with a pass to see her brother. McCracken requests that she look after Norah. Ellis lends a scissors with which Mary Ann cuts of a lock of McCracken's hair. A front cloth showing the exterior of the Exchange is lowered and rises immediately to reveal the Scaffold, with the principal characters assembled. McCracken ascends and takes his place under the noose as the curtain falls.

One would need a heart of stone not to be moved by the final moments of this play. The death of any much-admired person is usually touching, but here we have the execution of a modest man from a comparatively ordinary background who stood for precepts of personal and national freedom in which he believed deeply. What Whitbread has done with consummate theatrical expertise – following far from adequate middle acts – is draw his story to a conclusion without the over-effulgent rhetoric of much of his other work. The fact that he does not even introduce dialogue into the last moments is a rare example (for him, and for melodrama generally) of the kind of restraint which is far more emotionally effective than a tirade of tears and verbal eloquence.

We know from the reviews that the play was well presented, whatever the conflicting opinions about its content. What one wishes for is a much tighter control of the action in the middle acts, where everything seems to have been thrown in including the Belfast kitchen sink. The opening act is so promising in its structure and utterance that one hopes one is going to be able to state that this is Whitbread's best play. The last act replaces this hope with the view that it easily might have been.

The Sham Squire

The squire of the title is Francis Higgins (1746-1802), the unscrupulous attorney-at-law who was earlier introduced to Whitbread's audience in *Lord Edward*. The play opened at the Queen's Theatre, Dublin, on 26 December, 1903.[140] The manuscript is not in the Lord Chamberlain's Collection in the British Library. It would be difficult to piece together an accurate description from the reviews in the Dublin newspapers, but *The Era's* Dublin correspondent gave a lengthy account of the plot, of which the following is a *précis*.

Although the background is the aftermath of the Insurrection of 1798 the story is domestic rather than politico-military and hinges on the love of Francis Higgins's ward Sheila Maguire for Neil O'Dare, who has been exiled to New South Wales for participation in the rising. Miss Maguire is the recipient of the unwelcome attentions of one Mike Dempsey, Higgins's nephew, but, it is hinted, more likely his illegitimate son. Higgins is incensed when Sheila spurns Dempsey; he informs her she is not the heiress she believes herself to be, but a pauper indebted to him for the necessities of life. Major Sirr (the same who appears in *Lord Edward*) brings the news that O'Dare has been drowned in a shipwreck. Aided by her faithful servants Hughey and Judy, Miss Maguire decides to flee. Naturally expecting this, Higgins plans to have her abducted to a castle in Galway, but O'Dare, not drowned, appears, and stating that they are already married (they are not) brings her to the home of her friend Lady Moynihan.

Higgins obtains a warrant for O'Dare's arrest, alleging that he helped Sheila to steal money. Major Sirr effects this arrest and conveys O'Dare to Higgins' Galway castle, but O'Dare is helped to escape by a sympathizer, Lord Wycombe. O'Dare then must discover the whereabouts of Sheila, and, finding her in a house in Templeogue with Higgins and Dempsey in attendance, he manages to rescue her. They prudently make a hasty marriage, but Higgins contrives to have them captured and conveyed to the dreaded Galway castle. O'Dare is placed in a dungeon, and Sheila confined to a room; she is said to have gone mad (and who would wonder?). Higgins decides that Sheila shall inadvertently murder her husband by poisoning his drinking water, after which Dempsey may marry her. When shown his apparently lifeless corpse and considering what she has done, she lapses into imbecility. O'Dare, however, is not dead: allowing himself to be placed in a sack, he 'comes alive', so frightening the bearers when borne towards the Atlantic, into which he is to be thrown, that they abandon him. The distraught Sheila is forced to wed Dempsey, but at the start of the ceremony, during a terrifying thunderstorm, O'Dare suddenly appears. Higgins immediately has a heart attack, from which he shortly expires. O'Dare and Sheila are happily reunited, and Hughey and Judy are married.

The critique[141] does not make clear why Major Sirr conveys his prisoner to a private dungeon rather than to the official public prison, and does not explain why there is a scene under the sea which was praised in another review. Joseph Holloway, however, has the final word on this play, unhampered by the possibility of the author taking him to court for defamation over a published article. 'It is simply a roaring burlesque on the typical sensational drama', he wrote on 31 December 1903.

> The writing was of the crudest, as was also the construction – each scene ended with a sort of pantomime rally-like rescue too absurd for anything save ironical laughter or mock applause. The characterization was nil, and the "old hands" of Kennedy Miller's company could not make anything of it, except burlesque melodrama ... *The Sham Squire* is a rotten specimen of Irish drama, or of any kind of drama in fact.[142]

If – as is most unlikely – Whitbread intended the work as a burlesque, no hint of this appears in the published reviews. Holloway's reaction is, to us, a timely reminder that plays are targeted at certain audiences, as horses are chosen for courses: here was an irritable punter in the wrong enclosure.

Sarsfield

Fig 12. James O'Brien as Terry Hogan in *Sarsfield* [Dublin City Library and Archive]. Admired by J.M. Synge for his Shaughran, O'Brien excelled in comic roles. On the closure of the Kennedy Miller company he formed the O'Brien-Ireland Combination with Ion Ireland. Among their young players were Cyril Cusack and Anew McMaster.

Sarsfield is undoubtedly Whitbread's most considerable play. It was the last in his series that recreated events centred round a celebrated historical figure. It also happened to be the play that opened in Dublin on the night prior to the first ever production in the Abbey Theatre, creating – we are in a position to observe with hindsight – a conspicuous watershed between the 'traditional drama of the Irish stage' (J.M. Synge's term for the patriotic melodramas) and the 'literary' theatre of which Synge was to become the first great exemplar. The text of *Sarsfield* was published privately by Séamus de Burca in Dublin in 1986 in memory of his father, P.J. Bourke, who was later a manager of the Queen's Theatre and wrote a number of patriotic melodramas himself in the early twentieth century.

The first production of *Sarsfield, A story of the Siege of Limerick,* was given by the Kennedy Miller company at the Queen's with a matinée at 2 pm on Monday, 26 December, 1904. The real 'opening' took place at 8 pm the same night. The only actor accorded billing was 'the great Irish comedian Mr. J. O'Brien' who played the Raparee, 'Galloping Hogan'.[143] By the first Wednesday the advertisements were already alluding to the play's 'enormous success'. The press reaction was evidently positive enough to encourage Whitbread to send the manuscript to the Lord Chamberlain with a view to production in Britain. A licence was granted on 17 July, 1905, for performance at the Metropole Theatre, Glasgow – this was sufficient to cover all theatres in Scotland, England and Wales. Newspaper advertisements show that henceforth *Sarsfield* received as much exposure as *Lord Edward, Theobald Wolfe Tone* and *The Ulster Hero,* with which it was usually performed night-about, often with one or two of Boucicault's plays to fill a week's run.

In regard to Whitbread's sources, it is likely that he had seen Boucicault's *The Rapparee, or, The Treaty of Limerick,*[144] on tour in the 1870s and that the story remained in his mind until he was on the *qui vive* for material for a new play – rather in the way that Oscar Wilde saw a revival of Boucicault's *A Lover by Proxy* and pillaged most of the plot for *The Importance of Being Earnest.*[145] Whatever prompted Whitbread to write a play with Sarsfield as the main character, it is most likely that he made use of two recently published books, Charles O'Kelly's *The Jacobite Wars in Ireland* (Dublin, 1894) and J.H. Todhunter's *The Life of Patrick Sarsfield* (London, 1895). Both of these draw upon previously published work, particularly the autobiography (1720) of Charles Clarke who was Secretary for War in Ireland at the end of the seventeenth century and was General Ginkel's chief adviser. O'Kelly's book deals with the military history of the period and supplies the names of some of the characters featured in Whitbread's play. Todhunter's biography[146] is much more specific as to the personalities of Sarsfield and his associates but is gravely lacking in colour. It may be assumed that whatever sense of character is to be found in the play is Whitbread's creation, mixed with borrowings from Limerick folklore.

The leading characters are the Duke of Wurtemberg (historically, Ferdinand Wilhelm, Duke of Württemberg-Neustadt) who was William III's adjutant in Ireland after the Battle of the Boyne. Whitbread makes him exceptionally boorish, creating an effective contrast to the courteous Generals Genkle (properly Ginkle) and Talmash. Wurtemberg – who has a leery eye for all the women – shares with Lady Rose Sydney the unpleasant but showy role of villain-of-the-piece. General Genkle is presented as a suave well-educated soldier, not at all unlike Shaw's General Burgoyne in *The Devil's Disciple* – which Whitbread would have seen at the Gaiety in Dublin in 1900. General Talmash and General Sir John Lanier also represent the good breeding and professionalism of the Williamite generals; historically, Talmash was one of the signatories of the Treaty of Limerick and Lanier was in charge of the cavalry detachment which failed to secure Sarsfield after the latter's brilliant *coup* at Ballyneety. Hans Oosterdam, Wurtemberg's 'major domo', appears to be a completely fictional character. He is a farcical stage-Dutchman.

The eponymous Sarsfield is General Patrick Sarsfield (c1655-1693), created Earl of Lucan by James II and leader of the Jacobite force in Ireland. His aristocratic background evidently rendered him acceptable in the leading Jacobite and Williamite houses: this socially advantageous attribute is made good use of in the play, where, in the period of truce that separated what were effectively two sieges, he and his noble opponents frequently meet. He was the chief negotiator of the Treaty of Limerick for the Jacobite/Irish side. Fortunately he is not depicted here as the conventional dashing hero; his daring is tempered by dignity; his relationship with Lady Honor allows of doubt. Although this is the name part it is not the largest; it provides a most desirable opportunity for an actor, for he must be of handsome bearing, must be well spoken and must possess the external qualities of authority – but this leader also has a thoughtful, not to say introspective, trait, which makes him much more interesting. Though he spends much of the play off-stage he is constantly spoken *of* by all the other characters and is therefore in the forefront of the spectator's mind throughout, so the part seems to be the largest.

Terry Hogan is undoubtedly the most original character and, except for his *soubriquet* 'Galloping' Hogan, is Whitbread's invention. The traditional 'comic Irish servant', he and his sweetheart Eilly Blake take the initiatives which preserve Sarsfield from the crafty designs of Wurtemberg and the amorous wiles of Lady Rose Sidney. Hogan is a figure of folklore; he is not even mentioned in the early accounts of the campaign and does not appear as a 'historical' figure until Maurice Lenihan's *History of Limerick* (1866). No commentator has been able to discover anything definite about his birth and death, or even his first name, which Whitbread has invented.[148] There is a considerable body of ballad and story relating Hogan's part in the success of the campaign: every Irish schoolchild used to know that he was responsible for guiding Sarsfield's detachment for forty miles by day and night from Co Clare, across the Shannon, and by obscure byways through East Limerick, where at Ballyneety they encountered the English ammunition train, blowing it up with great loss of life and immense loss of face to the opposing side.[149] Hogan could quite as easily have been written up by Whitbread as a romantic hero in a differently slanted drama, but Whitbread needed an amusing character somewhere in the work, and, as James O'Brien was the most popular comic actor of the time, the role was clearly moulded to his talents.[150]

While Genkle is supported in the play by eight Williamite officers, Sarsfield's entourage consists only of the wayward Hogan, who is not even a soldier but a 'a poor rapparee driven from house and home on the roadside. My stock confiscated or burnt by the Williamites ... ' and by two rustics, Parrah Ruadh and Oiney Rafferty. The absence of high ranking – or indeed of any – officers on the Jacobite side lends a kind of heroic quality to Sarsfield, dramatically isolating him, as if to infer that he was uniquely responsible for his army and for the future of his country.

Lady Honor de Burgh, the romantic female lead, was in real life the niece of Richard Talbot, Earl of Tyrconnell, James's commander in Ireland.[151] Historically, she did become Sarsfield's first wife. For the purposes of the drama she is staying in the country with her cousin, Lady Rose Sidney, an entirely fictional character. Impetuous and deceitful, Lady Rose lives with her father in Ballyneety Castle (there never was such a dwelling) which, we must assume, is situated hard by the place where Sarsfield destroyed the Williamite amunition train.

An important supporting character is the eccentric Molly-the-Pishogue, Lady Honor's long lost nurse. Cassandra-like in that she is supposed to have second sight, 'her mysteries, her black art' are referred to but not a great deal is made of them and she disappears from the second half of the play, which is a substantial loss. (This Molly bears a remarkably close resemblance to Molly McGuire in Hubert O'Grady's *The Gommoch*.) Molly's daughter, Eilly Blake, is Lady Honor's maid. She has a teasing sense of humour, an ever-present irritation to Terry Hogan, her intended. Parrah Ruadh is a hapless messenger sent by Sarsfield with a letter for Lady Honor which he delivers by mistake to Lady Rose with disastrous repercussions. He is a minor comical rustic.

Although military developments and political manoeuvrings form a plangent background, the drama is chiefly about the competition between two strong-willed women, Lady Honor and Lady Rose, for the attentions of General Sarsfield. While there is no historical basis whatsoever that Sarsfield was the focus of any such rivalry, to expect a hostile reaction from theatregoers in Dublin or anywhere else in 1904 because events and personalites of more than two centuries earlier had been unashamedly fictionalized would have been like expecting Elizabethan audiences to reject Shakespeare's *Henry V*. The Siege of Limerick lasted from August 1690 to October 1691, interspersed with periods of inactivity and negotiation, yet the play's time-scale has a feeling of Aristotelian economy, and, were it not for the note at the beginning of Act III – 'An interval of 11 months' – one would imagine that the entire action took place within a period of days. In fact, there is a very keen sense of dramatic compression, so much so that this interval is of no consequence and it is surprising that Whitbread bothered to include the note.

The Dublin reviews were entirely positive, the nationalist *Evening Telegraph* providing a lengthy and detailed description of the play which suggests that as well as attending the evening opening on 26 December the anonymous critic may also have seen the preview *matinée* and possibly may have read the text, such is the comprehensiveness of the piece. The heading is 'SARSFIELD – Mr Whitbread's new Irish drama'. Following praise for Whitbread's achievement in restoring and maintaining the high standards of the Queen's Theatre, the review proceeds:

> The production of a patriotic play, written with ability and sympathy, is a thing of which anyone might be proud. Mr Whitbread, as we all know, has achieved several successes of the kind, but none that is more greatly to his credit than that of 'Sarsfield' which yesterday and last night drew such crowded and enthusiastic audiences. The difficulties which face an undertaking of this kind cannot be lightly viewed. An author-manager has a responsibility of quite a stupendous kind to tackle. The work has to run the gauntlet of criticism from a by no means easily satisfied but rather a hypercritical audience. That applies to its sentiment and literary treatment. But then there is the adaptation of historical personages, the casting of the play to bring out its points with best effect. And finally, and by no means the least onerous and responsible elements remain, of staging, costuming and scenic surroundings to be undertaken. All these contribute to make such an undertaking one from which most people, save a very courageous and most capable man and a master of stagecraft, would be inclined to shrink ... Well constructed as to plot, with no anachronisms worth speaking of, full of incidents of life and boasting of a dialogue smooth, natural, witty and shrewd, it merits more than passing praise.

> The curtain rises on de Genkle (Mr Dane Clarke), commander of King William's army, and several of his staff discussing, in view of Limerick, the siege just raised and Sarsfield's gallant defence. As they are about to depart, an old woman, Molly the Pishogue (Mrs Arnott) and her pretty daughter Eilly (Miss Monica Kelly) arrive. The good looks of the latter attract the offensive attentions of the Duke of Württemberg (Mr Albert Sinclair) but she is saved by the unexpected arrival of the brave Sarsfield (Mr Robert Faulkner). He is attacked by the enraged German (sic) Duke whose onslaught is quickly terminated by the appearance of Lady Honor de Burgh (Miss Annie Hylton), afterwards the wife of the Irish leader, and her cousin Lady Rose Sydney (Miss Maude Tremayne). Lady Honor, with whom the Duke is deeply enamoured, learning the cause of the fracas, is deeply incensed, while her admiration of Sarsfield quickly develops into a tender feeling. Lady Rose, also smitten by the chivalrous Irish general, grows jealous of the attentions he bestows upon her cousin and conspires with the Duke to have him captured ... This attempt is frustrated later on by Sarsfield through the timely warning received from his faithful Gallopin'

Hogan, a bold Raparee (Mr James O'Brien). Sarsfield becomes the accepted suitor of Lady Honor, and on All Hallows' Eve, expecting his return, she has hung from her window her glove in the hope that her gallant lover will obtain it, thus doubly securing him to herself in accordance with the ancient legend. Lady Rose, imbued with spite and jealousy, schemes with the Duke, but unsuccessfully, to prevent this. The Williamites secure Sarsfield, who, however, is released by the faithful Hogan.

Sarsfield and Lady Honor have been wed, but the furious hate and bitter jealousy of Lady Rose pursues them to the end, her machinations invariably defeated by the increasing watchfulness of the bold Raparee and his sweetheart, Eilly Blake. The artful plans laid by Lady Rose to poison the mind of the gallant Sarsfield as to his lady's truth and honour are defeated and exposed by the confession of her accomplice, the Duke, in a very tragic scene. At the close we have the Treaty, and the departure of Sarsfield and the Irish Army for France.

A first performance, no matter how carefully prepared, is often little more than a dress rehearsal. In this case, no such idea could well enter the mind, for at the matinée every artist was 'letter perfect', the scenes followed in easy and natural sequence without the trace of a hitch or uncertainty, and the applause was loud and frequent. The two most important parts in the drama, apart from Sarsfield himself, are Lady Honor de Burgh and Lady Rose. To fill the latter, at any approach at success, requires the possession of quite exceptional power. It is an ungrateful character to play, in the sense that it is such an uncompromisingly unlovable one, and the faithful following of its text and the due fulfilment of the 'situation' demand a great strain on the faculties. It is, therefore, greatly to Miss Maud Tremayne's credit that she did so remarkably well, and brought out with such true dramatic instinct the varying phases of a part fraught with so many difficulties. Miss Annie Hylton was quite an ideal Lady Honor, graceful, sympathetic, unaffected and intelligent throughout. As a foil to the scheming, jealous, disappointed Rose, the drawing of this character is particularly effective and could hardly have been placed in more capable hands ...'[152]

This is astute criticism, for in fact Lady Rose is a stinker of a part – a female villain – and inappropriate casting of this role would have upset the equilibrium of the production completely. Lady Honor is less of a challenge in that the performer is not called upon to extend the bounds of credibility almost to bursting point, but the character is very far from the conventional *ingénue* and the actress must possess a wide emotional range, which Annie Hylton clearly did. It is interesting to see the critic give pre-eminence to two women's parts, and also to see regular members of the Kennedy Miller company assessed on their work in a new play, rather than in yet another revival.

Within the opening twenty minutes all the main characters have been introduced and the chief motifs announced. There is a high level of political and sexual tension from remarkably early on; the discussion of allegiances is interspersed by flirtatious and sometimes highly provocative innuendo. These tensions are alleviated from time to time by physical action, such as captures and escapes, and by comic dialogues that are as neatly dovetailed with the more earnest material as anything in Boucicault.

One of the more serious motifs is that Eilly Blake has to make up her mind whether she will leave Ireland or face an unknown future in France with Terry Hogan. Potent arguments are put forward on both sides. When the Treaty of Limerick is signed by Genkle and Talmash (for the Williamites) and Sarsfield (for the Jacobites) mass emigration of the Irish soldiers and their dependants follows. Eilly's decision to go with Terry, who is passionately loyal to Sarsfield and to the cause, signals the end of the play. 'My heart's broke, so it is, not knowing what to do. I daren't lave me mother all alone in the Country; sure she'd die of grief'. Terry's comic exasperation gives an added poignancy to an exceptionally well-scripted exchange and of course Eilly does abandon her mother and her country to accompany Terry into the unknown.

The final scene at Thomond Bridge, with a background representing King John's Castle, has what would later be known as the 'Treaty Stone' conveniently placed centre stage to serve as a writing desk. There is a verbal skirmish between Genkle and Sarsfield over certain clauses of the Treaty, but diplomacy is restored and they sign. Sarsfield states that if the Treaty is violated, their names will be forever tarnished. All Irish soldiers taking part on either side are allowed to decide which king to serve – 3,000 join William and 20,000 join James, which means exile abroad for the latter.[153] A boat approaches to convey Sarsfield and his entourage, including Eilly Blake and Terry Hogan, to the ships. Genkle gallantly hands Honor on board. Sarsfield makes a final speech uniting Ireland and France in brotherhood and love, and bids farewell to his native land. There is no stage direction, but one assumes the boat moves off to the accompaniment of music, cheers and tears, as the curtain falls.

The finale is a consummately vivid theatrical moment, the more so having regard for the composition of the original audience. The destitution which most of the Wild Geese faced in Europe, having 'spread the grey wing on every tide', is not openly stated, for Whitbread was never concerned with aftermaths. Whitbread may be commended for the subtlety with which he presents the nationalist view for his particular audience – and, no doubt. for the Lord Chamberlain's reader. Sarsfield's opponents are never referred to as 'the English' but 'the Dutch'. It is true that William III was a Dutch monarch and that some of his troops had followed him from the Netherlands, but the overall perception of the play is that the direction of the anti-Jacobite (for which read anti-Irish) campaign is coming from London. There are countless highly disparaging ('politically incorrect') references to the 'Dutch': the audience would have read this as 'foreigner' or 'Sasanach'. Yet Whitbread does allow his characters a few overt political pronouncements:

> It's a pity to see the old stock [ie Catholics of mainly Norman descent] all on the side of the enemy, Terry,' muses Sarsfield, to which Terry replies, 'it is that, your honour: but sure ye can't blame thim: if they didn't every acre they have would go to some creature of William's.

Sarsfield is almost as strong, allusive and entertaining as anything by Boucicault. One cannot but surmise what would have happened if Lady Gregory had been introduced to Whitbread and had taken him in hand, instructing him to forego the highfalutin' trappings of melodrama and concentrate on the character and speech of the country people. Had she done so, the tyro National Theatre Society would have had a truly professional dramatist ready-made, and therefore (one would fantasize) less need to rely on the sequence of fumblingly amateurish plays which it produced in the early 1900s, for want of anything better.

The *Irish Times* critic remarked that *Sarsfield* was 'perhaps the best play to come from the fertile pen of Mr Whitbread ...'[154] It is interesting to note that while the *Irish Times* covered the opening performance on the page normally associated with music, drama and other entertainments, the Abbey Theatre's earliest productions were reviewed on the page devoted to social events – as if the content of the Abbey plays was of less interest than news of who had promoted them and who was present in the audience. The ultra-

Unionist *Dublin Daily Express* ignored the play completely: but the mistrust was mutual, for the Queen's Theatre did not advertise in the *Express*. The *Express* was represented at the opening of the Abbey Theatre, which did advertise in its theatre column, and gave favourable mention to the performances in *On Baile's Strand* and *Spreading the News,* but was distinctly cool the following night about the 'allegory' of *Cathleen ni Houlihan,* 'which has been seen before'.[155]

Press notices apart, the only contemporary comment which has been found is in the unpublished diary of the architect Joseph Holloway for 4 January 1905. He states that his family went to the Queen's but he arrived late as he had been attending a rehearsal of Synge's new play *The Well of the Saints* at the Abbey, and so he missed the first act and part of the second. He found *Sarsfield* to be 'an ordinary melodrama, with the names Sarsfield, Limerick and the Treaty Stone thrown in, giving some local colour'. He continued, '... substitute any other [name] for "Limerick" and all trace of Irish Historical Drama would evaporate from the work.' Holloway failed to note how much the Irish characters, with their dialogue and mannerisms, give a truly racy-of-the-soil feeling to the piece and no substitution for Limerick of Rhodes or Rochelle – to name the locations of other 'siege' dramas – could remove the force of this essential element.[156]

The end of Whitbread's career

Whitbread's further plays, produced after the establishment of the Abbey Theatre, do not come within the remit of this survey. They are of little significance anyway. The last performances to take place at the Queen's under his management were a revival of Boucicault's *The Rapparee* and an afterpiece called *Sold* by J.H. Cousins, both given on 18 March, 1907. Cousins had already had two plays produced by the National Dramatic Company, a forerunner of the National Theatre Society. Whitbread retired to Scarborough, where he had spent the earlier years of his life. A company called 'Whitbread's Irish Players' appeared at the Theatre Royal, Dublin, in 1909, prior to the reopening of the Queen's: Whitbread obviously saw a continuing niche for his work, but did not pursue this line after the new Queen's management took over – there may have been a contractual agreement not to do so. As we have seen, he did not stop writing, though *The Soldier Priest* did not add to his achievements if we are to believe the comment of the Lord Chamberlain's reader, quoted earlier.

Mr. KENNEDY-MILLER.

Fig 13. J. Kennedy Miller [*Irish Playgoer*/National Library of Ireland.] From 1888 to 1906 he successfully ran one of the only two unsubsidized theatre companies ever to produce exclusively Irish plays on tour in major metropolitan theatres. (The other was Hubert O'Grady's.)

When he died, *The Era* wrote that he

> might be said to be the last of a certain school of Irish dramatists, or writers of a particular form of Irish drama. We have, it is true, several Irish dramatists who have done excellent work, but that work is on rather different lines.

The obituarist must have been thinking of Colum, Fitzmaurice, Gregory, Robinson, Synge, Yeats and others. The piece continues:

> Whitbread made a speciality of Irish patriotic drama, dealing with incidents and characters connected with Irish revolutionary movements of the past. Many of the plays which he wrote are sufficiently well known so that it is only necessary

to point out that while they displayed strong patriotic feeling they did little to encourage anything like race hatred. It might be imagined that J.W. Whitbread, being an Englishman, took up the writing of Irish plays because they were good to suit his customers. This is only partly true, for it is no exaggeration to say that he loved the old Dublin and its people, and that to the last he had hopes of some time or other resuming his connection with that city ...[157]

Given Whitbread's enormous contribution to the life of the Irish theatre, it is curious that the Irish newspapers did not make much of his passing. It is true that he had not produced anything new that was memorable since the first production of *Sarsfield* twelve years previously; as well as that, he was living in retirement in the north of England – yet the comparative neglect by the national press seems nothing short of dismissive. During their lifetimes not even O'Casey or Shiels achieved as many performances of their own plays in Ireland as did Whitbread. Nothing printed in the Irish papers attempts anything like the serious valedictory assessment of *The Era*; and with the demise of the *Irish Playgoer* in 1900 there was now no dedicated medium of theatrical record.

After Whitbread's retirement from management of the Queen's Theatre in 1907 *Sarsfield* was taken up by P.J. Bourke who produced it sporadically until the 1920s, by which time the need for plays with a patriotic message had evaporated; in any case the cinema was taking over popular entertainment. It is interesting to note the presence of 'Peter MacCormac' as Gallopin' Hogan in the 1920 cast; born Peter Judge, he later changed his stage name to F.J. McCormick and it was in this guise that he became the Abbey Theatre's greatest actor of (probably) all time, creating the roles of Seumas Shields in O'Casey's *The Shadow of a Gunman*, Joxer in *Juno and the Paycock*, Jack in *The Plough and the Stars*, the title roles in George Shiels's *Professor Tim* and Yeats's *King Oedipus*, linking, in this rather tenuous way, the popular Irish melodrama with the Abbey Theatre's radical artistic agenda.

7 | TRULY IRISH: A CORNUCOPIA OF IRISH PLAYS AND PLAYWRIGHTS

Born to Good Luck by Tyrone Power
The Irish Tutor by the Earl of Glengall
Peep o'Day by Edmund Falconer
The Rebels by J.B. Fagan
The Rose of Rathboy by Dan Fitzgerald
Caitheamh an Ghlais, also known as *The Wearing of the Green,* by Walter Howard and Chalmers Mackey

We have now considered the work of the two most prolific Irish dramatists of their time – or rather, the most prolific after Boucicault, who died in 1890 – O'Grady and Whitbread. Of the other titles given in the introductory list the texts of almost all are available in the Lord Chamberlain's Collection in the British Library, but there are disappointing omissions. For example, a copy of the hugely popular *Rogue Reilly* by E.C. Matthews, which was repeatedly performed in Ireland during the period, could not be traced; nor could *Shamus*, subtitled *The Spy of the Glen*, which has a further subtitle *Spéidhóir na Glanna* (*sic*) that suggests a folkloric source; it may have been written by Calder O'Byrne, the touring manager who produced it.[158] Another is *The Old Land* by Robert Johnson which won the prize offered by Whitbread in 1902 for 'a new Irish play'. It was produced by Kennedy Miller at the Queen's on 13 April, 1903, its award-winning status heavily advertised. The sparse reviews do not tell us much about its content and nothing about the author. The *Northern Whig* remarked of the Belfast run that 'it deals with incidents associated with the Irish rebellion of 1798 and bears a strong resemblance to *Lord Edward* ...' – thus we have Whitbread selecting a play that must have been strongly influenced by his own work.

Born to Good Luck by Tyrone Power

The only play by William Grattan Tyrone Power (1797-1841) to have survived on the professional stage into the era of the Irish Literary Renaissance – it was revived by Kennedy Miller at the Queen's in 1895 – was this short comedy for which Power wrote a highly entertaining part for himself as Paudeen O'Rafferty.

Born to Good Luck began its sturdy life at Covent Garden in 1832. Set in Naples during carnival time, the central intrigue concerns a collection of Neapolitan would-be lovers: young Count Manfredi is amorous in a 'melancholy kind of way' of Margaretta, Count Malfi's daughter, who is engaged to Count Corandino. Malfi is pursuing, in a 'frisky' kind of way, 'a rich cunning old widow, the Countess Molina'. Manfredi is considering murdering Coradino with the help of two 'bravoes', Rufio and Carlos. The latter are nervous about carrying out this commission and seek the help of 'a devilish strong-built Irishman' whom they encounter on the quay who confesses to having stepped onto the wrong boat at Howth. As young O'Rafferty is a little the worse for drink and has run out of cash he accepts their money but fails to do the deed. Later, Malfi tells O'Rafferty that he has a job for him: to woo Countess Molina on his behalf. As he is young and handsome she may listen to him. O'Rafferty arrives at Molina's house in a sedan chair, asking for 'the Countess of Mullingar', but finds her so 'accursedly ugly' he forgets his prepared speech – but he is on his best behaviour and she is attracted to him. O'Rafferty triumphantly emerges from the Countess's house and, seated in the Sedan chair, overhears Manfredi again plotting Coradino's death. Manfredi leaves, O'Rafferty steps out of the chair and with the help of the chairman overpowers Rufio; they confine him in the chair and there is a processional exit.

At a grand reception Malfi believes that the occupant of a mysterious chair will be Molina – but who should step out but O'Rafferty and Molina, in wedding garments! Following many expostulations and explanations, O'Rafferty exposes Manfredi, who is removed by guards. Coradino and Margaretta are united. Malfi appears unruffled by the loss of the Countess. The Irishman discloses himself, in a final speech, as 'the descendant of kings'.

With its eighteenth century continental setting the feeling is highly reminiscent of R.B. Sheridan's comedy *The Duenna*. The principal difference is that while the action of *Born to Good Luck* is similarly tricked out with songs and dances, the real focus is on the Irish character and not on the intrigues of the various lovers. Power would have been very much aware of the possibility of an Irish tour and the need to gain the approbation of his fellow-countrymen; furthermore, being of the *matinée-idol* brand of actor, he never wrote a part for himself that was in any way unsympathetic.

As language is central to the style of the comedy, one does wonder that use was not made of the difficulties which an Irishman would have encountered with Italian. (The only reference to any Italian word is in an aside about 'macaroni'.) O'Rafferty is described early on by Malfi as 'a hungry, houseless, hot-headed Hibernian'; he describes himself as lacking 'the price of a potato in my pocket'. There is only one discernible political allusion, in this case a veiled reference to the prevailing deportations. When the Countess enquires 'Pray sir, have none of your family ever travelled before?', O'Rafferty replies, 'Oh yes, mam; and such attention is paid them, they are always sent abroad at the expense of the Government.' This would have drawn much hilarity in Ireland. In Kennedy Miller's 1895 Dublin production, according to the *Evening Telegraph* of 3 September, 'Mr Breen, as Paudeen O'Rafferty, kept the house in continual laughter'.

The Irish Tutor
by Richard Butler, second Earl of Glengall

This slight piece, which may be categorized as romantic farce, was written by Richard Butler, Earl of Glengall, of Cahir, Co Tipperary. He was 28 at the time of the first production at The Theatre, Cheltenham, and subsequently at the Theatre Royal, Covent Garden, in 1822. *The Irish Tutor* was often revived as an afterpiece. One wonders why Kennedy Miller should have thought it necessary to follow so lengthy a play as *The Shaughraun* with an 'added attraction', yet this he did in the final week of 1899 at the Queen's Theatre, Dublin. He also gave it at other venues in the years preceding and following.

The setting is an English country house and garden at no specified date. Mr Tillwell is desirous of hiring a tutor for his son Charles who has just come down from Westminster School. Charles is in love with his cousin Rosa, who returns his sentiments; both resent having to study. Dr Flail, the local school teacher, is disappointed to learn that Mr Tillwell has promised the post to a Dr

O'Toole who has arrived – as Mary, Rosa's Irish companion-maid, says – 'without thrunks, portmantils or vallases'. Mary recognizes him as her long unseen love Terry O'Rourke of Ballyraggett, but does not disclose herself to him. Terry is alarmed to find that Charles is not a child and knows 'Latin, mathematics, algebra, metaphysics and logic'. Mr Tillwell instructs the tutor that his obligation to Charles is more to 'form his manners' and 'make him fit for society'. He confides that he intends that Charles should marry Rosa, but not yet.

Mary makes herself known to the tutor. At first he is much embarrassed at finding himself in this situation, but she assures him that she will keep his secret. Mr Tillwell is surprised to come upon them in what looks like a compromising pose but Terry explains himself in a preposterously roundabout way, to which Mr Tillwell responds that 'You Irish gentlemen of talent have extraordinary methods of communication'. Dr Flail questions him on his system of education, to which Terry again replies in a roundabout way – this time to disguise his lack of any such system. Terry becomes nervous and then aggressive, and Dr Flail angrily takes his leave. Terry explains to Mr Tillwell that Dr Flail was trying to hide his ignorance.

Terry, discovering that Charles has no interest in tutorials, owns up as to who he is. They become friends, Terry agreeing to cover for Charles when he takes Rosa to a village dance. Mary reports that she saw Dr Flail hand Mr Tillwell a letter, the contents of which seemed to annoy him. Terry makes an assignation with Mary to meet at the village dance.

The four young people meet on the Village Green. Terry is persuaded to play the fiddle. There is a production number with Terry dancing on a barrel while fiddling, the full assemblage dancing to his tunes, until: Mr Tillwell appears, accompanied by Dr Flail, who has informed on the young people's presence at the dance and furthermore that he has discovered that 'Dr O'Toole' is an impostor. This time Terry's explanatory blather is insufficient to calm the duped parent and the irate schoolteacher but Charles speaks up for Terry, the outcome being that Dr Flail agrees that his niece should marry Terry O'Rourke. It follows that the goodnatured Mr Tillwell agrees that Charles should marry Rosa. All join in a country dance.

This *dénouement* must be one of the least satisfactory and ill-contrived of any play imaginable. One would like to assume that the Lord Chamberlain's copy was not the final version. Little is made of the Irishness (or pseudo-Irishness) of O'Toole/O'Rourke – though the (largely undeveloped) notion that an Irishman's best method of extracting himself from a spot of bother is verbal. The play is more revealing in its period attitude to social class than to nationality: O'Toole/O'Rourke is described by Mary as always having 'lived as a gentleman'. He is immediately accepted by Charles Tillwell as an equal, and Mr Tillwell is concerned that he should not be accounted among the servants of the household.

Those who make a study of the beginnings of the National Theatre Society might be surprised to learn that in March 1900, only ten weeks after Kennedy Miller's professional revival at the Queen's, W.G. Fay's Comedy Combination gave *The Irish Tutor* at the Coffee Palace Hall, a favourite venue for light theatrical entertainment. The *Irish Playgoer* of 22 March praised Fay's O'Toole/O'Rourke as 'very funny, without any buffoonery or undue exaggeration'. (Once again we find a critic using the word made dreadful by Gregory and Yeats, 'buffoonery'.) Frank Fay was 'effective' as Dr Flail. Dudley Digges (also an Abbey player-to-be) played Charles. 'Everyone', pursued the reviewer, 'seemed to be thoroughly well pleased with the strong Irish flavour of what they had heard and seen.' One wonders how the sternly nationalistic Frank Fay, who was at this time writing scathing reviews of professional productions of stage-Irish plays in the *United Irishman,* could have justified his own participation in what to him must have been a travesty.

Peep o' Day by Edmund Falconer

This persistently popular piece was first performed at the Lyceum Theatre, London, in 1861, when it ran for 346 nights. It was revived by Kennedy Miller at the Queen's Theatre, Dublin, in June, 1901, and also on tour, when it was advertised as having 'played at Drury Lane': it had indeed been played there, but not since 1870, and then by another company.

Edmund Falconer (1814-1879) was an Irish actor who flourished in London at mid-century. He played Danny Mann in the first English production of Boucicault's *The Colleen Bawn* and would therefore have had the Boucicault tune in his head while writing. His other popular Irish plays (not professionally revived in Ireland during the period of this study) were *Galway go Bragh* (Drury Lane, 1865) a dramatization of Lever's novel *Charles O'Malley;* and *Eileen Oge* (Princess's Theatre, London, 1871) which in structure is very much a precursor of the Whitbread type of Irish melodrama but

Fig 14. Mrs Glenville in a character part with Kennedy Miller's Company [Dublin City Library and Archive]. Another player admired by J.M. Synge, Mrs Glenville was Mrs O'Kelly in *The Shaughran*, the Widow Moloney in *The Old Land* and Molshee in *Peep o' Day* (above).

is distinguished by a genuinely diverting *motif* whereby an English servant is ridiculed by some of the Irish characters for his use of his own language. *Eileen Oge* is a better constructed piece than *Peep o' Day* but Kennedy Miller probably chose the latter because *Eileen Oge* too much resembles the Whitbread plays that were already in the company repertoire; and *Peep o' Day* would certainly have provided more challenging, not to say outlandish, parts for his leading players. The critic Clement Scott described Falconer as 'a most excellent Irish comedian' but 'the most long-winded author that the stage has ever known'.[159]

In Act I, Stephen Purcell, the local tithe-proctor, arrives at the Kavanagh cottage (in an un-named locality in 1798) to tell Kathleen Kavanagh that his father will not wait much longer for the rent: Kathleen's father is dead, her mother ailing, her half-brother Barney O'Toole out at work and her brother Harry on a trip to Dublin to try to sell his writing. Purcell's real motive is to make advances to Kathleen, who gracefully sidesteps the issue. Later a well-to-do neighbour, Mr Grace, brings his daughter Mary to say farewell to the Kavanaghs for she is going to school in Dublin for three years; this is a real blow to Harry for he and Mary are sweethearts. He will not allow her to promise to be 'true to him' as she must keep a free mind. Purcell eavesdrops on their conversation. When the Graces are taking their leave Mr Grace reminds all that there will be a curfew due to the threatened rebellion. Purcell approaches Harry – who has had an advance on his writing – for the rent; in a man-to-man chat Purcell discloses that he is a member of the United Irishmen, and asks Harry to hide some papers as he expects to be searched. Harry foolishly agrees. Once Harry has departed Purcell fires a shot in the air. Harry is stopped by a patrol and searched as the likely source of the shot and the UI papers are found. He is arrested and transported.

Seven years later, Barney O'Toole informs the priest, Fr O'Cleary, that since Harry was transported his mother has died and his sister Kathleen has been abducted by Purcell, who now declares her dead while making advances to Mary Grace. The priest advises the Peep o'Day boys to cease their activities as pardons are expected. Barney recognizes a poor passer-by as Kathleen – she says she is looking for Purcell and is not his wife. Barney tells Kathleen that Mary is not giving Purcell any encouragement; he determines to seek Purcell for an explanation. Barney meets Mary, who appears to be walking out with a Captain Howard, but Mary discloses that she 'waits for one' of whose innocence she is certain. At the annual Pattern, Purcell approaches Barney with money to get 'the boys' to abduct Mary: Purcell's plan is to make a show of rescuing her, and then arrange a hasty marriage. Barney pretends to accept but informs the Peep o' Day boys of this vile scheme and they agree to engage in a faction fight in which Purcell's supporters will come out the worse. There is much singing and drinking. The fight takes place but Father Cleary orders the boys to desist when it appears that Purcell is likely to be seriously wounded.

At the beginning of Act III Purcell is advised by his retainer, Black Mullins, that his marriage to Kathleen is illegal because the priest was a poseur; his planned marriage to Mary will be deemed illegal due to absence of consent. Kathleen suddenly appears, having overheard the foregoing, and berates Purcell. Purcell and Mullins leave, telling Kathleen they will return shortly; she soon finds she has been locked in and suspects she may be murdered. On a country track, Captain Howard is being 'guided' by Red Murtough – another of Purcell's henchmen – to Mary Grace's house. The nature of the desolate terrain makes him suspicious: he threatens Murtough, who draws a pistol; they struggle, another shot is heard and Murtough falls. Howard's saviour is Harry Kavanagh, who agrees to carry a note to Miss Grace explaining the delay as the Captain has to return to barracks due to word of a Peep o' Day attack.

Barney O'Toole and Harry Kavanagh – indeed returned from exile – meet. Barney fears that as a result of his having saved the Captain's life Harry may lose Mary. Barney has received a note from his sister Kathleen which both recognize as a forgery. At the Old Quarry Kathleen rightly assumes that the freshly dug grave is intended for herself. She pleads with Mullins for her life and attempts to flee. Harry and Barney appear. Harry swings from a cliff by means of a convenient branch, knocks the spade from Mullins's hand and strikes him down. There are exclamations of 'Brother!' 'Sister!'. In the final act Purcell and his masked henchmen have bound Mr Grace and Mary, but Harry and Barney intercept them. Purcell shoots Harry and escapes, but Harry is only grazed. The redcoats arrive, having been alerted by Purcell, but are surrounded by the Peep o' Day boys. Purcell calls for mercy, but Harry enquires what mercy did Purcell offer to his family? In the ensuing fracas Barney shoots Purcell. Harry and Mary are reunited, but Mr Grace protests that his daughter must not marry into a family whose son is a rebel and whose daughter has been dishonoured – but Kathleen enters and exclaims that she was Purcell's lawful wife and it was not a 'false priest' who married them but the redoubtable Fr Cleary, who is now present to say so! But Harry remains a rebel! – no, the papers were planted on him, and though he is sympathetic to the cause the Lord Lieutenant has provided a free pardon – as well he might, Harry having sustained seven years of transportation. Mr Grace then bestows Mary upon Harry. Nothing is said of the hapless Captain Howard, who simply fades from the story.

When Joseph Holloway saw Kennedy Miller's revival of *Peep o' Day* at the Queen's he noted in his journal that it 'only went to show how poor an effort at Irish drama it is when compared to Boucicault's fine racy efforts in the same line'. He found it 'stagey'.[160] It is true that *Peep o' Day* does not remotely measure up to *The Colleen Bawn,* in which Falconer must have been appearing at the time he was writing *Peep o' Day,* but it is far less 'stagey' – in the sense of ludicrously theatrical – than many another successful drama of its time. Some of the scenes are well constructed, building to genuine suspense; the set pieces, such as the Pattern and Fair, should be lively if imaginatively choreographed, which evidently they were not in Kennedy Miller's production.

The political/historical element is quite muted. The background of the Insurrection of 1798 is not made clear for the (original London) audience – it is simply assumed that there is 'a rebellion' going on somewhere. More curiously, the title is not explained – the Peep o' Day boys were an agrarian society of Protestant protest, but the title seems to convey something much less seditious, such as the idea of the rising sun. Ultimately Holloway's point is well made: Falconer was no Boucicault. *Peep o' Day* suffers from a plentiful lack of wit.

The Rebels by J.B. Fagan

It is particulary interesting to find an Irish patriotic melodrama written by an Irishman who later became an influential force in the British theatre establishment. James Bernard Fagan (1873-1933) was born at Graiguenaverne, near Monasterevan in the Queen's County, the son of Sir John Fagan JP – exactly the background against which the Roman Catholic landlord class is depicted in so many plays of the period. He went to Clongowes Wood College and thence to Trinity College, Oxford, where he was a founder member of the OUDS. He abandoned a law career on joining Charles Benson's touring company in 1895 – it was the Benson management which the Irish Literary Theatre engaged to present its first two productions in Dublin in 1898. Fagan also acted with Sir Herbert Beerbohm Tree at Her Majesty's Theatre, London, in at least five productions. Later he went into management himself, producing plays by Lennox Robinson, Sean O'Casey and George Shiels in London following their initial success at the Abbey Theatre – for which he generously provided funds in times of financial stress. He opened the Oxford Playhouse in 1923: Tyrone Guthrie credited Fagan as having been an enormous encouragement to himself and to the young Flora Robeson and John Gielgud there.[161] A conspicuous career as a West End playwright and *impresario* followed. It is extraordinary that he did not write his autobiography; nor was he the subject of a biography.

The Rebels is Fagan's earliest known play. Lady Gregory and W.B. Yeats would certainly have placed it in their 'buffoonery and easy sentiment' classification had they seen it. It was first presented by Mrs Lewis Waller's company at the Metropole Theatre, Camberwell, on 4 September, 1899. Mrs Waller played the part of the heroine, Norah Bagenal. She then took it on tour in tandem with *The Three Musketeers,* opening at the Gaiety Theatre, Dublin, four weeks later, *The Rebels* occupying the final three performances of the week.

The setting is Dunleckney House on the east coast of Ireland in 1798, the neighbouring countryside, Kilmainham Gaol in Dublin and St Olaf's graveyard in Stoneybatter. Squire Bagenel of Dunleckney, his young son Ned and his daughter Norah are all involved in one way or another with the Insurrection on the insurgents' side. Hervy Blake, the leader of the local force, is believed to have 'an understanding' with Norah. It emerges that Captain Armstrong of the Yeomanry is the chief representative of British military power. Two interesting characters from the lower orders are 'Dark' Michael Ogie, a blind pedlar, and Mick Rafferty, the village tailor. We are very much in the country of J.W. Whitbread's later plays.

At a convivial gathering in Dunleckney House there is a toast to 'men of all ages who fell in freedom's cause'. They hope that the next time they all meet 'it will be in a free country'. Hervy Blake is expected; it is probable that he will shortly lead the local contingent to Dublin. Young Ned Bagenal gives orders for his new uniform to be delivered. He expresses suspicion that Captain Armstrong, who is among the throng, may not be at one with their aims. Armstrong also appears to be casting a roving eye on Ned's sister Norah; when Norah returns from riding she remarks regretfully to her brother that Hervy Blake has eyes for no one but Ireland.

This last conversation is noted by Armstrong, who meets Michael Ogie, the blind pedlar to whom he had entrusted a letter to Dublin Castle. Ogie reports that the letter was stolen; for Armstrong, this means that the British military will lack intelligence of what is obviously an imminent uprising.

Hervy Blake arrives and is welcomed by Bagenal. He tells Norah that after the planned 'events' he will have 'something particular' to say to her. She gives him a shamrock charm. Rafferty delivers the new coat to Ned, telling him he put 'a letter' in the pocket – the letter he snatched from Ogie. Ned reads the letter and recognizes Armstrong's handwriting; he thanks Mick Rafferty for saving their lives.

Armstrong notices Rafferty and senses that he may be here about the letter. He finds the uniform with his letter in its pocket and throws it in the fire. A Colonel Desmarets arrives from France and is received at dinner by all singing the *Marseillaise*. Ned rises and declares that there is a Judas among them: he names Armstrong but can not now find the letter, which he thought was in his pocket and was to be his proof. Armstrong calmly refutes the charge. The embarrassed Ned becomes hysterical and a fight with pistols ensues in which Ned is shot. Armstrong and his friends leave. It is known that Armstrong wears armour, so it was not 'a fair fight'. Dying, Ned gets Norah to promise that she'll let Hervy 'take care of her'. The room is illuminated by bonfires lighted outside to signal the Rising. Ned dies in Hervy's arms. Hervy cries 'Vengeance!'

Act II takes place four months later. Following a disastrous battle at Naas, Hervy Blake is on the run. The maid Bridget lets slip to Ogie that Norah is going to be married. Ogie divines that this will be to Blake, so he may be able to claim the £1,000 reward for informing if Hervy turns up. Hervy's horse arrives riderless with blood on the saddle; Norah and her family believe he must be dead – but he soon appears, wounded but in good spirits. He and Norah engage in a tender conversation – he swears that he was saved by her shamrock charm! Father Teeling, a priest who, like Hervy Blake, is on the run, performs the marriage before the household. It is announced that the redcoats are coming. Fr Teeling rushes off with Rafferty to a place of hiding. Norah presses a spring and a picture frame opens disclosing a chamber into which Hervy retreats.

When Armstrong and his soldiers arrive Norah is disarmingly polite, taking care to mention that she is married to Hervy Blake. The men withdraw, but they capture Father Teeling who is hanged from a lamp standard. The act ends with Armstrong declaring that unless Norah discloses the whereabouts of her husband his blood will be on her hands. Hervy then appears at the top of the staircase to announce 'Hervy Blake is here!' as the curtain falls.

In Act III we learn from the medical officer of Kilmainham, Dr Considine, and a gaoler, that Hervy Blake is to be hanged next day. The doctor was a fellow student of the condemned man; they have an emotional scene before Norah is admitted. She lays blame on herself for agreeing to let Hervy come to her house. When she and Dr Considine are leaving they observe men waiting to remove the corpse of a suicide. The distraught Norah impulsively conceives a plan: Hervy will be the corpse and will be carried out. Norah tearfully requests a final private word with her husband, to which the embarrassed gaoler agrees in order to be done with her. Then, while the gaoler is assisting the hysterical Norah to the exit, Hervy slips into the dead man's cell from which he and Considine remove the corpse to Hervy's cell and then Considine wraps Hervy in a shroud. Pallbearers arrive and place 'the suicide' in a coffin, Considine explaining 'Hervy's' still form as being due to emotional prostration. Armstrong arrives to interview Hervy but has no warrant and is not admitted.

The scene changes to the vaults of St Olaf's church where two body-snatchers notice a moving corpse! They recognize Hervy as one of the insurgent leaders and helpfully administer brandy. Approaching voices are heard and Hervy and the body-snatchers run off – but it is Dr Considine with Norah, come to release Hervy. Armstrong then arrives with soldiers, having learned of Hervy's audacious escape from Kilmainham; the doctor explains that they have come to pay tribute to the dead. The soldiers brutally ram their swords into the coffin. Norah faints, for she believes Hervy is alive in it.

In Act IV news confirming the execution is awaited at Dunleckney. Rafferty arrives from Dublin to say he believes Hervy is to be buried alive and then will immediately be exhumed. (The audience is aware that Hervy has already escaped.) There are tense comic exchanges among the servants as plans are made to prepare a boat to convey Hervy, dead or alive, to France. Then Norah arrives with her father: they are convinced that Hervy died in the pierced coffin. Armstrong and soldiers follow with Dr Considine, he chained for his part in aiding the escape. When the military have gone and Norah is relating the dire story to her maid a shape is seen at the window: it is Hervy! There is an emotional scene and much subdued rejoicing before Norah again conceals him behind the picture.

Rafferty is dispatched to inform the insurgents of their leader's safe return. Hervy emerges from concealment to say that he intends to kill Armstrong in revenge for the death of Ned. He hides again as Armstrong is heard returning. Armstrong wishes to make Norah his own (now that she is a widow). He asks Bagenal for his daughter's hand, at the same time disclosing that he has a warrant for the old man's arrest as a rebel – clearly he is making a deal. Norah snatches the warrant and tears it up. She states that she *will* be Armstrong's wife! – at the thought of which her father collapses, for he does not yet know that Hervy is alive. 'Dark' Ogie arrives to collect his share of Hervy's blood money, which Armstrong refuses to pay. Ogie then informs him that from henceforth he may consider himself an outcast, eerily laying a curse on him.

Left alone, Armstrong considers himself the victor. Hervy steps out of the picture frame in a shaft of moonlight. Armstrong believes it is a ghost. Hervy drags Armstrong's armour from him and challenges him to a fair fight with swords. Hervy runs Armstrong through, as Norah appears at the top of the staircase. The insurgents rush in, having overcome the soldiers who surrounded the house. Hervy bids a temporary farewell to Norah and leaves for France. 'Ned, you are avenged' breathes Norah, pressing Ned's picture to her lips.

This is an effective and intelligently written melodrama of somewhat Gothic disposition. In many respects it is a better play than any of Whitbread's – there are fewer incredible incidents and certainly fewer tiresome and seemingly endless captures and escapes – in other words it is more believable: but then, one of the foundations upon which melodrama is built is that of fantastic incredibility. Perhaps the fact that Fagan's hero is fictional inhibited the kind of *réclame* that surrounded Whitbread's historical plays. Hervy Blake is an attractive and courageous leader, but his name on the billboards would have been as nothing beside those of Tone or McCracken. It is probably fair to say that had Fagan been associated with Kennedy Miller's company *The Rebels* would have been toured in repertory alongside the plays of Boucicault and Whitbread, but having his work initially produced by such a well known London *impresario* as Mrs Lewis Waller meant that it was tied to whatever else she might be doing, and, in any case – one might remark with pardonable prescience – he had no intention of continuing to write in this old-fashioned vein: he would later capture the West End by more up-to-date means.

Fig 15. J.B. Fagan [Oxford Playhouse] *The Rebels* is his earliest known play. A West End impresario, he brought several Abbey Theatre plays to London.

The Rebels received an appreciative review in *The Era*. Every member of the cast was favourably mentioned – even those who played the body-snatchers: as it happened, theirs were the only two Irish names on the programme and they were described as 'worthy of warm praise for the quietly droll way in which they did their work' – but Mrs Waller received a begrudging notice for her acting: 'Mrs Lewis Waller sustained the part of Norah Bagenal with care, and with the confidence and technical skill of a practised artist' – as much as to say that she was too old for the part.

The Era assessed the content of the play thus: '*The Rebels* does not belong to the class of "regulation" Irish melodrama. It is rather better written than the average well made and theatrically effective Hibernian piece, to which, however, *The Rebels* is inferior in sensationalism. It has a fairly interesting story, and its incidents are genuinely dramatic ... The comedy, too, is quite subordinate to the serious element, which is serious indeed; as, truly, the rebellion in 1798 was, both in its intention, its attempt, and its punishment'.[162]

The Rose of Rathboy by Dan Fitzgerald

Dan Fitzgerald's name appears as an actor on the playbills of the H.W. Sheldon Company which operated from an address in Clapham Junction and was continuously on the road throughout the British Isles at the turn of the twentieth century. He is not mentioned in theatrical reference books save as author of *The Rose of Rathboy*, in which he played a very small supporting part. This play, which opened at the Princess of Wales Theatre, Kennington, on 11 September, 1899, arriving in Dublin for a successful three-week run at the Queen's two months later, has no social or political pretensions beyond the incidental turning out of the tenant farmer O'Neill and, in the background, a parliamentary election for which the issues are not stated. It is clearly conceived purely as entertainment and on this level it certainly succeeds – especially in its depiction of a louche society with a definitely *dégagé* attitude to bigamy, bankruptcy and homicide. One could certainly make the case for its historico-literary relevance by comparing its picture of the hedonistic world of Paris and the Rathboy mansion with similar *milieux* depicted by George Moore; the parallel might even be made that the Rathboys, like the Moores, were Roman Catholic landlords – but, in the event, *The Rose of Rathboy* is Moore *manqué*.

Described on the playbills as 'A modern Sensational Irish Drama', the play opens in the salon of the fashionable Hotel Seine in Paris where Lord Patrick Cecil O'Hara and his bride Mary, *née* O'Neill, are living following their clandestine marriage, for the old Earl would certainly not approve of Mary as wife for his heir. She, formerly known as 'The Rose of Rathboy', is the daughter of a gentleman farmer who is also unaware of her present circumstances. Patrick is in financial difficulties due to backing the wrong horses at Longchamps and is bailed out by his friend Lionel Vernon. He has become acquainted with a certain Captain Leech who claims to be the natural son of the old Earl. Patrick's faithful servant, the elderly Martin Desmond, is uneasy about the presence of Mary's personal attendant, a Madame Latour, having observed her curious connection with Leech – but when he tactfully discloses his suspicions Patrick takes no notice. Leech overhears this conversation and takes the earliest opportunity of propelling Martin off the hotel balcony into the Seine.

A telegram arrives from the Earl, who senses that he is dying, summoning Patrick to Rathboy and suggesting that he should marry the wealthy Lady Betty Fitzgerald. In Ireland, Patrick assigns the care of his wife to Madame Latour in a rented house in Clontarf while he goes on to Rathboy. Leech becomes what appears to Mary to be a permanent resident. She shortly gives birth to a baby boy. Leech's aim, it transpires, is to make Patrick believe that his wife has died; Leech will then dispose of Patrick so that he can claim the Rathboy estate as the Earl's natural son; one assumes that he intends to marry Mary whose legitimate son by Patrick will make his claim all the more sure. Madam Latour, on Leech's instructions, gives Mary a potion which causes her to go into a remarkably deep swoon. Patrick – now Earl of Rathboy – hurries to Clontarf on being acquainted with his wife's death. He berates Madame Latour for her failure to look after Mary but really blames himself. Mary, alone, wakes to discover that she is dressed in a shroud and that the door and window are locked. Madame Latour passes her a letter, purportedly from Patrick, repudiating her and informing her that henceforth she will be looked after by the honest Frenchwoman. Mary's 'funeral', undertaken by the helpful and efficient Leech, takes place, the devastated Patrick not knowing that the coffin is empty.

At Rathboy, the sad secret widower receives a letter from Martin Desmond disclosing that he was saved from drowning in the Seine and urging Patrick to come to Paris – but not to divulge his destination to Leech, now employed as the Rathboy land agent. Leech is at present in the process of terminating the lease of Michael O'Neill (Mary's father). Leech receives a note from Madame Latour enclosing a letter she intercepted from Mary to Patrick – Mary is, not unnaturally, trying to escape, and will not accept that Patrick has disowned their marriage. Leech, interrupted while reading this interesting correspondence, mistakenly tears up the note from Madame Latour and lets fall Mary's letter which is picked up by a house guest, Mr Chisholm, a lawyer who is standing for parliament. Lady Betty Fitzgerald ponders on the cause of Patrick's apparent sadness. He discloses to her that he was secretly married and that his wife has died. Lady Betty is sympathetic. Patrick leaves for Paris.

Mr Chisholm reads Mary's letter and divines (wrongly) that O'Neill's missing daughter of three years must be Mrs Leech – 'Madame Latour' having recently 'married' Leech. Chisholm enquires of Leech why he is removing O'Neill from his farm – it is 'simply' that he has a more suitable tenant in view. Chisholm then seeks the parish priest's confidential advice on Mary's letter. Father Hyland decides he must inform O'Neill that his daughter is alive but her whereabouts unknown. Following a confusion of information and speculation at the O'Neill homestead a coach-horn is heard and Mary arrives with her child: O'Neill is astonished to learn that his daughter is Countess of Rathboy! but he has to give her the distressing news that her husband believes her to be dead and is now said to be engaged to Lady Betty. Mary shows Father Hyland Patrick's letter of repudiation which is easily seen to be in Leech's handwriting.

Mary withdraws when Leech returns to the O'Neill farmhouse with the eviction order. Father Hyland requests Leech to inform O'Neill where his daughter is. Leech is astonished when O'Neill brandishes Mary's recent letter. Mary comes forward. Then Martin Desmond enters, 'back from his grave in the Seine!' 'Take your hat off in the presence of Lady Rathboy!' orders Martin, to a trembling Captain Leech.

Leech goes on the run. His companion – alias Madame Dupré, alias Mrs Leech – warns him by telegraph from Paris that she is under arrest and that he should avoid that city. He decides to catch the Cork train and sail to New York, but Patrick catches up with him and informs him that his 'career is at an end'. Leech pleads that they are half brothers, but Patrick says his mother had proved that this is not so. Police remove Leech. Lady Betty withdraws from her engagement to Patrick without animosity and marries his helpful friend Lionel Vernon. It is established that Patrick is innocent of any ill intention. His fault, or flaw, is his gullibility. Patrick praises Mary for not losing faith in him. The play closes with the door opening and the elderly retainer, Martin Desmond, carrying in a little boy: it is Patrick's son, whom he has never seen.

The critic of *The Era* was not encouraging. 'We fear that staunch admirers of the type of Irish drama made popular by the late Dion Boucicault will feel sadly disappointed with Lord Patrick Cecil O'Hara, afterwards Earl of Rathboy, for he is most lamentably lacking in the bold, dashing, devil-may-care qualities which specially distinguish the heroes met within the series of plays written by the author of *Arrah-na-Pogue* ...'[163] The description of Patrick is exact, but the critic is unfair about the style of the play for it is clearly not intended as a Boucicaultesque Irish melodrama but rather a West End drama with an incidental Irish inclination. The critic does report that the piece was well received by its London audience.

When playing at the Star Theatre in Liverpool in September, 1899, it had an unusually strong rival in O'Grady's *The Fenian* at the New Rotunda, but both appear to have done good business.[164]

When *The Rose of Rathboy* reached Dublin – carrying 'eleven tons of scenery' including backdrops showing the Hill of Howth, Kingstown Harbour and the Wicklow Mountains as viewed from Clontarf – it was taken by the press on its face value rather than on what it might have been. The *Evening Herald* felt it was 'full of well constructed scenes', which indeed is the case.[165] One may speculate to no avail upon whether or not the busy background electioneering scenes in the village of Rathboy created a spark in the mind of George Bernard Shaw, igniting a flame that resulted in the hilarious election at Ballycullen in *John Bull's Other Island*.

Caitheamh an Ghlais, by Walter Howard and Chalmers Mackey; also known as *The Wearing of the Green*

No other available script demonstrates the strengths of popular Irish melodrama better than *Caitheamh an Ghlais*, while disclosing few of its weaknesses. Its social criticism may not possess O'Grady's searing commitment, yet its implication is unambiguous. It may lack the rousing patriotic sentiment of Whitbread's later plays, yet its distinctive political stance is all the more effective for not being so obvious. Its story and structure make use of the accepted conventions in a clear and at all times absorbing way – there is a happy absence of *longueurs,* of contradictions in character-drawing and situation, and of confusions occasioned by ineffective dramaturgy. Its comic element, far from being appended in order to lighten a dull passage and amuse at all costs, is closely bound up with the plot and is used sparingly to excellent effect as a means of heightening certain key moments of dramatic tension.

Described in the catch-all billing as '*An Irish operatic comedy-drama*', the musical requirement is given in the stage directions in a way that emphasizes this essential and obvious component of melodrama. The play starts with '*An old Irish song – at the end of song "calls for a jig" ... During the jig the bells of the chapel are heard tolling for evensong – dance stops – all uncover.*' Exeunt crowd, presumably to the chapel, and the story begins. During a later mimed passage, when Norah sorrowfully brings a sprig of shamrock to Gerald, we read '*Music pp till curtain*', after which

'*[Music] changes to lively for change of scene till Barney on*'. There are many such instructions that recall Shakespeare's '*Here a dance*'.

The title has sometimes been confused with *The Wearin' o' the Green* (also known as *The Boys of Wexford*) by E.C. Matthews. All its appearances in Ireland were advertised as *Caitheamh an Ghlais* and were at the Queen's Theatre, Dublin, for a week each in June 1898, November 1899, November 1900, and August 1901. What is very remarkable is that the Irish language title was also used at the Theatre Royal, Belfast, in December 1899, without translation. When on tour outside Ireland it was advertised in the English version and on some playbills there was a declaration that it was 'the only piece with the above title duly licensed by the Lord Chamberlain' – an obvious tilt at Matthews. Chalmers Mackey, co-author and leading actor (he played Barney O'Hea and his image appeared on the posters) asserted ownership of the work in a note on the Lord Chamberlain's copy. His collaborator, Walter Howard, who jointly managed the touring company, is listed by Nicoll as having written four other plays, none of them Irish.[166]

The setting is the neighbourhood of Killarney in the late eighteenth century. Sir George Courtenay is the local landlord. His son, also George, is enamoured of Norah McGrath, daughter of the late Captain McGrath and fostered by the McDermott family who regard her as one of their own. The McDermotts were dispossessed of their lands over a century ago and now live in penury as tenants of Sir George. Shamus McDermott, the only son remaining, is a man of poetically introspective nature who is deeply involved in 'the movement' for liberty. Following precedent, Sir George's land-agent, Michael Kenny, is the ill-disposed and rapacious villain-of-the piece, ably assisted by an unscrupulous lawyer called Conor Martin. The comic lead is Barney O'Hea; he bears the name of the hero of Samuel Lover's ballad 'Barney O'Hea' though that song is not introduced in the only available script. Barney is courting the vivacious and outspoken Biddy Maginn – a broth-of-a-girl if there ever was one.

It has come to Sir George Courtenay's notice that his son is taking too close an interest in Norah McGrath. Sir George will pay the fares of the McDermotts and Norah in order to put an end to anything that might arise from this unsuitable attachment. As the McDermotts do not wish to leave, Kenny, the land agent, will present a bill for arrears of rent. Kenny has a grudge against Mrs McDermott because she rejected his proposal of marriage twenty-five years ago. Barney O'Hea, who owns his own house and can not be evicted, will give the McDermotts shelter if need be. Kenny delivers the eviction notice and becomes the butt of comically insulting remarks from Barney and his sweetheart Biddy.

Norah has a moonlight tryst with George. She tells him that tonight they must part for ever for she has finally decided to emigrate in order to be less of a burden on her foster-mother and foster-brother. She has written a letter to Mrs McDermott to this effect. George vows that he will seek a way of changing matters. He takes the letter and puts money in the envelope as a temporary measure so as they can pay the rent. Kenny appears in the background and observes the transaction. Norah leaves the envelope in the cottage for Shamus to find, and she and George go off to the chapel – it would seem to be married. It appears that Shamus has been in love with Norah for years, but has said nothing. Kenny informs Sir George that his son gave money to Norah. When landlord and agent visit the cottage Shamus returns the money, under the impression that Sir George is trying to buy Norah's favours.

Act II takes place a year later. Barney finally manages to propose to Biddy who accepts him on a number of humorous conditions. It emerges that Mrs McDermott and Shamus are now living in a cave and Norah and Gerald have not been heard of since their marriage. Shamus is pining for Norah, whatever the circumstances. Biddy is of the opinion that the marriage will not last. In a short landscape scene Sir George tells Kenny he has heard George is in Dublin, 'in a bad way'. If he renounces Norah, Sir George will allow him his inheritance; if not, Kenny will become his heir. Kenny is delirious with excitement.

The returned wanderers, George and Norah, stop at the river bridge leading to the entrance of Ballymore Castle. They notice watch fires in the distance and believe them to be an advance force of a threatened rising of which Shamus McDermott is the leader. Sir George appears at the gate and enquires of his son who 'that woman' is, to which George replies 'my wife'. George pleads that they be taken in, but seeing that his father is impervious, he and Norah leave. When Sir George appears to relent, Kenny informs him that he overheard George making slighting remarks about him. The lawyer, Conor Martin, arrives with a new will, which Sir George signs. Martin takes the papers indoors. 'And I'll own Ballymore at your death, Sir Gerald?' enquires Kenny. 'You will.' – 'Then I own it now!' cries Kenny, stabbing Sir George and pushing him over the parapet into the river.

At that moment Conor Martin returns, to witness the murder. Kenny attempts to stab Martin, but Martin grabs the knife and throws it into the river. 'Your secret is safe with me!' says Martin, declaring that they can cooperate to mutual advantage. They go off together, as George returns for a final talk with his father and enters the castle unhindered. Shamus creeps onto the bridge and springs on George as he comes out, not having found his father, but George knocks him senseless. Norah appears. George says he has taken some money, to which she replies that she will return it; he exits 'in a frenzy' and then Norah discovers the stunned Shamus, who is recovering. Kenny rushes from the castle shouting that they've been robbed. Shamus grabs the money from Norah to save her from being accused. Kenny sees Shamus with the money and orders servants to apprehend him, but as they move to do so Barney appears on the bridge and covers Shamus's retreat with a pistol.

In Act III Kenny is gleefully ensconced in Ballymore Castle – he can now afford to be generous, and plans to give George £1,000 to go away. The reading of Sir George's will takes place with George, Kenny and the lawyer Martin present. George, not knowing he has been disinherited, tells Kenny his services will not be needed any further at Ballymore, but the reading is a surprise to both men for George has certainly been disinherited but will be reinstated if his marriage to Norah is annulled; Kenny has been left a shilling and a rope to hang himself! Kenny leaves, muttering imprecations. George renounces his fortune as he will not be parted from Norah. Martin gives the (reasonable) advice that as the chapel has been burnt down and there is no proof of the marriage having taken place, George could keep Norah as his mistress and retain the estate. They are interrupted in this delicate conversation when a messenger arrives with a warrant for the arrest of Shamus McDermott 'as a rebel in arms against the king', delivered to George who is now, by inheritance, a county magistrate. George will not arrest Norah's foster brother, but Martin warns him that in failing to do so he becomes a rebel himself.

Martin is glad to see the McDermotts in difficulties, for, like Kenny, he was jilted by the present Mrs McDermott in their youth. Norah comes in; Martin explains the will and advises her that George wishes her to renounce their marriage. If she agrees, she is to leave a bunch of shamrock – his first gift to her. She goes off, and when George returns Martin informs him that Norah wishes to separate from him provided he gives her £100 a year 'for her silence'. The scene ends with music and a mimed sequence with a distraught George and a trance-like Norah who re-enters and leaves the bunch of shamrock, after which she swoons.

Outside Biddy McGrath's cottage, Barney brings the news that Shamus has been arrested. There is a rumour circulating that Shamus murdered Sir George and that Kenny and Martin were witnesses. Shamus passes by under guard; Biddy rushes out with a drink for him and Shamus requests her to comfort his mother. Barney resolves to rescue Shamus.

In the hut where Mrs McDermott is living Biddy consoles the old woman. Shamus suddenly appears: before reaching prison he was rescued by a band of 'the boys' masterminded by Barney, and hopes to sail on the midnight tide. Norah arrives, much depressed, to say she is not George's wife. Shamus, parting, expresses his undying love for her. As Shamus is about to leave, George and Martin arrive with soldiers, one of whom strikes Shamus senseless. Norah implores George 'by the memory of any loving word spoken' to spare Shamus. George exclaims to the soldiers, 'Place the irons on my wrists, Shamus McDermott goes free!' Curtain.

Act IV opens in Biddy's cottage where we learn from Biddy and Barney that George's fine action did not succeed for the law took over and Shamus was removed to jail, tried, and sentenced to be hanged for murder, on the testimony of the two lying witnesses. The resourceful Barney has a plan. He has obtained permission from the sergeant to deliver a wardrobe of new clothes for Shamus to wear on the scaffold. There is much comic by-play as Biddy plies the sergeant with whiskey. Barney gets into the box. As two soldiers carry the box out, Barney lifts the lid and kisses his hand to Biddy – aficionados will have recognized a Boucicaultesque touch.

The box of 'clothes' is duly delivered to Shamus who is chained in his prison cell. Martin comes in to confirm the sentence. There is a curt exchange about 'law' and 'justice' – Shamus states that Ireland has almost forgotten the meaning of the word 'justice', but there is another which has taken its place; 'oppression'. Martin foolishly boasts of the murder of Sir George Courtenay and to having masterminded the severance of George and Norah. Suddenly George steps forward – it is not explained how he managed to enter the cell – crying 'You have confessed too soon!' They fight with swords, and just as it seems that George is being overcome, a hand comes out of the clothes-box and aims a pistol at Martin, who falls dead. Norah enters, Ophelia-like, singing snatches of sad songs. (How she passed the guards is not explained either.) In mime, she gives him the sprig of shamrock, and he takes another from his bosom and gives it to her.

Kenny enters, followed by soldiers who have come to escort Shamus to the scaffold. In his farewell speech, Shamus bestows Norah on Gerald. The soldiers march him off, leaving Kenny to attend to the dead Martin. Kenny is gratified that the only witness to his crime is dead. Then Barney speaks from inside the box, accusing Kenny of murder! Kenny screams, believing this to be the voice of Martin's ghost. A soldier comes in. Kenny says he does not wish to miss the execution, and follows the soldier out. Barney steps out of the box, to find that he is locked into the cell. Martin, not dead, groans!

Barney, who heard everything and still has the pistol, urges him to confess, saying that it will be better for him, and Martin, faint from his wound, agrees to reveal who is the real murderer of Sir George.

Shamus is brought to the scaffold in the prison courtyard before a large crowd which includes his mother, Norah, George and Kenny. He makes an impassioned speech of farewell. Barney rushes in to announce they have 'the wrong man!', closely followed by the now very weak Martin, who offers 'the deposition of a dying man'. He whispers that he saw Michael Kenny throw Sir George Courtenay from the bridge at Ballymore Castle, and then expires. An officer accepts this as evidence without question and orders Shamus to be released, informing him that until the signing of the proper papers he is under military protection. 'And whose protection am I under?', enquires Barney. 'Mine!' declares Biddy. Barney then steps forward to the audience and says, 'Biddy says I'm under her protection, and if she can't keep me in order I'll ax yez to place me under yours – then I can't go wrong – and with Biddy for my wife and you for my friends and Master Gerald and Miss Norah and Shamus by my side, I'll be the happiest boy in all Ireland!' There is lively music and the 'operatic-comedy-drama' ends.

It is clear that Chalmers Mackey was closely identified with the part of Barney O'Hea and that the piece was seen as a vehicle for his talents. Frank Fay wrote a highly obtuse, if deeply considered, review in the *United Irishman* following the December 1899 revival. Fay, an admirer of Mackey's acting, gave his play an inordinately

Fig 16. Chalmers Mackey [Dublin City Library and Archive] Popular throughout the British Isles as the Shaughran, his performance as Barney O'Hea in his and Walter Howard's *Caitheamh an Ghlais* was applauded on over 5,000 nights.

finicky dismissal, declaring, 'I don't see anything particularly Irish about *Caitheamh an Ghlais* ...' Yet to advertise a popular theatre show in the Irish language in all sections of the press was unprecedented at the close of the nineteenth century, demonstrating that the language revival must have been sufficiently advanced as not to require the printing of an English sub-title. (One can imagine Mackey and Howard, on reading Fay's review, enquiring, 'If the content is not "Irish", what is it? – Portuguese?') Fay also objected to the use of the term 'operatic' in the billing, pointing out pedantically that 'an opera is something quite different from a costume melodrama into which a few songs, more or less appropriate, have been introduced ...'[167] He certainly had a point there, but one expects an element of hyperbole in advertising and it does seem that Fay was attempting to break a butterfly upon a wheel. There is something distinctly hypocritical in Fay's stance, for he had himself produced and appeared in works of considerably inferior quality, such as *The Irish Tutor*.

8 | QUASI IRISH: A GALLERY OF IRISH PLAYS BY BRITISH AND AMERICAN AUTHORS

Most of the following plays do not attain the quality of the work of Fagan, Mackey, O'Grady and Whitbread, but the scripts seen may have been drafts. One has to bear in mind Boucicault's remark that 'plays are not written: they are rewritten'. The texts found of these plays would certainly have been altered in rehearsal.

(1) Plays of English provenance:
The Green Bushes
Kathleen Mavourneen
Bally Vogan
The Boys of Wexford
An Irish Gentleman
On Shannon's Shore
The Rebel's/Patriot's Wife
The Shamrock and the Rose

(2) Plays of American provenance:
Dear Hearts of Ireland
McKenna's Flirtation
Our Irish Visitors
Muldoon's Pic Nic
My Native Land

(1) Plays of English provenance.

The Green Bushes, or, *100 Years Ago* by John Buckstone

Of the early nineteenth century 'Irish' plays which were in continuous production until the early twentieth century by far the most popular was *The Green Bushes* by John Buckstone (fl.1825-65), a successful English writer of melodramas, pantomimes and burlesques. It was first produced at the Adelphi Theatre, London, in 1845 – the centenary of the second Jacobite rising, at which time the action is evocatively placed. Among its many revivals were those by Isabel Bateman's company at the Gaiety in Dublin in 1895, by Kennedy Miller at the Queen's in 1898, 1899, 1900, 1901, 1902 and 1904, and by Chalmers Mackey at the Queen's in 1900.

The Green Bushes has a picaresque quality which at first glance would seem to be more appropriate to a work of prose fiction, but the epic range of its development is undoubtedly operatic – the scenes of American exile remind one of Balfe's opera *The Maid of Artois* (1836), an early stage adaptation of Prévost's novel *Manon Lescaut*. The element of the touring Wild West show puts one in mind of Irving Berlin's still-to-be-written *Annie Get Your Gun!* This is to say that in total its tone is more than somewhat eclectic.[168]

The action starts on the O'Kennedy family estate in Ireland where George O'Kennedy enlists the help of a horse-jobber known as Wild Murtough to enable his elder brother Conor, a Jacobite activist, to escape the redcoats. George wishes his brother out of the way so as he can take over the family estate, and he hopes that Conor's wife Geraldine will follow him to whatever destination is chosen; the ensuing thought is that George will marry Geraldine's foster-sister Nelly O'Neill and they will together take possession of the ancestral home. Conor would prefer to sail for France to join the Irish Brigade but ill winds drive his ship to America. For the present Geraldine and her baby daughter remain in Ireland under George's 'protection'.

In the American wilds Conor becomes a trapper, forming a relationship with an Indian lady, Miami, and her companion Tiger Lily. In due course Geraldine arrives after a lengthy search; she reports that as George 'believes' Conor to be dead he has cast her out along with their daughter Eveleen, who for the present is in the care of Nelly – the latter having spurned George's advances. Miami is devastated by the discovery that Conor has a wife and contrives his death with the help of a rifle belonging to Messrs Grinnage and

Gong, artistes in a travelling show – but a wealthy French visitor, Madame de St Aubert, witnesses the murder.

Back in Ireland three years later Madame de St Aubert's carriage breaks down outside the dwelling of a poor blacksmith and his wife. This couple have been looking after a child who was left with them by a passing stranger who gave them money for her lodging but never returned. While the smith is repairing the coach the peripatetic Frenchwoman is intrigued by a locket which the child shows her. Hearing the story of the child's abandonment she offers to bring her up – to which the poor couple agree. In Dublin, Nelly – distracted at having lost the child entrusted to her by Geraldine – calls at George Kennedy's town house and is disgusted to find that Murtogh and his likes are being entertained there. She hears that there is no news of little Eveleen. George is also trying to learn the fate of his brother's child in the hope that he may now legally inherit Conor's estate; it appears that he bribed Murtogh to dispose of Eveleen but Murtogh either can't or won't say if she is still living. They argue, and a tearful Nelly overhears this altercation.

The American show-people arrive by ship. Tiger Lily, carrying a rifle and wearing a man's hat, is now married to Mr Gong. Mr Grinnage has read an advertisement seeking information on the death of a gentleman in America; believing the deceased may be Conor O'Kennedy he seeks the reward from George. At the same time a distressed passenger from the ship takes lodgings nearby: it is Geraldine. She hears a song and recognizes the singer as her foster-sister Nelly. There is an emotional reunion, Nelly admitting the loss of Eveleen but stating she suspects her to have been abducted, not killed, by Murtogh. Grinnage and the Gongs call on George and describe his brother's death in Mississippi; they say that Mme de St Aubert will corroborate. George calls at this lady's lodging where she confirms his brother's death. He supposes that Conor's daughter must also be dead – but Nelly's voice is heard singing, a child runs in, listens at the window, calls to Nelly to come up and Nelly and Eveleen are united – thanks, ultimately, to Madame. George realizes Eveleen must truly be his brother's child and declares that nothing has gone right for him since he got into bad company with Murtogh! Constables arrive and remove the latter for 'kidnapping and horse-stealing'.

Madame de St Aubert is surprised to learn that Geraldine is back in Ireland. She is sent for, and immediately recognizes her daughter – again thanks to Madame, who reveals that with his last breath

Conor begged her to protect Geraldine. George apologizes to Geraldine and restores Conor's property to her and Eveleen, electing to seek his fortune elsewhere. Madame de St Aubert dies, leaving her wealth to Geraldine and Eveleen.

This preposterous tale survives on the interaction of its motley array of characters – Irish gentry and peasants, Indians, showpeople, soldiers, an aristocratic Frenchwoman and her *entourage*. What begins as a conventional drama of familial jealousy and loyalty has imperceptably metamorphosed into impure fantasy. The undated version printed in *Dick's Standard Plays* shows the piece to be wildly inconsistent in every way, varying from the realism of a scene at a fair in Ireland to an almost balletic sequence in frontier America. If for us the Irish setting and characters are the chief focus of interest it can not be denied that the mansion and country town could really be anywhere: it would have fallen upon the scenic artist to provide authentic backgrounds and on the actors to create whatever accent or brogue was within their capabilities. The only remarkable Irish character is the tricksy horse-jobber Wild Murtogh (an incessant performer on the uileann pipes) who prefigures certain types of which Boucicault would make more effective use fifteen years later. The politico-historical backgound – the Jacobite rising, and Conor's desire to join the Irish Brigade in France – is not developed.

The extraordinary popularity of *The Green Bushes* in Ireland was probably due to its luxuriant theatricality rather than its preponderance of Irish characters and partly Irish setting. Frank Fay, reviewing Kennedy Miller's 1899 revival, felt that its day was 'probably over', noting that the audience treated it with 'amused toleration' though the actors in some of the roles – particularly Monica Kelly as Nelly O'Neill and Georgie Whyte as Miami – were 'great favourites with the house'. Fay thought that Frank Breen merely 'satisfied the audience as Murtogh', keeping 'some of his mannerisms in the background'. He appreciated the performance of Herbert Glenville as George for 'not getting on melodramatic stilts'[169]. One would have thought that melodramatic stilts would have been the only stage devices that would render the piece viable.

Kathleen Mavourneen by **William Travers**

First produced at the Pavilion Theatre, London, in February, 1862, this play was consistently popular in the British Isles and the United States until the early twentieth century. It was revived by the

Kennedy Miller Company at the Queen's Theatre, Dublin, on 17 February, 1896, with Monica Kelly as Kathleen O'Connor, the curtain falling 'upon a perfect storm of applause'.[170] William Travers, noted for having provided the earliest English libretto for *Il Trovatore*, is listed in Nicoll as the author of twenty-nine plays, this one his third, all receiving their first productions in England. It is mentioned so often (though never described) in Odell's *Annals of the New York Stage* that one wonders if it might have originated in America, but the feeling is definitely English, not Irish.

Kennedy Miller's publicity described *Kathleen Mavourneen* as 'the Beautiful Irish Comedy in Three Acts'. The story seems to be original – certainly it has no connection with the well-known ballad of the same name. It reads like the prototype English melodrama, for it has all the distinguishing marks of that genre – there is nothing Irish about it save the title and the names of most of the characters. There is a 'Squire' (not a term used in Ireland) and a comical neighbour called Billy Buttoncap who is much more of a Mummerset-type yokel than an Irish rustic of the Gommoch variety. The country dialogue is entirely lacking in the colour and vitality of contemporary plays by Irish authors.

A wise woman has predicted that one day the lovely Kathleen O'Connor will become 'a fine lady'. Squire Bernard Plinlimmon calls at the O'Connor farmhouse with his sister Dorothy; it is clear that he has notions of Kathleen, and it emerges that she is also attracted to him – but Kathleen has a conscience about her long-standing friend Terry O'Moore and is anxious that, should she marry the nobleman, he may be seriously distressed. Dorothy makes Kathleen the present of a fine cloak which Kathleen puts on, imagining herself at the County Ball. A letter is delivered, containing a ring and a proposal of marriage from Plimlimmon. When Terry arrives and sees the cloak and the ring Kathleen is much confused, but Terry believes they are suitable wedding gifts from the gentry and asks her to name the day. She requests time to consider.

The second act takes place in a handsome apartment in the Plinlimmon mansion. Kathleen is 'a rich man's wife' but has not found happiness for it transpires that her husband finds her an embarrassment when in company. When Plinlimmon learns that due to foolish investments he is financially ruined, he envisages a wealthy marriage as the only solution. There is a Miss Onslow who will save him. He informs Kathleen that they are not legally married because the 'priest' was a paid impostor. He then writes to her offering an annuity if she will depart. She faints, and as she does so Father O'Cassidy appears, revives her, and tells her that he performed the marriage ceremony, substituting himself for the impostor priest engaged by Plinlimmon! This intelligence enrages Plinlimmon who engages a man known as Black Rody to murder Kathleen at a desolate spot and make it look as if her coach was attacked; Black Rody is to be sure to dig her grave first. Having dug the grave, Black Rody and accomplices await their victim. She and Plinlimmon enter, their coach having 'broken down'; he pretends to walk on to reconnoitre. Rody approaches Kathleen and before dispatching her informs her that her husband has paid for her death! The men seize her, but the broken-hearted (though ever vigilant) Terry emerges from the rocky landscape. There is a fight, during which Terry kills Rody and hurls the other two men off the cliff. He then comforts the lady – whom he did not until now recognize as his own Kathleen! When Plinlimmon returns there is a confrontation: Terry and he fight, and Plinlimmon is killed. Soldiers suddenly appear and arrest Terry for murder.

Act III begins in a prison, where Father O'Cassidy speaks to the governor of Terry's unblemished reputation. When Kathleen comes to say farewell she blames herself for what has happened and vows never to love another. The dreaded execution bell sounds and the governor leads Kathleen gently away. The scene then changes to the O'Connor cottage, where Kathleen is asleep on a chair. She wakes. It was all a dream! Terry is heard singing outside. When he enters he asks for Kathleen's answer, which is 'Yes!' Country folk assemble in holiday attire for the announcement of the wedding. Kathleen shows Terry Plinlimmon's letter proposing marriage, and when Plinlimmon duly appears among the merrymakers Terry courteously declines his proposal on Kathleen's behalf. Plinlimmon, not in the least discommoded, tells them his proffered engagement ring may be taken as a wedding gift: they are at liberty to sell it and use the money to secure Terry O'Moore's farm. Terry then addresses the audience: 'I venture to say that you're glad I've got my Kathleen and that she gave me such a favourable answer to the question I asked her on St Patrick's Eve!'

Unlike other Irish melodramas by English authors – *Bally Vogan, The Rose of Rathboy, On Shannon's Shore* – there is no 'political' content whatsoever, not even the regulation reference to 'the bad times that are in it'. It very much resembles the anonymous English melodrama *Maria Marten* in general tone and also in certain incidents – the wise woman's prediction that the heroine will meet a young man of means, and the grave being dug in order to accommodate her corpse, seem to have been borrowed directly from that work. Bernard Plinlimmon, as he appears in Act II, bears a striking resemblance to William Corder of *Maria Marten* – but then he could be said to resemble any villainous nobleman of English melodrama. The 'twist' which makes this element of the tale 'all a dream' may be seen either as imaginative or ridiculous – it does not much matter which – but at least the dream sequence, which takes up more than a third of the play, allows for much exciting action, without which there would be little drama to speak of. One assumes that the members of the Kennedy Miller company played with their natural Irish accents, lending verity to the billing that announced their production as 'the beautiful Irish comedy'.

Fig 17. Monica Kelly as Kathleen in *Kathleen Mavourneen* [Dublin City Library and Archive]. Better known for her comic servants and confidantes, Monica Kelly created the parts of Eilly Blake in *Sarsfield*, Kitty Malone in *Lord Edward* and Peggy Ryan in *Theobald Wolfe Tone*.

Bally Vogan by **Arthur Lloyd**

The British theatre manager Arthur Lloyd is credited by Nicoll as having written five plays. *Bally Vogan* is the only one with an Irish title – we know from a glance at the first page that the author had little knowledge of Ireland for the principal location, a country mansion, is described as The Hall, a particularly English appellation. It was presented in Ireland by Lloyd's own company several times, one of which, at the Queen's Theatre, Dublin, in March 1897, coincided with the period of this survey. In essence a society drama, it includes an element of mystery and detection. There is a considerable amount of mild criticism of the colonial regime, especially the need to reform the landlord-tenant relationship. *Bally Vogan* was first performed at the Tyne Theatre, Newcastle-upon-Tyne, on 25 July 1887, billed as 'an Irish drama in Four Acts'.

The chief distinction of *Bally Vogan* is its strong plot. It appears from the manuscript to be very carelessly structured for it opens in the quaint rural village of Bally Vogan, after which there is a scene set in London containing characters who are not connected in any way with what has gone before and appear to be fugitives from another play; later, there is a scene on a rocky island off the Australian coast which also seems to be misplaced – but, much later, the strands slowly coalesce. It is entirely likely that these and some minor technical deficiencies were radically emended in rehearsal – otherwise *Bally Vogan* could not have been so successful. There is a clever production trick in that one actor plays the lookalike parts of the Irish landlord's son Gerald McMahon and the London forger Jim Branson.

Norah O'Sullivan's mother supposes that her daughter is taking a romantic interest in either her cousin Pat Hogan, a poet, or perhaps in Mr McCrindle, the new land agent at Bally Vogan Hall, but Norah has set her sights at a higher social level for it is the landlord's son, Gerald, who is the object of her hopes – and Gerald has responded positively. McCrindle divines this and reports his view to Sir Gerald McMahon who most civilly suggests to Gerald that if he still has a wish for Norah after three years in the army there will be no paternal objection. McCrindle is certain that during Gerald's absence Norah will change her mind. Sir Gerald and his son make a tour of the village, flanked by the local MP Major Redmond and his handsome but vain daughter Kate – clearly assumed by all, including herself, to be 'a good match' for Gerald. Gerald's army commission is announced, there are cheers, merriment and country dancing, and Pat Hogan is prevailed upon to recite a poem. It is a happy townland.

The scene changes to a London lodging-house, where Jim Branson and his obsequious clerk Timothy Littlejohn, also known as Sleeky, are planning to cash a forged cheque and emigrate to Australia, leaving Branson's mistress, Mary Power, behind. Mary overhears. Her wish is to accompany Branson as his wife. She threatens to report his forgeries to the police if he refuses to marry her. Branson shoots her and departs, but Mary is only slightly wounded; she recovers and informs on him.

Four years pass. Sir Gerald is dead, having left his estate to Gerald, of whom nothing has been heard other than a rumour that the ship on which he and Pat Hogan (who travelled as his servant) foundered *en route* from Melbourne. Mrs O'Sullivan has been unable to pay her rent but McCrindle excuses her in order to please Norah, to whom he subsequently proposes – but she rejects him.

An English visitor to the Hall, the Hon. Bobby Bowser, 'a modern chappie', pays court to Kate Redmond, assuming that she now has no thoughts of Gerald. Meanwhile, on a rocky island in the South Pacific, Gerald encounters Branson and Sleeky: they believe they are the only survivors of the wreck of the *SS Pandora*. Sleeky draws Branson's attention to his remarkable likeness to Gerald; they plot that, if rescued, Branson will pass himself off as Gerald and claim his inheritance. A ship is sighted. Branson shoots Gerald and he and Sleeky are rescued.

News reaches Bally Vogan that 'the young master' has returned! Norah O'Sullivan can not understand his change of heart, for he is to marry Kate Redmond. All, including Kate, find Gerald curiously altered. Mrs O'Sullivan tells McCrindle that her daughter will never accept him so he dangles the threat of eviction over them. Branson – for it is indeed he, impersonating Gerald – informs McCrindle that he is appointing a Mr Dunn (*alias* Sleeky) as his new land agent. McCrindle is shocked, and Kate speaks sternly to her fiancé about the abrupt way in which he dismisses his employees. Norah returns a locket which Gerald gave her, and asks for the return of a ring: 'What ring?' enquires 'Gerald'. Kate Redmond enters, enquires about the locket and asks why Gerald gave it to Norah? 'Gerald' then intimates that Norah stole it. Norah responds by telling Kate that if she marries such a man, God help her!

The alienated McCrindle lurks in Bally Vogan, seeking revenge. He overhears 'Gerald' telling 'Dunn' that 'nobody but you will ever know the new Sir Gerald McMahon is Jim Brandon the bank forger!' – 'Nobody but me!' declares McCrindle, stepping forward. After a heated parlay McCrindle agrees to remain silent for a share of the late Sir Gerald's money. Mrs O'Sullivan then waits on 'the new master', appealing to him as his oldest tenant on the matter of the rent. 'Gerald' and McCrindle decide to evict the O'Sullivans, and Sleeky is sent, much against his will, to inform the police that Norah is a thief. There is consternation in the village as officers come to arrest Norah. A bearded gentleman in the crowd announces: 'That girl is innocent!' He removes the beard and cries that he is 'Gerald McMahon, the heir of Bally Vogan!', but McCrindle responds, 'Arrest that man: he is James Branson, the London bank forger!' Constables arrest the real Gerald. (The stage direction reads: 'Branson, Sleeky and McCrindle grin in triumph'!)

In the final act a senior police inspector from London interviews Gerald and concludes that he is an impostor. In a short scene in the garden of The Hall Branson orders Sleeky to disappear, because the London policeman will certainly recognize him. Sleeky says that he intends to reform, and goes. In The Hall Major Redmond presides over an improvised court at which Norah is accused of theft; her solicitor states that she was 'unjustly and maliciously accused'. The solicitor then recounts the shipwreck story – which appears to be an irrelevancy until he declares that he can produce 'Mr Dunn' and 'Pat Hogan': Sleeky is brought in and introduced as Mr Dunn and the 'solicitor' then reveals himself as Pat Hogan! Sleeky apologizes for his part in the proceedings and then reveals Branson (still thought to be Gerald) as the perpetrator of several crimes, but by this time Branson has fled – inevitably so, for the actor playing the two Geralds could not appear as both at the same time.

Pat and the real Gerald – who recovered from the shooting – had met on the Pacific island after the departure of Branson and Sleeky and were rescued by another ship. Gerald is reunited with Norah and it is likely that Kate Redmond will seek consolation with Bobby Bowser, 'the modern chappie'. The story of the personification of Gerald McMahon by Jim Branson would not have seemed so improbable to audiences who would recall the notorious case of the 'Tichborne Claimant' only a few years earlier; it is likely that the playwright had that lawsuit in mind. In *Bally Vogan* Arthur Lloyd certainly created a riveting drama. If the Irish element seems spurious, it would not have done so to the great majority of his audiences, who saw his play in British theatres.

The Boys of Wexford, entitled The Wearin' o' the Green when first produced, by E.C. Matthews

E.C. Matthews, another British actor-manager-playwright, wrote six plays between 1887 and 1900,[171] of which *Rogue Reilly* and *The Boys of Wexford* were on Irish subjects. At the first performance in the Queen's Theatre, Dublin, on 21 June 1896, the author played the part of Terry Shiel, with Tom Nerney as Old Barney, Mrs Matthews as Oonagh Mulvain and Frank D'Alton (father of the distinguished Abbey Theatre dramatist Louis D'Alton) as Black Shawn. Quite why it was called *The Boys of Wexford* is not clear because there is no reference to the Wexford insurrection although the period is 1798; the Co Clare yeomanry are in evidence.

The copy in the Lord Chamberlain's Plays is clearly an early draft, possibly submitted because nothing else was available when it was remembered that a licence had not been issued for touring in Britain. The critic of the *Irish Times* wrote that 'the plot from beginning to end was well carried out',[172] but the *Freeman's Journal* felt that the play was 'spun out at great length' and the plot was 'squalid' – yet the general tone of the review is favourable.[173] When *The Boys of Wexford* was seen in Glasgow two years later the *Evening Citizen* described it as treating of 'certain phases in the life of the Irish peasantry about a hundred years ago when the country was stirred by agitation and rebellion. Mr Matthews, however, has not imported too much of the historic element to his work. There is just a leaven of it here and there to keep matters right, and the imagination of the author does the rest ...' [174] The Glasgow correspondent of *The Era* wrote of the same production that there were 'flashes of Hibernian wit – instead of what usually passes for it in many pieces which are described as Irish ...'[175]

One wonders about the latter; but one also senses that the play was better appreciated outside Ireland than inside. Joseph Holloway, who attended the Dublin opening, was far less well disposed than any of the Irish or British critics: he felt that the whole piece needed 'pulling together'.[176] Certainly that is the impression gained from an attempt to read the manuscript, in which 137 pages are covered in very poor handwriting with many emendations and erasures. There is no list of characters so it is not possible to compare what was originally intended with the names on the playbills. It would be unfair, however, to dismiss the work on the grounds of the illegibility of parts of the script and a resulting number of apparent improbabilities in the action. The inconsistencies would certainly have been repaired, else the piece would not have survived three years of touring. The following *précis* of the plot may or may not be entirely accurate.

The Shiels parents have two sons – Dermod, who is destined to be 'a gentleman' and upon whom much hard-earned money has been lavished, and Terry, who has remained on the family farm. Oonagh Mulrain's late father wished her to marry one of the Shiels brothers. He had a preference for the more promising Dermod, but when this intelligence is conveyed to Oonagh by Old Barney, a family retainer, she already has her eye on Terry, who is 'a bit wild', and attractively so. Oonagh has another suitor in Mr Howard, a 'government agent', whose advances she pertly avoids for it is generally known that Howard is engaged to Lord Castlerock's daughter. Dermod is given to gambling, and in a drunken evening with Howard he loses £5,000 at cards. Howard has joined the Yeomanry, 'to have a pot at your rebel countrymen!' as he laughingly declares – something far from Dermod's taste. At his wits' end on how to repay the 'debt of honour' Dermod forges his father's name on a cheque. When the fraud is discovered Old Shiels acknowledges the signature as being his own in order to save his son from the law. Terry Shiels, though in love with Oonagh, abandons his hopes of marrying her so that her considerable wealth may restore his brother's fortunes – and Dermod accepts this situation even though his romantic thoughts are directed towards a lady called Molly Bawn, who, as it happens, is the daughter of a certain 'Black Shawn', an accomplice of Howard.

In Act II Mr Howard has hopes of inheriting a fortune from the local landlord Lord Heathcote; he inveigles Dermod into a quarrel with Heathcote, hoping that a duel will result in Dermod killing the latter. Oonagh is opposed to Dermod taking part in a duel, and furthermore believes that he is not for her and should marry his sweetheart Molly – but Molly is convinced that he should fight the duel like a gentleman. Heathcote, believing the matter to be too trivial, refuses to fight. Howard then shoots Heathcote in the back and publicly accuses Dermod of murdering him. Black Shawn, in Howard's pay, is a 'witness' and swears that Dermod is the culprit. Black Shawn has been assigned to hunt down a priest called Father John, who is on the run under the prevailing penal laws. Dermod is cast into prison to await trial for murder, but Terry, ever the magnanimous and loving brother, makes a false confession to the effect that he committed the deed, and therefore obtains Dermod's release and takes his place. Dermod marries Molly amidst – given the circumstances – surprising jollification.

In Act III a 'penitent' Black Shawn, apparently on his deathbed, asks for a priest but will accept none other than his former quarry, Father John. When the priest arrives Black Shawn springs out of bed and assaults him, so that he subsequently dies. The onus, naturally, is on the perpetrator of all these crimes, Black Shawn's employer, Howard. Black Shawn turns on his master, and both Terry and Dermod are acquitted of any part in the murder of Lord Heathcote. In the final scene at Howard's house, Howard, in monologue, decides to flee the country, taking Oonagh with him. Oonagh repeats that she will not be his wife, to which he retorts that she will be his mistress! Kathleen – Old Kit, one of the servants – has overheard the foregoing and informs on Howard. Terry arrives in time to rescue Oonagh, and Howard's servants are happy to seize him. Terry and Oonagh are united.

An Irish Gentleman by D.C. Murray and John L. Shine

David Christie Murray was a New Zealander. Nicoll identifies his earliest play as *Ned's Chum*, performed at the Opera House, Auckland, in 1890, but he is not mentioned in the *Dictionary of New Zealand Biography*. John L. Shine is listed as having written four plays, this being one of them, but he was much better known as an actor and singer.[177] The first performance of *An Irish Gentleman* was at the Globe Theatre, London, on 9 June, 1897; it arrived at the Theatre Royal, Dublin, on 27 June, 1898, with the 'Entire Globe Theatre Company'. That it transferred to Dublin's largest theatre demonstrates its popularity.

The form is not that of the multic-scenic melodrama but of the three-act *boulevard* comedy in which each act is played in a single box set. Structurally, *An Irish Gentleman* fits quite neatly into the new school of writers of the 'well-made play'. As a theatrical piece it achieves what it sets out to do: to tell an unusual story in a light-hearted manner. If there is any thesis, it is that the 'Irish gentleman' is, of his nature, charming, kind-hearted, generous and witty, but with a distinctly careless attitude to domestic economy. Gerald Dorsay, 'a young Irish gentleman of sheltered means', is also a very good judge of whiskey. The play could be said to be about a man who is not a drunkard but has a serious drink problem, but Murray and Shine do not adopt the moralizing tone of 'Mr Smith', author of the famous American melodrama *The Drunkard*.

The Irish Gentleman is unusual in its careful plotting. Important characters are always established in the dialogue some time before their first appearance, and later in the play such characters never enter with improbable suddenness unless there is a practical reason. The personnel are moved on and off the stage with unobtrusive skill. (It should be unnecessary to mention such essentials were it not for their absence in so many plays of the time.) There are also sub-textual *nuances* – for example, on the first entrance of Gerald Dorsay's cousin, Dillon Dorsay, there is no overt suggestion that he may be a rival for the hand of the heiress Ellaleen Dunrayne, yet there is an undoubted 'feeling' that this may be so. *Nuance* is hardly a property of melodrama, and this is not a melodrama, though there are the kind of melodramatic moments one finds in, for example, Wilde's *A Woman of no Importance* (1893). Some of the dialogue is quite aphoristic – pale in comparison with Wilde, yet it would not be unreasonable to suppose that the collaborators had been attracted by his society comedies. 'I hate people who are only "doing their duty"', observes Gerald's orphaned *protégée,* the unconventional Constance. 'Whenever people talk like that you may be sure they mean something nasty' would be Wildean were it not for the final word.[178]

The first and third acts take place at Park Dorsay, Gerald Dorsay's country house in Ireland. Among the house guests is the young Lord Avon, who Gerald helps by paying one of his debts, though with the warning that his name 'is not good at the bank'. A Mr Daley Doyle arrives and is shown to the kitchen where the butler gives him a meal, perceiving that he may be in need – this turns out to be the case for Doyle is an old school chum of Dorsay, 'down on his luck'; he is intensely embarrassed because he is employed to serve a writ on Gerald but Gerald blithely accepts the writ and even lends Doyle £100 to assist him and his family to emigrate to New Zealand. Another guest at Park Dorsay is a lawyer named MacQuarrie who is gradually revealed to have had a past in dubious financial dealings and is described by a perceptive visitor as 'a former jail-bird'. (MacQuarrie, it emerges later, had the drafting of the will of the late Blake Dorsay of New Zealand who left his money to whichever of the cousins, Gerald and Dillon, would marry

Ellaleen Dunrayne: but MacQuarrie has changed the will in favour of Dillon.)

Gerald is delighted to welcome his cousin, Dillon Dorsay, from New Zealand. There are in fact a number of connections with that colony, for Ellaleen Dunrayne has been there on a visit with her aunt, where she met Dillon. Ellaleen appears to be deeply in love with Gerald, but we learn from the servants' talk that she would gladly consent to marriage if only he would stop drinking to excess. Such an alliance would save the declining Park Dorsay estate. Further writs are served on Gerald. Ellaleen perceives he is in trouble: when she comes of age in six months' time she can advance him money, but he will not hear of it; she tells him he has let his generosity ruin him and urges him to 'take stock of himself', a diplomatic reference to his drinking.

Gerald is about to be dispossessed. MacQuarrie cunningly suggests to Dillon that he do a 'helpful cousin' act with a loan but Dillon takes this further than MacQuarrie intended and offers Gerald a position on his sheep station. Gerald, touched by Dillon's 'kindess' at first refuses but changes his mind when he privately considers that Ellaleen will be a neighbour on another visit with Mrs Dunrayne. He says goodbye to the old home of ten generations.

The second act is set on Dillon's station in New Zealand where Gerald has become the very successful manager. He has kept his pledge with Ellaleen and is entirely off the drink. He has brought his Irish servants with him, and also his amusing hoydenish niece Constance. Lord Avon arrives – on a tour motivated by his desire to reacquaint himself with Constance, whom he met at Park Dorsay. Avon's minor financial difficulties have evaporated for he has inherited his father's seat in the House of Lords; he now wishes to employ Gerald to run his Irish estate. Gerald is undecided. Avon arranges a surprise party for Gerald's birthday to which Ellaleen and her aunt are invited. Constance, in her *faux-naïf* way, tells Gerald she believes Dillon doesn't like him, and she certainly doesn't like his friend Mr MacQuarrie. Gerald is delighted by a visit from Daley Doyle, now prosperously settled and working for a firm of solicitors nearby. Doyle insists on paying back Gerald's loan; he also expresses doubts about Dillon and MacQuarrie. There is a short conversation between Dillon and MacQuarrie during which Dillon complains of Gerald, 'that fellow drives me mad! Always and everywhere gratitude, gratitude, gratitude! until I feel as if I could take him by the throat and tear his life out!' Dillon has genuinely fallen in love with Ellaleen and wishes Gerald out of the way. MacQuarrie decides to put whiskey and a strong drug in Gerald's tea so that he will appear drunk before Ellaleen.

Gerald enjoys the party and confirms to Ellaleen that he never touches a drop. There is singing and dancing. Gerald tastes the whiskey in the tea – all the men's tea is traditionally laced for the sheep-shearing – and decides he must tell Ellaleen as a matter of duty, but the drug takes effect and he falls into a stupor. Dillon 'diplomatically' informs Ellaleen and her aunt that Gerald is 'the worse for wear'. The ladies leave, Ellaleen in tears. Constance subsequently finds the discarded phial in a tree trunk where she stores *trouvailles* and Avon realizes what has happened. Gerald implores Avon to take him back to Ireland as his agent as he has disgraced himself for ever with Ellaleen. Avon agrees. When MacQuarrie nonchalantly asks him if he's been asleep, he replies, 'I'm just beginning to wake'.

The setting for Act III is Park Dorsay where MacQuarrie and Dillon call on Ellaleen and her aunt who are now living there as tenants since Gerald is running the Avon estate. Dillon proposes to Ellaleen. She tells him that she esteems him, and shakes hands, but the answer is 'no' for she has decided to enter a convent. Dillon attacks MacQuarrie verbally for initiating the whole proceedings and declares he will reveal his mean-minded tricks – but MacQuarrie demonstrates how this would also put Dillon in jail. Lord Avon and Constance return from New Zealand to join the Dunraynes and are surprised to see MacQuarrie and Dillon. Dillon rushes off in a state. Constance annoyingly enquires of MacQuarrie why he left Gerald in that dreadful condition? And what is he doing here? He blusters and goes off to 'comfort' Dillon.

Mrs Dunrayne enters to receive her visitors. Avon swears that Gerald is teetotal and what the ladies witnessed was the effect of a drug – the dregs of the phial have been analysed. Mrs Dunrayne says that under no circumstances will her niece receive Gerald. When Gerald arrives Avon and Constance find it extremely difficult to inform him of Ellaleen's decision. Later, Mrs Dunrayne asks Gerald if he has forgotten that he admitted to having taken drink? She then discloses that although Ellaleen will be retiring from the world she has generously bought Park Dorsay for him, and he is once again owner of his ancestral home. Gerald, left alone, muses that he could not bear to live here without Ellaleen. Daley Doyle arrives and takes Gerald off for 'a quiet word'. He is now a member of the New Zealand firm that administered Uncle Blake's will and he has much interesting information as to what has been going on. Doyle produces the will and shows it to Dillon. There is an immediate confrontation with MacQuarrie, which Ellaleen hears as she descends the staircase, pausing to take in the whole story. Gerald is too much of a gentleman to prefer charges. He announces that 'their attempt to ruin me helped to make a man of myself'. There is a lovers' embrace, the convent forgotten.

> GERALD: Please heaven under my own roof tree I'll live and die ...
> ELLALEEN: An Irish gentleman!

Following the London premiere, a reviewer in *The Era* exclaimed: 'I sat and glowed and let dramatic criticism go hang. If the London public still care for a capital specimen of the stage Irishman, Mr Shine is their man ... Vigorously written and extremely well played. Miss Eva Moore's emotional heroine is particularly good. Erin go bragh!'[179]

George Bernard Shaw was of a different mind on the Irish qualities of the play. Writing in the *Pall Mall Gazette,* he felt *An Irish Gentleman* was

> a typical product of our theatre. It has been evident for some time that we have in Mr Shine a comedian capable of restoring the popularity which Boucicault won for sketches of Irish character on the English stage. Accordingly ... Mr Shine ... calls in Mr Christie Murray to act as penman, and manufactures a "drama" with heroes, heroines, villains, Irish retainers, comic relief, incidental songs and all needful accessories for the exploitation of his talent. And I have no doubt that Mr Shine and his backers were convinced that they had a fortune in their product although they would have laughed to scorn a proposal to invest three shillings in an Ibsen production. Fate was in her ironical mood on the first night. Neither Mr Shine nor any other of the Stage Irishmen raised a smile. All honors went to the Scotch villain (Mr J.B. Gordon) and to Miss Eva Moore, who was very charming and very English as the heroine ...[180]

The play may have been a disaster in Shaw's suave view, but the coldness of that first audience must have given way to something quite different when 'word of mouth' reached the regular theatregoers.

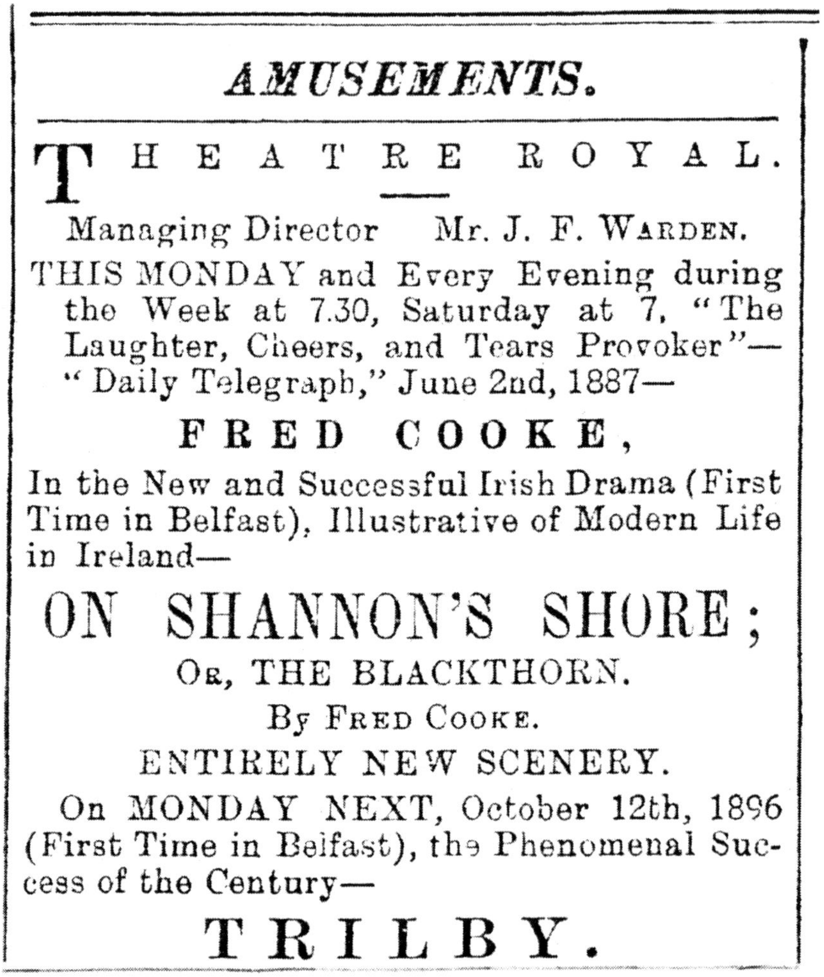

AMUSEMENTS.

THEATRE ROYAL.

Managing Director   Mr. J. F. WARDEN.

THIS MONDAY and Every Evening during
the Week at 7.30, Saturday at 7, "The
Laughter, Cheers, and Tears Provoker"—
"Daily Telegraph," June 2nd, 1887—

FRED COOKE,

In the New and Successful Irish Drama (First
Time in Belfast), Illustrative of Modern Life
in Ireland—

ON SHANNON'S SHORE;

OR, THE BLACKTHORN.

By FRED COOKE.

ENTIRELY NEW SCENERY.

On MONDAY NEXT, October 12th, 1896
(First Time in Belfast), the Phenomenal Success of the Century—

TRILBY.

Fig 18. 1895 Belfast Advertisement for *On Shannon's Shore* [*Northern Whig*/ Belfast City Library] One of several plays by English authors exploiting the vogue for bizarre Irish topics.

On Shannon's Shore, or, *The Blackthorn* by Frederick Cooke

On Shannon's Shore came out at the Prince's Theatre, Reading, on 14 February, 1895. It was first seen in Ireland on 12 August of the same year at the Queen's Theatre, Dublin; the following week it was at the Theatre Royal, Belfast. If ever a play was replete with 'exciting and amusing incidents' this is it: but there are far too many, leading the reader down false alleys from which it is hopeless to try and discern a return route. Granted, the theatre audience does not have time to ponder inconsistencies in the way a reader will, for the next piece of stage business is already in motion and new avenues and *culs-de-sac* are opening up.

Following the first Dublin showing the *Evening Telegraph* reported a confusing plot in which 'some of the scenes were very unreal and exaggerated ...'[181] Another harsh criticism was made in the *Irish News,* though for a different reason. The publicity announced that *On Shannon's Shore* was 'illustrative of modern life in Ireland'. This reviewer pointed out that

> many of the incidents belong to the traditions of past years. The Whiteboys are introduced somewhat prominently, and, as far as knowledge of present day affairs permits, there does not seem to be any revival of that order.[182]

This is a put-down: the author and company are being told that things are not like this in Ireland now, just in case they hadn't noticed.

Six years later the *Irish News* again worried this bone of contention when the same company gave *On Shannon's Shore* in Belfast. The advertising was still 'incorrectly' describing the piece as dealing with 'modern life'.[183]The little matter of English actors playing Irish parts was also adverted to: 'The Irish accent is apparently not considered an indispensible particular ...for it is noticeably absent'. In other words, Mr Cooke and his company were being told they were talking through their Sasanach hats.

The period is probably meant to be that of the agrarian disturbances of the last quarter of the nineteenth century. The location is Limerick city and county. The chief characters are Turlough O'Hanlon, a dodgy magistrate; Hyacinth O'Neale, a young gentleman in love with Norah O'Riordan, daughter of a publican, Brian O'Riordan; Barney na Boccaun, the O'Riordan's serving-man, on ticket-of-leave from jail for a crime he did not commit; Mary O'Shanahan, Barney's sister, 'wronged' by Turlough O'Hanlon; Gerald O'Neale, Hyacinth's uncle and guardian and a staunch supporter of law-and-order; and Shaun and Andy, members of a local illegal organization.

Turlough O'Hanlon will do anything to obtain the hand of Norah O'Riordan, the publican's lovely daughter. Shaun, a secret member of an illegal organization, informs O'Hanlon that the orphan Hyacinth O'Neale is also in love with Norah, but his guardian, Gerald O'Neale, is against the match. It transpires that Shaun and 'the boys' are planning to dispose of the same Gerald O'Neale that night in the Hag's Valley. O'Hanlon gives Shaun a sword with 'H.O'N.' engraved on the hilt: if this weapon is used, Hyacinth will be blamed and subsequently executed. Shaun will be well paid.

Gerald O'Neale advises his nephew Hyacinth not to set his heart on Norah but on one Oonah O'Malley: this match will repair the family fortunes. Norah and Hyacinth declare their love for each other. Uncle Gerald angrily accuses Hyacinth of being one of 'the boys' but Hyacinth states that he is merely in favour of 'bettering my poor neglected countrymen'; he deplores the 'misguided violence' of members of the illegal organization. Gerald receives a note with a skull and crossbones drawn on it but he dismisses the threat and declares that he'll have the perpetrators of all evil acts transported.

Norah's father, Brian O'Riordan, scolds her for shunning the advances of Turlough O'Hanlon; she reminds him that the same Turlough is a rake, and that he was responsible for the undoing of poor Mary, the sister of their serving man Barney. O'Hanlon arrives at the O'Riordan pub and is annoyed by Barney's attempt to put him off a visit by humorous sallies, hitting him with a stick. A tussle ensues, O'Hanlon calls Shaun who puts a stop to the affray with threats of what may happen to Barney.

On the road to the Hag's Valley, Gerald O'Neale thanks O'Hanlon for his company and will now press onward. He declares that his nephew Hyacinth is no longer beneath his roof. Hyacinth receives a message wrapped round a stone – it is from Barney, warning him that if he wants to save his uncle's life he must speed to the Hag's Valley, which he immediately does. Outside a hut in the valley Shaun and Andy are taking a drink as O'Hanlon arrives by boat. Mary, O'Hanlon's abandoned wife, appears, in reminiscent mood, informing the audience that she has been in foreign lands but has returned determined to expose O'Hanlon. 'You will not!', declares the latter, stepping from behind a rock and instructing Shaun to hold her captive. She seizes a pistol, shouting that she will frustrate the murder of Gerald O'Neale which she knows they have planned. Shaun fears her cries will be heard by O'Neale, who must be near.

Gerald arrives to find Shaun holding Mary and Mary clobbering Shaun. Shaun calls for Andy who emerges drunkenly from the hut and runs Gerald through with a sword – this is what was originally intended, for the sword has the 'H.O'N.' initials on it – but what was not intended was that Mary should be present as witness. Hyacinth arrives, having heard a cry, to find his uncle dead. He shouts for help. O'Hanlon enters and accuses Hyacinth of murder. A patrol arrives and is welcomed by O'Hanlon; Captain Clinton recognizes the corpse as that of Mr O'Neale, whom he was to meet here (it is not stated why). O'Hanlon accuses Hyacinth of murder, but the corpse stirs: Gerald O'Neale is not dead.

O'Hanlon claims that Hyacinth has a financial interest in his guardian's death, but the honourable English officer refuses to arrest him, having known him since boyhood. O'Hanlon, as magistrate, accuses Clinton of failure to do his duty, drawing his attention to Hyacinth's autographed sword. The Captain is then obliged to arrest his friend. However, Barney enters, brandishing the scabbard as proof that Hyacinth did not do the deed – the significance of this is obscure. O'Hanlon asks, 'But who will credit the oath of a ticket-of-leave man?' – 'I will', responds Clinton. Hyacinth declares that at trial he will exonerate himself. All exeunt, leaving Shaun, hiding in the hut, to proclaim that Hyacinth will hang for murder. 'For the murder you committed – not if my evidence can prove it!' declares Mary from the shadows.

The second act begins in an 'Oak Chamber' in O'Hanlon's house. O'Hanlon and Shaun expect that Hyacinth will be hanged for murder. Mary overhears that she will never be able to prove her marriage to O'Hanlon, an event which occurred in Switzerland. She confronts him with her marriage certificate, declaring, 'You have felt how Mary O'Shanaghan can love – now you shall feel how Mary O'Hanlon can hate!' – but O'Hanlon tears up the document and throws it in the grate, calling his servant Molly to light the fire. This the wily Molly does, but not before she has collected and pocketed the fragments. Mary leaves via the window. A shot is heard and O'Hanlon falls senseless – Mary has retained the pistol from the mountain hut: did she do it? (It is not explained.)

In the Officers' Room in Limerick Barracks it is learned that the boat carrying Gerald O'Neale sank without trace. Only a miracle will prevent Hyacinth from being found guilty of murder. Norah is announced to Captain Clinton by his batman Jerry – 'A hIrish hindividual is hanxious for a haudience' – and is surprised at how well she is received. She hopes that circumstantial evidence will be insufficient to have Hyacinth committed. The captain concurs, agreeing that Hyacinth should be allowed a visit from the priest of his own parish. O'Hanlon – evidently recovered from the shooting – is shown in, drunk, and disgusts Clinton by attempting to kiss his 'old friend' Norah.

Captain Clinton receives a note from the priest saying he can not come to the prisoner because his clothes have been stolen – 'What a strange impulsive people the Irish are!', he remarks, thinking no more about it. At the prison, Barney enters dressed as the priest and is admitted. Norah is heard singing outside, and Hyacinth kisses her through the bars. O'Hanlon arrives in the corridor with a sergeant, having obtained an order for Hyacinth to be moved to secure accommodation on Spike Island, but he agrees Hyacinth's removal should not take place until the priest has departed. The priest then emerges from the cell – but it is Hyacinth in the priest's clothes. O'Hanlon and the sergeant enter the cell and stumble over Barney, who jumps up, runs out and locks them in. Curtain.

Act III opens in a rocky pass, where Shaun appears to be digging a grave for the delirious Hyacinth. Barney arrives, knocks Shaun senseless and helps Hyacinth to escape. In another location at the entrance to a cave O'Hanlon appears with six followers and asks 'Judy' – who is Mary in disguise and whom he does not recognize – to admit them to the cave, which she apparently does. Shaun is there and pretends his wound is a result of a fall. Inside the cave, where Mary is in charge, Shaun explains that when Barney succeeded in rescuing Hyacinth from the prison cell he put him on an American schooner, but the ship was driven on the rocks in a storm, and Hyacinth was found on the shore. Enquires O'Hanlon: 'And of course you put him comfortably to bed?' Replies Shaun: 'We did. With a shovel.'

Mary accuses Shaun of murdering Gerald. She denounces O'Hanlon, removes her disguise and proclaims that she is his wife. Shots are fired. Hyacinth rushes in and also denounces O'Hanlon, before making a speech in which he calls for honesty in all dealings, thanking 'that same Providence that saved me from the scaffold and also rescued me from a living grave'.

Time has passed before the opening of Act IV. Hyacinth O'Neale has been abroad, an outlaw with a price on his head, but he returns to see 'his Norah'. In a tactfully comic speech Barney informs Hyacinth of Norah's forthcoming marriage to O'Hanlon. Hyacinth is devastated and vows to kill O'Hanlon. Norah's father has heard the story of Mary O'Hanlon, but has dismissed it. A sergeant arrives in search of Hyacinth, for his return has been rumoured. Barney holds the sergeant in humorous blather to give Hyacinth time to get away.

There is a large attendance for the wedding of Norah and O'Hanlon in 'an old chapel'. Mary is among the crowd. The ceremony is performed. Then Mary sees Hyacinth observing the proceedings and urges him to 'claim his promised bride'. As the procession starts to leave the chapel Mary denounces O'Hanlon, stating that she is his wife. He replies that she has no proof. Mary produces the remnants of her marriage certificate. Constables arrive to arrest Hyacinth. Captain Clinton follows, and enquires upon what authority the arrest is being made? – the warrant for the arrest of the murderer of Gerald O'Neale, of course! – but Gerald O'Neale suddenly appears, having been saved from drowning! Gerald blesses Hyacinth and Norah. Shaun decides to turn Queen's evidence if need be. O'Hanlon collapses and is ignominiously removed in a wheelbarrow.

It is significant that *On Shannon's Shore* only played a total of three weeks in Ireland in the decade 1895-1904, though it was regularly on tour in the rest of the British Isles.[184]

The Rebel's Wife, or, *A True Irish Heart*; also known as *The Patriot's Wife* by Frederick Jarman

Frederick Jarman wrote twenty-two plays that are listed by Allardyce Nicoll; this is the only one with an Irish title. When playing in Britain it was advertised as *The Rebel's Wife*, in Ireland as *The Patriot's Wife*. The somewhat shadowy leading character is Myles Byrne, 'a young Irish patriot'; the inspiration must have come from the very real figure of Myles Byrne (1780-1862) who at the age of eighteen commanded the pikemen at the battles of Arklow and Vinegar Hill, subsequently emigrating to France. His *Mémoires* were published in Paris in 1853. The Myles Byrne of this play does not possess anything like the articulate authority of his historical namesake – in fact, the true hero of the play is Andy McGuinness, a boy soldier who is probably the author's invention.

The manuscript in the Lord Chamberlain's Collection is exceptionally difficult to read. The following description is therefore rudimentary and at times conjectural, but it is included here because the play has some moments of real pathos and some of the comic dialogue is unusually rich.

Shamus Byrne bemoans the absence of news of his son Myles, who may have died in battle, though Barney McGuinness reports that 'the boys' are driving 'the dirty Yeos into the say'. Jacob Daly takes note of any treasonable ejaculations such as 'God save the patriot army!'. Shamus tells Jacob he should 'go to the dairy, where you'd curdle the milk with your sour face'. Barney's young grandson,

Andy, reports that the English have surrounded the camp. The remainder of the action is influenced by the defeat at Vinegar Hill and Myles Byrne's fugitive existence. Myles was formerly an officer in George III's army so is officially a deserter. He is captured, court-martialled and sentenced to death. A kindly British officer, Major Fitzgerald, gives mitigating evidence, but Myles is sentenced to death. Myles marries his childhood sweetheart Kathleen McGrath in prison. He subsequently manages to escape due to the ingenuity of young Andy. Myles is secret witness to the murder of his father by his 'treacherous enemy' Captain Hunter Gowan, a local landlord, but is powerless to do anything.

Myles Byrne leaves for France, following an affecting parting scene with Kathleen; her devotion has kept him alive and in touch while on the run. He will return when the dust has settled, so to speak. It appears that Gowan has every reason to wish Myles dead, for he is a relative and should inherit the Byrne farmstead in the event of Myles' death, but now Myles' bride will inherit so Gowan insinuates himself upon her – with no success. Andy McGuinness, 'a real chip of the rebel brood' as Gowan angrily describes him, is himself a kind of spy; he keeps watch on the activities of Captain Hunter Gowan and Jacob Daly. He has a way of deliberately annoying Gowan by singing 'The Boys of Wexford' any time the latter approaches. Byrne's associates are seen by Gowan as 'infernal traitors'; 'No sir,' says Andy, 'it's no relations of *yours*, but Father Currin'; 'Oh, that cursed papist!'; 'Yes sir, the papist who saved the Protestants of Wexford Bridge.' Sardonic exchanges of this kind keep what seems to be a turgid story going, while at the same time enhancing the play's patriotic drive.

A boat is expected bringing Shamus with French support (presumably to restart the insurrection). Kathleen is so uneasy she is unable to eat. There is no substantial news of Shamus, and young Andy is also absent on some mission connected with the revival of the fighting spirit. Fitzgerald has news that Myles is nearby but was surprised by Gowan; however, he was helped to escape by 'a lad' (Andy) and in doing so they killed an English soldier – a further crime on Myles' head. Myles and Andy appear, the former splendidly arrayed in a green uniform. Andy describes what happened to the English soldier; 'I didn't mean to kill him quite dead, but he struck me wid his sword ... and then somehow he got mixed up with my pike and he died!' Soldiers arrive; Myles and Andy hide in a rick of turf. Kathleen pretends to have been asleep in bed and has seen no sign of her husband. Gowan states that a man and a boy have definitely been seen. The soldiers stick their bayonets in the turf and exeunt. Myles is safe, but Andy has been pierced. 'Mine was only a little Irish heart, but it was true,' he whispers as he expires. Myles and Kathleen subsequently decide to go to France. 'May the memory of your love and devotion, little Andy, bring happiness to the Rebel and his Wife'. (Presumably in the version played in Ireland the final line was 'the Patriot and his Wife'.)

After such a cursory reading it would be unfair to denigrate this play unduly, but it does seem to creak at all its hinges save those of comic exchanges that help to promote the rebel/patriotic theme. What is very interesting indeed is its apparent out-and-out nationalistic stance, especially coming from an English author for performance on the extensive British circuit. *The Era* reviewed *The Rebel's Wife* when it was presented at the Royal West London Theatre, Marylebone: this critic was completely won over by the element which he refers to as 'patriotic', meaning 'patriotic Irish'. He also noted that 'as the informer, Mr Edward Rainer (as Jacob Daly) stirs the feelings of the spy-hating gallery and pit', demonstrating that this section of the London audience was so much on the side of what the dramatist was presenting it did not matter that they were booing the English and cheering the Irish.[185]

What can be read of this play serves to demonstrate that there was a discernable vogue in the West End and British provinces for plays with an Irish setting; in this Jarman was simply following a fashion.[186] At a very early stage one notes the similarity of the topic of the fugitive '98 insurgent to Whitbread's *The Insurgent Chief* – Whitbread may well have taken some points from this work. The kindly British officer, Major Fitzgerald, is generically allied to Whitbread's Captain Airlie in the same play.

In Dublin, Frank Fay saw *The Patriot's Wife* in 1900 when it was at the Queen's. In his regular article he dismissed it as 'this concoction'; it was 'one of the worst I have ever seen, and much of the acting is too wicked for words'.[187] In complete and therefore rather startling contrast, Joseph Holloway found it 'most exciting, interesting and stirring'. Holloway, of course, was interested in an enjoyable night out, while Fay was concerned with dramaturgical issues and with the projection of Irish nationality on the stage. Holloway was relieved, however, that the English cast did not attempt Irish accents. He enjoyed the 'sweet tuneful rendering of

The Boys of Wexford which apparently took the audience's fancy, as 'they joined in the choruses with a will' – it is unlikely that this had happened outside Ireland and the visiting players must have been impressed by the public participation.

The Shamrock and the Rose by **Walter Reynolds**

Walter Reynolds wrote at least nine plays, one other of which has an Irish title, *Sweet Innisfail* (Huddersfield, 1891)[189]. It was not seen in Ireland during the period under review, if at all. It is perplexing to find references in the dialogue of *The Shamrock and the Rose* which suggest that it may have been inspired by the prose fiction of William Carleton, but searches through Carleton's works and Barbara Hayley's remarkable bibliography do not disclose a story containing the same characters. Carleton's fictional town of Findramore (an amalgamation of Fintona and Dromore, Co Tyrone) is the location.[190] There is also mention of the actual town of Carrickmacross, which features in several of Carleton's *Traits and Stories* (1830). The tone of the play, however, lacks anything of Carleton's gift for hard-edged realism laced with the kind of humorously pragmatic utterance by means of which the peasants express, and in expressing conceal, their true opinions.

The Shamrock and the Rose is a genuine barnstorming melodrama of the 'murder in the red barn' variety set in the Irish rather than the English countryside. We must assume that the author chose an Irish locality because of the vogue for plays set in so remote and bizarre a land. It is a very long play, replete with dialogue that can only be described as blather – each sequence could fulfil its function with half the number of words. *The Era* was able to state that between the play's first showing in Huddersfield and its arrival at the Grand Theatre in London, 'sundry excesses have been lopped off and the piece has been strengthened in many places'.[191] Frustratingly, these changes were not identified. In spite of the evident professionalism of the writing, the text in the Lord Chamberlain's Plays carries an excessive load of comicalities – such as Dandy Dunraven and his accomplices stealing the uniforms of the drunken policemen and confronting the villain, a device used to better effect by Whitbread in *The Irishman* only two years before.

When presented at the Grand Opera House, Belfast, in March 1896, none of the four city dailies gave anything like a full description of the production, but the advertising stated that it had already achieved over 2,500 performances in Britain and so it must have been as 'gloriously successful' as the publicity claimed. When Joseph Holloway saw it fifteen months later at the Queen's in Dublin he found much of it 'too grotesque for anything,' adding in his humorous mixed-metaphor manner that 'an English company in Irish drama is like a fish out of water, and never open their mouth but they put their foot in it – without their "brogue" on unfortunately – and make a hash of the Irish dialect.'[192]

The heroine is Rose Riversdale, an English orphan who lives with her uncle and guardian, Dr Riversdale, attended by their garrulous housekeeper Peggy Rafferty, at Lindisfarne House, probably in south Ulster. Johnny Desmond, a tenant farmer, is in love with Rose – although acutely lacking in personality, he is, in effect, the hero. There is an English visitor called Fitzwilliam. Dandy Dunraven ('a broth of a boy') is courting a traduced woman called Morna Moore. On the less than reputable side are Mixy Mulchahy, a 'Mergency Man;[193] Nicholas Flint, a process server; and his son Stephen, a government spy.

At the rise of curtain we learn that there is much lawlessness in the neighbourhood due to the absence, in London, of the local landlord. Mixy Mulchahy calls on Dr Riversdale to be present to certify an eviction ordained by Nicholas Flint. Flint appears and is coolly received by Rose who deplores evictions – he enquires how her 'pretty head can be so full of prejudice' against him. He insinuates that his position as magistrate could influence the authorities against her uncle continuing to hold the position of dispensary doctor. He then admonishes the doctor for hiding food in a creel of turf for one of the dispossessed – 'encouraging pauperism'. Flint suggests that Rose would make a good match for his son Stephen – a union which Dr Riversdale can not countenance.

Rose is outraged when her uncle tells her of Flint's impertinent suggestion. Dr Riversdale is not entirely sure that her interest in Johnny Desmond, a well known member of an agrarian reform league, is for the best, but his principal concern is for Rose's happiness 'in these perilous times'. Desmond brings a gift of shamrock for Rose, for it is St Patrick's Day.

In the second act Dandy Dunraven's beloved Morna Moore is tricked into marriage by Stephen Flint, her expectation being that as a result her mother will not be evicted – but she is evicted and dies shortly afterwards. The Flints cheat Dandy of his holding and he is reduced to penury. In a nocturnal clifftop incident Nicholas Flint is murdered – it is assumed the deed was done by Desmond and members of the No Mercy League. Rose conceals Desmond, but he is discovered, arrested and imprisoned. The intrepid Dandy successfully organizes his escape.

In the third act Stephen Flint informs Morna that their marriage was not legal. Distracted – for she sees herself as a 'dishonoured woman' – she flees from the neighbourhood but Dandy seeks and finds her and leads her to the old waterside mill where he is at present lodging. He tells her that 'the father of the man who cheated you has been murdered', adding that in spite of the darkness he managed to hit the murderer with a spade, so he should be identified by a scar. Examining Morna's 'marriage lines' Dandy notices something remarkable and so he sets off to find the priest who allegedly married Morna to Stephen Flint. Stephen, suspecting Morna may have been given refuge in the mill, approaches with Mixy Mulchahy. He finds Morna and expresses 'sorrow and remorse' and will now marry her: she scornfully declares there is no need, for she is his wife! – to which he responds that the priest was an impostor. She shows him letters he addressed to her as his wife. In the act of violently snatching the letters his hat falls off, revealing a deep scar. Morna screams that he is a parricide, to which he replies that he will now have to kill her. There is a fearsome struggle which Mixy hears; he rushes in, striking Morna as she falls. The two men realize that they 'will hang for this' and so place Morna's body in a chest while they go in search of a boat in which to remove her. Dandy returns to hear Morna's moans. As her assailants are returning he joins Morna in the chest. Stephen has secured a boat and the chest is lowered into it my means of a winch. 'Now open it and pitch her out!', cries Stephen; but Dandy jumps forth and knocks Stephen and Mixy into the mill race.

In the fourth and final act Dandy tells Rose that Desmond is safe in a cave. Stephen and Mixy – apparently none the worse for their wetting – overhear. Peggy, the Lindisfarne housekeeper, is distraught because an English visitor, Fitzwilliam, whom she fancies, has been removed by police on mistaken suspicion of spying. He is quickly released and returns to bewail his Irish adventures in a comic scene. Desmond suddenly arrives, followed by 'the whole British army!' – four soldiers who are searching for him who are kept at bay by the humorous Dandy while Desmond makes himself scarce.

Mixy Mulchahy is aware that Dandy will be required to tell all he knows about the murder and gives him money to keep silent and also to reveal Desmond's hiding place. Dandy takes the purse and makes off; as two constables attempt to catch him the two halves of his tail coat split and he escapes.

Desmond conducts a highly proper love scene with Rose. Stephen arrives with police but dismisses them when he notices that Rose is in the house. He warns her that she may be arrested for concealing a felon, promising her that this will not happen provided she grants him certain favours. She reacts angrily. He summons the policemen, Desmond is called forth, but the 'police' fail to arrest him for they are Dandy and friends in stolen uniforms.

Before a lawyer, Stephen declares that Desmond had quarrelled with his father and his coat was found at the scene of the murder. Dandy relates his story of having hit a man in the dark: Stephen bears a mark on his head which he dismisses as a bite from a dog – but Dandy has further evidence: Nicholas Flint walks in! Stephen is therefore an attempted parricide; but it also emerges that he did kill someone in the darkness, an unfortunate local man who was escaping from the police dressed in Nicholas' clothing. Dandy then accuses Stephen of the attempted murder of his wife, Morna – who now appears, accompanied by a (real) priest. Stephen Flint is arrested, and the play is drawn to a close with predictable explanations. England and Ireland both have 'something to forgive', says Desmond; 'And to forget', adds Fitzwilliam. Dandy has the final words: 'True for you, Mr Englishman, for the time has come when all our differences will be ended by the union of ...' – 'The hands', says Fitzwilliam, taking Peggy's; 'And the hearts', says Desmond, taking Rose's; 'Of the Shamrock and the Rose!', concludes Dandy, embracing Morna. Curtain.

(2) Plays of American provenance.

In the teeming theatre programmes offered to the Irish public at the turn of the twentieth century plays with an American background are not unexpected. They range from frequent revivals of Boucicault's *The Octoroon, or, Life in Louisiana* (first produced in 1859) to innumerable adaptations of Harriet Beecher Stowe's *Uncle Tom's Cabin* (first published in 1852) usually mounted by London managements. What has been unexpected – though it should not have been – are contemporary plays that might be described as 'Hiberno-American', a repertoire now totally forgotten in Ireland and possibly in the United States as well.

During the decade under review five such plays were given in Ireland. They were: *My Native Land* by William Manning, *McKenna's Flirtation* by Edgar Selden, *Our Irish Visitors* by Thomas E. Murray, *Muldoon's Pic Nic* by Harry Pleon, and *Dear Hearts of Ireland* by Myles McCarthy. They range from the mawkishly nostalgic to the amusingly optimistic. *McKenna's Flirtation* is by far the most interesting for it gives a remarkably detached and entertaining picture of life in an upwardly mobile Irish community in New York City.

My Native Land by William Manning

This play is described in the *Stage Cyclopaedia* as 'Anglo-American', rather than 'Hiberno-American'.[194] Manning was almost certainly of English extraction. The earliest performance found was at the New Bowery Theatre, New York, in 1865. It appeared on tour at the Theatre Royal, Belfast, in the week starting 22 December, 1895. The setting is a rural landscape in Ireland and the streets of a city in the United States.

It is curious that *My Native Land* was only given for one week in Ireland during the period under review while it was widely seen and presumably applauded in the United States and Britain, for it is no worse than several of the other more frequently performed plays of Irish content. One would like to think that this was on account of the superior intelligence of the Irish managements and audiences – but it is much more likely to have been due to touring logistics. The play can best be described as 'uneven'. Most of it is standard melodrama, with genuinely suspenseful moments paralleled by an assemblage of customary improbabilities – such as almost the entire Irish population of the play happening to meet within minutes in an American city. Its unevenness is compounded by the fact that the last act is almost entirely written as farce – with impersonations, mistaken identities and people appearing from nowhere at comically inopportune moments – all very well in the farcical context, but the audience is expected to keep in mind that the central and serious issue is that these people are exchanging a lifetime of oppression in Ireland for a future of liberty in America.

The Blakes – Andy, Winnie and their ailing daughter Nannie – are almost destitute, and are considering emigration to America. The landlord, Mr Cunningham, is pressing for the rent through his agent, Norry Boyle. Andy believes Norry will do anything to destroy him because they were both suitors for the hand of Winnie. Myra

Pyne, an American visitor at the Cunningham mansion, is troubled by the Blake family's plight. She has inherited a fortune from her late father who specified that she should marry young Eardley Cunningham but only 'if she finds him worthy'. On a country walk she encounters the intensely humanitarian Dr Magee who has just come from attending to Nannie Blake. Myra and Dr Blake between them have ready cash which they press on Andy Blake, but Norry Boyle observes this charitable act and steals the money from the Blake's cabin – Andy, therefore, is unable to pay the rent and constables remove him to jail where Nannie stays with him though Winnie remains at home. Both Eardley Cunningham and Norry Boyle have designs upon her person. When Eardley hears that Dr Magee and Myra Pyne have colluded to help the Blakes he realizes that he may have a rival in the good doctor; this is most alarming for him as he needs to marry Myra in order to pay his gambling debts.

The plot is highly circumstantial, but beneath its twists and complications there are characters of flesh and blood with real emotions and anxieties. The story continues with Eardley interviewing Winnie, whom Norry has urged to seek a position on the domestic staff of the Big House; she is hired, but once installed finds herself helpless from Eardley's advances. She accuses Norry of setting her up but he laughs and locks her into her room. Myra hears her screams and releases her, telling her that Dr Magee has gone to bail out her husband. Myra borrows Winnie's cloak; when Eardley returns and approaches 'Winnie' she discloses herself, regards him haughtily and exits with meaningful dignity.

Andy Blake is released with Dr Magee's help but when he discovers that Eardley Cunningham has been tormenting his wife he gives him a thrashing and is again arrested. A charge of assault is brought by Eardley in a court presided over by Eardley's father. Dr Magee and Myra Pyne give evidence of gross provocation in support of Andy and the case is dismissed; the elder Cunningham declares that Eardley has brought disgrace upon their house. Eardley attempts a reconciliation with Myra for he desperately needs what her marriage portion will bring, but she dismisses him. He produces a pistol which she knocks from his hand. Andy rushes in and takes Eardley by the throat but the gun goes off and Eardley falls. Constables appear and seize Andy, but Myra, ever in control, pronounces that Eardley committed suicide.

While lodging in a refuge provided by Myra Pyne the Blakes receive a letter from the lawyer of the late 'Uncle Murphy' in the

United States containing bank notes that will cover their passage. The exhausted Andy does not believe he will live to see the day when they will escape from their present situation and falls in a swoon. Fortunately the kindly Dr Magee is at hand. Norry Boyle, who observes everything, enters the cabin unseen and again steals the Blakes' money. The doctor forces cash upon Andy and urges him to leave for America before he is arrested for firing at Eardley. He will look after his wife and daughter and see that they follow later. An elderly peasant comes to the cabin seeking food but expires within minutes – 'The oppressor's heel has stamped on him!' declares the departing Andy. Norry arrives ahead of the ubiquitous constables, observes the corpse and, assuming it to be Andy's, departs. The audience sees Andy kissing his wife farewell 'at the back'.

The final scenes take place in an undisclosed American city. Norry Boyle has arrived, personating Andy Blake before Uncle Murphy's lawyer, Mr Stebbing. Norry's moneylending accomplice Moses Solomons comes from Ireland to tell Norry that Mr Cunningham has become aware of his frauds and has sent Moses to identify him in the US courts – but Moses will rather befriend him for a share in the Murphy estate. Moses informs Norry that Andy is not dead and may be in America, and that his wife and daughter are probably on their way. Legal difficulties arise with identification. It is decided that Moses' wife Rebecca will impersonate Winnie. Rebecca does not play the part to perfection, becoming confused and supposing she is pretending to be Mr Stebbing's wife. Mr Stebbing is embarrassed and suspicious.

When Winnie and Nannie arrive from Ireland they are horrified to see Norry. Winnie observes an angry confrontation between Norry and Moses in a bar. The scene is punctuated by the comings and goings of a barman called Pompy (presumably black) who keeps repeating the line 'There's something wrong somewhere!' to comic effect. Winnie steps forward and informs Norry and Moses that she is going for the police, but Norry makes a heartfelt plea for forgiveness, promising an end to her suffering if – in a ruse which he says is designed to save Andy – she will only swear that she is Norry's wife. Winnie foolishly agrees. Mr Stebbing seeks testimony from 'Norry's wife', but he has posted two detectives nearby. Winnie is about to declare that Norry is 'Mr Andy Blake' when – in the nick of time – Andy appears. Winnie faints. There are the predictable disclosures, resulting in extradition orders for Norry and Moses. The play ends with Winnie overcome that Andy is finally safe and their troubles are at an end. 'Yes, darling,' says he, 'beneath the American flag I shall find that sympathetic freedom which is denied me in my native land!'

Except for Myra Pyne, most of the characters are conventional even if their motivations are genuinely absorbing. Myra is a person who is prepared to take matters into her own hands: it might not be wholly incongruous to make a case for her as a cousin of the Ibsenite new woman. Unfortunately she disappears from the story when the action moves across the Atlantic – one assumes she stays in Ireland to marry the philanthropic Dr Magee. One sympathizes entirely with the tribulations endured by the Blake family, impotent at the mercy of every kind of crooked manipulator, but their misfortunes fall so thickly that (at least as a reader) one longs for them to succumb without further ado or else triumph – but in either case quickly and be done with it.

The Irish News, in a carefully non-committal review in which the actors were praised, felt that the comic element in the last act was 'not too far-fetched to deserve the verdict of grotesque' but that the play was 'in some ways a travesty of the Irish character'.[195] One is tempted to wonder if the piece might not have been written as a pastiche of every Irish play ever presented, *à la* Martin McDonagh a century later. The best scene is one in which Eardley and Norry taunt the hapless Winnie, who is the prisoner of the former and a possible sexual plaything of the latter. This scene is tinged with a high degree of sadistic eroticism and was presumably played with that in mind.

The American component is a disappointment. The subject of emigration as a solution is not developed in the early scenes and only when the unexpected *epistola-ex-machina* arrives from Uncle Murphy's lawyer does the possibility of escape from the dire regime seriously present itself. The farcical scenes in the American lawyer's office and the bar do nothing to assist the drama. There are only two lines of any resonance that relate to the American *motif* – the final line, already quoted, and a remark of Myra's to the effect that 'the poor exiles of Erin are the pillars of the stars and stripes!'.

McKenna's Flirtation by Edgar Selden

The earliest performance found was at the Amplion Theater, New York City, on 7 May, 1888, but it may have appeared elsewhere earlier. It was produced in Britain by the Edwin Garth-George Bates partnership who toured it from 1892 until at least 1898. It was at the

Theatre Royal, Belfast, for one week each in 1895 and 1898. The setting is the interior and exterior of the McKenna Flats, a new housing development in Harlem, in the Ryan mansion nearby, and in the Pleasure Park on the East River. Timothy McKenna I is a widowed building contractor whose son, Timothy II, is in love with Mary Ellen Ryan II, daughter of a retired milk supplier, Michael Ryan, and his wife Mary Ellen I who is described as 'a victim of Circumstances'. Greenleaf Blackstone Kent is 'a shyster lawyer' and Willet Chase is 'a society chappie'. The McKenna home is looked after by Anastasia McGovern, Timothy I's sister-in law. There are four other ladies – Marmie Fogarty, Maggie Casey, Sadie Monohan and Annie O'Brien: the names of the entire cast tell us a great deal.

This is a light comedy with a mildly satirical element laced with musical interludes set in an Irish urban enclave. 'Ireland' is hardly mentioned; nor are 'traditional' Irish themes such as emigration/immigration, Roman Catholicism, working-class poverty; there is definitely no tearful backward look to the valley of Sliabh na mBan. If any members of the older generation in the play contributed to the Fenian movement it is not mentioned here. These people have done well; they can relax with people from other cultures such as Willet Chase (who is probably a WASP and indeed may be a future founder of the Chase-Manhattan Bank). None of the songs rendered at a party in the Ryan home is Irish but seem to be popular American ballads of the day – 'When our dinner-hour comes round' or 'Kate's Sweetheart'.

As to language, however, the middle and older generation employ 'Irishisms' extensively. A line like the misogynistic Ryan's '... it is the clattering tongue of woman that sent thousands of men dangling between heaven and earth at the end of a rope' has a rhythmic intensity not unknown in conventional Irish playwrighting. Patrick McQuirk, a hod carrier, indulges in verbal convolutions suggesting that English is his second language – 'He'll be back in a while ago agin!' Malapropisms and mispronunciations abound as freely as in any play by an Irish author from Sheridan to O'Casey – such as Aunt Anastasia's grand response when being shown over the new Ryan mansion – 'The aquarium is simply magnolius!'

The picture which Selden gives of the 'lace curtain Irish' – he would not have known the term – must be, one feels, entirely accurate. These are people who have raised themselves up through hard work and (no doubt) hard graft and who have established themselves in an expanding commercial and entrepreneurial world.

McKenna is constructing apartment blocks, not working as a navvy. Ryan has built up a milk distribution business, an important service industry in a growing metropolitan area. The new home into which he has just moved is not a cold-water flat in the Bronx but undoubtedly one of those spaciously porched and ostentatiously pinnacled houses that are now so greatly admired by historians of American vernacular. The older ladies are intensely snobbish in the manner of those who have climbed into a new social milieu; a neighbour, Mrs O'Donnell, admits that she 'may not be Mrs Langtry' though she 'might be!' It will be at least another two generations before they can marry into the New England meritocracy and produce a President of the United States.

It is the characterization and the depiction of the social background that places *McKenna's Flirtation* above the normal run of popular plays of the period. The plot is entirely inconsequential and hangs upon the delivery, loss and reading of letters designed for other people – there is much confusion between the McKennas, father and son, who are both called Timothy, and the Ryans, mother and daughter, who are both called Mary Ellen . Much comedy is extracted from the relationship between the two older men – McKenna and Ryan; they are buddies but their friendship is based on continual bickering on subjects from cigars to economics. Ryan is in mental turmoil because he suspects his wife is 'all dressed up' in order 'to stagger McKenna' though in fact she is doing nothing of the kind. When he unburdens himself of his domestic woes to the spinster Anastasia McGovern she believes he is propositioning her – she is vexed and informs Ryan's wife which causes endless misapprehensions. Mary Ellen II flirts obtrusively with the effete Willet Chase in order to pay back what she believes is the disloyalty of Timothy McKenna II. At a grand party in the Ryan's new house there is much drinking, dancing and singing – four of the lady guests are clearly in the play as a hired quartet. Having taken too much drink Ryan challenges McKenna to a duel. This will take place next day in the park but they are too embarrassed when the time comes to drop the challenge and so a comic duel that nobody wants – like that of Sir Andrew Aguecheek and Viola in *Twelfth Night* – ends in pandemonium when McKenna deliberately tumbles into the lake. Ryan is sought for murder by the 'State Coroner' who is actually a vexed McKenna in disguise. In the confusion the nature of the misdelivered letters is gradually and satisfactorily explained. All engage in 'an old-fashioned cushion dance'.

The songs and dances probably pleased the audience more than the play for it is in the light of hindsight that one discerns ethnic, social and period subtleties. *The Belfast News-Letter* reported that:

> *McKenna's Flirtation* is of the nature of a general entertainment without much pretension save to raise a laugh and enable a summer hour or two to be spent without the trouble of being required to do any thinking ...[196]

The *Northern Whig* took the play rather more seriously, its reviewer placing it as 'an intermediary course in a superior menu', the 'intermediary' lying between 'cup-and-saucer comedy' and 'burlesque'. In this respect, 'Edgar Selden requires no apology'. The *Whig* went on to say that the company responsible 'left nothing to be desired', praising the acting, singing and stage presentation.[197] It is a pity that Belfast did not have a Joseph Holloway to consign his private views to a journal.

Our Irish Visitors by Thomas E. Murray

Described as 'The American Musical Farcical Comedy constructed for laughing only', *Our Irish Visitors* was given twice in Ireland during the period under review, in the week starting 13 May, 1899, at the Cork Opera House and at the Theatre Royal, Belfast, in the week of 29 July in the same year. The earliest record found was of a production at Miner's Theater, New York, in October 1883.

As will be seen, there is a remarkable similarity between this play and *Muldoon's Pic Nic*. Neither has anything approaching a strong story line, and motifs which one might expect to be developed are forgotten – for example, the 'theatricals' which the ladies are so excited about are never performed (unless they are part of one of the unspecified 'speciality acts'). Both these plays are made up of a series of burlesque sketches interspersed with musical numbers, and both leave a great deal to what is 'to be worked out in rehearsal'. They are closer to vaudeville than to any strict form of drama, such as farce. *McKenna's Flirtation*, by contrast, is a well structured play.

There is a curious sharing of incident between these three plays in that all contain near-drownings and the two older male characters, McGinnis and Gilhooly, in each are pals who spend much time in argument and exaggerated bouts of violence. All three also share a social-climbing element, and the importance of education as a means towards social and commercial success is stressed. This *motif* is strongest in *Our Irish Visitors* where language plays a significant, and at times hilarious, part. Mrs

McGinnis remarks of Arabella that 'the eddication she has would paralyse yeh!'. Both McGinnis girls have been to Vassar College where they have learned to speak nicely: 'Every one of them big words,' declares their mother, 'cost their father ten dollars apiece!' McGinnis is never quite sure of the name of the college to which he has sent his daughters at such formidable cost, referring to it on different occasions as 'See Saw' and 'Vaseline'. Using one of the big words she has learnt there one of the girls remarks 'I came here with celerity' – her father explains 'that must be some friend she met at Warsaw College'. When relating an incident, Arabella uses the term 'incongruity', upon which Gilhooley immediately states in an aside 'That must have cost thirty dollars'.

Act I. In the Gilhooley Guest House it is Mrs Gilhooley and the maid Dorothy who keep the place going: Colonel Gilhooley inclines towards the bottle and their daughter Sally puts on airs – complaining that her breakfast of 'pork and hominy' is not suited to a lord's daughter: for there is a tradition that they are descended from Irish aristocrats. While her mother goes to chase a cow out of her flowerbed, Sally and the handyman Fritz do a 'speciality' (ie song and dance act) in which Dorothy joins, for she once worked in show business and hopes to return to that *milieu*. Fritz, the Dutch handyman, is keen on Dorothy. He has difficulties with English and it is only after much trying that he manages to pass on the message that a party of five adults and two babies are on their way. The visitors are Jeremiah McGinnis, a New York alderman, his wife, two daughters, Arabella and Cinderella, two babies and a friend called Sammy Tupper. Colonel Gilhooley recalls that 'the Gilhooleys came to America first class. McGinnis was sent over as ballast.' The two men question each other about their army careers, with slights on both sides. It is clear that neither served in any army. While Mr and Mrs McGinnis are settling in, the lively Sammy Tupper arrives with the two McGinnis daughters. Fritz announces that the circus is in town and a bear has escaped. Arrangements for dinner are made. Where is McGinnis? – he is dragged on by the seat of his pants by – the bear! Curtain.

Act II. Cinderella McGinnis plays the piano to which Sally performs a dance. Arabella McGinnis complains that in this remote place there is no one to flirt with. Sally announces that she and Dorothy are organizing some theatricals: the ladies of all ages will be required as coryphées. The older ladies go to dress while the girls engage in a 'Double Speciality' followed by a ballad from Arabella.

Then Colonel Gilhooley, McGinnis, Fritz and Sammy do a mock ballet, with a Highland Fling as an encore. A 'Yankee salesman' called Salem arrives; he figures these people must be loaded with money. He mistakes Gilhooley for McGinnis: he has a plan to get more votes for McGinnis, for a consideration. He then asks Gilhooley for change of $10 – but Gilhooley sees the bill is counterfeit and when he proves this to the Yankee the latter nonchalantly suggests that he pay for his lodgings with it – still not realizing that he's talking to the landlord. Gilhooley throws Salem out of the window, takes his wallet from his coat and throws that after him. Mrs McGinnis comes in and she and Gilhooley indulge in a little flirting. He admires her dress, but says she'd look wonderful in red. She leaves to change into red. McGinnis hears of this and enters with a red dress and bonnet, which he puts on over his own clothes. Gilhooley returns and 'makes love' to the supposed 'Mary Ann McGinnis'. A lengthy dialogue follows, full of ambiguous remarks. When Gilhooley realizes that he has been fooled he challenges McGinnis to a duel. 'Pistols!' says McGinnis. 'Cannons!' says Gilhooley, but they shoot at each other with pistols. When McGinnis falls, Gilhooley believes he has killed him and hides in the chimney. Fritz rushes in, pursued by Salem on another money-tendering racket, and also hides in the chimney. Gilhooley fires a shot in the chimney. The ladies rush in in a fright. There is 'a tableau to be explained at rehearsal'. Ultimately one discerns that those in the chimney climbed out by the roof, for they later re-enter in bathing costumes, describing how McGinnis was escaping by boat, Gilhooley fired at it, McGinnis tumbled out and Fritz saved him from drowning. 'Then follow specialities'. Drinking together, Gilhooley and McGinnis become bosom buddies. Gilhooley admits that he is not descended from lords, but McGinnis knew that anyway. There is a 'medley', followed by a quadrille.

The critic of the *Cork Constitution* felt that *Our Irish Visitors* 'might close in the middle or begin at the end as far as consistency and story are concerned'.[198] The *Northern Whig* was in general agreement:

> *Our Irish Visitors* cannot be criticized from the ordinary standpoint of dramatic representations. It is exactly as the bill announces it – a miscellaneous combination of farce and music ...[199]

On the topic of 'Irishness', the *Constitution* goes on to state somewhat pedantically that 'it is built somewhat after *Muldoon's Pic*

Nic ... hugely enjoyed in America, and even in this country where playgoers do not appear to be able to see that they are laughing at what is generally a gross caricature of the mannerisms or eccentricities of their race ...'

In spite of the declared Irish ancestry of the characters and the use of Irish colloquialisms by some of them, these are American plays that expose a particular section of Americanized society. A review in the *Irish News* refers to *Our Irish Visitors* as 'an American musical farce', praising the use of 'several pleasant American melodies'. It is from this notice that one learns that the author took the leading role of Colonel Gilhooley, and that unlike the majority of 'Transatlantic' plays it was not mounted by a London management but was the genuine New York product.[200]

Muldoon's Pic Nic by Harry Pleon

The earliest performance found was at Pastor's Theater, New York, on 1 May, 1879. Authorship is in doubt. Harry Pleon was a theatrical entrepreneur who is credited as having 'arranged and produced' *Muldoon's Pic Nic*, which most resembles an extended music-hall sketch the content of which – like *Our Irish Visitors* – certainly changed from tour to tour depending upon what speciality and musical items were available to pad it out. It was approved by the British censor in 1886, and so great was its popularity there were at one time three productions on tour simultaneously throughout the British Isles. Between 1897 and 1901 it was seen five times in Belfast, three times at the Theatre Royal and once each at the Alhambra and the Grand Opera House. .

The only threads which hold *Muldoon's Pic Nic* together as a play are the preparations for the pic-nic and the romantic love interest between Kitty Muldoon and her gentleman caller, Augustus (who is not accorded a second name). Socially, the piece discloses a rather more lowly level of the Hiberno-American class structure: the Muldoons have not done quite as well as the McKennas or the Gilhooleys – but social climbing is part of their agenda: Mrs Muldoon knows that if Kitty marries Augustus – who clearly comes from a moneyed background – this will change. The importance of education is again a *motif* – Kitty's mother tells her she must use grand words, such as 'epistle' instead of 'letter'.

The text in the LCP Collection is fragmentary. Denis Muldoon is a businessman who lives with his wife and two daughters, Kitty and Cora, in New York. They have a housemaid called Ada McGlacklinn

– theatregoers with a penchant for identifying how Irish names change when removed to America will note 'MacLochlainn'. All is bustle as the Muldoons prepare for the christening of their baby son to which 'all the elite of the Irish aristocracy' have been invited. Muldoon has invited a young man, Johnny O'Brien, whom he believes to be a more suitable beau for Kitty than Augustus, but she describes him disdainfully as 'a dude'. The male guests congregate in a pub where there is an exhibition of wrestling, as well as singing and dancing. One of the men puts a toy dog on a poodle's chain.

Back at the apartment, Augustus arrives with his present for Kitty, a poodle, and is much disconcerted to find that it has metamorphosed into a toy. Kitty would much prefer something that reminded her of him – such as a monkey. Augustus proposes marriage, and Kitty accepts. Hearing Muldoon returning from the pub he hides behind the piano where he is trapped while Cora plays for her father and his friends. He attempts to escape when they fall into a drink-induced sleep. Later, Muldoon tells Kitty he will give her anything within reason but she mustn't marry a 'diddly-fal-lal' chap like that. Names are considered for the child: 'Isaac' and several others are quickly rejected. A procession leaves gaily and unsteadily for the park.

There is singing and dancing in the park. Augustus takes Kitty for a row on the river. When the donkey-cart bearing the elder Muldoons arrives it upsets them onto the path. In spite of their rivalry, Johnny and Augustus sing a duet. Muldoon leaves to take refuge in the pub. His wife is mortified at having to walk home. It appears (from almost illegible notes) that some members of the party fall into the river. In the Muldoon apartment Augustus and others arrive after a soaking – it is clear that they were the victims of the aquatic escapade. Evidently Augustus saved a Mr Mulcahy, an elderly friend of Muldoon's, from drowning. Mr Mulcahy urges Muldoon 'in return for his good deed, give him your daughter's hand in marriage!' A note reads, 'All agree. Shake hands. Three cheers for Mulcahy. Three-handed reel. Curtain.'

The poorly presented script, the second half of which is little more than dashed-off notes, does at least emphasize the idea that this almost plotless play is intended as a framework upon which to hang knockabout business, comic repartee, songs and dances. The success of the work was therefore dependent upon the talents of the performers for improvisation, solo and choral singing, and solo and ensemble dancing. *Muldoon's Pic Nic* does not have pretensions as publishable comedy: it is an entertainment of the moment. On its earliest visit to Belfast it was described by the *Northern Whig* as 'a successful burlesque'. This critic, taking a somewhat superior stance, thought that

> the action of the play is not governed by any artistic law, and the delightful characters which reigned supreme in one or two of the scenes affords (*sic*) a unique opportunity for the individual talent – descriptive, vocal and dramatic – which to some extent compensates for the absence of the higher forms of artistic portrayal

– whatever those may be.[201] Another review, better suited to the kind of piece which *Muldoon's Pic Nic* is, covered the production at the Alhambra Theatre three years later: on this occasion the 'Nono Bland and Nono Transatlantic Combination' gave what must have been a shorter version because the Alhambra was a variety house where straight drama was rarely seen, and this policy is borne out by the rest of the evening's programme which included Francesco the Juggling Marvel, Jennie Bason the Coon Comedienne, and Mademoiselle Leo Ville the Lady Jester and sleight-of-hand Illusionist. With proper regard for the main piece of the night the *Irish News* reported that

> the company at once enrolled themselves in the favour of the audience by their performance of the well-known and ever-popular *Muldoon's Pic Nic* ... On the whole a more side-splitting interpretation of the 'Hibernian absurdity' has never been witnessed in Belfast.[202]

Dear Hearts of Ireland, or, *The Dear Little Shamrock* by Myles McCarthy

Described as 'A domestic Comedy Drama in 3 Acts', this play was passed as suitable for performance in Britain on 30 November, 1900. It has been variously attributed – William Manning's name appears in some references – but 'Myles McCarthy' is given on the incomplete submission to the Lord Chamberlain. This is somewhat hesitatingly confirmed by the reviewer from *The Era* who attended the first British performance at the Crown Theatre, Peckham, on 3 December of the same year, observing that 'Mr Myles McCarthy, who is, we understand, the author of the play, gave a bright, breezy rendering of the part of Barney Flynn ...'[203] Three months later, on reaching the Theatre Royal, Belfast, it was announced in the daily papers as 'the Great American Success', the bills describing Myles

McCarthy as 'the Irish Singing Comedian' without, however, attributing authorship.

Only forty-four pages are extant, unless full copies may be preserved in collections other than the British Library. The scene is 'the Whin Rock' at an undisclosed location, where Rose O'Moore is amusedly berating a vagabond Frenchman, Bullay, for making love to every woman he meets; she tells him he should join the Constabulary and make a decent living. A certain Barney ('the life and soul of the village') is in love with Rose but for the moment is absent on mysterious business in Dublin. Mr Fitzgerald, father of Roger Fitzgerald who is on the run for allegedly murdering Squire O'Reilly exactly two years ago today – it is Hallowe'en and there are preparations in train for music and dancing – is determined to support his son should he appear. Driscoll, a kind of scrounger, is desirous of marrying Fitzgerald's adopted daughter, Henriette; he confides to his retainer (or accomplice) McShane that there is the difficulty of Henriette having been promised to Roger, but the men agree that it is unlikely Roger will ever return. Driscoll fears that 'the boys of the three-leaf badge' will carry Henriette off to wherever Roger is in hiding. Driscoll observes Fitzgerald putting money aside for his 'poor boy'. He accosts him and acquaints him of his wish to marry Henriette. Fitzgerald dismisses the notion – 'I would as soon ask the dove to mate with the serpent!'

Barney returns from Dublin, and, between making amorous advances to Rose, declares that he has the greatest bit of news. McShane assumes the news must be about Roger. Both McShane and Driscoll wish to attend the Hallowe'en party in Barney's house but they are not admitted. When Henriette steps out for a minute she is intercepted by Driscoll who lies to her that he has news of Roger. She reproaches him for taking advantage of her by this means and he tells her he has learned it was she who did the murder! – McShane was his informant. Henriette is much discomposed; Driscoll lays hands upon her but Bullay emerges from the shadows and separates them. Henriette supposes Driscoll wants money to keep quiet about the alleged shooting; he agrees this is the case but he also wants her, and seizes her again. This time Barney rushes out of the house and sends Driscoll packing. He consoles Henriette, and Nora consoles him. At the moment when all are speaking fondly of the fugitive Roger, the latter suddenly appears: his advent was the 'great news' which Barney was keeping to himself. There is suitably muted rejoicing, and a brief love scene between Roger and Henriette, after which she tells Roger that Driscoll knows she committed the murder. (Old Fitzgerald is unaware of the circumstances, which were that Roger had intervened when Squire Reilly was attempting to abduct Henriette and she shot him inadvertently; Roger later took the blame in a written submission, and then went on the run.) Henriette believes that if she and Roger get married Driscoll will cease his solicitations.

It is decided that Roger should hide in the barn. Later, Driscoll returns to pester Henriette. This time she appears complaisant, saying she needs time to consider and will write when she has decided upon a date. Driscoll's suspicions are alerted when he observes Rose bringing soup from the house to the barn: when he asks who it is for, Barney makes a comic scene out of it, saying he always drinks his soup out of doors, offering a sup to Driscoll, who declines. Driscoll attempts to bribe Barney for information on Roger, but Barney throws the money back at him. Later, Driscoll returns to observe Roger sneaking into the house and grabs him, declaring that he knows all. 'Give up Henriette, and you shall go free!', declares the enflamed Driscoll. Roger cries for help, Barney rushes in and holds Driscoll, and Roger makes himself scarce.

There the script tantalizingly ends. Some further incidents may be gleaned from the reviews. Evidently McShane lures Roger to a mountain peak (probably at the behest of Driscoll) where they fight with knives. Roger is the victor but both he and Barney are removed to gaol by some soldiers. Driscoll presses Henriette to marry him. She consents, but 'on the day of reckoning ... Driscoll is denounced and is shot trying to make his escape.' Presumably Roger and Barney are released and marry, respectively, Henriette and Nora.

There appears to be no American element in this turgid work – one therefore assumes that it is simply a play with an Irish setting originally intended for the American market. According to the *Northern Whig* the period is 'between 1790 and 1815' – this information may have been given on a playbill, but is not in the manuscript. Except for the fact that Roger is said to be a member of the 'boys of the three-leafed badge' one might have thought from reading the first act that there was no political element either, but the period, as disclosed by the *Whig,* suggests that Roger may have taken part in the Insurrection of 1798 and possibly also in the Emmet rising. [204]

The *Whig* found *Dear Hearts of Ireland* to be 'a production in which romance and comedy are most agreeably associated, and the interest of the audience is well maintained during the prologue and three acts ...' The *Irish News* noted 'many interesting and exciting situations, while at the same time giving a very acceptable interpretation of Irish habits and character ...'[205] The latter notice proves that the reader of forgotten plays should be chary of dismissing the content of any on the evidence of a poor or fragmentary copy: the *Irish News*, of all papers, would have been the most likely to pounce upon what its readership would have seen as distortions of 'Irish habits and character'. It is also salutary to recall that the Warden family, who ran the two most important Belfast theatres with efficiency and discernment, would not have booked *Dear Hearts of Ireland* if its touring reputation had disclosed it to be of inferior quality.[206]

ENVOI

The view that there existed in Ireland at the turn of the twentieth century a popular, socially significant and professionally presented native drama has been greatly strengthened by further research. As it turns out, the variety of the classes of play produced, and the extent of their distribution throughout the British Isles – and sometimes to North America and Australia, often amounting to over 1,000 performances and in some cases to 5,000 per play – has surprised even the present writer.

The question must be, why have we not heard of the majority of these plays, except in passing? – for very few, other than Boucicault's famous 'Irish trilogy' and plays that deal with the lives and exploits of military and political leaders, have been given recognition by commentators. The reasons quickly become obvious. The 'hero' plays are easily remembered by their titles even if they have not been read. Others are forgotten simply because they were not very good. By far the greatest number vanished because they were not published: they were written for performance with a view to sustaining the immediate needs of a company or a theatre, after which the players would pass on to the next piece. There was no thought whatsoever that anything as pretentious as 'dramatic literature' was being created.

There is scant evidence to support the notion that the work of the Irish Literary Theatre and its successor the National Theatre Society (the Abbey) drove this kind of popular drama from the boards by its insistence on high artistic ideals and its appeal to a distinctly literate community. The Abbey drove nobody away for the unpalatable reason that aside from early performances of *The Playboy of the Western World* and the first performances of Sean O'Casey in the 1920s it experienced considerable difficulty in filling its own seats.

While Yeats and his colleagues, by writing the history of their own movement in a messianic tone of self-aggrandizement almost before it happened, did refer obliquely to unidentified Irish plays as epitomizing 'buffoonery and easy sentiment' there is nothing to show that any of these people actually attended such demeaning productions. (Later, Synge did so, appreciating the strengths of the 'traditional drama of the Irish stage': what we know of Synge in the midst of the early Abbey *galère* rather emphasizes his good sense.) In any case Yeats did not need to exclude the popular drama from consideration for another reason: the political need for plays containing a strong element of aspiration towards national independence ended after 1922. Furthermore, the type of subjects which this drama had exploited were now much better served by the new medium of the cinema. Plays like *On Shannon's Shore, An Irish Gentleman* and *The Priest Hunter* read like draft scripts for fantastic action-packed motion pictures yet to be envisaged.

Some unexpected – though this should not have been so – *genres* disclosed themselves. One of these was the 'Hiberno-American' drama – plays usually set in the United States where Irish people – whether recently arrived or establishing themselves in first or second generation positions of influence – form almost the entire cast and create the dramatic interest. A nostalgic look to the Old Country has not been found: rather, the persons depicted anticipate working with success in the Land of Liberty. While only five of these plays have been read because they were the only ones presented in Ireland during the period under review, it is clear from other titles seen that there is much similar material in collections in the United States.

Another source for rewarding study would certainly be the plays of English authors which are set in Ireland, introducing Irish social and historical themes. As has been seen, eight plays in this category have been noted as having been produced in Ireland in the decade 1895-1904. What is most interesting is that successful English playwrights took it upon themselves to treat of Irish subjects when they clearly had little knowledge of Irish affairs save what they read in the London newspapers or gained from (probably) the novels of Lever and Carleton and (presumably) the plays by genuine Irish writers. Ireland provided something unusual as a recipe for drama that was at once close to hand yet comfortably remote: rebellion, revolution, famine, eviction, agrarian agitation, political assassination – contemporary topics hardly to be found in rural Shropshire or urban Bath – that was colourful and could be made entertaining enough to engage the public at the Princess's Theatre in Glasgow or the Royal Standard in London.

There is also a fascinating subject for a scholar trained in linguistics who possesses an understanding of the nuances of the Irish language and the dialects of Hiberno-English. Most of the plays here are replete with 'Irish' phrases, some of them direct translations from Gaelic, others that are derivations and still more that are indeterminate or possible invented by the authors. One supposes, for example, that the playwright Hubert O'Grady must have had a knowledge of the Irish language that stayed with him during a career spent almost entirely outside Ireland – how else would he have called the evil priest-hunter in the play of that name Mac An Easpaigh, if not as a wry joke? – but who in his English audience would have appreciated it? There should also be much of interest to be gained from an analysis of the ubiquitous 'Irish bulls', 'quare talk' and sheer colourful blather. What makes these speech forms (if that is what they are) work on the stage is the vibrancy of the characters who utter them – but for that again there is much to be said for the language creating the characters.

One of the most rewarding aspects of this survey for the present author has been the 'discovery' of several very good plays in the popular *genre*. Among these are *The Rebels* by J.B. Fagan which turns out to have been the earliest work by this Queen's County-born West End impresario who presented the Abbey Theatre plays in London. Another is the utterly West-Endish drama *An Irish Gentleman* by Christie Murray and John L. Shine which was so successful in its initial London run that it transferred to the largest Dublin house, the Theatre Royal. Perhaps the most absorbing – not to say moving – has been *Caitheamh an Ghlais* by Walter Howard and Chalmers Mackey which contains all the elements of melodrama in good (but not over-abundant) measure: a patriotic story, a touching love-motif across the social divide, a particularly interesting 'felon' on the run who is not the nominal hero, and two of the most amusing comic characters in all the plays read who assist rather than hinder the development of the plot. *Caitheamh an Ghlais* was almost permanently on the road in major theatres in Britain as *The Wearing of the Green* for six or perhaps seven years. Overall, there is a general sense of the emerald gem set in the crown of confident theatricality. Yet undoubtedly the most rewarding work has been in the rediscovery of all the plays of Hubert O'Grady that appear to be in existence: only two have previously been accorded serious critical study and there has been no attempt heretofore to seek the man behind the plays lauded in the leading theatres throughout the British Isles.

INFORMATION ON FIRST PRODUCTIONS OF IRISH PLAYS which were subsequently – or in some cases initially – presented professionally in Ireland in licensed commercial theatres during the decade prior to the opening of the Abbey Theatre. Dates of first productions are the earliest found in the British Isles; a very few plays may have been performed earlier in the United States and where this is known the appropriate American date is given. (Productions by the Irish Literary Theatre, the National Theatre Society, and other groups which contributed to the formation of the Abbey Theatre are not listed here.) All of the following plays were revived, some of them many times, in Dublin, Belfast and Cork during the period under review.

Author	Title	Year and Venue of Ist Production	Textual Source
DB Aylmer	Shamus a' Glanna	21 Aug 1876 Queen's, Manchester	Apparently lost
Dion Boucicault	The Colleen Bawn (after Griffin)	29 Mar 1860 Keene's Theatre, NY	OUP 1972
	Arrah-na-Pogue	7 Nov 1964 Theatre Royal, Dublin	Dicks' Standard Plays 1883
	The Shaughran	14 Nov 1874 Wallack's Theatre, NY	CUP 1984
	Kerry	7 Sep 1871 Prince's, Manchester	Apparently lost
	The Omadhaun	24 Nov 1877 Queen's, London	mss. L/LCP
	The O'Dowd	17 March 1873 Booth's, New York	mss. L/LCP

Dion Boucicault, Julius Benedict, John Oxenford	The Lily of Killarney	2 Feb 1862 Covent Garden	Boosey & Co 1882
John Buckstone	The Green Bushes	27 Jan 1845 Adelphi, London	Dick's Standard Plays
FJ Conyngham	Our Irish Visitors	1 Oct 1883 (earliest found) Miner's, NY	mss. BL/LCP
Frederick Cooke	On Shannon's Shore	14 Feb 1895 Prince's, Reading	mss. BL/LCP
JB Fagan	The Rebels	28 Sep 1899 Metropole, Camberwell	mss. BL/LCP
Edmund Falconer *né* O'Rourke	Peep o' Day	9 Nov 1861 Lyceum, London	French's Acting Edition NY (19c., no date.)
Dan Fitzgerald	The Rose of Rathboy	16 Oct 1899 Princess's, Kennington	mss. BL/LCP
Glengall, Earl of	The Irish Tutor	12 July 1822 Cheltenham Theatre	Dicks' Standard Plays
Fred Jarman	The Rebel's/ Patriot's Wife	8 Dec 1898 New, Consett	mss. BL/LCP (incomplete)
Robert Johnson	The Old Land	18 Apr 1903 Queen's, Dublin	apparently lost
Miss LeFanu-Robertson	A Daughter of Erin	19 Aug 1901 Theatre Royal, Dublin	apparently lost
F.Gould	The Father's Oath	24 Oct 1893 Princess's, Glasgow	apparently lost
J.Sheridan LeFanu CV Stanford GH Jessop	Shamus O'Brien	2 Mar 1896 Opera Comique, London	TCD M4 -96-900

Arthur Lloyd	Ballyvogan	25 July 1887 Tyne, Newcastle	mss. BL/LCP
Myles McCarthy	Dear Hearts of Ireland	3 Dec 1900 Crown, Peckham	mss. BL/LCP
Chalmers Mackey & Walter Howard	Caitheamh an Ghlais	22 June 1896 Queen's, Dublin	mss. BL/LCP
Wm Manning	My Native Land	1885 New Bowery, NY	mss. BL/LCP
EC Matthews	Rogue Reilly, or, The Four Leaved Shamrock	26 Feb 1894 Her Majesty's, Aberdeen	Apparently lost
	The Boys of Wexford	21 June 1896 Queen's, Glasgow	mss. BL/LCP
Christie Murray & John L Shine	An Irish Gentleman	9 June 1897 Globe, London	mss. BL/LCP
Hubert O'Grady	The Gommoch/ The Wild Irish Boy	16 Mar 1877 Theatre Royal, Stockton	mss. BL/LCP
	(The) Eviction	24 Jan 1880 Princess's Glasgow	mss. BL/LCP
	Emigration	14 May 1883 Princess's, Glasgow	Journal of Irish Literature, Jan 1985 and mss. BL/LCP
	The Famine	28 Apr 1886 Queen's, Dublin	J of Irish Lit. Jan 1985 and mss. BL/LCP
	The Fenian	1 Apr 1889 Princess's, Glasgow	mss. BL/LCP
	The Priest Hunter	3 Apr 1893 Queen's, Manchester	mss.BL/LCP
	A/The Fast Life	26 Oct 1896 Rhyl Theatre	mss. BL/LCP
J Pilgrim	Paddy Miles [the Limerick Boy]	22 Apr 1836 Sadler's Wells	Apparently lost
Harry Pleon	Muldoon's Pic Nic	10 May 1880 Pastor's Theater NY	Dick's Standard Plays

Tyrone Power	Born to Good Luck/ The Irishman's Fortune	17 Mar 1832 Drury Lane	Dicks' Standard Plays
Walter Reynolds	The Shamrock and The Rose	7 Oct 1891 Royal, Huddersfield	mss. BL/LCP
Edgar Seldon	McKenna's Flirtation	7 May 1888 Amphion, NY	mss. BL/LCP
William Travers	Kathleen Mavourneen, or, St Patrick's Eve	28 July 1863 Winter Garden, NY	mss. BL/LCP
JW Whitbread	Shoulder to Shoulder	8 Nov 1886 Theatre Royal, Limerick	mss.BL/LCP (first act only)
	(The) Race of Life	21 Nov 1887 Queen's, Dublin	mss.BL/LCP
	True to the Last	16 July 1888, Elephant & Castle Theatre	mss.BL/LCP
	Hero of Heroes	12 Aug 1889 Queen's, Dublin	Apparently lost
	The Irishman	4 Nov 1889, Elephant & Castle Theatre	mss. BL/LCP
	Miss Maritana	Queen's, Dublin	mss. BL/LCP
	The Nationalist/ A True Son of Erin	21 Dec 1891 Queen's, Dublin	W.J. Alley Dublin 1892
	All Hallow's Eve	21 Dec 1891 Queen's, Dublin	Apparently lost
	Spectres of the Past/ The Spectre of the Past	30 Jan 1893 Queen's, Dublin	Apparently lost
	Lord Edward, or, '98	20 Mar 1894 Queen's, Dublin	Ed. CHerr Syracuse UP 1991 and mss. BL/LCP
	The Victoria Cross	7 Sep 1896 Queen's, Dublin	mss. BL/LCP

	Theobald Wolfe Tone	26 Dec 1898 Queen's, Dublin	Ed. CHerr Syracuse UP 1991 and mss. BL/LCP
	Rory O'More (after Lover)	16 April 1900 Queen's, Dublin	apparently lost
	The Insurgent Chief	31 Mar 1902 Queen's, Dublin	mss. BL/LCP
	The Ulster Hero	12 Jan 1903 Queen's, Dublin	mss. BL/LCP
	The Sham Squire	21 Dec 1903 Queen's, Dublin	apparently lost
	Sarsfield	26 Dec 1904 Queen's, Dublin	Ed. Séamus de Burca Dublin 1986

BIBLIOGRAPHY

Reading:

The essential reading material for this study has been the texts of the surviving thirty-four plays performed in Ireland during the period under review, listed and described in the foregoing.

Books Consulted:

Archer, William, *English Dramatists of Today and Yesterday* (London: Sampson, Law, Marston, Searle & Rivington, 1882).

Bell, Sam Hanna, *The Theatre in Ulster* (Dublin: Gill & Macmillan, 1972).

Boardman, Gerald, *American Theatre* (Oxford: Oxford University Press, 1994).

Booth, M.R., *Hiss the Villain: English Melodrama* (London: Herbert Jenkins, 1965).

---, *English Nineteenth Century Plays*. V vols. (Oxford: Oxford University Press, 1969).

Boylan, Henry., *A Dictionary of Irish Biography* (Dublin: Gill & Macmillan, 1978).

Brown, Stephen J., *A Guide to Books on Ireland* (Dublin: Hodges, Figgis, 1912).

---, *Ireland in Fiction* (Dublin: Maunsel, 1916).

Byrne, Miles, *Memoirs* (Dublin: Maunsel, 1906).

Campion, J.T., *Michael* Dwyer, *the Insurgent Captain* (Glasgow: Cameron 7 Ferguson, 1869).

Clarence, Reginald. *The Stage Cyclopaedia* (London: The Stage, 1909).

Connolly, S.J. *The Oxford Companion to Irish History* (Oxford: Oxford University Press, 1998).

Culligan-Hogan, M.J. *The Quest for Galloping Hogan* (Hampton NH: Tyrone Press, 1994).

De Burca, Séamus, *The Queen's Royal Theatre Dublin* (Dublin: de Burca, 1983).

Dickson, Charles, *The Life of Michael Dwyer* (Dublin: Browne & Nolan, 1944).

Duggan, G.C., *The Stage Irishman* (Dublin: Talbot Press, 1937).

Fawkes, Richard, *Dion Boucicault* (London: Quaretet, 1979).

Fay, Frank and C. Carswell, *The Fays of the Abbey Theatre* (New York: Harcourt, Brace & Co., 1935).

Fitzpatrick, W.J., *The Sham Squire* (Dublin: Kelly, 1866).

Fitz-Simon, Christopher, *The Arts in Ireland* (Dublin: Gill & Macmillan, 1982).

---, *The Irish Theatre* (London: Thames & Hudson, 1983).

Foster, R.F., *Modern Ireland 1600-1972* (London: Allen Lane, 1988).

Frazier, Adrian, *George Moore* (Hartford CN: Yale University Press, 2000).

Gregory, Augusta, *Our Irish Theatre* (New York: Putnam, 1913).

Grene, Nicholas, *The Politics of Irish Drama* (Cambridge: Cambridge University Press, 1989).

Gwynn, Stephen, *Irish Literature and Drama* (London: Nelson, 1936).

Handley, Elaine, *Melodramatic Tactics.* Stanford 1995.

Handley, J.E., *The Irish in Modern Scotland* (Cork: Cork University Press, 1947).

Hayley, Barbara, *A Bibliography of the Writings of William Carleton* (Gerrard's Cross: Colin Smythe, 1985).

Herr, Cheryl, *For the Land they Loved.* (Syracuse NY: Syracuse University Press, 1991).

Hogan, R. and Kilroy, J., *The Irish Literary Theatre* (Dublin: Dolmen Press, 1975).

---, *Laying the Foundations* (Dublin: Dolmen Press, 1976).

Hogan, R.and M.O'Neill (Eds), Joseph Holloway, *Impressions of a Dublin Theatregoer* (Carbondale: Southern Illinois University Press, 1967).

Jenkins, Anthony, *The Making of Victorian Drama* (Cambridge: Cambridge University, 1991).

Kavanagh, Peter, *The Irish Theatre* (Tralee: The Kerryman, 1940).

Kilgariff, Michael, *The Golden Age of Melodrama* (London: Wolfe, 1974).

Killen, John (Ed.), *The Decade of the United Irishmen* (Belfast: Blackstaff, 1997).

Krause, David (Ed.), *The Dolmen Boucicault* (Dublin: Dolmen Press, 1976).

Madden, R.R., *The United Irishmen* (London: Madden & Co., 1842).

Mander, R and J.Mitchenson, *London's Lost Theatres* (London: Hart-Davis, 1968).

Martin, F.X. and T.W. Moody, *The Course of Irish History* (Cork: Mercier, 1967).

McNeil, Mary,*The Life and Times of Mary Ann McCracken*. (Belfast: Blackstaff, 1997).

Mercier, Vivian, *The Irish Comic Tradition* (Oxford: Oxford University Press, 1962).

Moore, Tom, *The Life of Lord Edward Fitzgerald* (London: Longman, Rees, Orme, Brown & Green, 1831).

Morash, Christopher, *A History of the Irish Theatre 1601-2000* (Cambridge: Cambridge University Press, 2002).

Mullen, Donald, *Victorian Plays 1837-1901* (Cambridge: Cambridge University Press, 2002).

Nicoll, Allardyce, *A History of English Drama* (London: Cambridge: Cambridge University Press, 1930).

O'Connor, Frank, *The Backward Look* (London: Macmillan, 1967).

O'Connor, Frederick. *A Shop on Every Corner* (Liverpool: 1955).

O'Donnell, Ruan, *The Rebellion in Wicklow* (Dublin: Irish Acadamic Press, 1998).

O'Driscoll, Robert, *Theatre and Nationalism* (London: Oxford university Press, 1971).

Odell, G.C.D., *Annals of the New York Stage* (New York: Columbia University Press, 1931).

O'Kelly, Charles, *The Jacobite War in Ireland* (Dublin: Sealy, Briers & Walker, 1894).

Peter, Bruce, *Scotland's Splendid Theatres* (Edinburgh: Polygon, 1999).

Pakenham, Thomas, *The Year of Liberty* (London: Hodder & Staughton, 1969).

Rehill, Frank, *The World of Melodrama* (University Park PA: Penn State University, 1967).

Ryan, Philip, *Lost Theatres of Dublin* (Westbury: Badger Press, 1998).

Scott, Clement W., *The Drama of Yesterday and Today* (London: Macmillan, 1899).

Shaw, George Bernard, *Our Theatres in the Nineties* (London: Constable, 1932).

Sheedy, Kieran, *Upon the Mercy of Government* (Dublin: RTE, 1988).

Sherson, Erroll, *London's Lost Theatres of the Nineteenth Century* (London: John Lane, the Bodley Head, 1925).

Simms, JG., The Williamite Confiscation in Ireland (London: Faber, 1956).

Slowey, Desmond, *The Radicalisation of Irish Drama* (Dublin: Irish Academic Press, 2008).

Smith, James L., *Melodrama* (London: Methuen, 1973).

Synge, J.M., (Ed. Ann Saddlemyer) *Collected Letters* (Oxford: Clarendon Press, 1983).

Todhunter, John, *The Life of Patrick Sarsfield* (London: Unwin, 1895).

Trotter, Mary, *Ireland's National Theatres* (Syracuse NY: Syracuse University Press, 2001).

Vaughan, W.E., *Landlords and Tenants 1848-1904*. (Oxford: Clarendon Press, 1984).

Wanchope, Piers, *Patrick Sarsfield and the Williamite Wars* (Dublin: Irish Academic Press, 1992).

Watt, Stephen M., *Joyce, O'Casey and the Irish Popular Theater* (Syracuse NY: Syracuse University Press, 1991).

Wearing, J.P. ,*American and British Theatrical Biography* (Metuchen NJ: Scarecrow Press, 1979).

Welch, Robert, *The Oxford Companion to Irish Literature* (Oxford: Oxford University Press, 1999).

Wilmeth, Don (Ed.). *Cambridge History of American Theatre*, Vol.II (Cambridge: Cambridge University Press, 1999).

Yeats, W.B. *Autobiographies* (London: Macmillan, 1955).

Daily Newspapers:

Irish News, Belfast, Every issue 1895-1904.

Evening Telegraph, Dublin, Ditto

Cork Constitution, Cork, Ditto

Northern Whig, Belfast, Issues that allude to certain plays under scrutiny

The Irish Times, Dublin, Ditto

Freeman's Journal, Dublin, Ditto

Daily Express, Dublin edition, Ditto

Evening Herald, Dublin, Ditto

Bradford Argus, Ditto

Glasgow Citizen, Ditto

Glasgow Evening News, Ditto

Weekly Newspapers:

The Era, London. All issues 1895-1904 that report the performance of plays identified in this study, whether in London or the provinces, of which Ireland was accounted a part. Also some earlier issues that relate to the initial productions of such plays.

The Irish Playgoer, Dublin. All issues. The paper flourished only from November 1899 until May 1900.

The United Irishman, Dublin. All issues 1899-1902 to which Frank Fay contributed theatre reviews.

The Graphic, London. Issues that allude to certain plays under scrutiny.

Middlesex Independent, London, Ditto

Connaught Telegraph, Castlebar, Ditto.

Limerick Chronicle, Ditto.

Waterford Star, Ditto.

Important Articles In Periodicals:

McCormick, John, *Origins of Melodrama*, in: *Prompts Magazine*, Dublin,
    for September 1983
Pine, Richard, *After Boucicault*, in: *Prompts Magazine*, Dublin, for
    September 1983
Synge. J.M.: Article on *Irish Drama* in Academy of Literature Magazine,
    London, for June 1904
Watt, Stephen M (Ed.),*The Famine* by Hubert O'Grady and Act I of
    Emigration by Hubert O'Grady in: *The Journal of Irish Literature*,
    Newark NJ, for January 1985
Watt, Stephen M., 'Boucicault and Whitbread' in *Eire-Ireland*, St Paul MA,
    for Fall 1983

Manuscript Sources:

Almost all the plays have been read in the (usually handwritten)
versions submitted to the Lord Chamberlain's Office, London, now
preserved in the Lord Chamberlain's Plays collection in the British
Library. Where other editions have been read, this is noted.

Extensive use has been made of the Holloway Papers in the
National Library, Dublin. Joseph Holloway (1861-1944) claimed to
have attended every play presented in Dublin from the age of
seventeen, except when prevented by illness or absence from the
city. For example, in 1896 he attended 124 productions at the Gaiety
and Queen's Theatres – during one week he saw six Shakespeare
plays at the former; 15 concerts at the Leinster Hall (which had
temporarily replaced the Theatre Royal); 8 recitals at the
Molesworth Hall; 12 variety shows at the Empire and Tivoli
Theatres; 28 'miscellanies' – lectures, debates and evenings of
amateur talent and elocution; and two 'entertainments' at the XL
Café. He contributed reviews (unsigned) at different periods to the
Daily Express (Dublin edition) and the *Irish Times*. He was the
architect responsible for the adaptation of the Mechanics' Theatre
and adjacent buildings as the Abbey Theatre in 1904, when his
technical advisor was W.J. Fay.

ENDNOTES

1 Yeats, W.B., 'The Man and the Echo' in *Last Poems*.
2 The *Irish Theatregoer* described the opening of *Maeve* by Edward Martyn and *The Last Feast of the Fianna* by Alice Milligan at the Gaiety Theatre, Dublin, on 22 February, 1900, as 'Irish Literary Theatre draws two blanks on opening night'.
3 Philip Ryan, *Lost Theatres of Dublin*. Dublin 1998.
4 Plays by Shaw and Wilde, first produced in London, went on the circuit amost immediately. In spite of Wilde's name being removed from the posters the plays remained in production – *A Woman of No Importance*, *Lady Windermere's Fan* and *The Importance of Being Earnest* all appeared in the larger Dublin theatres with London casts.
5 In 1895 there were c.190 licenced theatres and music halls in the greater London area and c.380 in the 'provinces', which included Ireland.
6 Information from the indispensable British weekly *The Era* which listed all professional productions throughout the British Isles.
7 The other three were Mrs Henry Wood's *East Lynne*, Bulwer-Lytton's *The Lady of Lyons* and a dramatization of Harriet Beecher Stowe's *Uncle Tom's Cabin*.
8 J.E. Handley, *The Irish in Modern Scotland* (Cork 1947).
9 Glasgow Evening News, 9 August 1905.
10 *The Era,* 2 September 1899.
11 *Academy of Literature Magazine*, 11 June 1904.
12 Joseph Holloway, NL Mss.1798(1). This is a catalogue number, not a date.
13 Mary Trotter, *Ireland's National Theatres*. Syracuse 2001.
14 Frank Fay and C. Carswell, *The Fays of the Abbey Theatre* (London 1935).
15 O'Keefe's considerable *Wild Oats* (Covent Garden, 1791), which has no Irish content, was produced at the National Theatre, London, and the Abbey Theatre, Dublin, in the 1960s.
16 Christopher Fitz-Simon, *The Irish Theatre* (London 1983).

17 Samuel Lover was an accomplished miniature painter and a member of the Royal Hibernian Academy. When his sight failed he moved to London, reinventing himself as a professional Irishman. His touring entertainment *An Irish Evening* contained recitations and songs of his own composition such as the evergreen *Molly Bawn* and *The Low-backed Car*. His novel *Handy Andy* went into many editions.

18 M.R. Booth, in *Place, Personality and the Irish Writer* (Gerrard's Cross: Colin Smythe, 1977), believes Falconer was influenced by Boucicault's Irish plays, but almost all of Falconer's pre-date Boucicault's.

19 Richard Fawkes, *Dion Boucicault* (London 1979).

20 Christopher Fitz-Simon, *The Irish Theatre*. London 1982.

21 David Krause, Introduction to *The Dolmen Boucicault* (Dublin 1964).

22 This was the inspiration for the courtroom scene in Shaw's *The Devil's Disciple* (1897).

23 Richard Fawkes, *Dion Boucicault*. London 1979.

24 *United Irishman*, January 1900.

25 *Evening Telegraph*, 16 November 1896.

26 *Irish News*, 16 March 1896.

27 NL Mss.No.1796. Joseph Holloway (1861-1944) was the architect of the renovation of the Mechanics' Theatre for the Abbey Theatre in 1904. An inveterate playgoer, it is estimated that his unpublished diaries extend to 28 million words. Professor Robert Hogan extracted relevant entries for *Joseph Holloway's Abbey Theatre* (Carbondate 1967) and *Holloway's Irish Theatre* (Dixon 1968). Of somewhat prim disposition, he did not care for plays in which any whiff of marital or sexual irregularity might be detected – he objected to the character of Nora Burke in Synge's *In The Shadow of the Glen* (1904) though he praised the performance of Máire ni Shiubhlaigh. He excoriated Denis Johnston's satirical ballet *Le Chèvre Indiscrète* (Gate Theatre, Dublin, 1931). His remarks on many of the patriotic melodramas are valuable in that they add the private critical element of the observer in the stalls.

28 There was no official stage censorship in Ireland., but the authorties could revoke a theatre's licence on grounds such as fire hazard or inadequate sanitation.

29 The Home Rule Bill was was first passed in the Commons (but defeated in the Lords) in the year prior to the play's first production.

30 *Evening Telegraph*, 12 November 1888.

31 *Freeman's Journal*, 8 September 1896.

32 This was the same Lord Roberts (1832-1914) who was Commander of the British forces during the second Anglo-Boer war. He was created Earl in 1901.

33 W.B. Yeats, 'September 1916' in *Collected Poems*.

34 *Northern Whig*, 27 January 1903. The *Whig* employed an unusually erudite critic during this period who may have come from the academic

world. The Public Records Office for Northern Ireland believes that the paper's administrative archive was destroyed when the paper ceased publicatio so it has not been possible to name this contributor.

35 *Irish News*, 17 January 1903.

36 *The Ulster Hero* returned to Belfast nine months later following an English and Scottish tour, for five nights only, the Saturday being reserved for a special performance of *The Colleen Bawn* to commemorate the 100th anniversary of the death of Gerald Griffin, upon whose novel *The Collegians* (1829) Boucicault had based his play.

37 NL Mss.No.1800. The proceedings of the Irish Transvaal Committee are frequently reported in the *Evening Telegraph* at this time. It met in the rooms of the Celtic Literary Society, 32 Lower Abbey Street, Dublin, and collected funds for Irishmen who were fighting for the Boers. The main male character in Sebastian Barry's play *The Only True History of Lizzie Finn* (1995) is one Robert Gibson from a landed Protestant family who is disgraced among his caste for fighting for the Boers against the British.

38 Cheryl Herr, *For the Land they Loved* (Syracuse 1991).

39 *Mary* Trotter, *Ireland's National Theatres* (Syracuse 2001).

40 *The Old Lady Says 'No!'* was first produced at the Peacock Theatre, Dublin, by the Dublin Gate Theatre Studio, in 1929.

41 Allardyce Nicoll, *A History of English Drama* (London 1946).

42 The *Essay on Irish Bulls* by Maria Edgeworth and her father Richard Lovell Edgeworth came out in 1802 and demonstrated that the spoken 'bulls and blunders' of Irish people were 'produced by their habit of using figurative and witty language' and not by accidental misuse of English. The prose fiction of Edith Somerville and 'Martin Ross' published almost a century later provides an extraordinarily accurate transcription of rural Irish speech in English.

43 The humorist and songwriter William Percy French (1854-1920) reported a Cavan man's exclamation on first seeing a tricycle – 'a commodious utensil'.

44 It is significant that the author-managers Walter Howard and Chalmers Mackey gave an Irish language title to their melodrama *Caitheamh an Ghlais* ('The Wearing of the Green'). BL/LCP 53607.

45 As far as can be ascertained this was never done during the period under discussion though Dublin Castle attempted to ban Shaw's *The Shewing-up of Blanco Posnet* at the Abbey Theatre in 1909 with embarrassing absence of success due to having to deal with no ordinary theatre manager in Lady Gregory.

46 The only recorded birth in Limerick in 1841 which may be remotely ascribed to Hubert O'Grady is for one Hugh Grady who was born in St Michael's parish on 14 November (Limerick City Library.) It was common for the O in Irish names to be omitted. He may have changed

the name Hugh to Hubert when he entered the theatrical profession, it having a more showy ring. The occupation of the father of this child is not given; the mother's name was Margaret Robinson. The Limerick Christian Brothers do not have a record of the names of pupils going back as far as 1841.

47 *The Era*, 23 December 1899.
48 Frederick O'Connor, *A shop on Every Corner* (Liverpool 1955).
49 *The Era*, 23 December 1899.
50 Ibid.
51 Richard Fawkes, *Dion Boucicault* (London 1979).
52 *Irish Playgoer* for January 1900.
53 *The Era*, 23 December 1899.
54 NL Ms.44461.
55 Allardyce Nicoll, *A History of English Drama* (London 1946).
56 Others were the Irish Theatre Company, the National Players, the Irish National Dramatic Company, the Irish Literary Society Drama Group, the Cork National Theatre, the Ulster Literary Theatre and the groups which developed to become the Abbey Theatre – the Irish Literary Theatre and the National Theatre Society Ltd.
57 First performed at the Princess's Theatre, London, in 1857. No copy appears to have been preserved.
58 *The Era*, 23 December 1899.
59 Ibid.
60 *Bradford Argus*, 7 October 1899.
61 Holloway: unpublished letters Vol.II NL.
62 Denbeighshire County Library.
63 Peter Kavanagh, *The Irish Theatre* (Tralee 1940).
64 Stephen Watt, *Joyce, O'Casey and the Popular Irish Theatre* (Syracuse 1991).
65 Among the most notorious is the Abbey Theatre's rejection of Brendan Behan's *The Quare Fellow*.
66 The Evicted Tenants Act of 1907 enabled the Land Commission to provide holdings for tenants who had been evicted since 1878 – the year prior to this play's composition. The National Land League was inaugurated in 1879 by Charles Stewart Parnell, Michael Davitt and Andrew Kettle, its chief precept being that 'the land of Ireland belongs to the people of Ireland'.
67 *The Era*, 1 February 1880.
68 Mr Small of Dublin's stage designs were admired by reviewers all over the British Isles, mainly for O'Grady's Irish National Company and the Kennedy Miller Combination.
69 *Glasgow Evening Citizen*, 27 January 1880.
70 In Ireland the railways were still being developed, only reaching Rosslare in 1882 and Donegal in 1889.

71 *Freeman's Journal*, 2 June 1881.

72 'Comic effects like pelting the villain with sods of turf not only allowed the play to slip past the censor but also pointed to the Irish peoples' ability to survive with spirit the social disaster of famine and emigration'. – Mary Trotter, *Ireland's National Theatres,* Syracuse 2001. Like Professor Watt, Dr Trotter does not seem to have envisaged further acts of this play.

73 *Evening Telegraph*, 13 December 1886.

74 *Joyce, O'Casey and the Popular Irish Theatre.*

75 Chris Morash, in *Bullán* for Spring 1997.

76 *Irish News*, 25 May 1901.

76 *Glasgow Evening Citizen*, 18 July 1899.

78 There is a distinct similarity between this Irish bull and one made by Captain O'Blunder in Thomas Sheridan's *The Brave Irishman* (1738) when the hero remarks, 'and when I wake up in the morning I find myself asleep!',

79 'Two-faced Tim'.

80 *The Era*, 22 April 1993.

81 *Evening Telegraph*, 10 October 1899.

82 *The Era*, 23 December 1899.

83 *Evening Herald*, 22 December 1899.

84 *Limerick Chronicle*, 22 December 1899.

85 *Irish Playgoer* for January 1900.

86 See bibliography.

87 BL Mss.LCP 43408.

88 Ibid.

89 Christopher Fitz-Simon, *The Irish Theatre* (London 1982).

90 BL Mss.LCP 53276.

91 *Irish Times*, 31 January 1893.

92 *John Bull's Other Island* was commissioned for the Abbey Theatre in 1904 but not performed there until 1916. In the meantime it was produced by the Vedrenne-Barker management in London (Court), Dublin (Gaiety) and elsewhere.

93 *The Era*, 21 June 1916.

94 *Irish Times*, 1 April 1993.

95 Seamus De Burca, *The Queen's Royal Theatre, Dublin* (Dublin 1983).

96 *Daily Graphic*, 19 February 1990.

97 Bourke Poster Collection, Dublin City Archive.

98 Authors of popular plays generally did not have their work printed because of the difficulty in collecting royalties from other companies.

99 Frank Fay, and C.Carswell, *The Fays of the Abbey Theatre* (London 1935).

[100] The best known stage plays with McCracken as central figure are Jack Loudan's *Henry Joy McCracken* (Ulster Group Theatre, Belfast, 1945) and Stewart Parker's *Northern Star* (Lyric Theatre, Belfast, 1984).

[101] *Irish Playgoer* for November 1899.

[102] *The Old Land* was first performed at the Queen's Theatre, Dublin, on 18 April 1903.

[103] NL Ir 882389. It is bound together with miscellaneous unrelated pamphlets.

[104] *Limerick Chronicle*, 9 November 1886.

[105] *Irish Times*, 11 October 1887.

[106] *United Irishman* for July 1900.

[107] *Irish News*, 4 December 1900.

[108] Matcham also designed the Grand Opera House, Belfast, in a kind of Hindu-Baroque style. It opened in 1895 and, after many vicissitudes, is still the most sumptuous theatre in Ireland.

[109] In the mid-twentieth century a stage setting disclosing realistic representations of upper and lower rooms as well as the exterior of the building was known in the profession as 'an Arthur Miller set' but the convention had been established in nineteenth-century melodrama.

[110] *Evening Telegraph*, 21 November 1889.

[111] *United Irishman* for September 1899.

[112] NL, Dublin.

[113] *Irish Times*, 28 December 1891.

[114] *Evening Telegraph*, 28 December 1891.

[115] NL Mss.1798(1).

[116] NL Mss.1795.

[117] *Freeman's Journal*, 8 September 1886.

[118] During a particularly fierce engagement there is a stage direction for 'Machine to imitate bones cracking'.

[119] Cheryl Herr, *For the Land they Loved*.

[120] *Evening Herald*, 27 March 1994.

[121] *Evening Telegraph*, 28 December 1895.

[122] *Irish News*, 8 December 1896.

[123] NL Mss.1795.

[124] Whitbread sticks closely to a description of this incident in Tom Moore's *The Life of Lord Edward Fitzgerald*, written thirty-three years after Fitzgerald's death. Moore used eye-witness accounts.

[125] For the Land they Loved.

[126] Louisa Connolly (1742-1821) was a noted philanthopist, wife of Sir Thomas Connolly, Speaker of the Irish House of Commons. She was also Lord Edward's aunt and therefore Whitbread probably felt that her inclusion in the deathbed scene was justified, though in fact she was not present.

[127] The Irish Texts Society and the Irish Literary Theatre were founded in 1898; the annual Oireachtas cultural festival and the Dublin Feis Ceóil had been inaugurated the previous year. It was no accident that in the following year Arthur Griffith gave his weekly newspaper the title of *The United Irishman*.

[128] *United Irishman*, 26 August 1899.

[129] NL Mss.1800.

[130] The present writer's maternal grandmother, Maude O'Connell Fitz-Simon, Honorary Secretary of the United Arts Club when WB Yeats was its President, was nonetheless a fairly regular attender at the Queen's Theatre. She referred to the patriotic melodramas as 'the real Irish plays'.

[131] Oliver Bond was an Ulster wool merchant who joined the United Irishmen in 1798; arrested for high treason in 1791 he was sentenced to death but died in prison. Robert Emmet was involved in the UI as a student; he fled to the continent in 1799, returning to organize the unsuccessful rebellion in 1803 for which he was hanged. The Rev. William Jackson was a radical journalist who sought French participation in 1792, was charged with high treason, found guilty and committed suicide in 1795. (Whitbread has altered the chronology, for Tone did not go to France till after Jackson's death.) John Keogh was a businessman and a member of the Catholic Committee; he was arrested in 1796 for associating with the UI but soon released. Henry Joy McCracken is described by Whitbread in the stage directions as being present on stage but he does not speak in this play. The barrister Leonard McNally defended Tone, Emmet and Tandy in court but turned informer and received a Secret Service pension until his death in 1820. Archibald Hamilton Rowan was a wealthy landowner who joined the UI and was defended by Curran at his trial for sedition in 1794; he escaped to America and was pardoned after the Act of Union (1801). William Russell, Tone's close friend in this play, was an army officer stationed in Belfast; was arrested in 1798 and sent to Fort St George; released in 1802 he immediately involved himself in plans for Emmet's rebellion; he was sentenced to death and hanged in Downpatrick.

[132] Mary Trotter, *Ireland's National Theatres* (Syracuse 1991).

[133] Séamus De Burca, *The Queen's Royal Theatre* (Dublin, 1883).

[134] No publication date is given but the Local History Librarian for Wicklow belives it was 1869.

[135] The scene of the shooting of Captain Airlie is similar to the shooting of Colonel Tracey in O'Grady's *The Fenian* where the internal witness is taken for the external marksman.

[136] The William Hume of Humewood House of the time was a liberal landlord who brokered several deals between the Castle and the UI and

was not murdered. Later in the play Hume applies for a pardon for Dwyer.

137 Most of the important twentieth-century plays with Ulster locations and essential Ulster motifs by Ervine, Friel, McGuinness, Mayne, Mitchell, Parker, Reid, Shiels and others were initially produced in Dublin. Parker's superb *Northern Star* is a notable exception.

138 NL Mss.1801.

139 The cotton mill was one of a number of McCracken and Joy family businesses. One wonders if Whitbread deliberately placed it on the Falls Road in order to make a political/demographic statement: A protestant-owned mill in a Roman Catholic neighbourhood. The actual factory was in Castle Street.

140 The play is based on W.J. Fitzpatrick's *The Sham Squire; and the Informers of 1798*, published in Dublin in 1866 shortly after RR Madden's celebrated four-volume work on the UI. Fitzpatrick was also the biographer of Bishop Doyle of Leighlin.

141 *The Era*, 2 January 1904.

142 NL Mss.1803.

143 Rapparee, from the Irish *rapaire* meaning a pike, was the term given to dispossessed Catholics who waged a guerilla campaign against the new social order created by the land confiscations of the mid-seventeenth century.

144 First produced at the Princess's Theatre, London, which had accommodation for 1,700 patrons. Its most famous manager was Benjamin Webster who produced three of Boucicault's plays, *After Dark, The Streets of London* and *The Rapparee*, as well as revivals of Falconer's *Peep o' Day*.

145 Boucicault's *A Lover by Proxy* was first produced at the Haymarket Theatre, London, on 21 April, 1842. Boucicault's biographer Richard Faulkes states that it was frequently revived.

146 John H. Todhunter (1839-1916) was a person of considerable importance in the Celtic Revival. He published more than twenty books, many of them promoting the idea of a glorious Irish cultural past. His play *The Land of Sighs* was produced by Miss Annie Horniman alongside W.B. Yeats's *The Land of Heart's Desire* at the Avenue Theatre, London, in 1894. The poster was designed by Aubrey Beardsley. Todhunter is known today mainly for his poem *Aghadoe*, and barely for that.

148 Not even Matthew J Culligan-Hogan in *The Quest for Galloping Hogan* (New York 1979).

149 J.G.Simms, *The Williamite War in Ireland* (London, 1956).

150 While with the Kennedy Miller company from c.1891 to c.1904 he generally played the 'broth of a boy' parts. It was of O'Brien's Shaughran that Synge wrote in the *Academy of Literature Magazine* for June 1904

that he 'put a richness in his voice that it would be useless to expect from the less gutteral vocal capacity of the French and English comedians, and in listening to him one felt how much the modern stage has lost in substituting impersonal wit for personal humour.'

[151] Simms, as above.

[152] *Evening Telegraph*, 27 December 1904.

[153] Simms, as above.

[154] *Irish Times*, 27 December 1904.

[155] The right-wing *Dublin Daily Express* was in fact the local edition of the *Daily Express* of London. It did not review Irish plays at the Queen's Theatre. It ignored, for example, the fund-raising drive to erect a monument to Wolfe Tone, dilating rather on upon 'Viceregal Court Mourning for the late Royal Highness the Dowager Duchess Alexandrina of Saxe-Coburg Gotha'. By ignoring 'patriotic' plays at the Queen's, Royal and Gaiety theatres its readership – which would have included officials of the colonial regime at the Castle – may have been unaware of this cell of nationalist ferment.

[156] NL Mss.1803(1).

[157] *The Era*, 21 June 1916.

[158] *Northern Whig*, 19 May 1903.

[159] Clement W. Scott, *The Drama of Yesterday and Today* (London 1899).

[160] NL Mss. 1798.

[161] Tyrone Guthrie, *A Life in the Theatre* (London 1960). Fagan's chief plays were *The Prayer of the Sword, The Dressing Room, The Happy Island, The Improper Duchess* and *And So To Bed*, a play with music based on the Diaries of Samuel Pepys; it was revived many times in the West End up to 1951.

[162] *The Era*, 9 September 1899.

[163] *The Era*, 23 September 1899.

[164] *Liverpool Echo*, 5 September 1899.

[165] *Evening Herald*, 24 October 1899. This critic consistently referred to 'Athboy', a town in Co Meath. This may be an indication of the general level of critical attention.

[166] Allardyce Nicoll, *A History of English Drama* (London 1946).

[167] *United Irishman*. This notice was for the December, 1899, revival of *Caitheamh an Ghlais*.

[168] An operatic version of *The Green Bushes* was produced at the Princess's Theatre, London, in 1893 with music by Hayden Parry and lyrics by John Hollingshead, but it was short lived.

[169] *United Irishman*, 16 September 1899.

[170] *Irish Times*, 18 February 1896.

[171] Nicoll, as above.

[172] *Irish Times*, 22 June 1896.

[173] *Freeman's Journal*, 23 June 1896.

174 *Glasgow Evening Citizen*, 27 June 1899.

175 *The Era*, I July 1899.

176 NL Mss.1795.

177 Nicoll, as above.

178 Wilde would have written 'You may be sure they mean something else'!

179 *The Era*, 12 June 1897.

180 Reprinted in *Our Theatres in the Nineties*. London 1932. Shaw's oft-expressed views on the Stage Irishman are best exemplified in his superb preface to *John Bull's Other Island*, 1907.

181 *Evening Telegraph*, 13 August 1895.

182 *Irish News*, 6 October 1896.

183 Ibid. 16 December 1902.

184 Cooke's *Under the Czar* was exceptionally popular in the West End and on tour, visiting Dublin at least twice. Fortunately Cooke did not have to run the gauntlet of the St Petersburg press.

185 *The Era*, 24 June 1899.

186 One quickly realises that Jarman had little knowledge of the Irish background – e.g. no Irish person refers to a 'fairy ring', but to a 'fairy fort' or a 'rath' or 'lios'. English fairies tend to be perfectly charming while Irish ones are noted for their ugly demeanour.

187 *United Irishman*, 4 March 1900.

189 Nicoll, as above.

190 Barbara Hayley, *A Bibliography of the Writings of William Carleton* (Gerrard's Cross, 1985). Carleton's *Traits and Stories* were pre-Famine, and this play is vaguely set at the time of the agrarian disturbances of the late 1870s – but this does not preclude a plot influence.

191 *The Era*, 1 October 1892.

192 NL Mss.1892.

193 Emergency Men were financed by the Emergency Committee of the Orange Order to work farms from which the tenants had been evicted.

194 Reginald Clarence, *The Stage Cyclopaedia* (London 1911). The name of the chief character in *My Native Land*, Andy Blake, suggests an affinity with Boucicault's play of that name – but there is no connection.

195 *Irish News*, 23 December 1895.

196 *Belfast News-Letter*, 12 July 1898.

197 *Northern Whig*, 20 August 1895.

198 *Cork Constitution*, 14 May 1895.

199 *Northern Whig*, 30 July 1895.

200 *Irish News*, 30 July 1895.

201 *Northern Whig*, 9 March 1897.

202 *Irish News*, 31 April 1901.

203 *The Era*, 8 December 1900.

204 *Northern Whig*, 26 March 1901.

205 *Irish News*, 26 March 1901.

[206] It may be worth placing *Dear Hearts of Ireland* in its socio-theatrical context by noting that in the week prior to its Belfast showing the same theatre was presenting a new London production of Wilde's *Lady Windermere's Fan*. This emphasizes the extraordinary variety of productions available to the theatres on the circuit. One might suppose that one of these plays would have been mainly to the taste of residents of the Falls Road and the other to the Malone Road, but there must have been consumers who attended from both neighbourhoods in the way that, e.g., the Gaiety Theatre in Dublin today will offer the Royal Shakespeare Company in *Hamlet* followed by the Irish musical *Riverdance* without reference to imagined social or demographic demarcations of the potential audience.

INDEX

Carysfort Press was formed in the summer of 1998. It receives annual funding from the Arts Council.

The directors believe that drama is playing an ever-increasing role in today's society and that enjoyment of the theatre, both professional and amateur, currently plays a central part in Irish culture.

The Press aims to produce high quality publications which, though written and/or edited by academics, will be made accessible to a general readership. The organisation would also like to provide a forum for critical thinking in the Arts in Ireland, again keeping the needs and interests of the general public in view.

The company publishes contemporary Irish writing for and about the theatre.

Editorial and publishing inquiries to:
Carysfort Press Ltd.,
58 Woodfield,
Scholarstown Road,
Rathfarnham,
Dublin 16,
Republic of Ireland.

T (353 1) 493 7383
F (353 1) 406 9815
E: info@carysfortpress.com
www.carysfortpress.com

HOW TO ORDER

TRADE ORDERS DIRECTLY TO:
Irish Book Distribution
Unit 12, North Park, North Road,
Finglas, Dublin 11.

T: (353 1) 8239580
F: (353 1) 8239599
E: mary@argosybooks.ie
www.argosybooks.ie

INDIVIDUAL ORDERS DIRECTLY TO:
eprint Ltd.
35 Coolmine Industrial Estate,
Blanchardstown, Dublin 15.
T: (353 1) 827 8860
F: (353 1) 827 8804 Order online @
E: books@eprint.ie
www.eprint.ie

FOR SALES IN NORTH AMERICA AND CANADA:
Dufour Editions Inc.,
124 Byers Road,
PO Box 7,
Chester Springs,
PA 19425,
USA

T: 1-610-458-5005
F: 1-610-458-7103

The Fourth Seamus Heaney Lectures, 'Mirror up to Nature':

Ed. Patrick Burke

What, in particular, is the contemporary usefulness for the building of societies of one of our oldest and culturally valued ideals, that of drama? The Fourth Seamus Heaney Lectures, 'Mirror up to Nature': Drama and Theatre in the Modern World, given at St Patrick's College, Drumcondra, between October 2006 and April 2007, addressed these and related questions. Patrick Mason spoke on the essence of theatre, Thomas Kilroy on Ireland's contribution to the art of theatre, Cecily O'Neill and Jonothan Neelands on the rich potential of drama in the classroom. Brenna Katz Clarke examined the relationship between drama and film, and John Buckley spoke on opera and its history and gave an illuminating account of his own *Words Upon The Window-Pane*.

ISBN 978-1-9045505-48-8   €12

The Theatre of Tom Mac Intyre: 'Strays from the ether'

Eds. Bernadette Sweeney and Marie Kelly

This long overdue anthology captures the soul of Mac Intyre's dramatic canon – its ethereal qualities, its extraordinary diversity, its emphasis on the poetic and on performance – in an extensive range of visual, journalistic and scholarly contributions from writers, theatre practitioners.

ISBN 978-1-904505-46-4 €25

Irish Appropriation Of Greek Tragedy

Brian Arkins

This book presents an analysis of more than 30 plays written by Irish dramatists and poets that are based on the tragedies of Sophocles, Euripides and Aeschylus. These plays proceed from the time of Yeats and Synge through MacNeice and the Longfords on to many of today's leading writers.

ISBN 978-1-904505-47-1 €20

Alive in Time: The Enduring Drama of Tom Murphy

Ed. Christopher Murray

Almost 50 years after he first hit the headlines as Ireland's most challenging playwright, the 'angry young man' of those times Tom Murphy still commands his place at the pinnacle of Irish theatre. Here 17 new essays by prominent critics and academics, with an introduction by Christopher Murray, survey Murphy's dramatic oeuvre in a concerted attempt to define his greatness and enduring appeal, making this book a significant study of a unique genius.

ISBN 978-1-904505-45-7 €25

Performing Violence in Contemporary Ireland

Ed. Lisa Fitzpatrick

This interdisciplinary collection of fifteen new essays by scholars of theatre, Irish studies, music, design and politics explores aspects of the performance of violence in contemporary Ireland. With chapters on the work of playwrights Martin McDonagh, Martin Lynch, Conor McPherson and Gary Mitchell, on Republican commemorations and the 90th anniversary ceremonies for the Battle of the Somme and the Easter Rising, this book aims to contribute to the ongoing international debate on the performance of violence in contemporary societies.

ISBN 978-1-904505-44-0 (2009) €20

Ireland's Economic Crisis - Time to Act. Essays from over 40 leading Irish thinkers at the MacGill Summer School 2009

Eds. Joe Mulholland and Finbarr Bradley

Ireland's economic crisis requires a radical transformation in policymaking. In this volume, political, industrial, academic, trade union and business leaders and commentators tell the story of the Irish economy and its rise and fall. Contributions at Glenties range from policy, vision and context to practical suggestions on how the country can emerge from its crisis.

ISBN 978-1-904505-43-3 (2009) €20

Deviant Acts: Essays on Queer Performance

Ed. David Cregan

This book contains an exciting collection of essays focusing on a variety of alternative performances happening in contemporary Ireland. While it highlights the particular representations of gay and lesbian identity it also brings to light how diversity has always been a part of Irish culture and is, in fact, shaping what it means to be Irish today.

ISBN 978-1-904505-42-6 (2009) €20

Seán Keating in Context: Responses to Culture and Politics in Post-Civil War Ireland

Compiled, edited and introduced by Éimear O'Connor

Irish artist Seán Keating has been judged by his critics as the personification of old-fashioned traditionalist values. This book presents a different view. The story reveals Keating's early determination to attain government support for the visual arts. It also illustrates his socialist leanings, his disappointment with capitalism, and his attitude to cultural snobbery, to art critics, and to the Academy. Given the national and global circumstances nowadays, Keating's critical and wry observations are prophetic – and highly amusing.

ISBN 978-1-904505-41-9 €25

Dialogue of the Ancients of Ireland: A new translation of Acallam na Senorach

Translated with introduction and notes by Maurice Harmon

One of Ireland's greatest collections of stories and poems, The Dialogue of the Ancients of Ireland is a new translation by Maurice Harmon of the 12th century *Acallam na Senorach*. Retold in a refreshing modern idiom, the *Dialogue* is an extraordinary account of journeys to the four provinces by St. Patrick and the pagan Cailte, one of the surviving Fian. Within the frame story are over 200 other stories reflecting many genres – wonder tales, sea journeys, romances, stories of revenge, tales of monsters and magic. The poems are equally varied – lyrics, nature poems, eulogies, prophecies, laments, genealogical poems. After the *Tain Bo Cuailnge*, the *Acallam* is the largest surviving prose work in Old and Middle Irish.

ISBN: 978-1-904505-39-6 (2009)   €20

Literary and Cultural Relations between Ireland and Hungary and Central and Eastern Europe

Ed. Maria Kurdi

This lively, informative and incisive collection of essays sheds fascinating new light on the literary interrelations between Ireland, Hungary, Poland, Romania and the Czech Republic. It charts a hitherto under-explored history of the reception of modern Irish culture in Central and Eastern Europe and also investigates how key authors have been translated, performed and adapted. The revealing explorations undertaken in this volume of a wide array of Irish dramatic and literary texts, ranging from *Gulliver's Travels* to *Translations* and *The Pillowman*, tease out the subtly altered nuances that they acquire in a Central European context.

ISBN: 978-1-904505-40-2 (2009)   €20

Plays and Controversies: Abbey Theatre Diaries 2000-2005

Ben Barnes

In diaries covering the period of his artistic directorship of the Abbey, Ben Barnes offers a frank, honest, and probing account of a much commented upon and controversial period in the history of the national theatre. These diaries also provide fascinating personal insights into the day-to- day pressures, joys, and frustrations of running one of Ireland's most iconic institutions.

ISBN: 978-1-904505-38-9 (2008)   €35

Interactions: Dublin Theatre Festival 1957-2007. Irish Theatrical Diaspora Series: 3

Eds. Nicholas Grene and Patrick Lonergan with Lilian Chambers

For over 50 years the Dublin Theatre Festival has been one of Ireland's most important cultural events, bringing countless new Irish plays to the world stage, while introducing Irish audiences to the most important international theatre companies and artists. Interactions explores and celebrates the achievements of the renowned Festival since 1957 and includes specially commissioned memoirs from past organizers, offering a unique perspective on the controversies and successes that have marked the event's history. An especially valuable feature of the volume, also, is a complete listing of the shows that have appeared at the Festival from 1957 to 2008.

ISBN: 978-1-904505-36-5 €25

The Informer: A play by Tom Murphy based on the novel by Liam O'Flaherty

The Informer, Tom Murphy's stage adaptation of Liam O'Flaherty's novel, was produced in the 1981 Dublin Theatre Festival, directed by the playwright himself, with Liam Neeson in the leading role. The central subject of the play is the quest of a character at the point of emotional and moral breakdown for some source of meaning or identity. In the case of Gypo Nolan, the informer of the title, this involves a nightmarish progress through a Dublin underworld in which he changes from a Judas figure to a scapegoat surrogate for Jesus, taking upon himself the sins of the world. A cinematic style, with flash-back and intercut scenes, is used rather than a conventional theatrical structure to catch the fevered and phantasmagoric progression of Gypo's mind. The language, characteristically for Murphy, mixes graphically colloquial Dublin slang with the haunted intricacies of the central character groping for the meaning of his own actions. The dynamic rhythm of the action builds towards an inevitable but theatrically satisfying tragic catastrophe. ' [The Informer] is, in many ways closer to being an original Murphy play than it is to O'Flaherty...' Fintan O'Toole.

ISBN: 978-1-904505-37-2 (2008) €10

Shifting Scenes: Irish theatre-going 1955-1985

Eds. Nicholas Grene and Chris Morash

Transcript of conversations with John Devitt, academic and reviewer, about his lifelong passion for the theatre. A fascinating and entertaining insight into Dublin theatre over the course of thirty years provided by Devitt's vivid reminiscences and astute observations.

ISBN: 978-1-904505-33-4 (2008) €10

Irish Literature: Feminist Perspectives

Eds. Patricia Coughlan and Tina O'Toole

The collection discusses texts from the early 18th century to the present. A central theme of the book is the need to renegotiate the relations of feminism with nationalism and to transact the potential contest of these two important narratives, each possessing powerful emancipatory force. Irish Literature: Feminist Perspectives contributes incisively to contemporary debates about Irish culture, gender and ideology.

ISBN: 978-1-904505-35-8 (2008) €25

Silenced Voices: Hungarian Plays from Transylvania

Selected and translated by Csilla Bertha and Donald E. Morse

The five plays are wonderfully theatrical, moving fluidly from absurdism to tragedy, and from satire to the darkly comic. Donald Morse and Csilla Bertha's translations capture these qualities perfectly, giving voice to the 'forgotten playwrights of Central Europe'. They also deeply enrich our understanding of the relationship between art, ethics, and politics in Europe.

ISBN: 978-1-904505-34-1 (2008) €25

A Hazardous Melody of Being:
Seóirse Bodley's Song Cycles on the poems of Micheal O'Siadhail

Ed. Lorraine Byrne Bodley

This apograph is the first publication of Bodley's O'Siadhail song cycles and is the first book to explore the composer's lyrical modernity from a number of perspectives. Lorraine Byrne Bodley's insightful introduction describes in detail the development and essence of Bodley's musical thinking, the European influences he absorbed which linger in these cycles, and the importance of his work as a composer of the Irish art song.

ISBN: 978-1-904505-31-0 (2008) €25

Irish Theatre in England: Irish Theatrical Diaspora Series: 2

Eds. Richard Cave and Ben Levitas

Irish theatre in England has frequently illustrated the complex relations between two distinct cultures. How English reviewers and audiences interpret Irish plays is often decidedly different from how the plays were read in performance in Ireland. How certain Irish performers have chosen to be understood in Dublin is not necessarily how audiences in London have perceived their constructed stage personae. Though a collection by diverse authors, the twelve essays in this volume investigate these issues from a variety of perspectives that together chart the trajectory of Irish performance in England from the mid-nineteenth century till today.

ISBN: 978-1-904505-26-6 (2007) €20

Goethe and Anna Amalia: A Forbidden Love?

Ettore Ghibellino, Trans. Dan Farrelly

In this study Ghibellino sets out to show that the platonic relationship between Goethe and Charlotte von Stein – lady-in-waiting to Anna Amalia, the Dowager Duchess of Weimar – was used as part of a cover-up for Goethe's intense and prolonged love relationship with the Duchess Anna Amalia herself. The book attempts to uncover a hitherto closely-kept state secret. Readers convinced by the evidence supporting Ghibellino's hypothesis will see in it one of the very great love stories in European history – to rank with that of Dante and Beatrice, and Petrarch and Laura.

ISBN: 978-1-904505-24-2 €20

Ireland on Stage: Beckett and After

Eds. Hiroko Mikami, Minako Okamuro, Naoko Yagi

The collection focuses primarily on Irish playwrights and their work, both in text and on the stage during the latter half of the twentieth century. The central figure is Samuel Beckett, but the contributors freely draw on Beckett and his work provides a springboard to discuss contemporary playwrights such as Brian Friel, Frank McGuinness, Marina Carr and Conor McPherson amongst others. Contributors include: Anthony Roche, Hiroko Mikami, Naoko Yagi, Cathy Leeney, Joseph Long, Noreem Doody, Minako Okamuro, Christopher Murray, Futoshi Sakauchi and Declan Kiberd

ISBN: 978-1-904505-23-5 (2007) €20

'Echoes Down the Corridor': Irish Theatre - Past, Present and Future

Eds. Patrick Lonergan and Riana O'Dwyer

This collection of fourteen new essays explores Irish theatre from exciting new perspectives. How has Irish theatre been received internationally - and, as the country becomes more multicultural, how will international theatre influence the development of drama in Ireland? These and many other important questions.

ISBN: 978-1-904505-25-9 (2007) €20

Musics of Belonging: The Poetry of Micheal O'Siadhail

Eds. Marc Caball & David F. Ford

An overall account is given of O'Siadhail's life, his work and the reception of his poetry so far. There are close readings of some poems, analyses of his artistry in matching diverse content with both classical and innovative forms, and studies of recurrent themes such as love, death, language, music, and the shifts of modern life.

ISBN: 978-1-904505-22-8 (2007) €25 (Paperback)
ISBN: 978-1-904505-21-1 (2007) €50 (Casebound)

Brian Friel's Dramatic Artistry: 'The Work has Value'

Eds. Donald E. Morse, Csilla Bertha and Maria Kurdi

Brian Friel's Dramatic Artistry presents a refreshingly broad range of voices: new work from some of the leading English-speaking authorities on Friel, and fascinating essays from scholars in Germany, Italy, Portugal, and Hungary. This book will deepen our knowledge and enjoyment of Friel's work.

ISBN: 978-1-904505-17-4 (2006) €30

The Theatre of Martin McDonagh: 'A World of Savage Stories'

Eds. Lilian Chambers and Eamonn Jordan

The book is a vital response to the many challenges set by McDonagh for those involved in the production and reception of his work. Critics and commentators from around the world offer a diverse range of often provocative approaches. What is not surprising is the focus and commitment of the engagement, given the controversial and stimulating nature of the work.

ISBN: 978-1-904505-19-8 (2006) €35

Edna O'Brien: New Critical Perspectives

Eds. Kathryn Laing, Sinead Mooney and Maureen O'Connor

The essays collected here illustrate some of the range, complexity, and interest of Edna O'Brien as a fiction writer and dramatist. They will contribute to a broader appreciation of her work and to an evolution of new critical approaches, as well as igniting more interest in the many unexplored areas of her considerable oeuvre.

ISBN: 978-1-904505-20-4 (2006)   €20

Irish Theatre on Tour

Eds. Nicholas Grene and Chris Morash

'Touring has been at the strategic heart of Druid's artistic policy since the early eighties. Everyone has the right to see professional theatre in their own communities. Irish theatre on tour is a crucial part of Irish theatre as a whole'. Garry Hynes

ISBN 978-1-904505-13-6 (2005)   €20

Poems 2000-2005 by Hugh Maxton

Poems 2000-2005 is a transitional collection written while the author – also known to be W.J. Mc Cormack, literary historian – was in the process of moving back from London to settle in rural Ireland.

ISBN 978-1-904505-12-9 (2005)   €10

Synge: A Celebration

Ed. Colm Tóibín

A collection of essays by some of Ireland's most creative writers on the work of John Millington Synge, featuring Sebastian Barry, Marina Carr, Anthony Cronin, Roddy Doyle, Anne Enright, Hugo Hamilton, Joseph O'Connor, Mary O'Malley, Fintan O'Toole, Colm Toibin, Vincent Woods.

ISBN 978-1-904505-14-3 (2005)   €15

East of Eden. New Romanian Plays

Ed. Andrei Marinescu

Four of the most promising Romanian playwrights, young and very young, are in this collection, each one with a specific way of seeing the Romanian reality, each one with a style of communicating an articulated artistic vision of the society we are living in. Ion Caramitru, General Director Romanian National Theatre Bucharest.
ISBN 978-1-904505-15-0 (2005)   €10

George Fitzmaurice: 'Wild in His Own Way', Biography of an Irish Playwright

Fiona Brennan

'Fiona Brennan's introduction to his considerable output allows us a much greater appreciation and understanding of Fitzmaurice, the one remaining under-celebrated genius of twentieth-century Irish drama'. Conall Morrison

ISBN 978-1-904505-16-7 (2005)   €20

Out of History: Essays on the Writings of Sebastian Barry

Ed. Christina Hunt Mahony

The essays address Barry's engagement with the contemporary cultural debate in Ireland and also with issues that inform postcolonial critical theory. The range and selection of contributors has ensured a high level of critical expression and an insightful assessment of Barry and his works.

ISBN: 978-1-904505-18-1 (2005)   €20

Three Congregational Masses

Seoirse Bodley

'From the simpler congregational settings in the Mass of Peace and the Mass of Joy to the richer textures of the Mass of Glory, they are immediately attractive and accessible, and with a distinctively Irish melodic quality.' Barra Boydell

ISBN: 978-1-904505-11-2 (2005)   €15

Georg Büchner's Woyzeck,

A new translation by Dan Farrelly

The most up-to-date German scholarship of Thomas Michael Mayer and Burghard Dedner has finally made it possible to establish an authentic sequence of scenes. The wide-spread view that this play is a prime example of loose, open theatre is no longer sustainable. Directors and teachers are challenged to "read it again".

ISBN: 978-1-904505-02-0 (2004)   €10

Playboys of the Western World: Production Histories

Ed. Adrian Frazier

'The book is remarkably well-focused: half is a series of production histories of Playboy performances through the twentieth century in the UK, Northern Ireland, the USA, and Ireland. The remainder focuses on one contemporary performance, that of Druid Theatre, as directed by Garry Hynes. The various contemporary social issues that are addressed in relation to Synge's play and this performance of it give the volume an additional interest: it shows how the arts matter.' Kevin Barry

ISBN: 978-1-904505-06-8 (2004) €20

The Power of Laughter: Comedy and Contemporary Irish Theatre

Ed. Eric Weitz

The collection draws on a wide range of perspectives and voices including critics, playwrights, directors and performers. The result is a series of fascinating and provocative debates about the myriad functions of comedy in contemporary Irish theatre. Anna McMullan

As Stan Laurel said, 'it takes only an onion to cry. Peel it and weep. Comedy is harder'. 'These essays listen to the power of laughter. They hear the tough heart of Irish theatre – hard and wicked and funny'. Frank McGuinness

ISBN: 978-1-904505-05-1 (2004) €20

Sacred Play: Soul-Journeys in contemporary Irish Theatre

Anne F. O'Reilly

'Theatre as a space or container for sacred play allows audiences to glimpse mystery and to experience transformation. This book charts how Irish playwrights negotiate the labyrinth of the Irish soul and shows how their plays contribute to a poetics of Irish culture that enables a new imagining. Playwrights discussed are: McGuinness, Murphy, Friel, Le Marquand Hartigan, Burke Brogan, Harding, Meehan, Carr, Parker, Devlin, and Barry.'

ISBN: 978-1-904505-07-5 (2004) €25

The Irish Harp Book

Sheila Larchet Cuthbert

This is a facsimile of the edition originally published by Mercier Press in 1993. There is a new preface by Sheila Larchet Cuthbert, and the biographical material has been updated. It is a collection of studies and exercises for the use of teachers and pupils of the Irish harp.
ISBN: 978-1-904505-08-2 (2004) €35

The Drunkard

Tom Murphy

'The Drunkard is a wonderfully eloquent play. Murphy's ear is finely attuned to the glories and absurdities of melodramatic exclamation, and even while he is wringing out its ludicrous overstatement, he is also making it sing.' The Irish Times

ISBN: 978-1-90 05-09-9 (2004)   €10

Goethe: Musical Poet, Musical Catalyst

Ed. Lorraine Byrne

'Goethe was interested in, and acutely aware of, the place of music in human experience generally - and of its particular role in modern culture. Moreover, his own literary work - especially the poetry and Faust - inspired some of the major composers of the European tradition to produce some of their finest works.' Martin Swales

ISBN: 978-1-9045-10-5 (2004)   €40

The Theatre of Marina Carr: "Before rules was made"

Eds. Anna McMullan & Cathy Leeney

As the first published collection of articles on the theatre of Marina Carr, this volume explores the world of Carr's theatrical imagination, the place of her plays in contemporary theatre in Ireland and abroad and the significance of her highly individual voice.

ISBN: 978-0-9534257-7-8 (2003)   €20

Critical Moments: Fintan O'Toole on Modern Irish Theatre

Eds. Julia Furay & Redmond O'Hanlon

This new book on the work of Fintan O'Toole, the internationally acclaimed theatre critic and cultural commentator, offers percussive analyses and assessments of the major plays and playwrights in the canon of modern Irish theatre. Fearless and provocative in his judgements, O'Toole is essential reading for anyone interested in criticism or in the current state of Irish theatre.

ISBN: 978-1-904505-03-7 (2003)   €20

Goethe and Schubert: Across the Divide

Eds. Lorraine Byrne & Dan Farrelly

Proceedings of the International Conference, 'Goethe and Schubert in Perspective and Performance', Trinity College Dublin, 2003. This volume includes essays by leading scholars – Barkhoff, Boyle, Byrne, Canisius, Dürr, Fischer, Hill, Kramer, Lamport, Lund, Meikle, Newbould, Norman McKay, White, Whitton, Wright, Youens – on Goethe's musicality and his relationship to Schubert; Schubert's contribution to sacred music and the Lied and his setting of Goethe's Singspiel, Claudine. A companion volume of this Singspiel (with piano reduction and English translation) is also available.

ISBN: 978-1-904505-04-4 (2003)   €25

Goethe's Singspiel, 'Claudine von Villa Bella'

Set by Franz Schubert

Goethe's Singspiel in three acts was set to music by Schubert in 1815. Only Act One of Schuberts's Claudine score is extant. The present volume makes Act One available for performance in English and German. It comprises both a piano reduction by Lorraine Byrne of the original Schubert orchestral score and a bilingual text translated for the modern stage by Dan Farrelly. This is a tale, wittily told, of lovers and vagabonds, romance, reconciliation, and resolution of family conflict.

ISBN: 978-0-9544290-0-3 (2002)   €20

Theatre of Sound, Radio and the Dramatic Imagination

Dermot Rattigan

An innovative study of the challenges that radio drama poses to the creative imagination of the writer, the production team, and the listener.
"A remarkably fine study of radio drama – everywhere informed by the writer's professional experience of such drama in the making...A new theoretical and analytical approach – informative, illuminating and at all times readable." Richard Allen Cave

ISBN: 978- 0-9534-257-5-4 (2002)   €20

Talking about Tom Murphy

Ed. Nicholas Grene

Talking About Tom Murphy is shaped around the six plays in the landmark Abbey Theatre Murphy Season of 2001, assembling some of the best-known commentators on his work: Fintan O'Toole, Chris Morash, Lionel Pilkington, Alexandra Poulain, Shaun Richards, Nicholas Grene and Declan Kiberd.

ISBN: 978-0-9534-257-9-2 (2002)   €15

Hamlet: The Shakespearean Director

Mike Wilcock

"This study of the Shakespearean director as viewed through various interpretations of HAMLET is a welcome addition to our understanding of how essential it is for a director to have a clear vision of a great play. It is an important study from which all of us who love Shakespeare and who understand the importance of continuing contemporary exploration may gain new insights." From the Foreword, by Joe Dowling, Artistic Director, The Guthrie Theater, Minneapolis, MN

ISBN: 978-1-904505-00-6 (2002) €20

The Theatre of Frank Mc Guinness: Stages of Mutability

Ed. Helen Lojek

The first edited collection of essays about internationally renowned Irish playwright Frank McGuinness focuses on both performance and text. Interpreters come to diverse conclusions, creating a vigorous dialogue that enriches understanding and reflects a strong consensus about the value of McGuinness's complex work.

ISBN: 978-1904505-01-3. (2002) €20

Theatre Talk: Voices of Irish Theatre Practitioners

Eds Lilian Chambers, Ger Fitzgibbon and Eamonn Jordan

"This book is the right approach - asking practitioners what they feel." Sebastian Barry, Playwright "... an invaluable and informative collection of interviews with those who make and shape the landscape of Irish Theatre." Ben Barnes, Artistic Director of the Abbey Theatre

ISBN: 978-0-9534-257-6-1 (2001) €20

In Search of the South African Iphigenie

Erika von Wietersheim and Dan Farrelly

Discussions of Goethe's "Iphigenie auf Tauris" (Under the Curse) as relevant to women's issues in modern South Africa: women in family and public life; the force of women's spirituality; experience of personal relationships; attitudes to parents and ancestors; involvement with religion.

ISBN: 978-0-9534257-8-5 (2001) €10

'The Starving' and 'October Song':

Two contemporary Irish plays by Andrew Hinds

The Starving, set during and after the siege of Derry in 1689, is a moving and engrossing drama of the emotional journey of two men.

October Song, a superbly written family drama set in real time in pre-ceasefire Derry.

ISBN: 978-0-9534-257-4-7 (2001) €10

Seen and Heard: Six new plays by Irish women

Ed. Cathy Leeney

A rich and funny, moving and theatrically exciting collection of plays by Mary Elizabeth Burke-Kennedy, Síofra Campbell, Emma Donoghue, Anne Le Marquand Hartigan, Michelle Read and Dolores Walshe.

ISBN: 978-0-9534-257-3-0 (2001) €20

Theatre Stuff: Critical essays on contemporary Irish theatre

Ed. Eamonn Jordan

Best selling essays on the successes and debates of contemporary Irish theatre at home and abroad. Contributors include: Thomas Kilroy, Declan Hughes, Anna McMullan, Declan Kiberd, Deirdre Mulrooney, Fintan O'Toole, Christopher Murray, Caoimhe McAvinchey and Terry Eagleton.

ISBN: 978-0-9534-2571-1-6 (2000) €20

Under the Curse. Goethe's "Iphigenie Auf Tauris", A New Version

Dan Farrelly

The Greek myth of Iphigenie grappling with the curse on the house of Atreus is brought vividly to life. This version is currently being used in Johannesburg to explore problems of ancestry, religion, and Black African women's spirituality.

ISBN: 978-09534-257-8-5 (2000) €10

Urfaust, A New Version of Goethe's early "Faust" in Brechtian Mode

Dan Farrelly

This version is based on Brecht's irreverent and daring re-interpretation of the German classic. "Urfaust is a kind of well-spring for German theatre... The love-story is the most daring and the most profound in German dramatic literature." Brecht

ISBN: 978-0-9534-257-0-9 (1998) €20